The Beantown Girls

ALSO BY JANE HEALEY

The Saturday Evening Girls Club

PRAISE FOR *THE BEANTOWN GIRLS*

"Equally heartbreaking and heartwarming, this meticulously researched book about the fascinating Red Cross Clubmobile program charmed me from page one. I fell in love with the characters and how Healey brought this important piece of WWII history to life. *The Beantown Girls* is must-read historical fiction about love, hope, friendship, and the resilience of the human spirit."

—Susie Orman Schnall, award-winning author of *The Subway Girls*

"A fantastic story of friendship, love, and bravery. Historical fiction at its finest, inviting the reader into little-known parts of our past and bringing it to bloom with characters we love right away."

—Camille Di Maio, bestselling author of *The Memory of Us*

"If you yearn for a sweeping, romantic, and altogether wonderful novel, look no further. If you like your novels filled with character, detail, and life, here is your next big read. If you want to see World War II from an entirely new perspective, settle in with *The Beantown Girls*, a brave group of young American[s] . . . who head for Europe in 1944. As they live and grow through one of the pivotal years in human history, you will grow to love them."

—William Martin, *New York Times* bestselling author of
Cape Cod and *Bound for Gold*

"Brilliantly written, *The Beantown Girls* captured me from the first page. The dangers of war mingle beautifully with the wide-eyed innocence of three young women who find themselves in extraordinary and sometimes harrowing circumstances. History is honored in this vital look at WWII told from a female perspective. This is an important book not to be missed!"

—Heather Burch, Amazon bestselling author of
In the Light of the Garden

"In *The Beantown Girls*, Jane Healey delivers a novel that whisks us to the final harrowing months of World War II in Europe, and brings it painfully, beautifully, heartbreakingly alive. Through the eyes of Fiona Denning, a Red Cross Clubmobile worker, and her colleagues, we witness firsthand not only acts of jaw-dropping courage and sacrifice, but also the romantic bonds that grow even during the horrors of war. Healey's superb research lets us see the decimated cities, smell the doughnuts and coffee handed out at great risk on the front lines, and hear the big band music—as well as the approach of the next bomb. I loved this novel!"

—Joy Jordan-Lake, bestselling author of *A Tangled Mercy*

"From the beginning of this inspiring novel, the reader is swept into a riveting story that combines the realities of WWII with the bond of true friendship and dedication to the highest cause, told from the little-known perspective of Red Cross Clubmobile girls. Jane Healey's extensive research and fine storytelling skills offer a page-turner that goes straight to the heart. Historical fiction at its best!"

—Patricia Sands, author of the bestselling Love in Provence series

"A fascinating novel about a little-known wartime sacrifice, *The Beantown Girls* is lovingly crafted, heartbreaking, and illuminated with hope. I couldn't put it down!"

—Ellen Marie Wiseman, author of *The Life She Was Given*

"Jane Healey's wonderful new work of historical fiction, *The Beantown Girls*, provides a fresh and heartwarming perspective on American participation in Europe during the closing years of World War II. The story follows a group of courageous young women who volunteer to serve coffee, donuts, and emotional support to Allied soldiers on the front lines. Jane masterfully captures the era with its style, music, fashion, and dialogue, and the reader is instantly whisked back to the

1940s. The engaging personalities of these girls in their Red Cross Clubmobiles are sure to captivate the reader. It's like *Band of Brothers* in Red Cross uniforms."

—Ronald H. Balson, internationally bestselling author of
Once We Were Brothers

"*The Beantown Girls* by Jane Healey tells the story of the brave women who served as Red Cross Clubmobile girls during World War II, offering comfort and a slice of home to our soldiers. A story of friendship and courage, *The Beantown Girls* will delight fans of historical fiction and women's fiction alike."

—Brenda Janowitz, author of *The Dinner Party*

The Beantown Girls

JANE HEALEY
Author of *The Saturday Evening Girls Club*

LAKE UNION
PUBLISHING

Published by Lake Union Publishing, Seattle

www.apub.com

Amazon, the Amazon logo, and Lake Union Publishing are trademarks of Amazon.com, Inc., or its affiliates.

ISBN-13: 9781542044523
ISBN-10: 1542044529

Cover design by Kirk DouPonce, DogEared Design

Printed in the United States of America

*Dedicated to the Red Cross Clubmobile girls of
World War II*

You must do the thing you think you cannot do.

—Eleanor Roosevelt

Chapter One

July 14, 1944
New York City

Dottie, Viv, and I stood together on the deck of the *Queen Elizabeth*, surrounded by a couple dozen other Red Cross workers and hundreds of US soldiers. The once-glamorous cruise ship, now painted a bland battleship gray for its current role as troop transporter, was making its final preparations for departure to Europe.

The three of us were enjoying the festive atmosphere as the people on the dock below waved up at the passengers shouting their final farewells to loved ones on board. We had said our good-byes to our families in Boston six weeks ago, but we waved and smiled back at the strangers wishing us well.

"I have to say, we all look pretty smart in these new uniforms," Dottie said, adjusting her light-blue Red Cross cap and nodding at Viv and me with approval. "Fiona, the color brings out the gray in your eyes."

"Thanks, Dottie," I said. "I agree, they aren't too bad."

"Not too bad except for these sensible black shoes they recommended that we buy," said Viv, looking down with a sour face. "They're horrible. Zero fashion. But yes, the uniforms are surprisingly spiffy."

"Sweetheart, you all look better than spiffy," a soldier next to us said, staring at Dottie as he gave a whistle. His two friends nodded in agreement. They had to be fresh out of high school. So many of these newly minted GIs looked like they were playing dress-up in their fathers' uniforms. Still, Dottie flushed a deep shade of pink and turned away.

"Oh, for God's sake, Dottie, at least say thank you," Viv whispered to her with a nudge. "She thanks you, honey," Viv said to the soldier with a smile, and now he was the one blushing.

"She's right," I said. "That's definitely not the last compliment you're going to get from a soldier. You better get used to it."

Dottie was about to reply, but an army band on the docks below struck up a raucous rendition of "Over There," and a rowdy group on the other side of us started singing along so loudly that it was difficult to talk over the noise.

I looked up at the decks above ours, at the hundreds of men pressed against railings like we were, waving good-bye to the crowds. Jostling and laughing with each other, they were all hiding their nerves beneath bravado.

And that's when I spotted my fiancé, Second Lieutenant Danny Barker, among the men on the deck above ours. My arms broke out in goose pimples despite the heat, and I felt a little faint. Tall and blond, he looked incredibly handsome in his US Army Air Force uniform. He was smiling and waving at the crowds below too, and it was all I could do not to scream his name and go running upstairs to him. I wanted to do it so badly my heart ached. But I held back calling to him, because deep down I knew. It wasn't him. It couldn't be. Danny Barker had been declared missing in action more than eight months ago, shot down in the skies over Germany.

The ship's horn blasted our departure from the dock, and more soldiers joined in the singing. Dottie and Viv didn't notice me gripping the rail of the ship with white knuckles as I tried to tether myself to reality. I was desperate to quell the feeling of panic that was bubbling up inside me. I shook my head back and forth, blinking a few times. When I looked up again, I realized that the soldier I could have sworn was Danny bore only a passing resemblance to him. He was tall and blond like Danny, but with sharp, angular features that were nothing like my fiancé's.

It was a hot July day in New York City, and the ocean air was tainted with the smell of diesel, cigarettes, and cheap cologne. I don't know if it was the humidity that made the atmosphere feel heavy or the emotions of the hundreds of soldiers on the ship with us, jumping up and down, yelling their final good-byes before heading off to war.

Some of the women in the crowds below had started to cry, clutching their handkerchiefs and straining to capture these last glimpses of their beloved sons, brothers, and sweethearts so they could remember them in the months to come. I felt grief in the pit of my stomach, grief that I had managed to push down for the past few months. But now that we were bound for Europe, it all came bubbling to the surface. *Oh God*, I thought. *What if this whole thing is an enormous mistake?*

I felt my face flush and thought I might throw up. I tugged on Dottie's arm. Viv was charming some of the men standing next to us with a story about learning to play Ping-Pong during our recent training in DC.

"I've got to find a bathroom," I said into Dottie's ear. "I'm feeling a little ill."

"Sheesh, it's kind of early to be seasick, Fiona," Dottie said. "We haven't even left the harbor yet. Fiona? Fiona!" Dottie called after me as I moved as fast as I could through the throngs of GIs, my hand over my mouth.

I heard greetings of "Hey, doll!" and "What's the matter, freckles?" from the dozens of men I pushed past. A couple of them graciously asked if I was okay.

I finally found a bathroom tucked into the space underneath the stairs to an upper deck. I slammed the door behind me and locked it, taking another deep breath as I splashed water on my face. In the small round mirror, I looked even paler than usual, making the freckles across my nose more prominent. I adjusted the pins on my new cap and smoothed down my newly shorn, shoulder-length hair. It was only then I noticed that my hands were shaking. I opened the tiny porthole above the toilet to let in some air and sank to the floor. I didn't throw up, but for the first time in many months, I began to cry.

In March, I had let Viv and Dottie drag me to see the Saturday matinee of *Jane Eyre* starring Orson Welles and Joan Fontaine. It had always been one of my favorite novels, so I reluctantly agreed to go. Before the movie started, we watched a short newsreel. The words *Now more than ever, your Red Cross is at his side* flashed across the screen with a familiar picture of a soldier standing next to a woman in a Red Cross uniform, the same one I was wearing today. It was followed by footage of Red Cross Clubmobile girls serving the troops all over Europe. There was a trio of these girls in Italy and then more footage of them in North Africa, happily serving coffee and doughnuts to soldiers out of a converted truck. There were other scenes of these women playing records and dancing the jitterbug with GIs against the backdrop of blown-out buildings. A voice-over began:

> *Our Red Cross Clubmobile girls must be single, college graduates, and over the age of twenty-five. They are handpicked for their looks, education, and personality. They are hardy physically and have a sociable, friendly manner.*

Seeing those women—traveling, directly helping the war effort—had stirred something in me that I hadn't felt since Danny had gone missing. It was a combination of hope and exhilaration. That feeling you have before the first day of college or when starting a new job. The newsreel had seemed like a sign from above. Maybe I could do something *real* in the war effort other than assemble care packages at the local USO. Volunteering for the Red Cross could be a way to honor Danny. And more than anything, it was a plan, a way forward—a way to try to find out what had happened to him the day his plane was shot down. Right after seeing that reel, I decided to apply to become a Red Cross Clubmobile girl.

I got up, looked at myself in the mirror, and said out loud to my reflection, "Nice job, Fiona. Did you think these soldiers *wouldn't* remind you of your missing fiancé? Did you think going to war was going to be a walk in the park? Get a grip."

I jumped at the sound of someone banging on the bathroom door.

"Fiona! Fi? Are you talking to yourself? Open up." I recognized Viv's raspy voice coming from outside.

"Fiona, we know you're in there," Dottie said in her high-pitched tone. "Open the door."

I wiped my tears and unlatched the door to see my best friends standing on the other side. Viviana was frowning at me, her violet-blue eyes studying my face. Dottie stood next to her, peering over her red horn-rimmed glasses, unable to hide her worry.

"Oh Jesus, Fiona, look at you," Viv said as she barged in with Dottie, locking the door behind them. "We've got to clean you up; no soldiers need to see you all swollen and tear-stained. We're supposed to be *boosting* their morale, not making them feel worse."

"Um, yeah, no kidding, Viv. Why do you think I'm hiding in the bathroom?" I answered as she started blotting my face with powder.

"Here, some fresh lipstick too. This coral color will look good on you, Fi; it's too light for my skin tone," Dottie said as she handed the lipstick to me. "Now, while Viv's fixing you up, do you want to tell us what's going on? Are you okay? Why did you rush off like that?"

"I'm sorry, girls. It's being with all these soldiers and seeing their loved ones waving good-bye. I'm not going to lie: it got to me," I said. "I also felt like I was going crazy because for a minute I actually thought one of the soldiers on the deck above us *was* Danny. It hasn't even been a year since he's been . . . he's been gone and . . . my God . . . It all just hit me . . . We're not at training in DC anymore; we are on the boat to England . . . *to the war*. I've been trying—I mean, I think I've been pretty strong about all of this, but just now? It was too much."

"Sweetheart, have a seat. We need to talk," Viv said as she slid down the wall underneath the porthole, pulled a pack of Chesterfields out of her pocket, and lit one cigarette.

"Are you seriously going to smoke in here, Viv?" Dottie asked, waving a hand in front of her face and grimacing. "Isn't that against the rules? No smoking while in uniform?"

"Who's going to rat on me?" Viv said with a smirk and a wink. Dottie let out a sigh and sat down against the opposite wall, where I joined her.

"Want a smoke?" Viv asked. "It'll calm your nerves."

I shook my head. Dottie patted my knee and said, "Fiona, honey, honestly? You've been so strong, it's been . . . well, it's been a little odd, frankly. You've been too calm."

Viv nodded and took a drag of her cigarette. "Dottie's right, Fi," she said. "You lost your fiancé in October, and for the past few months you've barely talked about it, even when we've asked. You've just been forging ahead. I'm kind of surprised you haven't fallen apart more, way before getting on this boat."

"He's missing, not lost," I said. "And I'm going to finally be honest with both of you because you're my best friends in the world and I couldn't have done this—couldn't have gone through applying or training, couldn't have gotten on this boat—without you.

"Danny is missing. He very well may be . . . he may be dead, but what keeps me awake at night is that I don't know *anything* for sure. The truth is, I'm hoping to find answers, or maybe even to find *him*. I know I sound crazy for even saying it . . . but I'm not sure I can live the rest of my life with 'missing in action.' So now you know. There's a lot of good reasons for us being here, but *my* main reason? It's to try to find out about Danny."

"Viv, you owe me five dollars," Dottie said, nudging her with her foot.

"What?" I said incredulously, hoping for a more thoughtful response to my confession. "Wait . . . you two made a bet about this?"

"We did and I do owe you, Dottie," said Viv with a laugh. "Fiona. Please. We've all been friends since the first day of college. Believe it or not, we know you pretty well by now. Dottie was sure that was why you were doing this."

"I thought I was losing my damn mind when I saw Danny on that deck. I'm a bit of a wreck now that we're actually on our way."

"Well, of course you're nervous and still grieving." Viviana looked me in the eyes. "Honey, you don't have to be so strong all the time. You're allowed to fall apart once in a while . . . but try not to do it in front of the soldiers, okay?"

"Never in front of the soldiers," I said. "My God, some of them are babies."

"I heard a bunch of them saying they graduated last month," Dottie added, chewing on a strand of her hair. "From *high school.* And I second what Viv said: we're here for you. You don't have to hide it the way you've been trying to these past few months. We'll get through this together. We're all nervous."

"I'm not that nervous," Viv said with a shrug as she tapped her cigarette, ashes sprinkling the bathroom floor.

"Shush, Viv, you know that even *you* are," Dottie said. "I am, for a lot of reasons, one being that I'm not nearly as outgoing as you and Viv. I think I barely passed that requirement in the personal interview. If I hadn't pulled out my guitar at the end, I'm sure they would have rejected me."

Dottie was right about that. She was not a fit for the "outgoing, friendly" persona the Red Cross was looking for. At some point she was going to have to talk to the soldiers and play her guitar, not just smile pretty and blush.

"Anyway, I understand you wanting answers about Danny," Dottie continued. "And the three of us are here together, for all the other reasons we've talked about."

"She's right," Viv said. "We all need this. It's been so frustrating seeing Danny, Dottie's brother, all our friends—men *our age*—get shipped off to war and we can't do anything to help them but assemble care packages and serve stupid frankfurters at the USO."

"Like you said yourself, Fiona, if Danny possibly gave his life to the war, you can—"

"I can give it one year. I know," I said with a sigh. I could give it a year. And I knew I could barely stand the thought of living one more day with my parents and sisters, feeling sorry for myself. And working at city hall with the rest of the staff constantly giving me looks of pity.

"And if we had waited too long, the war might be over," Dottie said. "And even if not, I'm not sure the Red Cross was going to come through Boston interviewing for Clubmobile positions again. We had to take the chance when we had it."

"We did," said Viv. "Ready or not, we're on our way to England. We just went through six weeks of training for these jobs. I had to learn to play badminton, for the love of God. There's no turning back now."

"I know, Viv. I'm sorry I lost it for a moment," I said, starting to calm down because, really, she was right. "What am I going to do, jump overboard? And God forbid you not get to use your newly acquired badminton skills."

"And remember," Dottie added, adjusting her cap, "it's kind of a big deal to be chosen for this. One of the girls just told me they only choose one out of every six applicants. One out of *six*. We went through that gauntlet of interviews and exams—it's a prestigious assignment."

"And parts of it might be *fun*, you know," said Viv. "Travel, adventure, our first trip to Europe—our first trip anywhere—and the three of us get to go together? When was the last time you really let yourself have fun, Fiona?"

"I know, I know. Thank you for reminding me," I said, giving them both a smile. "This is a fresh start. One that I desperately need."

"You got that right." Viv winked at me as she stood up and threw her cigarette in the toilet. Dottie jumped up, grabbed my hands, and pulled me off the floor.

The three of us stood squeezed in front of the mirror and did a quick check of ourselves. We were a study in contrasts. Dottie was petite with olive skin, rosy cheeks, and thick black hair like the rest of her Portuguese family. Her glasses only served to highlight her large dark eyes. Viv, on the other hand, was tall with dark-reddish-brown curls, high cheekbones, and full lips. I was the palest of the three by far, with green-gray eyes and those freckles across my nose.

"You should adjust your cap so you can see the highlights in the front of your hair, Fiona," Dottie said. My hair was light brown, but I had an odd chunk of blonde streaks in the front.

"Maybe I should adjust it right down in front of my puffy eyes so no one can tell I was crying," I said, frowning at my reflection.

We all jumped when someone started banging on the door loudly and we heard a voice say, "Hellooooo? Hello, Boston? Y'all in there? It's Blanche."

"As if we couldn't tell by that accent," I said, opening the door to see Blanche Dumond, a spitfire of a girl from New Orleans. She was curvy, blonde, and fast-talking. We had met her at training in DC.

"I thought I saw you heading this way," Blanche said, raising her eyebrows at me. "You okay, honey? You aren't looking so good."

"She's fine," lied Viv as we filed out of the bathroom. Blanche had become known as somewhat of a gossip among all of us newly initiated Red Cross girls.

"Uh-huh," said Blanche, unconvinced. "Anyway, a bunch of us are heading up to the officers' deck—they call it the Bird Cage. There's a bar and a club room and a piano. You want to join us? You need that red ID card they gave all of us to get in—only officers above captain and Red Cross girls allowed."

"Of course," Viv said. "I think we could all use a drink before the war. Hey, Dottie, you could play piano! Or you should go grab your guitar from our cabin."

"Um . . . no, that's okay, maybe next time," Dottie said, already turning pink at the thought of performing in front of anyone outside the elementary school where she taught.

"Well, let's go!" said Blanche, heading toward the stairs.

Viv and Dottie followed while I stood outside the bathroom.

"I'll be right there," I said, and they both stopped and looked at me, concern in their eyes.

"You promise, Fi?" Dottie asked.

"Yeah, yeah," I said. "I want to freshen up a bit more. You know, the eyes." I pointed to the puffiness I could feel underneath them.

"Okay, we'll see you there," Viv said, and they kept walking.

I went back into the bathroom, stood in front of the mirror, and put a bit of cool water on my swollen eyes. I reached into my pocket and felt for the folded letter. The last letter I had ever received from Danny before he was shot out of the sky somewhere over the forests of Germany. It was dated September 8, 1943. Danny went missing sometime around October 20. His family and I found out a month after that. I took the letter out of my pocket and started to open it, to read it for the thousandth time. I opened it halfway and saw my name at the top of the page in his familiar, terrible handwriting, but then I stopped myself. I looked up at the mirror, my puffy eyes staring back at me. I folded up the letter and shoved it as far into my pocket as I could.

I had already memorized it; reading it again wasn't going to help me now.

"You're doing this, Fiona," I said to my reflection. "Ready or not, you're doing this."

I applied the lipstick Dottie had given me, and the eyes looking back at me now had more resolve and strength than when I'd first walked into the bathroom. It was time to go to war. Hopefully to find answers. Maybe to find Danny.

Chapter Two

July 19, 1944

Sleeping on a narrow bunk bed in a tiny cabin with five other women meant falling asleep fitfully every night and waking up at odd hours, often from vivid, jarring dreams.

Danny and I were sitting on the large red-and-white-checked cotton blanket that I had spread on the lawn of the Bunker Hill Monument. It was a gorgeous but steamy day in late August, breezy with a faint scent of the ocean a few blocks away. He was leaving for Europe in three days. We had both been trying to ignore that fact, though it hung in the air between us, unspoken and heavy like the summer air.

He was lying on his side on the blanket, resting on his elbow as he bit into one of the apples I had bought off a pushcart earlier in the day. I shaded my eyes to get a better look at him; six foot one with long, athletic limbs, his dimpled cheek and almond-shaped blue eyes, his white-blond hair now cropped per military standards. I could still see a glimpse of the lanky, awkward nineteen-year-old I had fallen for sophomore year of college, but it was getting harder all the time. He looked up at me and smiled, running his finger down my bare arm, giving me goose bumps.

"How you doing there, Fi?" he said quietly, his dimple fading as his face became serious.

"I'm doing . . . I'm doing fine," I said, lying. "This was one of the best Saturdays I've ever had. Betty Grable was as good as I hoped she would be in *Coney Island*. And I had such a great time walking around the St. Anthony's Festival eating pizza and cannoli until we were stuffed, and now we're sitting here in the sun on this gorgeous summer afternoon . . . What more could I ask for?"

Danny kept looking at me, still serious. "Honey, it was a great day, the best, but we can't ignore the fact that I'm leaving."

That pit in my stomach. I studied his face, and then sighed.

"I know," I said. "I'm doing okay. I'll be all right. I'll miss you terribly; I'm already missing you if that's possible. But I'm sure I'm doing better than you are. I'm not the one going half a world away to fight in the war. How are *you* doing?"

I lay on my side across from him, resting on one elbow while I smoothed my green-and-white gingham skirt and tucked it under me so it wouldn't blow up in the breeze.

"I'm as ready as I'll ever be, I guess," Danny said, putting his apple core on the grass and reaching over to grab my hand. "Training is all done. It's what every guy our age has to do . . ." He squeezed my hand and looked into my eyes. "The hardest part is leaving you." He leaned over and gave me a long kiss.

"I'll keep really busy," I said, reluctantly pulling away in case my mother or one of her friends happened to walk by. "As you know, there's never a dull moment at the mayor's office; the days fly by. Mayor Tobin keeps piling more responsibilities on me by the minute.

"Of course, I'll help my mom and dad with my younger sisters. The twins are driving my mother crazy lately. Oh, and Dottie, Viv, and I are going to volunteer at the USO over at the Charlestown YMCA . . ."

"Uh-oh, don't let any soldiers at the USO try to steal you away while I'm gone," he said.

"It'll never happen," I said, giving him a playful shove. "I'll make it very clear that I'm engaged. Besides, they'll all be falling over themselves to get Viv's attention. And Dottie's too—they'll just mistake her shyness for playing hard to get."

"You three can be trouble when you're together," he said, smirking. "I might have to have a word with those two before I go."

"I think you mean we can be really *fun* when we're together," I said. He was looking at me, serious again.

"What?" I said, putting my hand on his cheek.

"I'm trying to memorize your beautiful face. Your freckles and your eyes that change shades with the weather. The patch of blonde in the front of your hair that you're always pushing out of your eyes. I'm going to miss your face so much."

"I'll miss your face too," I said, suddenly feeling my chest tighten and my eyes well up. "So much." I leaned down to kiss him again, blinking fast so I wouldn't start to cry.

"Fiona," he said, whispering. We were nose to nose. "We need to talk about the possibility . . . if something happens to me over there—"

"No," I said, sitting up, feeling physically ill at the words he was saying. "Nothing is going to happen to you over there. I know it in my heart. You'll be back in . . . in a little over a year . . . and we'll get married, and I'll *finally* move out of my parents' house, and we'll really start our life together. You'll finish law school, become a district attorney like you've always dreamed. We'll eventually have kids, maybe buy a small house outside of Boston. We can finally get a couple of Boston terriers . . ."

He was quiet. Staring out past the monument at something I couldn't see.

"I'm serious. You're going to be fine. And if you're not fine, I swear to God I'm going to come over and get you myself . . ." He was still quiet, so I kept talking. "This war has to . . . it's got to end sometime soon, right? It can't—" I was interrupted by the sound of a loud, deep horn. "What was that?"

"I'll be seeing you," Danny said, like he always did when we said good-bye. It was his favorite song. He looked up at me again and grabbed my hand like it was the last thing he'd ever hold.

"Why are you saying that?"

The horn sounded again.

I sat up, startled, and opened my eyes, nearly hitting my head on the bunk above me. I listened to the foghorn of the *Queen Elizabeth* and the quiet snoring of at least two of the six girls in our tiny cabin. I sighed and looked up at the bottom of the bunk above me where Viv was sleeping. Every time I woke from a dream about Danny, it was still a grim surprise.

I stayed in bed for another fifteen minutes before I realized I wasn't going to be able to fall back to sleep. It had to be well past midnight, but I needed to get some air. I felt around under my bunk for my uniform, which was neatly folded next to my shiny new steel helmet and gas mask. I got dressed lying down on my bed, grabbed my shoes, and opened the door of the cabin, slipping into the hall as quietly as I could.

The hall was dimly lit. I decided to make my way up to the Bird Cage, where my friends and I had been spending a good amount of time. We'd gotten to know some of the other Red Cross girls and soldiers—playing card games and singing songs by the piano. A few of the soldiers were decent musicians. Viv and I still hadn't been able to convince Dottie to contribute her talents.

I walked up several flights of stairs and relished the silence, which was interrupted by the foghorn at regular intervals. The *Queen Elizabeth* had been designed as a luxury cruise ship meant for about two thousand passengers per voyage. At the end of our first day on board, however, we were told there were fifteen thousand military men and about a hundred Red Cross workers heading to England via the vessel. This meant it was always loud and crowded. Everyone ate two mediocre meals a day in assigned shifts. There were never enough chairs, and while GIs would often offer to give up their seats for us, my friends and I were usually more comfortable just sitting on the floor picnic-style.

The late-night emptiness and quiet were a welcome change from the daytime hustle and chaos. As I reached the top of the stairs to the officers' deck, I stopped for a minute and listened. I heard someone playing the piano in the lounge. I walked toward it, pulling my jacket tighter around me. It was a cool, starless night, and the ship was surrounded by fog. As I got closer to the lounge, I saw a soldier sitting at the piano, his eyes closed, completely immersed in his playing. A lit cigarette sat in an ashtray next to him on the bench, along with a pack of Lucky Strikes. I recognized him by his red hair—he had been playing drinking songs on the piano a couple of nights earlier, and an enormous crowd of officers and Red Cross workers had been singing along. At the end of the night, the beer was still flowing, and verses of the song "Roll Me Over in the Clover" had become increasingly bawdy.

I opened the lounge door, walked in, and sat down on one of the oversized brown leather chairs to listen, tucking my legs underneath me. It smelled like stale beer, and there was an ever-present haze of cigarette smoke. A few officers were playing cards at a table in the opposite corner, and they all gave me nods and smiles.

The GI played the piano as if he were in a trance. Jazz. I knew the song. When he finished the piece, he turned and looked at me with a small smile. He had warm brown eyes.

"There's so few women on this ship, seeing you is like seeing a ghost."

"'Rhapsody in Blue'?" I smiled back.

"Yes," he said. "Very good. That's the one."

"I'm sorry to disturb your playing," I said. "I couldn't sleep and came up here for some air."

He waved his hand and took a drag of his cigarette. "It's fine. I've been coming up here every night. I like the quiet. Not a lot of quiet time on this boat."

"True," I said with a nod.

"Here, would you like a Krueger's?" He reached under his bench and grabbed a can of beer, offering it to me. "The bartender's off duty, but he left several six-packs for us night owls."

"Why not?" I said with a shrug, taking the can from him and cracking it open. "Thank you. Maybe it will help me sleep." I took a sip before adding, "You play beautifully. Are you a professional musician?"

"I am, thanks," he said. "I'm head of a swing band in Chicago . . . well, I was before this whole mess. Do you play?"

"No, but my friend Dottie, who's here with me, plays piano and guitar. She's incredibly talented. We've been trying to get her to play all week, but she's shy about it," I said. "My friends and I love swing, love the big bands. I'm Fiona, by the way. Fiona Denning."

"Nice to meet you, Fiona. I'm Joe Brandon," he said, reaching over to shake my hand. "You're one of the Red Cross girls, I take it?"

"Yes," I said.

"What are you going to be doing over there? Do you know yet?" he asked.

"My friends Viv, Dottie, and I will be in one of those Clubmobiles—in DC they said we'd most likely be sent to France. We have training in London for a couple of weeks, and they're going to officially assign us then. How about you?"

"Captain in the Twenty-Eighth Infantry Division," he said, lighting up a fresh cigarette. He had long fingers. Fingers meant to play piano. "I'm going to be heading up a band over there, believe it or not."

"I believe it, playing the way you do," I said. "Maybe my friends and I will get to see your band sometime."

"Maybe you will," he said, smiling at the idea. "Where are you from, Fiona Denning?"

That's how the conversations on board had started all week. *Where are you from? What do you do? Where are you headed over there?*

"I'm from Boston," I said.

"Ah . . . Red Sox fan?"

"Of course," I answered. "Cubs fan?"

"Are you kidding? From birth," he said. "What do you do with yourself in Boston?"

"I work—well, I *worked*—as an assistant in the mayor's office in city hall," I said.

"Did you like it?"

"I actually really did. And I was good at my job too," I said, thinking of my coworkers, all the girls in the office who had been so supportive after Danny went missing. "It was hectic, and every day was different, dealing with some crisis or another. But the hours flew by, and the people I worked with were nice. Mayor Tobin was a decent boss. Not perfect, but fair."

"So, what made you do this?" he asked. "I mean, I *have* to go. Guys have no choice. I'm always impressed when I meet girls like you who *want* to go to the war. Why'd you and—your two friends you said, right? Why'd you girls decide to do this?"

I paused and looked at him. This was another test. Since the beginning of the week, I'd been asked this question dozens of times. I had yet to share my story with the soldiers I had met on the ship. I swallowed the grief down. I hadn't been chosen as a Clubmobile girl so I could tell soldiers my sad story. I was there to help them get through the war, not remind them about its horrors.

"Yes, my two best friends from Boston's Teachers College are here with me. After seeing so many of our friends and family, so many men the same age as us, go over and do their part, it didn't seem right to be on the sidelines anymore.

"We went to a Saturday matinee a while back, and we saw this reel of Red Cross Clubmobile girls all over Europe and Africa helping the troops, and that did it. The three of us had to apply. My friend Viv was gung ho from the start. She loves art and design and got a job at this prestigious advertising firm in downtown Boston last year, but they hardly ever let her do anything except serve coffee. She figured if she's just going to serve coffee and doughnuts, it might as well be for the troops.

"But my friend Dottie, the shy one? She took some more convincing. She was a music teacher at an elementary school in Back Bay, in Boston. She loved her job, loved her kids, so she wasn't sure she wanted to leave them. It was the thought of me and Viv traveling the world without her that finally changed her mind. And she has a brother in the Pacific. A bunch of our friends from college are fighting too. We just felt like it was a great opportunity . . . And I'm sorry, I'm rambling on . . ." I felt my cheeks grow warm and took a sip of beer.

"No, I asked. I was curious," he said. "We've all got friends and family in this war . . . ," he said, running his fingers through his cropped hair. He pointed at me. "I bet your sweetheart is already over there too, right? Or in the Pacific or North Africa maybe? You must have a fella, a pretty girl like you." The foghorn punctuated his compliment.

I hoped he didn't see the shadow that crossed my face when he said it. I shook my head, probably one too many times, and said, "Thank you, but no. It was just the thought of being able to travel together and serve—we thought if the three of us could get accepted, how amazing would that be? How about you? Do you have someone back home waiting?" I was eager to change the subject.

"I do," he said, smiling even bigger than before. "Mary Jane Abbott. She's an English teacher with the prettiest brown eyes you've ever seen. Want to see her picture?" He was already reaching into his pocket for it.

"Of course," I said as he handed it to me. It was a picture of a striking dark-haired girl with enormous doe eyes. She was wearing an eyelet dress and laughing into the camera.

"She's beautiful," I said.

"She is." He sighed. "And maybe she'll actually wait for me."

"You really doubt that she will?" I asked, frowning.

"A little," he said, his smile fading. "I've heard too many stories. The Dear John letters guys over there get, telling them their girl's engaged or even *married* to someone else."

"I have a feeling she'll wait for you," I said. I wanted it to be true for this nice, handsome piano player. "I don't think you have anything to worry about."

"Thanks," he said, not reassured at all. He looked down and fingered a few of the keys.

He started to play again, and some of the other soldiers looked up in appreciation. It was "Moonlight Cocktail," a song that Glenn Miller's band had made hugely popular a couple of years before. It was still one of my favorites, and I watched as he closed his eyes and disappeared into the music. I'm not sure if it was the melody or the beer, but I felt much more relaxed than when the foghorn had jolted me awake.

"Well, I should try to go back to sleep, although I'm not sure I will," I said after he finished the song. "Between the foghorn and my friend Viv's snoring . . . oh, and I think I actually heard mice scurrying around our cabin tonight too. Ick." I made a sour face.

Joe laughed. "Good luck, Fiona Denning. It was nice to meet you." He stood up when I did and shook my hand.

"You too, Joe. Thanks for the beer. If I don't see you in the next couple of days before we disembark, good luck," I said.

"Thanks." He smiled and gave a small salute as I turned to go.

I was about to open the door to the deck when I heard, "Fiona!"

"Yes?" I said, turning back around to see Joe still standing by his piano. He walked over to me. "What's his name?" he asked, cocking his head to the side.

"What?" I said. I felt my cheeks turn pink.

"Your guy, the one you didn't want to talk about. What's his name? It's okay, you can tell me. This war's gone on long enough I can tell . . . I can tell when someone's lost someone."

"His name is . . . I . . . his name was . . . is . . ." I never knew how to say it—was he past or present? *He's lost, but is he gone?* "Danny. Danny Barker. He's my fiancé," I said finally. "He's a second lieutenant in the air force, in the 338th Bombardment Squadron. He . . . he went missing in October of last year. Somewhere in Germany. I found out in late November." I let out a deep breath. It was a relief to tell someone about it after keeping it such a tightly held secret all week. It felt good to acknowledge my grief.

"Missing . . . I'm sorry," he said. "Did you hear any more after that? Do you know—"

"That was all. His parents haven't heard anything since," I said. "It's been hard, the not knowing."

"I understand," he said, looking down and kicking at the hardwood floor. "I've lost a cousin. And one of my old friends from high school went missing in the South Pacific." He looked up at me, his eyes sympathetic. I blinked a few times to avoid shedding any tears in front of this man I had just met.

"So, for the first month after I found out, I was in a complete fog," I said, remembering my mother and sisters dragging me out of bed during that time, forcing me to eat dinner with them. The grief had swallowed me up, and I felt like I would never breathe again without the tightness in my chest, the ache in my heart. "You have to understand. We'd been going together since sophomore year of college. I'm a planner, and I had planned out my entire life with him. Danny had insisted we put our wedding plans on hold because of the war. So when I got the news . . . it almost broke me.

"When I started coming out of that fog and thinking more clearly, I felt restless," I said. "He's missing in action, but missing isn't dead. What the heck happened to him? Is he gone forever? What if he's hiding out in a village somewhere?

"So, I came up with a new plan. I decided I had to find out what happened to him. And I figured the best way to do that was to get myself to Europe, to the Continent. And for a woman, the Red Cross was one of the only options."

"So, the real reason you're going to war is to find your missing fiancé?" he asked, giving me a look I couldn't decipher.

"Well, yes, that is definitely the main reason," I said. "I've only just admitted it out loud to my friends who are here with me. It's not something I told anyone about. Don't get me wrong, I am proud to be in the Red Cross, to get this assignment, but yes, I do want to find answers about him."

"Even if it's not the answer you want?" he asked softly.

"Even if it's not," I said, the tightness in my chest returning. "I've thought about that. It's this not knowing that's the worst part. I feel like I'm in a limbo of grieving."

"It's impressive," he said, looking me in the eye with an intensity that made me blush again. "Doing this. I don't think a lot of girls would."

"Thanks, but I think most people would say I'm crazy," I said, giving him a weak smile. "I'm pretty sure my friends think I am. But they know when I've made up my mind."

"It's not crazy," he said, shaking his head. "This war is what's crazy. But what you're doing, if you have even a slim chance of finding out what happened to him, well, I don't blame you for trying. It's brave."

"I don't feel particularly brave," I said with a shrug. "Anyway, I just . . . I'm not here to share my sad story. That's not why they accepted me for this role."

"Yes, but then, some of us . . ." He looked down at his feet again, thinking. "Look, nobody in America is getting through this war unscathed. Nobody. You don't always have to keep quiet about your story when we get over there. This war has gone on long enough, most of us have a sad story or two by now. Sometimes it helps to talk about them. It makes everyone feel less alone."

"Thanks," I said.

"It's true," he said.

"Well, good night, Joe. I appreciate the talk." I didn't know what else to do, so I reached out to shake his hand again. He shook mine and put both palms over it and squeezed it before he let go.

"Me too. Good night, Fiona," he said. "Good luck."

I smiled and waved good-bye as the foghorn sounded again. "I'll keep an eye out for the Twenty-Eighth Infantry when I'm over there, Captain."

"You do that. And I'll be sure to look out for the three Clubmobile girls from Boston," he said.

Chapter Three

July 21, 1944
London, England

According to Viv, I slept on the train during the eight-hour ride from Scotland to Euston Station in London. She said she had drool on her shoulder to prove it. I couldn't recall sleeping at all. I only remembered being uncomfortable, squished together with Viv, Dottie, and a bunch of other Red Cross girls on the cold, blacked-out troop train all night long. I remember Dottie falling asleep on my shoulder, and I guess I must have fallen asleep on Viv's.

Our train had just pulled into London. We were marching through the station to the trucks that would take us to a Red Cross dorm for women, where we'd be staying for the duration of our Clubmobile training. The enormous station clock said the local time was 5:00 a.m.

"My stomach is growling," Dottie whispered as we stood in line. "I'm famished."

"What about your 'gourmet' K rations? The canned cheese product didn't look delicious?" I asked, not able to hide my sarcasm.

"I only ate the chocolate. I couldn't stand the look of the rest," she replied.

Dottie was wearing her helmet and her Red Cross–issued blue wool coat so she didn't have to carry them. She had her guitar and musette bag over one shoulder and her canteen and gas mask over the other. She looked like she was going to collapse under the weight of it all. We were awkwardly carrying all of our gear, but Dottie's petite size and her large guitar made it that much worse for her.

"The biscuits weren't too terrible," Viv said, letting out a huge yawn. "Happy for the mini pack of Chesterfields included."

"I almost smoked one hoping it would curb my appetite," Dottie said. "But I heard they're terrible for your vocal cords."

"Dottie, you won't sing in front of anyone anyway, so what does it matter?" Viv said. "One cigarette's not going to kill you."

"You can have my Chesterfields, Viv," I said.

"Mine too," Dottie said. "And that's not true; I sing in front of my students."

We exited the station through its enormous arches and walked toward the line of waiting army trucks. I inhaled the damp London air, refreshing after the stuffiness of the troop train.

"Hello! Hello! Red Cross, over here, this way!" Right outside the station there was a very tall woman in a Red Cross uniform holding a sign that read, *WELCOME RED CROSS GIRLS!* She kept calling out to us in a shrill voice, waving us over. There were already a couple dozen women from the ship standing with her.

"Hello, I'm Judith Chambers. I'm the Red Cross field director in charge of your orientation. Welcome." She gave us a warm smile and held out her hand to me, Viv, and Dottie. Judith Chambers was probably in her late thirties, well over six feet tall with a long face, sparkling blue eyes, and dark-brown, chin-length hair. She was the tallest woman I'd ever met.

"We're just waiting a few minutes for the rest of the group, and then I'll take you all to the trucks that will bring you to 103 Park Street in Mayfair," she said. "That's where you'll be staying for your eight days of orientation."

"Eight days?" Dottie asked, frowning under her helmet as it fell over her face. "I thought we were in London for two weeks."

"Yes, that was the original plan," said Miss Chambers. "But the Red Cross executive team, with input from the military, just made the decision to shorten the orientation period to get you girls out into the field as soon as possible. One of the reasons you were selected is because you're smart and well educated. I'm hoping you're all fast learners too. Ever operated a doughnut machine or driven a two-ton truck before?"

Nobody said yes. I looked around, and everyone was shaking their heads with facial expressions that ranged from anxious to amused.

Miss Chambers let out a laugh and waved her hand. "Of course you haven't! There's nothing to it—you'll all be fine."

Dottie raised her eyebrows at me and Viv, not convinced.

"Um . . . Miss Chambers," Viv said. "Why the rush to get us out in the field?"

"Well, we just don't have enough of you to go around," she said. "The Clubmobile program has exceeded our expectations in terms of popularity. The soldiers absolutely love it, so the military leaders want as many Clubmobiles as we can provide. We recently sent over four hundred women to the Continent after D-Day, and now we're understaffed across the United Kingdom."

"Wait . . . United Kingdom?" I said, feeling a rumble in my stomach that had nothing to do with hunger. "In DC we were told that we'd be sent to France."

"Yes, well, DC is always behind the times in terms of their information," said Miss Chambers with a smile. "In this war, we've got to be careful when sharing news about all of our comings and goings. The English countryside is probably your fate, at least for now. Possibly Scotland, but you'll know for sure in a couple of days." When I didn't smile back, she studied my face for a second before adding, "Are you okay—it's Fiona, yes? You look a little pale."

"I just had in my mind this whole time that we'd be going to France and then on to Germany," I said, not wanting to explain my real motivations. "Do you think we'll get to the Continent at some point?"

"My dear, while I can't predict the future, it's certainly a strong possibility," Miss Chambers said, watching my reaction.

"How long do you think we'll have to stay in the UK?" I asked, and I caught Viv giving me a look, telling me with her eyes to stop asking so many questions. I couldn't help myself, though. I was upset that we would be stuck in the UK. As Danny's last known location, Germany was where I needed to get to, however I could.

"I really can't say; things change on a dime in this war," Miss Chambers said. "So, it's somewhere in the UK for you for now, but that could change at any point, depending on the needs of our troops." She paused before adding, "Is that going to be a problem, Fiona? Why so anxious to go elsewhere? In the Red Cross, we need to go where our troops need us."

"Yes," I said. "Yes, of course." I looked down at my ugly black shoes, feeling my face grow hot. What was I going to do, have a tantrum about not going to the Continent? Still, I was devastated to hear that not only were we not going *now*, there was no guarantee that we would *ever* get there. My doubts and grief started creeping in again, and that familiar ache in my chest was back.

"Think of it, Fiona, the English countryside . . . ," Dottie said, putting an arm around my shoulder. Miss Chambers had moved on to answer questions from another girl. "We won't have to worry about not knowing the language, and we'll see lots of beautiful, um . . . gardens . . . and I don't know . . . English sheep? It will be great."

"Oh, yes, English sheep and rose gardens," said Viv with sarcasm, teasing Dottie. "It'll be swell. Cannot wait to see those sheep. Do you think they baa with an English accent?" Dottie swatted her arm, and they both started giggling, which made me smile despite myself. I was beyond disappointed, yet I had no choice but to put on a brave face for now.

"Okay, I think we're all here," Miss Chambers said after the last of the Red Cross girls from the *Queen Elizabeth* made it over to our group. "We should start heading to the trucks. I'm sure you're all tired and hungry and want to get—"

A terrible sound punctuated the air, like a police siren but higher pitched and more frantic.

She paused and looked up. There was another sound of something in the sky—a loud, low rumble like a motorbike, coming closer.

"What's that sound?" I asked.

"British Royal Air Force, right?" Dottie asked, looking at Miss Chambers.

"Miss Chambers, incoming buzz bomb," a young British soldier said loudly as he ran past our group. "We all need to take cover."

"What on earth is that boy talking about?" Blanche Dumond asked, snapping her gum.

GI drivers started jumping out of their vehicles, whistling and yelling. The groups of soldiers ahead of us turned around, running back toward the station. The rumble was louder still as more people around us started sprinting.

"Helmets on, ladies! Buzz bomb coming in!" A sweaty, pasty-faced American soldier hollered at us as he ran by.

Miss Chambers, her face pale, nodded at all of us. "Listen to what he says, ladies. Back into the station. Helmets on, hurry now, do not stop. We'll head to the great hall to take shelter."

"What the heck is a buzz bomb?" Viv breathlessly asked another soldier as we ran. He ran alongside us and was kind enough to grab some of Dottie's gear when he saw she was struggling.

"You'll learn soon enough; just get to safety now," he said in a sharp tone.

As we were about to enter the archway of Euston Station once more, the soldier handed Dottie back her gear and said, "Welcome to London!" as he rushed back out to usher more people into the building to take shelter.

Dottie tightened her helmet as she struggled to hold on to the rest of her gear again. Martha Slattery, a round-cheeked farm girl from Iowa we had just met on the crossing, hurried behind us with Blanche Dumond.

The train station was in utter chaos as civilians, soldiers, and Red Cross workers ran inside for cover, many of them hastily throwing on helmets as they tried to find a place to shelter from whatever was coming. Many soldiers were handing their helmets to civilian women and children, as a few officers yelled instructions, telling people where to go. The roar of the buzz bomb was so loud now it echoed in the cavernous train station.

We jostled our way into the station's magnificent great hall with hundreds of people heading in the same direction. But where to go? If the bomb hit the station, was anywhere inside truly safe? How big would the blast be? My stomach lurched, and I felt like I might throw up.

"Over there, ladies; head toward any of the alcoves—hurry!" Miss Chambers said, frantic, when she spotted us.

Our group scattered and ran to crowd into the various alcoves. I felt even sicker and more than a little naïve. Viv, Dottie, and I, along with Blanche and Martha, huddled in an alcove near the ladies' bathroom. Out of the corner of my eye, I spotted an impossibly petite person in a Red Cross uniform running toward us at top speed, helmet on, gear in hand. She squeezed in next to us.

"Hi, Martha; hey, Blanche." A girl I recognized from the boat plopped herself down next to Martha, who moved over to give her more room.

"I'm Frankie Cullen," she said, nodding at me, Dottie, and Viv. She was barely five feet, with wide-set light-brown eyes and shiny dark-brown curls peeking out from under her helmet, but there was a toughness about her despite her childlike size. She looked around, observing the scene without a trace of fear.

The roar continued to get louder, and more soldiers and civilians kept streaming inside the station to take cover. The British citizens looked fairly calm, but many of the young American soldiers who had just arrived with us looked horror-struck, as did many of the Clubmobile girls. More than one girl had started to cry.

"Jesus, it's so loud," Dottie said, tears in her eyes as she chewed on a strand of her hair out of what I suspected was a combination of nervousness and hunger. We were all listening and looking up at the gorgeous coffered ceiling high above us.

"But we're going to be fine, right? It can't be *that* close," I said, more to calm myself than anyone else. And right after I said it, the deafening roar stopped. The skies above the train station went completely silent. Now even some of the British men and women looked terrified. A few of the young American soldiers were blinking back tears. A baby's cries echoed off the walls.

"Brace yourselves! Brace yourselves and stay calm! Stay calm, stay low!" an army officer yelled to anyone who might listen.

I grabbed one of Viv's hands and one of Dottie's as we crouched even lower in the alcove.

An elderly woman sat near us in a tattered gray overcoat, wearing a helmet a soldier had just given her. She closed her eyes, put her hands together, and started to pray.

Welcome to London. The GI's words to us minutes ago echoed in my head.

And then the buzz bomb exploded right outside of Euston Station.

The blast was deafening, a sharper sound than I had expected. My ears were still ringing minutes after we realized it was over, which made the aftermath seem that much more surreal as I looked around at the expressions of terror on the faces of the people around me, hearing but not quite understanding what was happening. The sound of shattering glass came from somewhere on the other side of the station, where the blast had originated. And the baby that had been crying was now screeching. Hers wasn't the only scream I heard.

It took a few seconds for me to absorb that it was over and I could finally stop squeezing Dottie's and Viv's hands.

The old lady in the tattered coat was the first one near us to stand up. She handed back the helmet that had been loaned to her, brushed herself off, and walked away.

Other British civilians in the station followed suit. With looks on their faces like they were mildly embarrassed about the trouble, they dusted off their knees, said calming words to their children, and left the station to go about the rest of their day in their battered city.

Most of us who had just arrived from the US weren't holding up quite so well. The complexions of many of the young soldiers nearby had turned ashen in the aftermath of the bombing. One soldier crouched with his knees to his chest, his helmet covering his entire face as he stifled a sob.

Blanche had pulled out a cigarette and was trying to light it, but her hand was shaking so much she couldn't quite get the flame near enough to catch. Martha leaned over and tried cupping her hands around the lighter to help, but hers were shaking too, so it was hopeless. My heart was racing, and for the first time I considered taking up smoking. Anything to calm the jumpiness. I was sure I was wearing the same shocked expression as Viv and Dottie.

Only Frankie Cullen seemed completely composed, studying the scene around us like she was taking mental notes. She jumped up and started gathering her gear with an efficiency and earnestness I found annoying.

"Those buzz bomb jitters you're feeling?" Judith Chambers said, projecting her voice for all the Red Cross girls that were remotely within earshot. "It's normal—happens to everyone the first couple of times. I promise that will stop after a while."

She stood up and took off her helmet. "You won't even think about them after a few days. Come on now, make sure you have all of your things. It's time to head over to Park Street and get you all settled."

We all came out of our hiding spots, picking up our gear and once again heading out of the station. Weighed down by our gas masks, helmets, and everything else we were carrying, we looked like a bunch of droopy chicks, shocked and exhausted, as we followed Miss Chambers, our mother hen. I couldn't even speak for several minutes; the rest of the girls were silent too. It was our first up-close encounter with a war that we'd previously only known from the newspapers and radio.

"I need a drink," Viv said, breaking the silence as she chewed on her thumbnail. It was something she did only when she was nervous, a rarity for her.

Blanche laughed, put her arm around Viv's shoulder, and said, "Oh, sweetheart, we're all getting a drink after this baloney."

As we walked, I kept looking back toward the other side of the station, where the glass had shattered from the bomb's impact beyond it. Our train had arrived on one of the tracks on that side just an hour before. It was sheer luck that we hadn't been pulling into the station when the bomb struck. I tucked a lock of hair behind my ear and realized my hands were shaking too.

"Well, that would have been a hell of a way to go," Viv said, as if reading my thoughts. "Get all the way over here and then bite the dust on the first day?"

"No kidding," I said. "I still can't believe that just happened. You okay over there, Dots?" She was walking next to us with her head down.

"Yes, I was just thinking about what my parents would say," she said, her voice a whisper. "You remember how furious they were. They were so against me doing this with my brother already in the Pacific. This is *not* something I'm going to write home about."

This time, when we walked outside under the enormous arches of Euston Station, the London air smelled acrid, and an ominous-looking tower of dark smoke billowed from the other side of the building. We all looked up at the sky as we walked, listening for the siren to start up again.

Seeing that most of us were still traumatized, Miss Chambers kept talking as we went, raising her voice so that most of the group could hear her.

"Buzz bombs are V-1s. Pilotless bombs with motors," she said, in a matter-of-fact way that was unnerving. "The Germans launch them from the coast of France. They resemble small airplanes, and the tail end burns a steady bright light. When the motor cuts off, the bomb either falls straight down and explodes or drifts on awhile before falling and blowing up. One thing you learn quickly is that you're safe as long as you can *hear the motor*. The good news is, a buzz bomb destroys the object it hits, but not much around it."

"My neighbor told me about the buzz bombs in one of his last letters to me; he called them doodlebugs," Martha said. "People have been leaving the city in droves because of them. Be happy that we're only going to be in London for eight days."

"That feels like an awful long time if there are going to be bombs constantly dropping," Dottie said, looking like she was on the verge of tears again.

"Miss Chambers?" I said, raising my voice as we were walking several feet behind her. "How frequently do the buzz bombs strike?"

"They've been coming in increasing numbers this summer for sure, which is why so many women and children have been evacuated to the countryside," she said in a no-nonsense tone. "They usually come at night, though. Starting tomorrow night, after you've unpacked and settled in, you'll work in shifts of two girls at a time, watching for V-1s from the rooftop so you can warn everyone else to take cover if one is incoming."

"Seriously?" Blanche piped up. She and Viv were both on their second, shaky cigarette. "That's how we're going to know they're coming? A couple of us staring at the sky?"

"Seriously," said Miss Chambers, looking Blanche in the eye to make sure she knew she meant it. "As I said, all this will become routine to you soon. Ah, good, the trucks are all here. Climb in, ladies; let's get you registered at the club so you can get some sleep. I know you're all exhausted and hungry."

"Miss Chambers, I'll take the first shift," Frankie Cullen said, sitting next to me as we settled in for the ride. "I don't need that much sleep anyway. Hey, Fiona, why don't you join me tomorrow night?" She elbowed me.

"Um, sure," I said, my voice flat and on the edge of sarcasm. That was the last thing I wanted to do. I bit my tongue.

"Perfect, that settles it," Miss Chambers said with a nod. "Thank you, Frankie, Fiona."

Aside from Frankie, the rest of our crew was sullen and famished now that our long journey had concluded with a bomb scare. I felt physically ill from all of it, but perhaps still mostly because we weren't going to the Continent after all. I needed sleep so that I could think clearly again. And I needed a new plan now that we were going to be stuck in the UK.

I looked out the window at the streets of London, haunted by a war it had endured for four long years. As we drove, we saw gray buildings with boarded-up windows and piles of bricks stacked beside dusty bomb sites. Due to years of rationing, vegetable gardens were growing all around the Tower of London and St. James's Square. Most of the people on the streets, if they weren't in some kind of military uniform, were wearing mismatched, shabby clothes and shoes long worn through. The Londoners looked just as beaten down as the city itself.

A couple of the girls gasped as the driver took us by St. Paul's Cathedral, still standing majestically, though the buildings around it had been completely destroyed. Something about that cathedral among the ruins made me blink back tears.

"Imagine," I said to Viv and Dottie as we all gaped out the windows, "living under war conditions like this in Boston? For *years*? I don't know how they've managed it."

"You'd be amazed what the human spirit can endure, can adapt to. I know you're still in shock from the bombing, but I meant what I said: you'll all adjust to this new world in time," Miss Chambers said, looking around at us, her tone curt, calm, and professional. "And the English are as tough as they come . . ."

I thought of the Londoners at the station right after the bombing, going about their business as if a bomb dropping were just a huge inconvenience like a thunderstorm or a late train. How long had it taken them to get used to the air raid sirens and bombings as their new normal? How long would it take us?

Chapter Four

Dear Danny,

I should be writing to my parents and sisters right now. I promised them I would as soon as I arrived, but instead I'm writing to you, though of course I have no address. I have arrived in London for eight days of Red Cross training, and I've been wondering about what you would think if you knew I was here. You would no doubt think I was crazy for volunteering to go to the war. You would be worried about my safety and try to convince me to go home. But when you went missing, it turned my world upside down. What is my life without our future plans?

    While I've had my moments of doubt, coming here is better than doing nothing. My life stalled after you left. At least now I feel like I'm in forward motion after months of just waiting. Waiting for news about you. Waiting for life to happen to me. Too much waiting.

    I realize now how naïve I was to think that of all the men going to war, you were going to be one of the ones that would be okay. When I wake up in the morning, it sometimes takes me a few seconds to remember that you're missing . . . and my heart hurts all over again.

If you are anywhere, I'm much closer to you now geographically—but are you anywhere? I'm not on the Continent yet, but I'll get there.

Viv, Dottie, and I are currently rooming together in a spartan, college-dormitory-style room in a building the Red Cross has taken over. After our journey, and a close encounter with a buzz bomb, we had to wait in line for hours to register. When they finally assigned us rooms, I was so dead tired I don't even remember falling asleep. Dottie is still sleeping soundly next to me, curled up small like a cat. We decided to let Princess Viv have the other bed to herself because, believe it or not, she snores like a fat old grandpa, and she would have finagled it somehow anyway. Her snoring just woke me up, even though I'm still exhausted from the journey. It's about five p.m. London time, and I . . .

I jumped at the sound of a loud rapping on the door, and someone said hello in a sing-song voice from the other side.

"Hey, Boston! You gals awake in there?" I cracked open the door to see Blanche on the other side, blonde curls pinned and shiny, candy-apple-red lipstick perfectly applied. She looked fresh as a daisy compared to my groggy state.

"I'm barely awake; Viv and Dottie are still out cold," I whispered.

"Well, get them *up*, sweetheart," Blanche said with a smile. "We've got to see London while we can. Martha and Frankie are getting ready now. Meet us downstairs in an hour."

I rubbed my eyes. The thought of going anywhere besides back to bed wasn't appealing, but I had already learned that Blanche was not one to take no for an answer. "Where are we going?"

"Rainbow Corner," said Blanche.

"Rainbow what?" I asked, stifling a yawn.

"It's the Red Cross club in the West End, near Piccadilly. It is *the* place to go. Get the girls up." She looked me up and down, and added, "And you should definitely shower." As she was walking away, she said over her shoulder, "Also, we've got to wear our uniforms, or Chambers will flip her wig. But we can wear high heels."

∼

At dusk, the six of us hit the streets of London in our summer uniforms and heels. I was still tired but felt much better after a lukewarm shower and a change into fresh clothes.

"Blanche, you're sure we have to wear our uniforms when we go out for a night on the town?" Viv asked. "I brought a great new dress for nights like this."

"That's what the rest of the girls on our floor were saying," Blanche said. "We are going to a Red Cross Club after all. And do you really want to get on Miss Chambers's bad side on the first day?"

Viv sighed. "I guess not."

"Just so I understand, those buzz bombs could happen anytime, day or night?" Dottie asked no one in particular. "It could happen right this minute? I mean, a buzz bomb could land right in front of us?" She was scanning the sky with trepidation.

"We'd hear it coming and find somewhere to take cover," Frankie said in a matter-of-fact tone. "No use fretting constantly about it. God, I wish I could be up there, helping to shoot some of them down."

"Wish you could be up there? What are you talking about?" I asked her. Blanche and Martha had become friendly with Frankie on the *Queen Elizabeth*. I didn't know her very well yet, only that she took being a Clubmobile girl very seriously and was definitely a bit of an eager beaver for that reason. It got on my nerves.

"Didn't you know?" Blanche said, snapping her gum. "Frankie here learned to fly planes. She was gunning to be a pilot."

"That was the original plan—even got my pilot's license. I had applied to be one of those WASPs, the Women Airforce Service Pilots. But I was too damn short, so they rejected my application," Frankie said, bitterness in her voice. "They don't take anyone that's only five feet tall." She paused for a second before adding, "Of course, if I'd been accepted, it's not like they would have let me see any combat action. I'd be at a base in Texas or something. I'd rather be here."

London's West End was an enormous sea of humanity. We turned down the crowded street outside the club and made our way to the line at the front door.

"My neighbor, Tim, told me about this place in his letters," Martha said to me, excitement in her eyes as we followed the rest of the girls. She looked like she had just walked off the farm into her uniform. Her thick, chestnut-brown hair was pinned under her cap simply, her round cheeks flushed. She was wearing no makeup but for a swipe of natural pink lipstick. "Rainbow Corner is one of the biggest clubs in Europe. It's got hotel-style rooms upstairs, a dance hall, game rooms with pinball machines, a barber shop, a soda fountain, and American-style restaurants. It's one of his favorite places over here."

"Wow," I said, looking up at the five-story brick building. Across the entire facade, above the entrance and below three arched banks of windows on the second floor, were the words "American Red Cross Rainbow Corner" in huge red block letters on a white tile background.

Blanche was right—the Piccadilly Circus part of London was hopping. It looked like half the young people in Great Britain were out on this cool summer night. British girls wearing too much rouge chatted with American GIs. Canadian, Australian, and New Zealand accents could be heard as we walked the streets. French, Dutch, and Czech soldiers strolled together, talking and laughing in their respective languages. It was a melting pot of military and nonmilitary personnel, but with so many Americans in the area, it almost felt more like New York City than London.

"Girls! Red Cross girls! Come on up!" The man checking IDs at the door waved us over.

We stepped out of line and walked over to him. A few of the GIs waiting to get in whistled and nodded. Someone said, "Yeah, American girls!" when we walked up.

We all handed the man our IDs. I looked around, and for a minute I thought we were in trouble.

"You ladies must be brand-new," the squat, older man in the rumpled Red Cross uniform said.

"We arrived early this morning," I answered.

"Welcome to the European theater of operations, Fiona, otherwise known as the ETO," he replied, looking at my ID with a smile. "Now you know, Red Cross girls can skip the line, even on crazy Friday nights like this."

"I didn't know that, but now we do, thank you," I said.

"Time to relax and finally have that drink, ladies. Let's go," Blanche said, pushing us all inside with playful shoves.

More catcalls and wolf whistles met us as we walked through the doors. I looked over at Dottie, and she was already blushing. Viv just smiled and held her head high, winking at a couple of the guys as she passed by just to drive them crazy.

I caught Frankie rolling her eyes behind Viv's back, clearly annoyed. It wasn't the first time I'd seen her react that way. I could tell she thought Viv and Blanche were a little too flighty and flirtatious, like they didn't take our role here seriously enough.

In the reception area, a dark-haired woman was sitting behind a desk with a stack of paper and some pens. There was a young GI sitting with her, drinking a bottle of Coke. His mouth dropped open when we all walked up.

"Come in, come in; welcome to Rainbow Corner," the woman said. "I'm Adele, one of the regular volunteers here. So lovely to see more

American girls arriving." I guessed she was in her midthirties, with warm brown eyes and a kindhearted demeanor.

We all introduced ourselves, and Adele gave us a brief, well-rehearsed talk about the different areas of the club and the services available.

"We can get you tickets to a West End show, and we also offer tours of London," Adele said, and I could tell she was winding down her speech. "Do you have any questions?"

We all murmured our thanks and said no.

"I have to help this young man finish his letter to his mother now, but please don't hesitate to ask me anything at all. Welcome, and thank you for your service." And then, as we started walking away, she added, "Oh, and you're in luck. Since it's Friday, there's a fantastic band in the dance hall called the Hepcats—you can't miss them. I plan on heading in later for a dance or two," she said with a laugh.

"I want to explore this place," Frankie said. "Anyone want to come with?"

"Let's head in to see the band!" Dottie said, never one to turn down a chance to see live music.

"Sounds good, Dots," Viv said. "I need to sit and have a cold drink after that walk."

Blanche and Martha agreed to wander with Frankie, while Viv, Dottie, and I followed the sound of swing music. We entered a massive dance hall with high ceilings and cream-colored paneled walls covered with ornate plaster molding. Lights were strung across the width of it, and a crystal ball dangled in the center of the dance floor. There was a bar in the back corner, and the band was on a stage on the opposite side of the room from the entrance. Small tables and chairs were scattered near the walls around the edges of the room. The floor was packed with couples jitterbugging to the Hepcats' rendition of "Stompin' at the Savoy."

We squeezed our way up to the bar, where most of the men were more than happy to step aside and let us through—compliments, whistles, and "Hey, dolls" coming at us the whole time. Viv smiled and nodded, acting like a movie star responding to her fans. She even blew a kiss to a couple of young soldiers as we walked by, and one of them stumbled back, holding his heart. Dottie put her head down, blushing as red as the frames of her glasses, which only made some of the guys try harder for her attention. I followed behind them, giving the men a friendly smile as I realized I was searching the crowd for a tall blond second lieutenant I would never find there. If Danny were alive and able, he wouldn't have been at this club tonight anyway.

"What's your pleasure, ladies?" the bartender said when we finally made it up to the bar.

"A gin and tonic and two beers, please," Viv said.

"We've got warm British beer and cold American Cokes—no gin and tonics here," the bartender said with a wistful smile. "And the beer is only on Friday and Saturday nights—Red Cross rules." He dropped his voice to a whisper. "To be honest, I don't think the top brass even know we serve beer at all."

"I say, you ladies must be new here," a deep, British-accented voice called across the bar. We looked over at a—well, there was really no other way to describe him—a dashing man in a British Royal Air Force uniform standing to the right of the bar, holding a beer mug. He was tall, and with his accent, large dark eyes, and thick black hair, all I could think of was Cary Grant. He lifted his mug in a toast. "Welcome to London. So glad they've finally sent some more Red Cross girls over here. Can I ask, are there any young men left in your country? Because it seems like all of them are in mine."

"Almost all of them are gone. What's a British officer doing in an American club? Isn't that against the rules?" Viv said, clinking her glass against his. Dottie and I exchanged furtive glances that said, *This guy is a goner.* None of them could resist when Viv started flirting.

"Well, it's all about friends in high places, isn't it?" he said with a smile. "I'm Harry Westwood, invited by a few of my new American friends. Where are you all from?"

"All from Boston," Viv answered. "I'm Viv; this is Dottie and Fiona."

"Viv, like the actress Vivien Leigh?" Harry asked.

"Like Viviana Occhipinti," Viv said, giving him that sultry smile that had broken so many hearts.

"Lovely city, Boston, despite our country's beastly history there," Harry said.

"You've actually been there, then?" Viv said.

"One of my old chums went to Harvard, and I visited him while on holiday one summer," he said. He looked up and noticed something near the dance hall entrance. "If you'll excuse me, I've got to go see someone. Have a jolly good evening, ladies." He nodded, tipped his glass, and walked into the crowd.

I looked over at Viv, and I could tell she was miffed. No man ever walked away from her charms. No man ever walked away before she did.

"Well, he left in a hurry," Viv said, following him with her eyes. "I must be losing my touch. Let's go find a 'jolly good' table."

"Do you think he looked like Cary Grant?" Dottie asked when we sat down at a small, wobbly table in the corner of the room. "I kept thinking he looked exactly like Cary Grant."

"No way—you're not losing your touch, Viv," I said. "I've heard the Brits can be very standoffish."

"Oh, I don't really care," Viv said with a little too much emphasis, lighting up a cigarette and scanning the crowd one last time. "I've told you girls, I'm not here to meet my husband. I'm here to see the world. To have an adventure outside of the four square miles of Boston I live and work in. And, you know, actually contribute to the war and all that."

"Cheers, girls," Dottie said, clinking her mug with ours before taking a sip. "I can't quite believe we're in London. And listen to this band!" She craned her neck to get a better view of the stage. "Their pianist is amazing; do you hear that? He also happens to be gorgeous. It's *almost* enough to make me forget our close encounter with a bomb today."

"Almost but not enough," said Viv. "I've still got the jitters." She elbowed me and added, "So what's going on, Fiona? Dottie and I noticed you've been unusually quiet since we arrived. Are you that upset about the bomb today, or is it because we're stuck here in Britain? Or is it Danny?"

"A little bit of all that," I said, taking a sip of my beer. "But as far as being stuck in Britain, after sleeping on it, I think I know what we need to do."

"We?" asked Dottie.

"We," I said. "So, in eight days we're off to the countryside with the rest of the Clubmobilers that just arrived."

"Yes. And what's your grand scheme exactly?" Viv said, looking at me with skepticism.

"All we have to do, the only thing we really can do, is impress Miss Chambers with our skills," I said. "We have to be the best Clubmobile trio she has ever laid eyes on. We'll knock her socks off with our work ethic and our charm. She'll quickly realize our value and how amazing we are, and we'll be the first women in our group to be transferred to the Continent. I mean, how hard is this job going to be? We're college-educated, professional women for God's sake."

"I don't know, Fiona. I'm not sure it's going to be as easy as you think," Viv said.

"I'm telling you, it'll be a piece of cake for us," I said. "And we're already friends, so we work together well. Although, Dottie, you definitely need to get over your stage fright with the troops. Hellooo, Dottie? Did you hear what I said?"

Dottie was blushing and looking behind me, where the band had paused for a quick break. I turned around to see a tall man with reddish hair heading to our table. It took me a minute to place his face, and then I remembered him from my sleepless night on the *Queen Elizabeth*.

"Joe Brandon, the late-night piano player from the *QE*! How are you?" I said, standing up to greet him and make introductions.

"Ah, the Boston girls," he said. He pulled up a chair and sat down with us, and one of the white-coated members of the Hepcats came up behind him and handed him a bottle of beer.

"Nice playing there, Brandon," the band member said. "Don't tell Bernie, but you're way better on the keys. You can play with us anytime."

"Aw, I doubt that, Wayne," he said to the man. "But thanks, it was fun."

"Wait, that was you up there?" I said as Wayne walked away. "Dottie was just saying that you were amazing, and she knows music better than anyone."

I immediately regretted saying it because Dottie was visibly mortified. At least I had left out the part about how she also thought he was gorgeous.

"What's a piano player doing in the army?" Viv asked, covering for Dottie, who couldn't manage to squeak a word out.

Joe explained how he was captain of the army band of the Twenty-Eighth. He was looking at Dottie when he talked, but she could barely meet his gaze as she took a big gulp of her beer and fiddled with her glasses.

"Dottie, Fiona told me you play more than one instrument. Is that right?" Joe said, trying to put her at ease with a kind smile.

"I . . . yes . . . I do," said Dottie, her voice soft. "Guitar and piano . . . though not nearly as well as you. I also play clarinet, although that's my least favorite of the three."

"What do you like the best?" he asked.

"I think guitar," she said with a slow nod. "I brought mine, but I need to work up the nerve to play for the troops. Fiona was just saying that, and she's right. My usual audience members are under the age of twelve, at the elementary school where I teach music. It's a . . . it's just different."

"I'm sure the guys will love you. Trust me," he said, turning her blush up a notch again. "So, what are some of your favorite bands? What type of music do you like best?" Joe asked. Dottie started to relax as she talked about her love of Glenn Miller and the Andrews Sisters.

They continued to talk about music, their favorite songs and arrangements, different bands they'd seen live in Boston and Chicago. It was like Viv and I weren't even there. I was somewhat amazed that Dottie was talking to Joe at all. Viv kicked me under the table, and I knew she was thinking the same thing. Back in Boston, Dottie would sometimes excuse herself to the ladies' room when guys sat down with us at a club, just to avoid talking to them.

"I'd love to hear you play sometime, Dottie," Joe said, taking a last swig of beer and getting up from the table. "I'm heading to a pub a couple blocks down to meet up with some friends, so I've got to run. Then I'm out in a couple of days, but hopefully I'll run into you ladies again."

"I'm sure you will," Viv said. "Take care, Joe."

"It was really nice chatting with you," Dottie said, giving him a dimpled smile.

He paused, cocked his head, and looked at the three of us for a few seconds. "Are all girls from Boston this pretty?"

"Of course they are," I said sarcastically, shaking my head. "And yes, I'm sure we'll see you again. Take care of yourself."

When he walked away, Viv leaned over the table, patted Dottie's hand, and gave her a playful grin. "Well, if you talk to all the soldiers like that one, Dottie, you're going to be *just fine* over here. All of our worrying about you will be for nothing."

"Viv, it's only because he's a music guy," Dottie said. "Those types are easier to talk to for me."

"He's a *handsome* guy," Viv said.

"Yeah, he is," I said. "I didn't really think about it the night I met him on the boat, but he's good-looking."

"And he liked you," Viv said, nudging Dottie.

"He did *not*," Dottie said, hope in her voice.

Then I remembered about his girl from home, Mary Jane. *Oh shoot.* I was about to tell Dottie when the band started up again, this time playing "Moonlight Serenade," and the crowd erupted in wild cheers. A couple was dancing alone in the middle of the dance floor. It took me a second to realize it was Adele, the Red Cross woman from the front desk, and the dashing Brit Harry Westwood. They were mesmerizing as they waltzed across the dance floor, in perfect sync with the music and each other.

"Well, I'll be damned . . . ," Viv said. "Do you think that's his—"

"Girls, what the heck are you doing here in the corner?" Blanche said, barging up to our table. "As soon as they start playing something fun, you are all getting up and dancing. Martha and Frankie are playing pool upstairs with some GIs, but they'll join us soon."

"Okay, Blanche," I said, as she sat down. "Do you have any idea why they cleared the floor for those two?"

"Of course I know," Blanche said, thrilled to share this gossip. "Don't you know who Adele *is*?"

"No idea," Viv said, handing her a cigarette and pointing to Harry Westwood. "Is that her husband?"

"No, silly, she's a recent widow," Blanche said. "She was married to a lord. She's known over here as Lady Cavendish, but her maiden name is Astaire. As in *Fred Astaire*. She's Fred's sister *and* his original dance partner."

We all gasped in surprise and turned to watch the couple's final spin around the dance floor. She wasn't a kid anymore, but she was still a gorgeous dancer. When the music stopped, everyone started clapping and cheering, and Adele and Harry gave a quick bow before the band started up with the tune "Oh Johnny, Oh Johnny, Oh!" and the dance floor flooded with couples.

Blanche pulled me up by my hand and nodded to Viv and Dottie. "All right, ladies, we're going to grab some soldiers to jitterbug with and cheer 'em up before they head off to God knows what."

I'm not sure if it was the beer or her enthusiasm, but the three of us got up and followed her onto the dance floor, laughing the whole time.

Chapter Five

July 22, 1944

We didn't get back to our dorms at 103 Park Street until well after midnight, and I collapsed into bed next to Dottie after brushing my teeth, my feet sore from dancing in heels. So many of the officers and GIs at Rainbow Corner had been thrilled to have "real, live American girls" to dance with, and their enthusiasm was infectious. They kept begging us not to go home. For the first time in months, I forgot about everything other than jitterbugging with sweaty soldiers and laughing with my friends.

Seven the next morning came way too quickly. Dottie and I had to drag Viv, dead asleep and snoring, out of bed to get dressed so we could get to the Red Cross headquarters in Grosvenor Square on time. The air raid sirens started just as we arrived at the front doors.

"No worries, girls. Today's forecast is cloudy with just a slight chance of buzz bombs," I said to Viv and Dottie, trying to hide my nervousness at the sound of the siren as a receptionist directed us to head up the dark mahogany staircase to the training classroom.

"You're hilarious, Fi," Viv said, unamused. "I've already got the shakes just from hearing that damn siren. And I can't believe I can't smoke in class."

"I need coffee. And I'm never going to get used to the sirens," Dottie said, trying to glance out the windows as we climbed the staircase.

We found the classroom on the second floor. It was a lecture hall that had rows of chairs facing a lectern and chalkboard. As we worked our way over to three empty seats in the front, we waved and said hello, chatting with different groups of girls as we passed. I looked around for Blanche, Martha, and Frankie but didn't see them.

Ten minutes later, the door opened and Judith Chambers walked in holding some files, followed by two other women in Red Cross uniforms and two army officers. The hall quieted down as Miss Chambers took to the lectern. One of the women with her started writing on the chalkboard:

CLUBMOBILE TRAINING

AIR RAID PRECAUTIONS

ANTI-GAS PRECAUTIONS, TREATMENT, AND RESPIRATION DRILLS

FIRST AID REFRESHER

AMBULANCE WORK AND STRETCHER BEARING

GMC TRUCK DRIVING (INCLUDING BLACKOUT DRIVING) AND BRITISH DRIVER'S LICENSE TEST

DOUGHNUT AND COFFEE MAKING

"Good morning, ladies. A warm welcome to your first day of training in London," Miss Chambers said in a booming voice, smiling out at us. "The sirens are due to what we've dubbed the 'eight o'clock express' buzz bombs. They're hoping to catch military personnel on their way to breakfast or work. But not to worry. Someone will come to notify us if we have to be evacuated to the basement."

"Oh, swell," Dottie whispered to me. "At least if they ship us out to the country, there will be fewer buzz bombs, right?"

"I have no idea," I whispered back.

"We have a lot to pack into eight days of training, not to mention other required administrative tasks like dispensing your battle dress trouser uniforms, ration cards, and other necessities," Miss Chambers continued. "I'm going to break you up into—"

Just then, the door flew open, and a few girls jumped up in panic, no doubt thinking we had to evacuate. But it was Blanche, Martha, and Frankie. Blanche and Martha looking slightly disheveled and bleary-eyed. It was possible they had slept in their uniforms. And Blanche's alabaster complexion had a distinctly greenish hue.

"Oh boy, did either of you hear them come home last night?" Viv whispered, giving us an amused look. Dottie and I both shook our heads.

"Ahem." Miss Chambers gave them a tight smile as they all murmured apologies for being late. "Nice of you to join us, ladies."

Heads down, they hurried over and took seats a couple of rows behind us. Miss Chambers cleared her throat and gave them a pointed look before she began speaking again.

"Before I break you up into groups for training, now is a good time to discuss a few of the requirements of being a Red Cross Clubmobile girl. This is, as you know, a prestigious assignment, and you all went through a rigorous selection process. After completion of your training here in London, you will be out in the field, working very much on your own with the military except for check-ins by your section captain. And I will also be stopping by to evaluate on occasion to make sure things are shipshape in each group.

"In regard to your behavior, we hold you to the highest standards, and you all must abide by the rules of the Red Cross and the army, laid out to you in the guidelines you received in DC. Some of the most important guidelines to remember are, number one, follow the army's requests and regulations. And number two, adhere to a midnight curfew, unless special permission is granted. Number three? Always be on time. The army waits for no one. And being late in a war zone? That can put you in harm's way, or even get you killed."

She said this last part while looking directly at Martha, Blanche, and Frankie, who were all sitting low in their chairs, trying to hide under their caps. I turned and caught a glimpse of Frankie's face; she looked furious.

Other girls in the room started to squirm in their seats, whispering to each other. Viv glanced at me and rolled her eyes, fiddling with an imaginary cigarette. Dottie refused to look our way. She was a rule follower, and the buzz bombs had really gotten to her. Her olive complexion was pale, and she looked straight at the front of the room. Miss Chambers picked up every cue from her audience.

"Now, I know this all sounds harsh," she said, gripping the lectern and scanning the room, trying to make eye contact with as many of us as she could. "But understand that you have just arrived at the doorstep of a war you've only experienced in newspapers. In less than two weeks, you'll know more than ever what being close to the front lines of this conflict is like. This job is a privilege, but I promise you, it will challenge you more than anything you've ever done. You've got to be prepared. That's what the guidelines are for; that's what the training this week is for."

Nobody was whispering anymore. The room was silent while the sirens outside blared on.

"If it appears you cannot abide by the guidelines," Miss Chambers said, "or if we decide that you are not up to the assignment, understand that the Red Cross reserves the right to send you home immediately."

I held my breath at that comment. The atmosphere was tense and uncomfortable as we all looked around at each other, very uneasy now.

Nobody here wanted to go home. It wouldn't happen to us. I would make sure of it.

"Um, didn't we volunteer for this? And she's threatening to send people home on the *first day*? Way to boost morale, don't you think?" Viv said under her breath.

"Not exactly," I said. "But I'm not worried about being sent home."

Despite the warning, I still felt confident that Viv, Dottie, and I had the whole package. We had education, personality, and talents. Though Dottie was shy, I was sure she'd make up for that with her musical gifts. We would be fine.

"Fiona? Fiona, pay attention. They're breaking us up into groups for training," Dottie said, grabbing me by the arm. "We're in air raid precautions first. Let's go!"

~

"Jesus Christ, now I've seen everything!" Corporal McAllister bellowed as he walked over to Viv. She had her gas mask on and had pulled out a compact, arranging her curls fetchingly around the gray rubber. A bunch of us started laughing.

"There, that's better," Viv said, voice muffled behind her mask as she snapped her compact shut and put it in her pocket.

"Are you finished, miss?" McAllister asked. He was standing in front of her with his hands on his hips, chest puffing out, bald head shining in the afternoon sun. He had the weary look of a teacher who had lost all patience.

Viv gave him two thumbs up, which for no real reason made us all start giggling more. After spending the day in a first aid training refresher course and an air raid precaution lesson, we had just arrived by bus for our final session of the afternoon.

We were thirty minutes outside of London at the US military base Camp Griffiss in Bushy Park, the second largest royal park in

London. In peacetime, I was sure the park was lovely, but now much of its eleven hundred acres had been transformed for the war. Its ponds and fountains had been drained and covered with camouflaged netting to hide any topographical markings from the enemy. A landing strip for small aircraft had been built, as well as multiple tank courses, and there were anti-aircraft or "ack-ack" batteries everywhere you looked.

Feeling slightly ridiculous, two dozen of us stood in a muddy open field ripe with the smell of horse manure, as we attempted to put on our gas masks. We looked like alien creatures when we finally succeeded.

It had rained the night before, and the air was so muggy my clothes were sticking to me. The corporal had us take off the masks and put them on half a dozen more times to make sure we all knew how to wear and adjust them correctly.

Two jeeps full of GIs drove by the field. When they spotted us, the soldiers leaned out the windows and started whistling and hollering. We waved and blew kisses back at them with our masks on, which made them start cheering even more.

"Settle down, ladies," McAllister said with a grunt.

Dottie and I were watching now as the exasperated corporal helped Viv adjust her gas mask correctly for the sixth time.

"Driving lessons this week should be interesting," I said, as I tried to pull the tangled strands of hair out of my gas mask, "given that I've driven, oh, three times in my life."

I took a deep breath. Driving was the one thing that I was nervous about in all the training. I was a city girl and didn't even have a license.

"That's three more times than me," Dottie answered.

"The country girls will have had much more experience than us," I said.

"Yeah, Martha drives *tractors*," Dottie said. "And she's not the only one."

"Hey, Boston." Frankie came up behind us, whipping off her gas mask like she'd been doing it all her life. Her curls were sticking up in all directions.

"Frankie, what happened last night?" I asked.

"Honestly, I was ready to leave when you did, but Blanche and Martha begged me to stay," Frankie answered, rolling her eyes. "And then we were dancing, which was fun, but, shame on me, I completely lost track of time. Would you believe that club is open around the clock? We got three hours of sleep. And did you see the look on Miss Chambers's face? She was *not* happy with us. I'm still so mad at myself for agreeing to stay; I knew I should have left. I told those two that's the absolute last time I'm ever getting on Miss Chambers's bad side. I will not get kicked out. It's bad enough I was rejected from the WASPs."

"I'm not surprised Blanche wanted to stay," I said.

"Of course she did," Frankie said, shaking her head. "I swear the only reason that girl is here is to flirt with officers."

"But Martha's the one that surprises me," I said. "I didn't think the farm girl had it in her."

"Oh, Martha can *dance*," Frankie said. "She's not as good as that Adele Astaire, but she was knocking it out. Where do you even go to dance in Orange City, Iowa? In the cornfields? Every guy in the place wanted a chance to jitterbug with her. Anyway, we have rooftop duty tonight, Fiona. You ready for it?" Frankie asked. I had forgotten she had volunteered me.

"Sure, Frankie," I said, aggravated. *Do I have a choice?*

"All right, I want you eight," the corporal said, picking out me, Dottie, Frankie, and Viv along with four other girls. "You've all been chatty; you seem ready to be the first to go through the drill in the tear gas chamber." He pointed to the small wooden shack a hundred yards away.

"Right now?" Doris, a proper Southern girl from Alabama, said, frowning at the shed. "In our dress uniforms?"

"Yes, *right now* in your dress uniforms," McAllister said, imitating her voice, Southern accent and all. "You can't exactly take them off."

We trooped over to the sad-looking, windswept shack as he gave us the final instructions for the tear gas test. He led us inside, and we fumbled with our masks as fast as we could, holding our breath for as long as possible. In less than thirty seconds, the corporal led us out of the other side of the shed.

Choking, gagging, shrieking, and laughing, we stumbled out of the shed and tried to remove our masks.

"Now get down low to the ground and smell for gas before removing your masks," he said to us.

We were standing in a huge slick of mud behind the shed. We looked around at each other in our dress uniforms and just nodded to him. Nobody wanted to get too low.

"No, get down, WAY DOWN! Now!" he screamed.

The scream startled all of us, and I squatted with Viv and Dottie as Frankie, Doris, and the other three girls flung themselves down in the mud. I felt it dripping from my cheeks.

"What in God's name are you doing?" McAllister asked them.

"You said lay down!" Frankie looked up at him. "I'm doing what you said, I'm laying down."

"I said *way down*, not lay down," McAllister said.

"Well, from under the gas mask it sounded like *lay down*," Frankie said, exasperated, as she tried to push herself up out of the mud.

McAllister was red-faced, his thin mouth a tight line. But this time his stern expression started to crack. "I said . . ." And then he couldn't hold it. He had been biting his lip, but he broke into a smile and started to laugh, turning around and walking away to compose himself. That was all it took for the group of us to start howling with laughter.

Dottie was laughing so hard, she wobbled and fell back from her squatting position and went legs up, her bottom half fully soaked in mud and her glasses covered in so much muck we couldn't see her eyes. I looked over at Viv as she was trying desperately to extract herself from the mess and stay clean, but it was far too late; her skirt was splattered, and her shoes were barely visible. She was laughing so hard, tears streamed down her muddy face.

"Making doughnuts and driving has to be easier than this," I said to Dottie as Viv and I tried to pull her up, all of us still giggling.

"It better be," Viv said. "Look at what today has done to my nails. I've got to repaint them when we get back."

Dottie and I just looked at each other and rolled our eyes. If Viv's manicures survived the war, it would be a miracle.

❧

That night, back at Park Street, after a cold shower and a hot meal, I met Frankie up on the roof. I wouldn't have seen her sitting in the far corner on a wooden crate if not for the end of her cigarette glowing in the darkness. There was a nice summer breeze, and also that familiar acrid smell, a reminder that war was all around us.

"Hi," I said, walking up to her, still clutching the unopened letter that had been waiting for me when we got back from training.

"Hey, I found two crates to sit on," she said, motioning to a second one.

"Thank you. Any action so far?" I asked.

"Nah, quiet tonight. It looks so eerie out there—not a light in sight."

"Someday I'm going to return to London when the lights are back on."

"I was thinking the same," Frankie said.

"Where are you from anyway?" I asked. If we were going to be sitting there all night together, I figured I should get to know her better.

"Chicago, Illinois, only the best city on earth," she said. "Huge Cubs fan, of course."

"You're the second person I've met from Chicago. What did you do there?" I asked.

"I worked at Marshall Field's, the department store?" she said. "I was a salesgirl in their shoe department. I loved it, and I was so good at it. I was one of the top salespeople every month."

"Why does that not surprise me? So why leave to do this?"

"Well, I'm not a nurse, and they wouldn't let me fly," she said. "I needed to do something in the war. This job is the closest I can get to real combat."

"Why in the world would you want to be in actual combat?" I asked.

She was quiet for a moment. Even when she was sitting, her knee bounced up and down, constantly in motion.

"Ever since my husband, Rick, died in the war two years ago, I've been wanting to fight back," she said.

I peered over at her; she was observing the dark city. For a moment, I was at a loss for words.

"Frankie, I . . . I'm so sorry, I had no idea," I said. She was a war widow. I squeezed the letter tightly.

"It's okay," she said. "I thought Blanche had told you—she tells everyone everything." She paused for a moment before continuing. "Don't get me wrong, it wasn't okay for a long time. Rick was a bombardier in the US Army Air Corps, killed in North Africa in July of '42." She sighed. "I was so angry about it in the beginning. *So* angry. But you can't keep feeling that way, or it will drown you."

She paused for a minute, taking a drag of her cigarette.

"But the cliché is true, time heals—at least it's *started* to heal for me. And being here? It's exactly what I needed."

"I understand that," I said in a soft voice. We were both quiet for a minute, watching the sky. "Did Blanche tell you about my fiancé, Danny?"

Frankie nodded, looking me in the eye. "'Course," she said. "The not knowing must be torture. You must wonder all the time—where is he? Did he get out? Is he in Germany? Is he—" She stopped herself.

"Is he gone?" I said, finishing her thought. "It *is* torture."

I took a deep breath of the chilly night air before I started talking again. Now I understood Frankie's commitment to our role here in a way I hadn't before.

"I still have his last letter from October. I keep it in the bottom of my musette bag. I haven't read it in a while, because I practically have it memorized and it just makes me too sad. He always ended his letters 'I'll be seeing you . . .' Like the song."

Frankie nodded. We were part of a club nobody ever wanted to be a member of. But it was an immediate bond, one I was grateful to have here.

"Thank you for telling me about Rick. It's nice to talk to someone who understands. Viv and Dottie have been so supportive, but . . ."

"But they don't really get it," she said.

"No, and I hope they never do." I looked down at the envelope in my hand.

"Is that a letter from home?"

"Yes," I said. "From my family. And I'm dying to open it because I miss them so much, but I'm almost afraid to open it because they might have news about Danny. It's from my three younger sisters."

"You're really that afraid to open it?" she asked, holding her hand out. "Do you want me to do it?"

I thought about it for a second. "Would you? Please skim it to see if there's news of him, so I know." I handed her the envelope.

Frankie carefully opened it and held the letter up close to her face to read it in the glow of her cigarette. I caught a glimpse of my sisters' three different handwriting styles and the silly pictures they had drawn down the sides of the stationery.

"No. Nothing new about Danny. Right at the top of the letter your sister Niamh says, 'As of this writing, he is still considered missing in action.'"

I let out a sigh and realized I had been holding my breath while she was reading it.

"She would do that; she's good that way. It's torture, but . . . I can't help but have hope," I said.

"I understand," Frankie said. "Can I read it out loud to you? It's really sweet. How old are they?"

"Niamh is twenty-three; Deidre and Darcy are eighteen," I answered. "Sure, please read the rest."

Frankie read the letter aloud:

> *Now that we've got that out of the way, how are YOU? How was the trip over? Do you miss us yet? We're putting together a care package for you. What do you need? Deidre's knitting you a red scarf and mittens. Don't worry, we won't forget the Kotex! I can't believe . . .*

The air raid sirens started, and Frankie and I jumped. We stood and scanned the skies, looking for any V-1s heading in the direction of Park Street. She handed me back the letter. We kept searching, and I could feel my heart beating in my throat.

"Okay, if we spot one incoming, we ring the bell?" I said.

Frankie nodded. "We ring the bell, run downstairs to knock on everyone's doors, and then we all head to the basement, put helmets on, and pull pillows over our heads until it's over."

"Frankie . . . ," I said, pointing up to the horizon. I heard it before I spotted it—the tail end a steady, very bright-white light.

"Yeah, that one's coming close. Grab your helmet and let's go!" she said, throwing her own on and running to the staircase.

"Do you think we'll ever get used to this?" I asked, as we flew down the stairs to warn the others, the motorcycle-like rumbling in the sky getting louder by the minute.

"We don't have a choice."

Chapter Six

July 24, 1944

I stood next to Dottie and Viv, cracking my knuckles as we eyed the enormous, ten-ton GMC truck in front of us with suspicion. We had just changed into the army fatigues that Norman, our British driving instructor, had thrown at us when we arrived back at his garage at Camp Griffiss for the first day of our four-day driving and maintenance course. The final two days of training would be dedicated to doughnut and coffee making.

Our training would conclude with a ceremony featuring Harvey Gibson, head of the Red Cross in the European theater. Other Clubmobile trios, including Blanche, Martha, and Frankie, were scattered across the base getting their own private lessons with an instructor.

From the beginning, I had been excited about the idea of being a Clubmobile girl. But I was not excited about driving the behemoth in front of me.

"I'm not sure why we have to have these lessons now if we're staying in England and going to have our own driver here," Dottie said.

"Exactly," Viv said, looking down at the fatigues she was wearing with obvious distaste. "I wish we could skip this and get on to the doughnut making."

"The reason you're having lessons now is so you'll be ready if and when we need to send you over to Zone V," Miss Chambers said as she came around the corner of the garage with an athletic-looking woman, who was also dressed in a Red Cross uniform. The woman was tall, though not as tall as Miss Chambers, with blonde bobbed hair and a face my sisters would describe as handsome but not pretty.

"Well, that makes sense, then, Miss Chambers," I said with a smile. She had to send us to Zone V at some point. Trying to fake enthusiasm, I added, "We're really looking forward to our lesson as we definitely want to be ready for the Continent, er, Zone V."

Viv raised her eyebrows, signaling to me that I was laying it on a little too thick.

"I wanted to introduce you to Liz Anderson," Miss Chambers said. "She recently served with the Clubmobiles in North Africa. Liz is going to be the field captain for your newly assigned Clubmobile group, Group F. You'll be one of eight Clubmobiles in Liz's group."

Viv, Dottie, and I introduced ourselves to the woman who was our new boss and talked with her about where we were from and her experiences in Africa.

"I didn't even know we had been assigned a group yet," I said.

"Yes, well, we're here for a meeting to finalize the details, but we've almost got it figured out," Liz said. She gave us a warm smile. "I look forward to working with you. And trust me when I say that I know these trucks look intimidating, but you'll be fine once you get the hang of it."

"And you better get the hang of it quick—there's only a few days of training left," Miss Chambers said with a laugh. "You need to get those British licenses and pass Norman's written test, or you won't be going anywhere."

"Wait, there's a written test too?" Viv asked, looking at me and Dottie.

"Just some basic maintenance questions," Liz said, trying to reassure us, something Miss Chambers was definitely not doing. "How to check the oil and gas, how to keep the distributor clean—"

"The what?" Dottie and I both said at the same time.

"The distributor. Don't you know what it is?"

Norman walked over with a tool kit, his fatigues already smeared with black grease. He was in his sixties and spoke with a Cockney accent. The look on his heavily lined face told me he wasn't exactly thrilled to be teaching American girls how to drive. "See you got your fatigues on. Ready to get on with it, then?"

"Good luck, ladies." Miss Chambers's tone of voice said, *You'll need it.*

As the two women started to walk away, Liz turned around and mouthed, "You'll be fine," giving us a thumbs-up.

Almost two hours later, we were finishing up our lesson on the vehicle parts under the hood, or "the bonnet" as Norman called it.

"Now, tell me what 'at is and what 'at is," Norman said to me, pointing.

"Um . . . that is the doohickey, and those are the thingamajigs," I said, looking at him with a serious expression. He looked so frustrated, I had to break into a grin.

"Oh, I'm only teasing you, Norman," I said, patting his shoulder. "That's the carburetor, and those are the spark plugs."

Norman let out his breath and nodded. "'At's right. You Red Cross girls are going to drive me to drink."

Just then, another Clubmobile came barreling down the road toward us, the horn blaring and "Deep in the Heart of Texas" blasting out of the speakers.

"What in the name . . . ?" Norman said.

"Hey, girls!" Blanche and Martha were leaning out the windows of the Clubmobile, yelling and waving at us as they went by. Frankie was driving, clearly pleased with herself as she sat behind the steering wheel on the right-hand side of the car. Her instructor was sitting next to her, holding on to the dashboard, looking as though he was on the verge of a heart attack.

"See you later . . . if Frankie doesn't kill us first!" Blanche said, cupping her hands around her mouth and yelling loud enough for us to hear over the music.

"Goin' to have to buy ol' Alfie a pint tonight," Norman said, shaking his head. "I thought your lot were bad."

"Norman, sweetheart, when are *we* going to actually drive?" Viv said, batting her eyelashes at him so that he blushed. The maintenance lessons were necessary, but they were tedious and boring.

"Now that you gots an idea of what's under the bonnet, you've got to go under the truck next."

"I'm sorry, did you say *under* the truck?" Dottie said.

"Yes, all three of youse," Norman said. "You girls are going to be in the middle of nowhere someday in France or Germany, and you're going to thank ol' Norman when your truck breaks down and you ain't got a soul in sight to help youse. You've got to go under the truck; you've got to learn to change a tire. Then I'll let ya drive."

"You're right, we absolutely will. Thank you, Norman," I said. I knew he was reaching his limit with us.

"All right, ladies, let's get under here," I said, kneeling down next to the GMC. Just then, a jeep full of soldiers drove up and started beeping at us. We gave our usual waves and smiles when I heard, "Hey, it's Boston!"

Joe Brandon jumped out of the jeep and came running over. "Just wanted to say hi," he said, and I noticed he looked Dottie in the eyes when he said it. Norman grunted his annoyance at the interruption.

"Oh, hi, Joe," Dottie said, moving her glasses up her nose as she looked at him, the color creeping up her cheeks.

"Hey, girls, how are the lessons going?"

"'orrible," Norman said with a huff.

"We're not even done with maintenance," I said. "We're about to get under the truck before Norman here quits on us."

"*They're* about to get under the truck," Viv said. "I'm going to stay out here and take notes for them."

"You ain't doin' no such thing!" Norman said, arms crossed, but when he looked at Viv, he shook his finger at her and added, "Viviana . . . oh . . . oh, you girls need to stop the jokin'."

"Well, I won't keep you," Joe said. "But I'm playing with some of my band members at the Paramount Dance Hall on Sunday night, and I'd love for you three to come."

"Perfect," I said. "That's our last night in London."

"Can we bring friends?" Viv asked.

"You ladies can bring all the friends you want," Joe said, smiling, casting a shy glance at Dottie and kicking the dirt like a kid.

A guy from the jeep called to him that they had to get going.

"I'll let you get back to work," Joe said. "See you soon."

"See you soon," Dottie said, and Viv elbowed her as we said our good-byes.

"Oh, stop," Dottie said, elbowing her back.

"Stop what?" Viv asked. "He only had eyes for you, Dottie."

"She's right, Dottie," I said. And then I remembered that I still had to tell her about Joe's girl waiting at home . . .

"All right, all right," Norman said. "Under the truck now, too much to do."

I was the first to crawl under the truck, and I immediately whacked my head against what I was pretty sure was the axle. "Ouch," I cried, and a gob of grease fell on my face. And all I could think was, *Danny Barker, if you could see me now.*

Dottie and Viv joined me, and we all lay side by side under the truck as Norman yelled out the different parts we were required to grease.

"I can't believe how much grease has dripped on my face," Viv said. "It's disgusting. And a disaster for our complexions."

"I can't believe how many parts there are under here. Aren't we almost done?" Dottie asked.

"Dottie, while Norman is out of earshot, I need to tell you something," I said.

"What's that?" Dottie asked.

"Well, the night I met Joe Brandon on the boat, he told me he had a girl waiting at home," I said. "A teacher named Mary Jane."

"That wolf!" Viv said. "You'd never know it by the way he was looking at Dottie just now."

"I'm sorry, that's what he said at the time," I said. "I meant to tell you sooner, and I forgot. Maybe he's not with her anymore . . ."

"That's fine, Fiona, really," Dottie said, her voice quiet. "You girls were making something out of nothing."

"I agree with Viv. Not that he's a wolf, but he does seem to like you," I said. "So maybe she broke it off."

"Like I said, it's nothing. We're leaving soon, and I'll probably never see him again after London," Dottie said, her voice somehow hopeful and disappointed at the same time.

"Do you still want to go see his band play?" I asked.

"Why not? I'm sure they're going to be great," she answered.

"And we'll make sure you look absolutely beautiful that night," said Viv. "Blanche told me this morning that we're actually allowed to wear civilian clothes since it's our last night in London. It'll probably be the last night that we're allowed to wear a pretty dress for a long time. Joe Brandon will be eating his heart out."

"Oh, I don't . . ."

"Girls, ah you greasin' or gabbin' down there?" Norman called down to us. "I want to get some drivin' in before it gets dark."

I had wrapped my hair in a red kerchief to try to cover it, but several strands had escaped and were sticking to my neck. I could feel the grime and grease caked on my face, and my fatigues were filthy.

I spotted two large shiny black leather boots standing next to Norman's worn brown shoes as I crawled out. The sun had come out, and I had to shield my eyes to get a look at the officer. He was well over six feet with a broad chest, and his nose looked off-kilter, like it had been broken and put back together not quite the same. His thick black hair was cut military short, and he had big dark eyes with a small scar through one of his eyebrows. The boots were different than those of most GIs I had seen, and he had a distinct silver parachute badge on his chest and a patch with double *A* insignia on his shoulder.

"Oh, hi," I said, trying to at least tuck some of my hair back in my kerchief. I was sure that in that moment I looked like the opposite of a fresh-faced Red Cross girl. "We're just finishing up, Norman."

"Hi," the officer said, nodding, distracted. He was the first soldier not to smile at me. Now I was sure I looked even more of a mess than I thought I did.

"So, Norman, you think you'll be able to fix the jeep in the next few days if I bring it by tomorrow morning?" the officer asked. "We're heading out to Leicester soon."

"Yeah," Norman said. "For you? 'Course I will."

"Thank you, sir," he said. He looked over at me again, still no smile. "Red Cross?"

"Yes," I said. "Clubmobile. Leicester—that's in the Midlands, up north, right? I think we might be headed that way too."

"Oh?" he said. "Well, if you do, don't get yourself in any trouble out there. We don't need to be worrying about a bunch of girls driving trucks of doughnuts around the countryside."

"We'll have a driver there," I said, annoyed. I cocked my head and crossed my arms. "But what's the matter with girls driving trucks?"

"Nothing," he said, raising his eyebrows in amusement. "I'm sure you'll be perfectly fine; just take care of yourselves."

"Hey, can we come out now?" Viv called from under the truck. "I think we're done."

"I've got to go," the officer said. "Thanks, Norman. Good luck, uh . . ."

"Fiona. Fiona Denning," I said. "I'd shake your hand, but . . ." I looked at my hands covered in black grease and dirt.

"It's fine," he said. He held up his hands and finally gave me a tight, lopsided grin. "I'm Captain Peter Moretti, Eighty-Second Airborne. I've got to run. Thanks again, Norman."

He nodded and jogged off toward the administrative buildings on the opposite side of the field from the garages. Viv and Dottie had crawled out from under the truck and were brushing themselves off.

"Who was that?" Dottie asked.

"Some captain in the Eighty-Second. He doesn't think girls should drive trucks."

"Yup, he's totally right," Viv said.

"Viv!" I swatted her arm. "Not helping."

"Fella's not just any captain," Norman said. "That was Peter Moretti. He's a boxer from New York City. Heavyweight. He was risin' up the ranks before he ended up with the Eighty-Second. Almost fought Joe Louis."

"He *looks* like a boxer," I said.

"Those boys from the Eighty-Second just got back from Normandy," Norman said, shaking his head. "Thirty-three straight days of bloody 'ell, with no relief. Almost half of 'em are gone."

"Oh Jesus." Dottie sighed. "Dead?"

"Most dead. Some missin'. Don't matter, though, does it?" Norman said, waving his hand in sad resignation. "So brave and such good American boys. Ain't like some of your lot that's come over, drinkin', disruptin', and runnin' around with not-so-proper British girls. Eighty-Second Airborne is brilliant, though."

"Can we learn to drive this thing now, Norman?" Viv asked, trying and failing to wipe the grime off her face with her lacy pink handkerchief.

"All right, if you girls can change this tire in less than thirty minutes, we'll start drivin' lessons right after," said Norman.

"But that tire looks like it weighs five hundred pounds," I said. "There's no way we can lift it."

"Yeah, you can. Last bunch of Red Cross girls could," Norman said, looking at his watch. "You got thirty minutes. Get on with it, then."

"Come on," I said, as Viv let out a groan and Dottie looked like she might cry. "If we work together, we'll be done with this damn tire before we know it."

Chapter Seven

July 27, 1944

A fun fact about the Clubmobile trucks that we learned during our driving lessons is that, despite their size, the capacity of the tank is only four and a half gallons. Gas, or petrol, as the Brits call it, was so scarce in England, you could only get it at army camps. You needed to keep very careful track of how much petrol you had in the tank, or you risked running out of it "alone on a dark road somewhere, with bleedin' Nazi bastards comin' at ya," as Norman drilled into us.

If you were having any other sort of suspicious gas trouble, the first thing you were supposed to do was check the gas line and connection for leaks and dirt. Then you checked the functioning of the fuel pump. And if you still couldn't figure out what the heck was wrong with the damn truck, you checked the fuel pump to the carburetor.

During our training with Norman, he also taught us how to replace a worn-out bulb and check the battery and main cables, spark plugs, and all wire connections if there was electrical trouble. Changing one of the Clubmobile's massive tires had proved to be one of the toughest obstacles and took us much longer than thirty minutes, but we finally succeeded. I had joked to Dottie and Viv that we should open our own garage when we got back from the war.

It was our last day with Norman, and we were finally sitting for the written part of the driving exam, proving our newfound knowledge in these areas. It was a fifteen-question test that I felt confident we would all pass, and for the hundredth time I wished that was all we needed to get our British driving licenses.

After the written exam, Norman was going to take us on the driving test required to receive our licenses. I prayed he would pass us. Despite his best efforts, the three of us remained terrible drivers. Maybe if we had another week to learn, but our time was up. After doughnut training over the next couple of days, we would be on our way to the Midlands, ready or not. At least we would have a driver while we were in England.

We had spent the last three days driving the roads in and around Bushy Park. Dottie had proved to be way too nervous. She would freeze up and hesitate at the wheel, with a load of army vehicles beeping behind her. Viv had constantly gunned the engine and slammed the brakes, no matter how many times Norman yelled at her. Of the three of us, I was probably the best, which wasn't saying much. Driving the enormous truck felt awkward, and I didn't yet have a real sense of control at the wheel.

"Almost done?" Norman came into the tiny office in his garage, where the three of us were sitting at a small wooden table, finishing up the written exam. I was queasy from nerves, and the strong smell of petrol that permeated the building only made it worse.

"Done, Norman," I said with a smile, handing him my exam.

"All right, Fiona, you're the first to go, then. You ladies stay and finish," Norman said to Dottie and Viv.

"Wait, right this minute?" I asked.

"Yeah, we only got the morning before your lot have to head back to Grosvenor Square. Let's go," he said, already walking out the door.

"Good luck, Fi. You'll do fine," Dottie said.

"Yeah, definitely don't screw up," Viv said. "You're our best hope."

"Gee, thanks, Viv," I said with sarcasm.

I walked out to find Norman talking to the boxer turned army captain, Peter Moretti.

"She's all set for ya now. You'll find her round back, keys in the ignition," Norman said. "New carburetor, new battery, checked the spark plugs. That jeep ain't going to give you no more trouble under the bonnet."

"Let's hope so. Thank you for getting it done so quickly. Oh, hi." Moretti nodded to me, guarded and so serious. He was more mature, not like so many of the younger soldiers, who gave us huge, easy smiles and tripped over themselves to befriend some newly arrived American girls.

"Hello," I said. "Driving test this morning, for my British license. Pretty excited." I was doing that nervous thing, talking to fill the air. *Pretty excited? Shut up, Fiona.*

"Oh, I guess that's good," Moretti replied, clearly not excited for me.

"Good if she passes," Norman said, raising his eyebrows. "That's a big *if* right now if I'm bein' honest with ya."

"Jeepers, thanks, Norman. You're worse than Viv," I said.

Moretti just shook his head and, almost to himself, said, "Women aren't meant for war."

"I'm sorry, what?" I said, lifting my chin indignantly and looking up at his face, realizing he must be over six foot four. He was giving me a look somewhere between disapproval and skepticism.

"Women aren't meant for this. No offense, but you aren't built for war," he said.

"Honestly? Is *any* civilized person meant for war?" I said. "And lots of women are doing their part. What about the Land Army girls here, or the WAAFs? There are plenty of us working in the war, built for it or not."

"Yes, but your work isn't like those jobs," Moretti said, frowning at me, his tone tense. "At least the jobs those women do are actually necessary. You're here to serve *doughnuts*. And for officers, you're just another problem for us to worry about."

I felt my face grow hot, furious that he viewed us that way. *Unnecessary.* And of course, I was insecure. How many other officers viewed us as a nuisance they had to deal with?

Norman was watching this exchange, not hiding the fact he was entertained.

"Well, I'm . . ." I tried to retain my composure. I didn't want to give away just how upset I was. I breathed and crossed my arms in front of my chest.

"I'm really sorry you feel that way, Captain Moretti," I finally said. "I think we're going to prove you wrong. And if you and I do happen to be anywhere near each other in the countryside, I promise you *my* Clubmobile group will never be a problem for you. We'll stay out of your way."

He looked at me for a second, still serious, but then his mouth turned up in that lopsided grin.

"Yeah, we'll see," he said with a shrug. "I hope you're right."

"I know I am," I said, snapping back a little too harshly.

"Okay," he said with a wave good-bye. "I'll let you get to your test. Thanks again, Norman."

"Ta, Captain," Norman said. "Stay safe."

"I will, my friend," Moretti said. As he walked to retrieve his jeep, he turned around and added, "And Fiona?"

"Yes?" I said, still fuming. And surprised that he remembered my name.

"If we do run into each other again? You can call me Peter." He disappeared behind the back of the garage before I had a chance to answer. I stood there with my mouth open, still angry, and too late to have the last word.

Norman climbed into the passenger seat, which, to my American brain, was on the wrong side of the car. I was relieved we would have a driver in England. The opposite side of the road *and* the car had already proved too stressful.

"He's one of the best, ya know," Norman said. "Comes across as gruff, but those Eighty-Second boys . . ."

"I know, I know. The Eighty-Second Airborne is the best, top-notch, blah, blah," I said, my face burning when I thought of how dismissive Captain Moretti had been. "He didn't have to insult my entire reason for being here."

"You ain't got no understanding of what he's been through," Norman said. "I told youse, the Eighty-Second was over in Normandy for four weeks *without relief.* They lost so many blokes. And the things they seen . . . seeing their brothers blown up? You ain't got no idea what that does to a man. He's been beaten down by this war, he has. All he wants is to keep the men he's got left alive, and he don't want nothin' to distract him from doing that."

I looked at Norman, my anger receding. He was right, but I still hoped I didn't run into Captain Moretti . . . Peter . . . again.

"Now, ya ready, then?" Norman asked as I buckled in.

"Do I have a choice?" I said, feeling like I was going to throw up.

"Nah. Let's get on with it."

It was a humid, drizzly day, so of course I was already sweating from the warmth and nerves as I put the truck in gear, gassed the motor, and drove straight ahead. We drove by a group of GIs playing football in an open field, and they started cheering me on, whistling and calling out things like, "Yeah, Red Cross, you can do it!" It did nothing to calm my nerves, but I couldn't help but laugh.

We reached a hill, and I crossed my fingers that I didn't have to shift again to make it over the top, so of course I had to. The gears didn't mesh, I forgot to press the gas pedal at the right time, and there I was with Norman, stalled out, ten minutes into my test. I gave him a sheepish look and started to apologize, but he calmly grabbed the hand brake and said, "Relax. And remember to double clutch right away if you need to climb a hill like this one."

I nodded and took a deep breath. My dreams of confidently acing my driving test shattered, I stomped on the starter, the engine roared, and we took off once more. We went by barracks and huts and the mess hall. I was feeling better as we headed out toward the tank course and up over a hill, when a tree seemed to sprout up in the middle of the road as we came down the other side. I turned sharply to the right, cursing as we veered off the road, down through some bushes, surprising a couple of deer grazing. I managed to hit the brakes just before we ended up driving straight into a pond covered with camouflage netting.

I closed my eyes and heard Norman let out a long sigh.

"You think you're pioneerin' or somethin', Miss Denning?" he said, and I was relieved to hear amusement in his voice.

"I'm so sorry, it was just that tree . . . ," I said.

"Back it up now, turn it around," he said. "You can do that, can't ya? There's an actual road to the left, round that tree. Downshift in order to slow down without them brakes."

"Yes, that's right," I said, wiping away the sweat dripping down my forehead.

As I backed up, I glanced over at the deer, who were looking at me as if to say even they could do better.

We got back on course, and the rest of the trip was mercifully without incident. I drove through a few bomb craters, lots of mud and ditches, and we finally made our way to the smooth and steady roads around Camp Griffiss. I stopped the truck a few hundred feet away from the garage. If Norman wasn't going to pass me, I wanted to hear it from him out of earshot of Viv and Dottie. I wondered how many Clubmobile girls before me had flunked the driving test. I leaned on the wheel, my head resting against my hands, holding my breath for the verdict.

"Well, wasn't a complete disaster, was it, then?" Norman said, emphasizing "was it" with the now-familiar-to-me British inflection. He rubbed his hand over his face.

"Look, none of you are very good, are you?" he said, and I started cracking my knuckles, waiting. He paused for what felt like an eternity, looking out the windshield before finally adding, "But you'll get along all right if you have to."

"Yes!" I said, and without thinking about it, I leaned over and gave Norman a hug. "Thank you, thank you so much, Norman." When I pulled away, he was blushing but smiling.

"Promise me," he said, "you'll keep practicin'. You ain't ever going to get better if not. And you have to be if they ship you to France. You're the best hope of the lot, though Dorothy is pretty good under the bonnet— she's got that part figured out. Viviana is rather hopeless, isn't she? Used to fellas driving her round, maybe."

"Maybe," I said, feeling my stomach knot up again. "Are you . . . Do you think they'll pass too?"

"I think if they don't crash into nothin', yeah, they'll pass," he said. "Despite what the captain said, the army needs you girls too much for them *not* to. Now let's go get you that British license, then."

I wanted to hug him again, but I knew one hug was more than enough for our kind old British mechanic.

~

The next morning, the three of us were newly licensed despite ourselves as we reunited with a bunch of our Clubmobile friends for the final training session: doughnut and coffee making.

"Well, this will be much better than yesterday," I said to Viv as we walked into a cavernous garage where there were multiple stations set up with doughnut-making machines.

"Again, as long as it doesn't mess with my manicure, everything will be fine," Viv said.

"Hey, gals, Dottie says you're going to the Paramount Sunday night to see some music. Can some of the other girls and I join you?" Blanche said as she walked up behind us with Dottie.

"Of course," I said. "We're going to make Dottie look particularly glamorous that evening."

"Oh no, you don't really need to do that. It's fine," Dottie said, but it was clear she wasn't over her crush on Joe Brandon.

"Gather round, gather round, girls," Miss Chambers's distinct voice echoed off the walls when she called out to us from one of the stations at the opposite end of the garage.

"Very exciting, your final days of training before you head off," she said when we were all in a semicircle around the station. "In front of me is one of the machines loaned to the Red Cross by the Doughnut Corporation of America. The good news is they can produce massive amounts of doughnuts in a short period of time—forty-eight dozen an *hour*. The bad news is that they are delicate, temperamental, and filled with hot oil. We just had to send a girl home because of severe burns, so you must be *extremely* careful operating them."

"Lovely," I whispered under my breath.

"The whole process requires attention and skill and three people to keep it all going. Now pick a station with your crew, and we'll get started."

We took a station next to Blanche, Martha, and Frankie.

"Hey, gals, how were your driving exams?" Frankie asked. "Martha here was an ace—all that tractor driving, even the GIs were impressed. Blanche and I did okay in the end; we all passed easily. I saw you stalled out on that hill at Griffiss yesterday, Fiona, and I wanted to come over to help; I felt so bad. Did your instructor pass you?"

"Yes," I said. Just at that moment, Miss Chambers walked by, checking our machines to make sure the heat switch was on, and I saw her take note of this comment. I tried to shush Frankie with my eyes, but of course she was so busy fiddling with the doughnut machine, she didn't even notice.

"And Dottie told me about how you went off the road and almost hit a deer?" Frankie said, cringing. "You're so lucky he still passed you. Thank God you won't need to drive unless you're shipped to the Continent. Sounds like you're going to need some more practice before that."

Miss Chambers had moved on to other groups, but I was sure she had heard that too.

Dottie looked at me, apologizing with her eyes. She was about to speak when Blanche, lowering her voice, said, "Um, Frankie, honey, I think Fiona is too polite to tell you to shut your trap." She put a hand on her shoulder. "She doesn't want Miss Chambers hearing anything that will keep her from getting to the Continent at some point, you know?"

Frankie dropped the doughnut tongs she was holding, and her hand flew up to her mouth.

"Oh, Fi, I'm so sorry. I was just going to offer to go driving with you, to help you if I could," she said, and I knew she felt terrible. "But I don't think she heard me."

"No, she was only two feet from you. *Of course* she didn't hear," Viv said, her voice heavy with sarcasm.

"It's fine, Frankie," I said, my voice tight. "And I don't need you to go driving with me. Thanks anyway." After our talk on the roof, I understood why Frankie was so gung ho, but I couldn't help but be annoyed by the driving critique right in front of Miss Chambers. I was sure she had heard every word.

"Now, ladies, first mix the dough in the large metal cylinder bowls on your station," Miss Chambers said, standing at a doughnut station at the front of the room again. "To turn the premade mix into dough, you must weigh the doughnut flour and water carefully and take the temperatures of both. There's instructions at your stations, so let's get started."

"Wait, so we're in the field, there are four hundred GIs waiting in line for doughnuts, but we have to weigh *and* take the temperature of the water and flour every time? Is she serious?" Dottie said this to us in a soft voice as we placed the flour on a tiny scale.

"I know, that seems crazy," I said.

"Water that's too cold will make the doughnuts absorb too much fat," explained Miss Chambers, as she walked around the room. "Water that's too warm will make them even worse, so you've got to get it just right. Once you've got the measurements and temps right, you can start mixing."

"Um, Miss Chambers?" Viv said, smiling sweetly at our instructor.

"Yes, Viviana?" Miss Chambers answered, walking over to our station.

"We're ready to pour everything in the cylinder bowl, but I don't see anything to mix with. What should we use?" Viv said.

"You've got six hands between the three of you. That's what you mix with," Miss Chambers said, amused.

"Oh no, there's got to be a better way," Viv said, stepping back from the bowl in horror.

Miss Chambers shook her head. "No other way," she said. She pointed to the sifted flour and water. "Now mix them together with your hands. Go ahead, I'll walk the group through it."

"Me?" Viv asked. "Mix it by hand?" She was appalled at the thought as she looked at Miss Chambers and then down at her perfectly manicured crimson nails.

"Go ahead, Viv," I said, biting my lip to keep from laughing.

"Yeah, Viv, go ahead. Show us how it's done," Dottie chimed in, also trying too hard to remain serious.

"Yes, dear, let's go," Miss Chambers said, growing impatient at Viv's hesitation.

Viv grimaced as she poured the water and flour together. She stared into the mixture with dread, took a deep breath, closed her eyes, and plunged her beautiful hands in. Dottie and I could not even look at each other because we were both about to burst into laughter. Poor Princess Viv.

"That's it, really get in there," Judith Chambers said, towering over Viv as she peered into the bowl. "Those lumps that you feel? That's the sugar and eggs in the mix that make a good doughnut. You've got to work those lumps out of the dough."

"Work them out, Viv," Blanche said, and I realized she, Frankie, and Martha were also enjoying the show.

When Miss Chambers was satisfied with the job Viv was doing, she moved on to help the other groups. As soon as she walked away, we all burst into laughter.

"Yeah, yeah, have a good laugh. You gals all happy now?" Viv said, scowling at us with dramatic flair. "You better watch out, or I'll throw a lump at one of you. I cannot believe we have to do this in the field. I can't believe I have to do this to *my nails.*" She pulled one of her hands out of the bowl. It was a gooey mess. "Oh my God! Look at this; it's totally stripped my nail polish already. These doughnuts are going to be chock-full of bright-red nail polish chips."

"And made with love by a Clubmobile girl," I said, as we all continued laughing.

"*Love* is not the word I had in mind," Viv said. "This is disgusting."

"Okay, if your dough is mixed, attach the cylinder to the machine very carefully; it's finally time to make the doughnuts," Miss Chambers said to the group. She clapped her hands and, in a sing-song tone, added, "Get your tongs ready to go."

We attached the pressurized cylinder to the machine as best we could, although it didn't seem to be secure enough.

"Do you think that's on?" I asked Dottie as we struggled to screw it in.

"I think so." Dottie shrugged. Viv was pouting, trying to wipe all the dough off her hands.

And then, like a small miracle, the dough poured from the cylinder and started dropping into the oil in perfectly shaped circles. Dottie stood at the ready with her tongs, grabbing the doughnuts out of the oil and throwing them onto the cooling rack when they had achieved a golden-brown color. The garage filled with warm, humid air and an overpowering sickening-sweet fragrance as all the groups churned out dozens of doughnuts.

"*Blech.* Think we'll get used to the smell?" Martha said from the next station, covering her mouth with her hands. "It's making me nauseous."

"Me too," I said. "Maybe our noses will get numb to it."

"What's that hissing sound?" Viv asked, finally recovering from her mixing trauma and helping Dottie.

I heard a high-pitched whistle coming from somewhere in our machine.

"I don't know, that sounds weird," I said, trying to find the source. "Miss Chambers, our machine is hissing. Is that normal?" I called over to where she was helping some girls whose machine had already malfunctioned.

Miss Chambers whipped her head around at the question and, with a look of fear on her face, yelled to us, "Back away! Get away from that machine now!"

We all ran several feet back just as the hiss turned into an enormous boom and the cylinder bowl of dough flew off the machine and exploded into the air. Several girls screamed, and the three of us ducked and tried to shield each other from what was to come. The cylinder came crashing down with a loud clang, warped beyond repair.

So much dough. On our station, on the floor. On our clothes and aprons, even in our hair. It covered Dottie's shoes and splattered the front of Viv's shirt. I looked over and saw that the dough had hit

Blanche, Martha, and Frankie's station as well. The rest of the girls in the garage stared in horror, and the smell of extra greasy, overcooked doughnuts filled the room as several groups forgot to take theirs out of the oil in time.

Miss Chambers came running over. "Are you all okay?" she asked, taking a deep breath and surveying the damage.

"What the heck just happened?" Dottie asked. "It was all going so well and then—"

"You didn't follow the directions," Miss Chambers said with a sigh. "You need to secure the pressurized cylinder correctly, or it can blow up. *That's* what happened."

"Let this be a lesson for all of you," Miss Chambers said to the group. "Now, clean this mess up, ladies. When you finish, you can join the next station for the rest of training."

I rubbed my hands over my face, wiping a gob of dough off my cheek. Viv, Dottie, and I looked at each other. I was somewhere between crying and laughing. There was no doubt the three of us were making an impression on Miss Chambers, but not exactly the one I had planned.

Chapter Eight

July 30, 1944

I stood looking in the mirror in our tiny dorm bathroom and adjusted my Red Cross cap over the two combs in my hair, pulling the chunk of blonde strands down the side of my face in a flattering sweep. Some powder, blush, a touch of mascara, and a sweep of pink lipstick, and I was ready to go. It was the morning of the Red Cross Clubmobile presentation ceremony to the military, and it felt good to wear our dress uniforms and feel clean and pretty, not covered with mud, dough, or car grease.

"Fiona? You in there?" I heard Dottie call from outside the door.

"Yes?" I said, adding a little more blush but still failing to conceal my freckles. "I'm all done if you need to get in here."

"There's been a change of plan," Dottie said when I opened the door. She was standing in just her underwear and glasses, looking annoyed.

A few Clubmobilers hurried past us in various states of dress. A girl from New York named ChiChi stumbled and swore as she ran by, pulling on the high-waisted dark-blue pants that were part of the battle dress uniform. The Andrews Sisters were singing from the dorm's sole record player, and laughter and chatting spilled out of the rooms. There was a palpable sense of relief in the air now that training was over.

"What's the change?" I said.

"We have to wear our new battle dress uniforms."

"What? Why?" I asked. "Those are wool; we're going to be roasting."

"It's for publicity," Dottie said. "*LIFE* magazine is going to be there, and the Red Cross top brass want us to be in the uniforms we're going to be wearing out in the field. They want to get a bunch of photos of us holding doughnuts and stuff."

"But that's crazy. We're all going to be so sweaty and overheated, we'll be passing out."

"I know, it's ridiculous," Dottie said. "But we've got to go change now. The bus will be here in fifteen minutes."

"I'm wearing a clown suit," Viv said to us as we walked in the room. She was frowning as she twirled around and modeled the new uniform for us.

It included a short belted jacket with two deep pockets on the front and matching high-waisted pants, all in the same deep grayish blue as the Royal Air Force uniforms.

"I know they altered it to fit me, but I still don't like it," Viv said with a sigh. "Do you think we'll have to wear the jacket in this heat?"

"I'm sure we will for the pictures at least," Dottie said, slipping on the requisite white button-down shirt.

"Well, at least the hat's not bad looking," I said, taking off the cap I had so carefully adjusted and replacing it with the blue hat, which had a wider brim. "I think I like it better; at least it won't slide off my head."

"Fi, how are you doing? Are you still upset about the doughnut explosion?" Viv asked.

"Oh God, don't remind me." I put my head in my hands, reliving the moment, feeling the mortification all over again. I leaned against my bedroll. We had spent the whole day packing, and everything I owned, minus a few changes of clothes, was in my footlocker.

"I know training didn't go as well as you had planned . . ."

"*That's* an understatement . . . ," I said.

"But, Fi, this was *just* training. What better way to show her what a top-notch team we are than to work well in the field together?" Dottie said. "We'll be so good, we'll be noticed for all the right reasons."

"That's what I've been trying to tell myself," I said. "We will do better. And we're lucky we're already friends."

"No kidding," Viv said. "I heard three girls fighting like cats at doughnut training the other day."

"And I'll take driving lessons from our driver in the Midlands," I said. "One of us has got to get better at driving. I want ours to be one of the first Clubmobiles in this group to be sent to France. We have to be."

"We will be, I have no doubt," Dottie said, brushing her glossy black hair and putting her new hat on.

"Buses are here. Come on, girls, hurry up, let's go," Frankie said, as she ran by our door.

"All right, girls, time to meet the RC brass," I said. I put on my white gloves, threw my white scarf around my neck, and shut our door behind us for one of the last times.

～

The ceremony was grand, with more pomp and circumstance than any of us had anticipated. A large part of its impressiveness was due to the natural setting of the event. It took place at Royal Holloway, University of London, several miles outside of the city center, most likely by design, as the risk of buzz bombs dropping on us was somewhat diminished. On a gorgeous, expansive lawn, we assembled in front of an enormous brick building with spires that made it resemble a castle more than a college.

The sun managed to break through the clouds just as the ceremony began. We were lined up in our battle dress, white gloves, and scarves, trying our best not to look as sweaty and hot as we felt. Behind us, our newly painted Clubmobiles shined in the sun.

Miss Chambers was there, along with all the new Red Cross field captains, including our own Group F captain, Liz Anderson. Harvey Gibson, commissioner of the American Red Cross in Great Britain, was also on hand, as were most of the Red Cross headquarters staff and, of course, several high-ranking military officials.

The army band started to play, and the Military Police Battalion marched past us in perfect formation for the ceremonial review. They were resplendent in their white helmets, belts, and gloves, and I wasn't the only girl blinking back a tear as they passed.

Out of the corner of my eye, I noticed a photographer, dressed in a light-brown blazer and black fedora, taking pictures of us from various angles. He caught me looking over at him and waved. I gave him a small, close-lipped smile, and he snapped a couple more pictures, giving me the thumbs-up.

After the music ended, two of the generals came up to the podium and made some remarks about how grateful they were for the Red Cross, and for the Clubmobile program specifically.

Finally, Mr. Harvey Gibson, a stout, balding man with a warm, generous smile, approached the podium. The first part of the speech was for the dignitaries, but the final words were directed at us.

"We at the Red Cross are enormously proud of the Clubmobile program and of all of you, this latest class of Clubmobile girls. Our 'Doughnut Dollies.'"

"Ugh, why does he use that nickname? I hate it," I whispered to Viv. "It makes us sound like little girls in sailor dresses."

"Agree, it's totally awful," Viv said.

"You will be leaving London to serve our troops tomorrow," Gibson continued. "And it couldn't come at a better time as we are short-staffed after sending so many Clubmobilers to the Continent. The Clubmobile program is now two years old and hugely successful. It sprang from a simple idea, that the most useful service to the soldier in the field would be to bring him a symbol of the warmth of home when he needed it most. And that this could be done with a cup of coffee and doughnuts served by an American girl.

"Now, girls, trust me when I say I know doughnuts and coffee are merely your props, that you do so much just by being there. I thank you for leaving your homes and families behind to come here to volunteer for this important job."

With a round of applause, the ceremony concluded and everyone headed over to the Clubmobiles, where doughnuts and coffee were already waiting.

Our Clubmobile was named the Cheyenne. It was a newly refurbished, two-and-a-half-ton GMC truck with American-style gears and steering. The outside was freshly painted army green with "American Red Cross Clubmobile" in red-and-white block letters across the side, and there were two large windows from which we would be serving the troops.

We found our Clubmobile but could not find our driver, a British civilian named Jimmy English. He hadn't shown up at the ceremony to meet us for reasons nobody could explain.

Harvey Gibson came up to me just as I was pouring myself a cup of coffee out of an urn on a table in front of the Cheyenne.

"Hello. Harvey Gibson," he said, shaking my hand. He had an undeniable charisma and warmth. "I like to introduce myself to all of the new girls."

"Hello," I replied. "I'm Fiona Denning from Boston."

Mr. Gibson was about to say something when the photographer with the black hat snuck up behind me and said in a strong New York accent, "Hey, Mr. Gibson. Gary Dent, *LIFE* magazine. A picture with the young lady for the piece I'm doing?"

"Of course," Mr. Gibson said with a smile. We stood together. I tried to wipe some of the sweat off my face and gave the photographer an awkward smile.

"Perfect. You've got that all-American-girl look, freckles and all," Gary Dent said.

"Take as many as you need," Mr. Gibson said.

"Will do. Can I get a few of you two talking together? Just act natural."

"Of course," Mr. Gibson said. "So, Fiona, what made you decide to become a Clubmobile girl?"

What should I say? How much should I reveal at a time like this? I hesitated for a few seconds but decided to trust my gut.

"I'm here because my fiancé is missing in action," I said, and Harvey Gibson's jaw dropped open, almost imperceptibly.

"He's been missing since last fall," I continued, trying to keep my voice steady, my emotions in check. "His plane went down somewhere in Germany. And now I'm here because I wanted to do something."

"Wow, this is good stuff, keep talking." Gary, letting his camera dangle on the strap around his neck, pulled out a notepad and pencil. "What was the name of your fiancé?"

"His name *is* Danny Barker," I said. "He's a second lieutenant in the US Army Air Force, 338th Bombardment Squadron."

"Miss Denning, um, Fiona, I am so sorry about your fiancé," Harvey Gibson said, putting a hand on my shoulder. "And I admire you for being here."

"Thanks, Mr. Gibson," I said. "My friends Viv and Dottie are here too. We've all wanted to do something to help with the war effort. And we're happy this offered us a way."

"So am I. I'm sure you'll make your fiancé proud," he said, his eyes full of kindness, not pity.

"Where are these friends? Let's get a picture," said Gary.

"Right here," Viv said, raising her hand, and this time it was Gary Dent's jaw that dropped open as he started clicking away. Dottie joined us, putting her coffee down and taking off her glasses.

"Well, look at you three," Gary Dent said, whistling. "One with Mr. Gibson and then a few with just the three of you."

After a few clicks, Mr. Gibson stepped aside, and it was just us. People started looking over with interest. I saw Miss Chambers watching. She was standing with a few other Red Cross officials, and she did not look pleased.

"I feel like a movie star," said Dottie, giggling nervously.

"Turn your body to the side and your face to the camera, girls; jut your chin out just slightly like this," Viv said. "Trust me, it's the most flattering."

After he was done, we said thank you, and he ran over to Blanche and asked her to pose with a tray of doughnuts. She hammed it up, holding a tray in each hand and winking at him.

"Well, that was fun," Viv said. "Wonder if we'll make the final cut for the magazine."

"Enjoy the photo shoot, ladies?" Miss Chambers walked over to us as we refreshed our coffee.

"It went okay, I think," I said. "Good publicity, right?"

"Yes," she said. "A quick word with you, Fiona?"

Dottie and Viv gave me looks of solidarity as they walked away.

"I didn't know about your fiancé," she said in a quiet voice. "I'm truly sorry."

"Thank you, Miss Chambers," I said.

"Have you heard any news of him since you got here?"

"No, nothing." I felt that familiar ache in the pit of my stomach. "I thought I would have heard something by now."

"Well, I hope you do soon," she said. "I understand more than ever your wanting to go to the Continent. And I admire your tenacity in becoming a Clubmobile girl. But frankly, I've observed you and your friends this week in training, and—"

"Miss Chambers, please wait. I think I know what you're about to say," I said, holding up my hand. "Just hear me out. Our training did not go as well as I had hoped, trust me. But we will prove to be one of the best Clubmobile crews you've got. I promise you. I will work harder than anyone, and I'm really organized. And Viv? The guys are going to love her. Dottie can play any musical instrument you put in front of her. And they're hard workers too. We won't let you down."

"It's not about letting me down. It's about being ready," she said, frowning. "Being on the Continent in the midst of battle is very different than being here. You've got to be unflappable and have that Red Cross smile ready, even under the toughest circumstances. Are you sure you're up for that part? Emotionally, I mean?"

"Definitely," I said. It was like putting on a mask; I had to conceal my lingering uncertainty, my nerves and doubt. And my grief. This woman was the gatekeeper to the Continent. "You're asking because of Danny, am I emotionally ready? I am." *Am I?*

"You won't be reminded of your fiancé at every turn?" she asked, examining my face, trying to see through the mask.

I remembered that first day on the *Queen Elizabeth* when I'd seen Danny on the boat. It hadn't happened since, but that didn't mean it wouldn't ever again. I shook my head.

"I must admit, I'm surprised you made it through the interview process without this coming out. You're still grieving . . . understandably so," she said. I just looked at her. There was no use protesting. "Are you sure you can you handle soldiers who are traumatized and homesick? You don't know what it's like . . ."

"You're right, I don't know what it's like. But I can do this. I *need* to do this." My impassioned plea was as much to convince her as it was to convince myself. Because I did have fears of failing at this job, of not being ready, but she didn't need to know that.

"But I have other concerns," Miss Chambers said. "I have no doubt all the soldiers are going to love the looks of the three of you, but there's so much more to it. I happen to know you all barely passed your driving tests. And Viviana? I know you said she's hardworking, but I didn't exactly see that side of her during training.

"Dottie seems smart and capable, but she doesn't fit the extroverted Clubmobile personality profile. I'm shocked she was accepted, to be honest. She has to try to be more outgoing, and she needs to finally share these supposed musical talents that so far I've yet to see."

"We'll work on all of these things and then some," I said. "We can do this, Miss Chambers. We'll prove to you that we'll be ready for France." I felt my cheeks burning.

"Well, you talk a good game, but if the Continent is where you want to go, you'll have to *show* me," she said. "Or I'm afraid you'll spend the war on this side of the channel."

Chapter Nine

That evening was our final night in London Town, and the blacked-out city was once again alive and hopping with young people partying like it was New Year's Eve. On the dim streets were groups of soldiers from every Allied country, though once again it appeared the majority of them were Americans. And there were groups of civilian British girls seeking to escape the sad monotony of wartime.

In total, our crew of fifty-two Red Cross Clubmobile girls would be shipping out to our assignments all over the United Kingdom the next morning, but we planned to enjoy our last night in the city we had grown to love during our short stay.

"Girls, try to keep up. We're almost there," Viv yelled to me, Frankie, and Martha. She was up ahead with Dottie. About a dozen of us were walking the dark streets to the Paramount Dance Hall on Tottenham Court Road, where Joe Brandon's band was playing.

"I've heard you're quite the dancer, Martha," I said. "How'd you learn to dance so well?"

"My church group, believe it or not," Martha said. "We were looking for a way to raise money, so we started to organize these dances on the first Saturday of the month. It took some convincing to get decent bands to come play in Orange City. But then as word got out, young people from all over started coming—some from an hour or more away, just looking for something to do. So that meant we were able to attract even bigger bands. And then we started jitterbug contests. *That's* when I really learned to dance well."

"Maybe you can give me a few tips tonight. I'm barely good enough to get by," I said.

"Sure," Martha said. "I'm hoping Adele Astaire might be here. We could all learn from her."

"She was amazing," I said with a nod.

"You know who was *also* amazing?" Blanche asked, coming up behind us. "That fella she was dancing with that night. He was drop-dead gorgeous. Do you remember him?"

"I do; we had talked to him at the bar," I said, remembering the dashing British soldier named Harry Westwood who had caught Viv's eye for a second. "Hey, did any of you get any mail today?"

"Yes, I got a letter from my mother and one from my neighbor," Martha said.

"I got one from my parents too," Frankie added.

"Viv got one from her sister, Aria, who's due to give birth to her third baby any day, and Dottie even got a V-mail from her brother Marco—he's a navy firefighter stationed in the Pacific," I said. "But I got nothing in this batch. No news."

Every time the mail came, I got that tightness in my chest, anxiety I could feel down to my toes. I wanted to get mail, because I was starting to really miss my parents and my sisters, but I dreaded it at the same time because of the ever-looming possibility of bad news.

"I'm not going to tell you not to worry because you still will," Frankie said. "But I will tell you that I'm happy to sit and read any letters that come your way, like I did on the roof, just so you're not alone if the news is . . . is about Danny."

"Me too," Martha said.

"Just say the word," Blanche added.

"Thanks, girls," I said. In the Midlands, Frankie, Martha, and Blanche would be stationed nearby, and we were all happy about that.

We turned one more corner and reached the Paramount Dance Hall, the sidewalk beneath our feet vibrating from the sound of the big band coming from inside.

"Hey, dolls! You girls American Red Cross?" an olive-skinned soldier said as soon as we walked into the club. He was standing with a bunch of his fellow GIs, and they weren't even trying to hide their admiration, whistling and elbowing each other as they looked us up and down.

"You know it, darling," Blanche said with a dazzling smile. She looked beautiful; her blonde curls were pulled up on top of her head in an updo, and she was wearing a lovely emerald-green dress with flattering gathers at the shoulders.

"Where's your uniforms, then?" the soldier asked.

"Last night in town, so we're allowed to play dress-up," Blanche replied.

"Last night? You're breaking my heart," the soldier said, putting his hands on his chest, his face an exaggerated frown. "Promise me a dance?"

"If you're lucky." Blanche winked, and his friends laughed and teased him.

"Jesus, Blanche, enough. Get inside the club already," Frankie said, annoyed but amused as she gave her a shove.

It felt so good to wear something pretty and be out of uniform for the night. Viv's dress was a deep teal with an off-the-shoulder neckline, crossover detailing on the bodice, and a dropped waist that flattered every one of her curves. Dottie had a demure cream-colored swing-style dress with navy piping that made her look like the fourth Andrews sister. Martha's dress was a simple but flattering pink floral print. Frankie was wearing a dress that was black velvet on top with a full hot pink skirt.

And I was wearing my favorite black dress. It had a sweetheart bodice with spaghetti straps underneath a gauzy blouse overlay with cap sleeves. It was cinched at the waist with a black patent leather belt and had a slight fishtailed skirt. I had used a comb with a faux red rose to twist my hair up and to the side in the front; the rest of it fell in waves to my shoulders.

The hall was bathed in a smoky haze, the smell of cheap perfume and cigarettes mingling with the sour odor of stale beer. Joe Brandon had brought more than just a couple of his bandmates. He was up onstage, sweat dripping down his face as he played piano with a ten-instrument ensemble complete with a full horn section. Couples packed the dance floor, laughing and jitterbugging to the band's fantastic rendition of "Sing, Sing, Sing."

Miss Chambers's words were weighing on me, but I had promised Viv and Dottie I would try to relax and have fun on our last night here. I took a deep breath, self-consciously smoothed out my dress, and walked with my friends along the edge of the enormous dance floor. We finally found a couple of tables that we could push together, and a waiter in a white coat immediately came over to take our drink order.

A loud, rambunctious group of British RAFs were drinking pints of amber-colored beer and celebrating a birthday at the tables next to ours.

"He's really still got a girl at home?" Dottie was looking up at the stage as she asked. Her dark hair fell in soft waves around her face, and there was a wistful look in her eyes. Viv had done her makeup—winged black eyeliner on her lids and bright-red lipstick. She looked stunning but never believed it when we told her.

"I think so, and I'm so sorry you're disappointed," I said. "He certainly seemed to be flirting with you."

"It's fine," she said with a sigh and a wave of her hand. She turned away from the stage as the waiter brought our drinks. "Even if he was flirting, it's not like any of this matters—we're all going our separate ways."

"True," I said.

"Excuse me, I say, ladies, are these soldiers bothering you at all?" Harry Westwood, the RAF officer and Cary Grant look-alike, said. He stood behind Viv's chair and nodded over to the group of RAF soldiers next to us.

"They're fine," Viv said, giving him an amused look that told me she had definitely not forgotten him.

"Oh, it's Viviana, not Vivien, from Boston," he said, flashing her a broad smile that made Dottie kick me under the table. "How lovely to see you Red Cross ladies again."

"You too. I'm sorry, your name again?" Viv asked him, and I rolled my eyes at Frankie and Dottie because I knew she hadn't forgotten.

"Westwood, mate, come have a pint with us," one of the soldiers called to him. "Unless you're too good for our lot."

"Not at all," he said. "But I was hoping to ask Miss Occhipinti for a dance. And my first name is Harry. Shall we?" He put his hand out for her. Viv looked at it and then back up at him. It was like watching a movie unfold, these two gorgeous people, so confident, so used to getting people to do what they wanted.

"Why don't you have that pint, and I'll think about it," Viv said, smiling and giving him a wink. "We just got here. I want to talk with my friends for a bit."

They locked eyes, and I could tell he was a little put off, but then he laughed and said, "Very well. You think about it, Viviana."

"Are you crazy?" Blanche batted Viv on the arm after he walked away. "He's the most gorgeous guy in the joint. What are you waiting for? And besides, this group needs more to talk about. We need some scandals." Before the Red Cross, Blanche had been a gossip columnist for a New Orleans newspaper, which came as a surprise to exactly no one.

"Viv, he remembered your *last name*," I said. "We met him for what, a minute at Rainbow Corner?"

"Honestly, I didn't even remember your last name," Frankie said.

"That's why I know he'll be back," Viv said, sipping her gin and tonic. "This is payback for giving me the brush-off last time." She smiled and winked across the table at Blanche.

"You *are* crazy," Blanche said. "But I don't doubt he'll be back. That dress is smashing on you, as the Brits say."

"Thank you, honey," Viv said, lighting up a cigarette and offering one to Blanche.

I scanned the room, watching the dancing, the crowds of people talking and laughing. For a few hours, we were all pretending there wasn't a war going on outside the doors. And, once again, I looked for an officer I knew would not be there, and I felt the grief wash over me like a wave.

"I know what you're thinking about, or rather *who* you're thinking about. You get a certain look in your eye," Dottie said into my ear, patting my hand. "You try so hard to hide it. But it's okay, you're among friends. Miss Chambers isn't within earshot."

"I'm pathetic," I said, blinking back tears. "If Miss Chambers saw me right now, she'd send me home. Was I crazy to do this?"

"No, not at all," Dottie said. "When you told me you wanted to apply, I thought it was so brave. Your bravery made me decide to apply too. Part of the reason I'm doing this is to force myself to come out of my shell. Leaving my little brother and my parents, with Marco already stationed so far away? That was the hardest thing I've ever done. But I needed to do this too. For myself."

"I'm proud of you, Dottie," I said. "And my saving grace is having you and Viv with me."

"All right, finished my beer, who wants to go find some soldiers to dance with?" Martha said, slamming her beer glass on the table and jumping up from her chair. "Who's with me?"

"I'll come," Viv said. Blanche got up, as did a few other girls, including a somewhat reluctant Frankie, as well as ChiChi, Doris, and

Rosie, a crew from the Clubmobile Dixie Queen that we had gotten to know during our training.

"Wait, where did Harry Westwood go?" I asked, looking over to where he had just been sitting with the RAF officers.

"Missing. Maybe he brushed me off again," Viv said, acting nonchalant despite the disappointment in her eyes.

Dottie and I sat talking with the Clubmobilers who remained at the table, including Ruthie Spielberg and Helen Walton, two friends from North Dakota who could talk the bark off a tree. As Ruthie was telling a story, the hairs on the back of my neck stood up, and I felt someone watching me. I looked around the hall again and spotted a group of officers sitting in a dark corner on the opposite side of the dance floor. They were drinking beer, their faces serious as they talked quietly. In the middle of the group was Captain Peter Moretti. He was looking right at me.

I got aggravated all over again, recalling our conversation about women in war. I considered ignoring his stare, but I took the high road, waving and giving him a small smile. He just turned and started talking to the blond officer sitting next to him.

"How rude," I whispered under my breath.

"What?" Dottie asked.

"Hey, Boston girls, how are you?" Joe Brandon came over to our table and greeted us like long-lost friends. "So glad you came. Dottie, you going to join us up there tonight?"

"Never! I don't know how you do it," said Dottie with a laugh, her cheeks flushed at the sight of him.

Oh boy. It didn't matter if he had a girl at home, Dottie was smitten.

"Why aren't you onstage?" she asked him.

"I had one of my bandmates jump in for me so I could at least grab a beer or a Coke; it's so hot under the lights up there," he said, wiping his brow. "You girls want to come to the bar with me?"

"Sure," Dottie said, grabbing my hand and pulling me up.

At the bar, Joe ordered drinks for the three of us.

"Hey, Joe, have you heard from Mary Jane yet?" I said as he handed us our drinks. He had to come clean. I didn't want him breaking Dottie's heart. Joe looked at me and then at Dottie's face, turning pale.

"I . . . ," he said, taking a deep breath, nervously wiping his brow again. "Yes, I did yesterday for the first time. She's getting her classroom ready for the start of school."

"Your fiancée?" Dottie said.

"No, she's my girlfriend," he said in a quiet voice. "Dottie . . ."

They were looking deep into each other's eyes, and suddenly I was interrupting a private moment.

"I have to find the ladies' room," I said. "I'll be back in a few."

I made my way through the crowds to the ladies' room, which was in a narrow hallway near the front doors. There was a line, of course, so I queued up behind a gaggle of British girls who were swooning about some GIs they had just met. One of them was wearing lavender perfume that was so strong it made me gag a little.

"I thought you'd be out on the dance floor with your friends."

I looked up to see Peter Moretti, who was taking up more than half the narrow hallway with his broad shoulders.

"And I thought you'd wave back when I waved to you across the hall a few minutes ago," I said with a frown, feeling slighted and still annoyed by our last conversation.

"When did you do that? I didn't see you," he said.

"How come I don't believe you?" I stepped out of my place in line.

That lopsided grin again. "Honest, I didn't see you."

"Why aren't *you* dancing?" I asked.

"I don't dance."

"Ever?"

"Ever," he said. "I am a—well, I *used* to be a boxer, so I'm pretty good on my feet . . . but I don't dance."

"I heard you were a boxer. Norman is quite a fan."

"Norman's a good man."

There was an awkward silence as the line to the ladies' room moved up and guys pushed past us to get to the men's room.

"Well, see you," he said.

"Yes, I guess I'll see you in Leicester—or thereabouts," I replied.

He looked up at the ceiling, sighed, and said, "Yeah, you Red Cross girls are heading there too. They also sent a bunch of you over to Normandy with the troops in July."

"I'm sure you were thrilled about it," I said.

"It's nothing against you girls personally," he said. "I know I upset you the other day. But I just don't see the point of putting American women at risk so they can pass out doughnuts. It makes no sense."

"It's nothing against us, but you keep insulting my whole reason for being here," I said. "I know *you* don't see the value in it, but we must be doing something right or they wouldn't keep hiring more of us."

He shrugged. "I don't know. Again, no offense, I just don't get it. Maybe you just look like you're helping, and that's all that matters. Maybe it looks good in pictures for the folks back home."

I thought of the *LIFE* magazine shoot, and my face grew hot. *Did he know about that?*

"I'm not going to try to convince you," I said and, seeing that the line to the ladies' room had disappeared, decided to make my exit. "I don't think I could if I tried. I only hope someday you'll see our value. See you," I said and made a beeline for the swinging door of the restroom.

As soon as I walked back into the hall, Martha and Viv pulled me onto the dance floor. The band was playing again, and they had brought up a vocalist, a soldier named Marty. He was no Bing Crosby, but he wasn't half-bad.

"No more sitting in the corner, Fi," Viv said, squeezing my elbow. "We've got another guy out here that needs a partner."

"Any sign of Harry Westwood?" I said.

"Nope, disappeared," Viv said, shrugging. "His loss."

They introduced me to a fella named Timmy, a tall, skinny guy who didn't have a dance partner. Joe Brandon was back onstage at the piano, looking sullen. Dottie was laughing and dancing with a GI who didn't look old enough to shave.

Timmy proved to be a better dancer than he looked, and I actually relaxed and enjoyed myself as he gave me dancing tips and whirled me around the floor. The band had just started another song when Harry Westwood appeared again and rushed up to the stage. He signaled for the band to stop playing, and some of the soldiers in the audience booed. Harry grabbed the microphone and turned to the audience. The look on his face made the booing stop.

"Ladies and gentlemen, I regret to inform you that the club has to be evacuated immediately," Harry said, as he looked out across the crowd, calm, serious, and dignified. "It's too loud in here to hear the sirens outside. We have reports of an unprecedented number of V-1s coming into the city in the next twenty-four hours, and we need to take all the necessary precautions. Please exit the club in an orderly fashion and be cautious getting back to your lodgings. Be safe and God bless."

There was no panic in the crowd as people downed the last of their drinks, started finding their friends, and filed out of the Paramount. The feeling in the air was one of resignation. The carefree bubble of the club had just burst, and it was time to head back outside to the war.

The sirens were so loud outside, I was amazed we hadn't heard them. I brushed my hair back from my face with shaking hands. I had almost adjusted to the constant threat of bombs . . . but not quite.

"Viv, darling, there you are." Harry Westwood came up to us as we were waiting for the rest of the girls to file out. Viv gave me a sideways glance with her eyebrows raised.

"I can arrange for your group to get a ride to where you're staying on the back of one of the RAF trucks," he said. "My apologies as it's not exactly riding in style, but it will get you there safe."

"Okay, thank you; it's about two miles from here," Viv said. "There are eleven of us."

"Good," he said. "Gather the rest of your friends and wait right here. I'll be back." He disappeared into the crowds.

"*Darling?*" I said. "He doesn't even know you."

"Who cares, he's getting us home." She paused before adding, "And yes, it is a bit forward, but you have to admit, with that British accent? Anything sounds delicious." We both started laughing.

Dottie and Blanche came out, followed by Frankie, Martha, the chatterboxes Ruthie and Helen, the Dixie Queen crew, and the rest of our group. We were looking for the RAF truck when Peter Moretti stepped in front of me.

"Some of my guys have jeeps; we can bring you girls home," he said. "They'll be pulling up here in less than a minute . . ."

"Our chariot has arrived," Viv announced as a RAF pickup truck pulled up. Harry Westwood was in the passenger seat, and he jumped out and started helping all the girls climb into the back.

"Oh, it looks like we've got a ride," I said. "But thank you. It was kind of you to think of us."

"A RAF truck, huh?" he said, unmistakable annoyance in his voice. "Well, be safe and get home quickly. You're pretty exposed in the back of that truck, so stay low. Get shelter if you hear a V-1 even remotely close by."

"I'm sure we'll be okay," I said. It was a total lie, and we both knew it. No one was ever sure.

"I also just wanted to say I'm . . . I'm sorry if I offended you earlier. *Again.*"

"Don't worry about it. You know more about this war than I do." I relaxed after his apology, not even realizing how tense I had felt.

"Yeah," he said. "Now I . . ."

"Fi, come on, we've got to go now!" Frankie said, standing in the back of the RAF truck.

"Thank you again," I said.

I climbed into the back of the truck with my friends. As it pulled away, I turned back to see Peter Moretti looking at me; he nodded and gave me a small wave before heading into the crowds.

"Who was that, Fi?" Dottie asked as I sat down next to her.

"Oh, he's that captain with the Eighty-Second Airborne I met at Norman's garage. He offered us a ride too," I said. "But he's kind of a grump."

"He can't be all bad if he offered to get us a ride," Dottie said.

"I guess," I said with a sigh.

I didn't feel like talking about my discussion with him earlier in the night, especially in front of all the girls in the back of the RAF truck. I was pretty sure Martha and Blanche had each had one drink too many because they were acting like it was a party on wheels. We were totally exposed, with no helmets, but they just kept laughing, yelling, and whistling at all the soldiers we passed.

The sirens continued to blare as our RAF driver flew through the streets, which were packed with people and vehicles trying to get to safety. I couldn't hear the now-familiar rumble of the buzz bomb, but there was an undeniable tension in the air. London knew what was coming.

Chapter Ten

We made it back to 103 Park Street in no time, and Harry Westwood and the RAF driver helped all eleven of us jump out of the back of the truck. We hurried inside to get our gas masks and prepare to sleep in the basement if necessary.

"I'll see you again soon," Harry said to Viv, who was the last one out. He held her hand for a few seconds longer than was necessary.

"I won't hold my breath," Viv said with a wink and a smile.

When we entered the foyer, chatting and laughing, Miss Chambers and Liz Anderson were standing there waiting for us. We could hear footsteps and general chaos coming from the rooms upstairs.

"What's going on?" I asked. The rest of the group had gone quiet and seemed to have sobered up on the spot. Miss Chambers looked furious.

"What's going on is the city is under attack," Miss Chambers said. "What's going *on* is we've been waiting for you all to get back for over an hour. You'll be leaving in your Clubmobiles tonight. Although I seriously question if some of you should be going at all."

She looked at me when she said this, and I started to stare down at the floor but thought better of it and just returned her gaze, unblinking. I would show her. We would show her.

Meanwhile, everyone started asking questions, raising their voices as they tried to talk over each other. Liz Anderson raised her hand for quiet.

"Let me explain," she said in a calm, measured voice. She didn't appear the slightest bit rattled by our late arrival. "With the reports coming in regarding the barrage of V-1s that may be raining down on the city at any moment, we think the safer option is to head out to the Midlands tonight. We'll be meeting your assigned drivers at Camp Griffiss. I hope to God you're already packed because you've only got twenty minutes to get changed and gather all of your gear. Keep your helmets near you. We'll ring the bell if we all need to head to the basement." She clapped her hands together. "Now get moving, and I'll see you downstairs in twenty."

Frankie led us all in a mad dash up the stairs to our rooms. It was mayhem on the upper two floors as girls in various states of dress ran in and out of rooms, packing and getting organized. Footlockers, musettes, helmets, and gas masks were piled up outside some doors, all ready to go. You could feel the nervous anticipation, excitement, and fear in the air.

Dottie kept running to the window in our dorm room to listen for the too-familiar sound of V-1s as we changed and gathered our things. Viv was not completely packed, so I helped shove the rest of her belongings into her footlocker.

"Dottie, what did you say to Joe after I left you two?" I asked.

"He said he really liked me. He thought I was so beautiful," she said. "And I said, 'Thank you for the compliment, but what were you saying about your girl back home?'

"He thinks he loves her, had plans to marry her eventually. But he tried to convince me that since he's going to be away from her a long time, shouldn't we have fun in the moment because we're two people that like each other? And *then* he tried to kiss me. I excused myself and asked that young kid to dance with me to end the conversation."

"You made that kid's night," Viv said, laughing.

"I think I did," Dottie said with a smile. But then her smile faded. "I still have a terrible crush on Joe. He's handsome and so talented. And from the start, it was so easy to talk to him—you both know that never happens for me. But what kind of guy is telling his girl back home that he loves her while trying to kiss another one over here?"

"Good point. You did the right thing," I said. "And we're leaving anyway."

"True," she said with a sigh. "I can't help thinking about what it would be like to kiss him, though."

"Plenty of fish in the war, Dots. Fish that *don't* think it's okay to be unfaithful to their girl back home," Viv said.

"Five minutes!" Miss Chambers yelled up the stairs. "Trucks arriving in five."

We gathered up all of our gear, and out of habit I reached down to feel the letter in the bottom of my musette bag. Except I didn't feel it. I put my things down and opened the bag to get a better look.

"Fi, come on," Dottie said. "What's the matter?"

"The envelope with Danny's last letter to me isn't in my bag," I said, feeling frantic. "I don't know where I could have put it. It's not here."

Viv and Dottie dropped their things and started checking around the room, under the beds and in their own things. The letter was nowhere.

"I can't believe I lost it," I said, blinking back tears. "It's the last letter I have from him. How could I be so careless?"

"Go easy on yourself," Viv said. "We've been on the go since we left Boston. It's hard to keep track of everything."

"Yes, but it isn't like I lost a pair of socks," I said. "This matters."

"Ladies! Our rides are here," Liz called from downstairs.

"We've got to go," Dottie said, taking my hand. "You told me you hadn't read it in a while because it made you too sad."

"I hadn't read it since we were on the *Queen Elizabeth*."

"Ladies, what are you doing? You're about to miss your ride." Liz stood in our door, breathless. She looked at me. "Is everything okay?"

"Yes," I said. "I . . . I lost something, but maybe it's stuffed in the bottom of my footlocker or somewhere else in my stuff."

"Well, come on, then," Liz said, her impatience evident as she grabbed some of our gear and headed out the door.

I knew it was gone. But maybe Dottie was right. The letter had been like a weight, heavy in my musette bag, sadness and grief emanating from its tear-stained pages. If I was going to do this job right, maybe it was time to lighten my load a little. At least I still had the photograph of him.

We looked around our dorm room one last time, but I knew we had to leave. I bit my lip to hold back tears as we headed downstairs.

~

The three of us stood in front of our Clubmobile, the Cheyenne, with all of our gear, listening to the incredible snoring coming from the vehicle's cab. It was loud and nasal, punctuated by an occasional snort. Jimmy English, our designated British driver, was sound asleep, slumped over the steering wheel.

"I'm not sure I've ever heard someone snore that loud," I said.

"I could hear my father from three rooms over, but this man is worse," said Dottie. She tsk-tsked. "His poor wife."

We had arrived at Camp Griffiss minutes earlier with the rest of the girls. In addition to the eight Clubmobiles in Group F, there were two cargo trucks for supplies and a jeep and driver for Liz. We had just said our good-byes to Blanche, Martha, and Frankie as they drove away in their Clubmobile, the Uncle Sam, with their driver, a short, chubby fella named Trevor.

The air raid sirens were still blaring, and you could hear the occasional sounds of the ack-ack. We hadn't come close to any buzz bombs yet, but that didn't mean we wouldn't. I wanted to get out of the city as fast as we possibly could, which meant waking Jimmy English or driving the Clubmobile myself. I climbed up so I could reach into the window of the driver's side and tap him on the shoulder.

"Mr. English, hello? Time to wake up," I said in his ear. He responded with a loud, rumbling snore that reeked of alcohol.

"Oh God, he smells like he bathed in a tub of whiskey," I said, making a sour face at Viv and Dottie.

"You're joking," Viv said. "He's passed out drunk? That's fabulous. He's going to be in great shape to drive us over a hundred miles *in a blackout.*"

"We're the last Clubmobile here," Dottie said, as we watched the seventh Clubmobile drive away. "What are we going to do?"

"We're going to get the hell out of here somehow," I said. This time I stepped up to the cab, grabbed his shoulder, shook him, and in a very loud voice spoke directly into his ear. "Jimmy. Hello, Jimmy! Wake up, time to go."

He opened one eye and looked at me with a frown.

"What the hell do you want?" he said, in a Cockney accent like Norman's.

"We want to get out of London. Tonight. Don't you hear the air raid sirens? I'm Fiona, this is Dottie and Viv, and you're our driver."

"What time's it?" he asked, sitting up and rubbing his face. He had a spiky black forest of hair and at least three days of stubble on his face.

"It's time to leave. How long have you been passed out?" Viv asked, lighting up a cigarette.

"Give me a fag, will ya?" he said, looking at Viv's pack of Chesterfields. I jumped off the truck so he could open the door and get out. Viv handed him a cigarette and her book of matches. He was a lean, wiry guy with a compact build. From the lines around his eyes, I guessed him to be in his late forties.

"Ain't we leaving in the mornin'?" he said, looking at all of our gear on the ground. "What happened?"

"If you thought we were leaving in the morning, why were you sleeping in the truck now?" Dottie asked.

"Me mate dropped me here after the pub," he said with a shrug. "Already packed. Got no reason to go home if I got to be here at dawn."

"So you didn't even know about the decision to leave tonight?" I said.

"Red Cross lady came by. Is that what she was sayin', then?" he said, referring to Liz Anderson. "I was knackered. Didn't hear a word of it."

"You were dead asleep," I said. "And yes, we've got to leave tonight. Like now. We're the last ones here. Can you drive? Sounds like you've been at the pub."

"*Smells* like he was at the pub," Viv said under her breath.

"'Course I can drive," he said, standing taller.

"If you can't, we all took driving lessons," I said. "We have our British licenses. I can . . . I can try to drive us instead."

Viv and Dottie looked at me like I had lost my mind. I stared back at them, silently warning them not to contradict me. Truth was, I was terrified at the thought of driving, but careening through the country-side with a drunk Jimmy English was just as scary.

Jimmy burst out laughing. He stumbled back and kept roaring with laughter like it was the funniest thing he'd ever heard.

"What?" I said, crossing my arms. "What's so funny?"

"You? Driving *this*? In a blackout with only the cat-eye lights?" he said, wiping the tears from his eyes. "That's brilliant. Norman told me all about youse three." He pointed at me with his lit cigarette. "You wouldn't make it two miles, would ya?"

"Yes, we would," I said.

"No, we definitely wouldn't," Viv said.

"Quiet, Viv," I said.

"But she's right, Fi, we need him," Dottie said. "We need you, Mr. English."

"But he's still drunk," I said, pointing to him. His dark eyes were glassy and bloodshot. "You do realize that, right? And I don't think you'd disagree, would you, Mr. English?"

"Ain't gonna deny it," he said with a nod. "But I'm bettin' I'm a much better driver drunk than your lot is stone sober."

I was about to disagree when I heard it. And we all looked to the sky at the sound of the low rumble. It was getting louder by the second.

"That's it. That's them doodlebugs comin' in, isn't it?" Jimmy said, stomping out his cigarette. He sprang into action, grabbing our gear and loading it into the Clubmobile. "Ain't got no more time to argue, ladies."

"Jesus Christ," I said in a whisper as we loaded up all of our things. "We're really going to let this man drive us?"

"What choice do we have?" Dottie said. "We only passed our driving exams because Norman gave us a break, and I'm ready to stop shaking from buzz bombs. I want to get out of here."

"Amen, Dots," Viv said. "Time to go."

We climbed into the front, four across—it was tight but not terrible. I peeked through the small window into the back, at the tiny kitchen and all of our gear piled up. I suddenly saw a flash of movement and orange fur, and I jumped as it came leaping through the window right at us. Viv screamed.

"Whoa, kitty. Where in the world did she come from?" I asked. She had jumped onto Jimmy's lap.

"Oh yeah, that's me cat, Vera Lynn," Jimmy said as he fired up the Clubmobile. "Had to bring her too; ain't got no one to care for her."

Vera was a scraggly orange cat; her left ear was nicked at the top, and one of her green eyes was partially closed like another cat had punched her.

"You named your cat after Vera Lynn, the singer?" I said, eyebrows raised, not able to hide my amusement.

"What's the deal with Vera's eye?" Dottie asked.

"Oh no. *No.* I hate cats," Viv said, covering her mouth. In a muffled voice she added, "They steal your breath. Also, Vera needs a bath." She was sitting next to the window on the opposite side of the cab, and she moved like she was going to open the door and jump out. The cab of the Clubmobile smelled like cigarettes, whiskey, and stinky feline.

"Keep 'at door shut, miss. We're goin'," Jimmy said in a firm voice. I think the incoming buzz bombs had sobered him up, at least I hoped so. He kissed Vera on the head and threw her in the back as she meowed in protest.

Starting up the Clubmobile, Jimmy hit the gas so hard we all had whiplash. We drove out of the base into the pitch-black night, going easily over seventy miles per hour. Our semi-drunk driver navigated the roads and drove at a breakneck pace, as if the buzz bombs might make a direct hit on us. I said a silent prayer, terrified that if the buzz bombs didn't get us, Jimmy's driving surely would.

Chapter Eleven

July 31, 1944
Leicester, England

My eyes were still closed when I heard the sound of a rooster crowing right outside the window next to my bed, and I remembered we weren't in London anymore.

For the entire ride to Leicester the night before, I had gripped the door of the cab with white knuckles, certain we were going to crash into a cow or fence or oncoming car. By some miracle, Jimmy had managed to deliver us safely to our destination. We were billeted near one of the villages on the outskirts of the city of Leicester, in a stone farmhouse owned by a lovely widow named Mrs. Tibbetts. At three in the morning, we had finally stumbled into her home, sleepy and hungry. She greeted us at the door with a smile, fed us some savory tarts and tea, and sent us straight to bed.

Our bedroom was on the second floor, a long and narrow room with a slanted ceiling and three single beds in a row. It was her sons' room—all three of them were away in the war, one in Italy, two in the Pacific.

Dottie was already awake and standing by the window, where she had removed the blackout curtain. "Come see, Fiona."

We hadn't been able to see a thing when we arrived the night before. That morning the English countryside was breathtaking and such a contrast from London. There was a garden divided by a winding path—it was in full bloom, bursting with orange daisies, purple foxgloves, and pale-pink geraniums. Beyond the garden were rolling hills of various shades of green, spotted with herds of sheep. In the distance you could see a pond with some white geese lazily floating on the surface.

I opened the window and took a deep breath of the fresh country air. "This is lovely," I said. "Like out of a Jane Austen novel."

"Isn't it?" Dottie said with a smile. "I think we've got to wake Princess V." She gently shook Viv, who just grumbled and rolled over.

"Hello? Hello, good morning!" Mrs. Tibbetts knocked on our door and peeked in. "Oh, I'm so sorry," she said, pulling her head back. "I didn't realize you weren't dressed."

"It's fine, Mrs. Tibbetts," I said, stepping into the hallway in my pajamas and smoothing out my hair. "Good morning."

"Did you sleep well, dear?" she asked, hope in her voice. She was shorter than me, with light-blue eyes and brown hair streaked with gray. She had a round face and a very pretty smile.

"Yes, I did," I said. "Your home is beautiful. Thank you for letting us stay here."

"It's no trouble," she said in a lilting accent that was different than Jimmy's, though I couldn't identify exactly how. "And I'm happy to have the company. It's been too quiet with just me and the animals. I've started talking to them, for goodness' sake." She laughed. "There's tea and breakfast downstairs."

She smiled and patted my shoulder before turning to go. "And Jimmy will take you to Granby Street when you're ready to go."

"Jimmy's already here?" I said.

"Jimmy never left," she said. "He was in no shape to drive a minute longer, so I got him some blankets and he slept on the sofa."

"That was smart," I said. "Thank you."

"Not a worry. I'll see you downstairs."

I walked back into the bedroom to get dressed, put on some lipstick, and brush my hair. I was surprised to see Viv and Dottie almost ready to go.

"Please tell me she didn't say tea," Viv said, her voice even raspier than normal. "I need a strong cup of coffee, or I'm going to kill myself. Damn that rooster."

"I do prefer roosters to air raid sirens," Dottie said.

"We can get some coffee at the Red Cross club," I said. "We should go. Liz Anderson is meeting us there at nine to give us our assignments."

"Well, at least I have this pale-peach nail polish now, so when it chips into the batter, the soldiers won't be able to see it in their doughnuts," Viv said.

"You could actually *not* wear polish, Viv," Dottie said. "Nail polish chips in doughnuts is disgusting."

"Not wear any? Never," Viv said in mock horror.

I adjusted my hat and looked at the three of us in our battle dress uniforms.

"We look official," I said.

"I still think we look like we're wearing clown suits," Viv said.

"Oh shush, Viv." Dottie swatted her.

I laughed, and then felt myself getting a little emotional. "Thank you both," I said in a soft voice, looking at my two best friends. "For getting me this far. I couldn't have done it without you."

"We've got a lot farther to go, Fi," Dottie said. "But you're welcome."

"All right, all right," Viv said, waving her hand in the air and heading out the door. "You don't really need to thank us, but whatever, you're welcome. Now can we *please* go find some American coffee?"

∼

After a breakfast of Mrs. Tibbetts's own farm-fresh eggs, a fried tomato, mushrooms, and toast, a quiet and sober Jimmy and his very vocal cat Vera drove us through the English countryside, past bursts of flowers and clipped hedges, past villages that looked straight out of a children's fairy tale. As we got closer to Leicester, it was clear that this part of England had not been spared the horrors of war. Buildings had been bombed out and had yet to be replaced, and the rubble had been cleared in some places, but the damage was still shocking. Jimmy explained that, like London, Leicester had suffered its own devastating damage from German air raids in late 1940.

Throughout the city, lampposts and curb stones had been painted with thick white stripes to help drivers navigate during the blackouts. I thought of Jimmy driving us the night before in that inky blackness, barely sober and with very little to rely on but his tiny headlights and the occasional marker. I'm not sure how he did it, but I was grateful.

Jimmy dropped us off and went to gas up the Clubmobile, and Liz Anderson met us at the front entrance of the Red Cross Service Club on Granby Street. To Viv's relief, she led us immediately to the dining hall to get steaming mugs of coffee.

"Now, which one of you is going to be captain?" Liz asked as we sat down at a table. She had a folder in front of her with *Cheyenne* written on the tab.

"Sorry, we haven't even discussed it yet," I said, a little embarrassed.

"*We* have actually," Viv said, pointing at Dottie and herself. "Fiona's captain, no question. Of the three of us, she's perfect for the job."

"Yup, Viv's right," said Dottie. "She ran the mayor's office in Boston; she's super organized. We nominate Fiona."

"Nice of you two to tell me ahead of time," I said, annoyed.

"Oh please, Fi, if one of us had the job, you'd end up with it anyway," Viv said.

"It's true," Dottie said.

Liz looked at the three of us, amused, as I paused to consider.

"No. What I *know* is that neither of you wants the job, and you're trying to flatter me into taking it," I said, giving them an exaggerated grimace. "Fine. I'll take it."

Liz gave me a quick refresher on the captain's duties we had reviewed in training, which included tedious tasks like making sure Jimmy kept the Cheyenne gassed up and running properly and keeping a weekly log of how many doughnuts we made and packs of cigarettes we dispensed.

"Okay, now to the good stuff." Liz pulled another sheet out of the folder. "Leicester is centrally located near several army installations. Each day of the week, you'll be assigned two or three locations. In the mornings, Jimmy will pick you up at Mrs. Tibbetts's and bring you here to the yard, where we keep the Clubmobiles—a.k.a. 'Doughnut Alley.' We have electrical hookups back there so you can make some of the doughnuts before you even get on the road.

"Now, since it's your first day, I was going to only assign you one camp instead of two, but I'm short-staffed and promised I'd get a crew to Huntingdon this evening. You up for it?"

Dottie and Viv and I looked at each other, the reality of it all making us nervous.

"Sure. Trial by fire, right?" I said.

"Great," Liz said. She looked at us, searching for words. "Finally, I wanted to mention, you aren't Miss Chambers's favorite Clubmobile group . . ."

"You've got that right," Viv said with a snicker.

"But you're going to be just *fine*," she said, giving us a reassuring smile. "Besides, you could serve them coffee grounds and stale dog biscuits, and they'd still be thrilled to see American girls."

Liz came with us, and we met Jimmy back at the Cheyenne in Doughnut Alley, where the air was thick with the now-familiar, cloyingly sweet smell of doughnuts and grease.

"Okay, I think you're all set," she said. "We had to hire some local women to come here to headquarters early in the morning to help supplement your own doughnut making, so you've already got several dozen to get you started. Jimmy did you load everything up?"

"Ya, I did, Miss Liz," he said. He was sitting in the front seat, smoking a cigarette. "Time to go."

"Major Bill O'Brien is your army liaison. He'll meet you at the first base to help you get situated," Liz said, handing off the paperwork. "If you run into any problems, he's your man."

"Liz, would it be possible to get some paints?" Viv asked, running her hand across the side of the Cheyenne. "I'd like to spruce this baby up."

"I think we can arrange that," Liz said, pleased at the idea.

We thanked Liz and said our good-byes. As we were pulling away, I called to her, and Jimmy stopped the Cheyenne, grunting his annoyance.

"Do you know when we're going to get another batch of mail?" I asked.

"I'm hoping by the end of the week," she said. "If I have any for you three, I'll drop it at Mrs. Tibbetts's."

"No news is good news, right?" Dottie said, trying to reassure me as we pulled away.

"I guess," I said. "I've only received that one letter from my sisters since we left the States."

"We'll be busy enough to keep your mind off any news," Viv said. "Although I think two stops on our very first day is way too much, frankly."

"What news you waitin' on?" Jimmy asked. He was quiet for a moment after I told him about Danny, but then he said with a nod, "Ah, well, hope you hear somethin' good soon."

"Thanks," I said quietly. I looked out the window at the blue skies and green rolling hills, the hedges and the flowers, wondering for the millionth time, *Where are you, Danny? Are you anywhere anymore?*

Our first stop was a half hour outside of Leicester, so we had Jimmy pull over, and then we climbed in back to prepare for our big debut. You had to hand it to Harvey Gibson—the interior design was impressive. The Cheyenne's compact kitchen included the doughnut machine, six coffee urns, and a stainless steel sink. There were space-saving drawers and cabinets for pots, pans, and utensils. There was a compartment with a Victrola that was hooked up to a loudspeaker and another compartment that held our record collection.

Dottie put a Bing Crosby record on the Victrola, and Viv was fixing her hair and lipstick, so I elbowed her to help me with the coffee urns.

"We're here, ladies," Jimmy said as we approached a virtual city of army tents. We pushed the two trap doors on the side of the truck up and out to create our serving counters. When we got closer, we spotted an officer in a jeep waving at us.

"Major Bill O'Brien?" I asked, leaning out the window as Jimmy pulled up beside him.

"At your service," he said. "The boys from the Eighty-Second are going to be happy to see you three. Where y'all from?" He was of average height with strong, rough-hewn features and a thick drawl.

I made the introductions.

"Yankee girls, eh?" he said, smiling. "We've got at least a few GIs from around Boston. I'm from Boerne, Texas, myself. Follow me, I'll show you where to hook up for water."

Jimmy drove behind Major Bill into the dusty tent city, and my stomach did a little flip.

"All right, ladies, this is what we came here for. Put on your ugly aprons. It's showtime," Viv said, handing us each one.

"Ready, Dottie?" I asked, squeezing her hand.

"As ready as I'll ever be," she said, chewing on her hair, her cheeks bright red.

"Promise me you'll play one song on the guitar?" I said, thinking of Miss Chambers's warning. "Just one, please?"

"Yes, you have to, Dottie, at least one," Viv said.

"Okay." Dottie sighed. "I think I can manage that without dying of embarrassment."

We leaned out of the Cheyenne and started waving and smiling. GIs peeked out from tents and looked up from cleaning their guns or shaving over water-filled helmets, then cheered when we passed. A couple of mangy-looking dogs started chasing after us. We went by a small muddy field, where a group of men was playing a game of pickup football, shirts versus skins. Viv whistled at them, and they went crazy.

Major Bill pulled his jeep up to the electrical hookup, and we parked right next to him. There were already men swarming the Clubmobile, waving their canteen cups in the air. One of them climbed onto the back and walked in.

"Hey, can I help?" the GI said. "I helped the last Clubmobile girls that were here."

"Sure," Viv said, handing him a tin of cream to open and stir into the coffee urn. "What's your name, soldier? Where you from?"

"I'm Private Edward Landon from Mesa, Arizona." He was a stocky, blond-haired boy who couldn't have been older than eighteen.

"Can you help us make some doughnuts for the next stop?" I asked.

"Sure," he said with a huge smile, so thrilled that we had taken him up on his offer. "I learned how with the Daniel Boone crew, before they left for France."

Viv turned on the Victrola and started blasting "Paper Doll" by the Mills Brothers over the speakers, and the soldiers cheered in delight. Dottie and I were on doughnut duty, handing out two apiece, while Viv and our new friend Edward started filling coffee cups. There had to be over a hundred soldiers surrounding the Cheyenne. Each conversation started out the same: "Hey, soldier, where you from?"

"I'm from Queens, New York," said a blue-eyed, black-haired soldier named Patrick Halloran, "but my buddy Tommy Doyle is from Boston. Hey, Tommy! Come over here, these girls are from Boston."

"No way. What part?" Tommy said, running over, an urgency in his voice. He looked more Italian than Irish. He had an olive complexion and deep-set brown eyes, a dimple in his right cheek.

"Charlestown," I said, smiling and handing him two doughnuts. "You?"

"Southie," he said. "You look like you're around my sister's age. Her name is Bridget Doyle."

"Hmm," Viv said. "Don't think I know her, but if she's as pretty as you are handsome, I bet she's popular."

This brought a roar from the crowd, and Tommy blushed, shaking his head.

"Come on in, Boston Tommy, and help us get these huge cans of lard off the floor," Viv said with a wink.

"Sure!" Tommy said.

Tommy rushed inside, pushing past another young soldier that I hadn't noticed. He was tall, standing at the back of the truck almost hunched over, with his helmet on and his carbine strapped to his back, looking at us all shyly.

"What's your name, hon?" I said.

"Sam. Sam Katz, I'm from Scranton, Pennsylvania," he said. He had a pale complexion and a distinct cleft in his chin. "It's so nice to see you gals."

"Well, Sam from Pennsylvania, would you like to help us pick some records for the record player, maybe pass out some candy?" I asked him.

"I sure would," he said, his face lighting up as he took off his helmet, revealing dirty-blond hair. "I'll help you gals with anything. Hey, a cat! What's your name, kitty?"

"That's Vera Lynn," I said. She was curled up on top of the record cabinet.

"You can put your gun down; I promise you don't need it to play records," I said, teasing.

His face got very serious, and he gripped the carbine on his back. "I . . . since our last, I've got to have it with me," he said, stuttering. "I, I know we're in safer territory, but . . . if you don't want me in here with it . . ."

"No, no, it's perfectly fine, really," I said, putting my hand on his arm. "Whatever you need to do, it's fine. How about putting on some Glenn Miller?"

I felt him relax as he let out a deep breath and nodded. Vera jumped down and rubbed up against him, and the two of them started going through our limited record collection.

After he was done with that, I handed him some gum, boxes of cigarettes, and packs of Life Savers and told him to pass them out to everyone waiting in line. I put another young GI in charge of the "guestbook," the state registry where GIs could sign their name and where they were from, so when we visited other units, soldiers could look through for friends from home.

This happy chaos went on for three hours as Tommy and Patrick helped us keep the six-and-a-half-gallon coffee urns full. When the doughnut machine was finally heated up, Edward from Mesa assisted us in mixing the eighteen pounds of doughnut flour with ten pounds of water. Our helpers were eager but not neat—the coffee, flour, water, and grease splashed all over our tiny kitchen, making a gooey mess, mucking up the floor and dripping down the cabinets, and soon everything stank of fried doughnuts. The boys loved the smell, but Viv, Dottie, and I were nauseated by it.

"Eau du Doughnut," Viv said as we finished making over five hundred doughnuts for the next stop. "I'll never get this smell out of my clothes."

"Got to leave at half past," Jimmy announced from the front seat at three o'clock.

"Okay, I think we're almost done here," I said. "Dottie, one song?" Dottie looked at her guitar resting against the doughnut racks.

"You play?" Tommy asked. "Please play a song. The guys will go crazy." He held his hands in prayer and was about to get down on his knees.

"Oh, for Pete's sake, all right," Dottie said, grabbing her guitar.

We turned off the music and the crowd started to boo. Viv put her hand to her mouth and whistled for quiet. One of the GIs cupped his hands and said, "Anything for you, gorgeous!"

"We've got a treat for you all before we go," Viv said. "Dottie Sousa is a fantastic musician, and she's going to play a song on her guitar for you." Dottie put her guitar strap over her shoulder and stepped up to the window next to Viv, and everyone started clapping.

I stood next to her on the other side.

"I'm not going to sing," she whispered to me through gritted teeth.

"You don't have to sing," I said. "Just play one song."

"What song?" she asked, looking at the two of us in a panic.

"'Don't Sit Under the Apple Tree,'" a GI called out. Other soldiers echoed this request.

"There you go," I said. "You know that one."

Dottie closed her eyes and took a deep breath.

"Oh, hell, Dottie, just *play*," Viv urged.

Her hands were shaking as she strummed the first notes of "Don't Sit Under the Apple Tree," and the soldiers started clapping. And then, a whole bunch of them started to sing.

The three of us looked at each other, surprised at the spontaneous sing-along. It was amazing to hear all these soldiers, in a dusty field in the English countryside, singing an Andrews Sisters song at the top of their lungs with pure joy. And the more they sang, the more comfortable Dottie became. The three of us, and even Jimmy, started singing.

The crowd clapped in delight when the song was finished, and the soldiers begged for more, but it was time for us to go. We waved goodbye to our new friends and promised to come back soon.

"Look at my hands," Viv said, clicking her tongue. Once again all the nail polish had worn off, and they looked raw and red from mixing the dough.

"I'm proud of you, Dottie," I said as we cleaned up the mess in the kitchen. "I know that wasn't easy for you."

"Me too," said Viv.

"Thanks," Dottie said. "I was terrified. But I felt better as I went along. All those soldiers singing was something to see."

"Why don't you sing *and* play for them next time?" I said. "I know you do it at school. I want to hear a solo; don't you, Viv?"

"No," Dottie said, shaking her head. "I can barely do that in front of my students."

"Before I forget, we were invited to an officers' dance on Friday night by Major Bill," Viv said. With a shrug, she added, "Might be fun. And maybe we can get Martha, Blanche, and Frankie to come."

We talked more about the day, exhilarated and relieved that we hadn't completely failed on our very first Clubmobile assignment. Viv dozed off on my shoulder. I felt myself nodding off too, when Jimmy announced we were at our next stop.

It was past five o'clock when we arrived at the base the US Army Air Force shared with the British RAF. We pulled up expecting an American officer to be waiting to greet us. Instead, we were greeted by Harry Westwood.

"You're coming in the jeep with me," he said, as the three of us looked at him with skepticism. I could tell Jimmy was more than happy to drop us and search for some whiskey, but even he hesitated.

"What in the world are you doing here?" Viv asked, with her hands on her hips, face flushed, and hair wrapped up in a red kerchief.

"It's a RAF base, my dear; we just let you Americans borrow it," Westwood said, smiling. "Come along now, we're going to watch some of your boys coming in. I'll explain what your job is here on the way; you won't need that big truck of yours."

"Yes, but why are *you* taking us?" Viv said, annoyance in her voice. "You're not even American."

"You don't say?" Westwood said. "I'm a RAF liaison officer, which means I may pop up in unexpected places whenever I please. In this case, the American officer who was supposed to be here took a two-day leave. He went to Stratford-upon-Avon with a lovely English gal he met. So here I am."

"Did you know it was going to be us three?" Viv said, still eyeing him with suspicion.

"Well, of course, I had no idea," Westwood said, feigning shock at the accusation. "How could I have known that?"

We asked him to give us five minutes to grab our helmets and some candy and cigarettes to pass out.

"Pretty sure he's lying," I said to Viv.

"Of course he's lying," she said. "He's here because I am."

"And . . . that bothers you?" Dottie asked.

"Yes," Viv said as she reapplied her lipstick and brushed her hair. "*No.* I don't know. I've no interest, really."

"Nobody would blame you for being interested," I said. "He's, well, he's pretty dashing . . ."

"Don't you *fancy him*?" Dottie said. "He really is the spitting image of Cary Grant. And that accent . . ."

"Oh please," Viv said with a wave of her hand. "I didn't come here to meet a man. I could have done that at home. I've been thinking lately that I may never get married. Look at my sisters—living in walk-up apartments in the North End, pregnant and fat with sniveling toddlers clinging to their legs. The only letters I've gotten from them? All they did was whine about their miserable lives. No thank you. I've got some living to do."

"Who has some living to do?" Harry Westwood said as we walked over to the jeep. He held each of our hands and helped us climb in.

"Nobody," said Viv, as he helped her in last, again holding her hand for a beat longer than necessary. "Explain what we're doing again, please?"

"I'm to escort you to the field line to watch your American flyboys come in after their mission, because you really ought to see it," Westwood said. "It's the Thirty-Sixth Bombardment Squadron, and they're brilliant. After they land, they're taken straight to the interrogation room at headquarters. I'll drive you over there. You're supposed to help them get over their jitters, calm them down, pass out some cigarettes, sweets, coffee, and doughnuts if you've got them. You'll help remind them they're in safe territory again."

We pulled up to the airplane hangars at the field line as the sun was starting to set. The sky was a gorgeous pink and purple, and a cool breeze was blowing. The air smelled like gasoline and grass.

Soldiers on bicycles arrived from all directions, many of them with dogs following behind. They sat together in small groups, leaning against their bikes, smoking cigarettes. Their mutts laid down at their feet.

The B-24s started to appear on the horizon, and for a moment it took my breath away.

"You okay?" Dottie said, touching my arm. We were all sitting on the hood of the jeep, watching the show.

"I am, yeah," I said. "It's something to see, isn't it?"

"It is," she said with a small nod.

I could hear the men nearby as they debated whether it was one of theirs or one returning to a nearby base. And then they started to count. Some of them were murmuring under their breath; others were counting as a group, calling out the numbers as if in prayer, collectively willing all of their planes to come back safely.

"Twenty-nine so far? That was twenty-nine, right?"

"I've counted thirty-one . . ."

As they started to land, a crew would run over and inspect each B-24 for damage. A few of the planes came in with one motor blown up; many were shot up with flak. One of the last planes in started to drop red flares just before landing.

"That means someone is injured," said Westwood, pointing to it. "An ambulance will be here any minute." He kept stealing glances at Viv, but she was staring at the sky.

"Oh no," Viv said. "I hope it's nothing serious."

At the sight of the flares, the atmosphere grew tense, and every one of the soldiers in the field stood up, pacing, swearing, and lighting up cigarettes, waiting to learn who it was and how grave the injury.

"You can see the buzz bombs, you can hear the ack-ack, you can talk to the soldiers at the bases, but this . . . ," Dottie said in a quiet voice.

"I know," I whispered, gazing at the plane with the red flares landing as an ambulance came speeding past us to attend to the injured.

We watched all of these American men coming back, filthy dirty, many of them shaking uncontrollably. Their friends breathed sighs of relief at their arrival, laughing and joking as they clapped them on the shoulders. My eyes filled with tears. It was humbling, witnessing the kind of bravery that many of these guys never knew they had until they got here, thrust into these circumstances because history required it.

As Dottie had sensed, I was thinking about my own brave soldier when I watched the planes come in. I would find out what happened to him; he deserved at least that after all he had sacrificed. And so did I.

Chapter Twelve

In our first week as Clubmobile girls, we were assigned two stops per day. Even though our days were over twelve hours long, they flew by. After serving the troops, there was always more work to be done—coffee urns to be filled, tins of lard and bags of doughnut flour to be lugged, floors to be scrubbed, and Lord knows how many pots and bowls and cups we had cleaned.

Some of the officers were dismissive upon meeting us, and it was clear they questioned our value and thought we were nothing more than an unnecessary distraction for their troops. But others were warm and welcoming, and the overwhelming gratitude from the GIs at every stop more than made up for the doubters.

I sat on my bed, finishing up my paperwork for the week. On Thursday, August 3, we made 1,833 doughnuts (with the help of the British bakers) and brewed 120 gallons of coffee in our fifteen-gallon urns. I knew the exact numbers per day, because in my new job as the Cheyenne's captain, I had to log these tedious details for the Red Cross brass. I silently cursed Dottie and Viv for volunteering me.

My hands were raw and red, a result of both hand-mixing the dough and washing dishes for so many hours. I had a couple of burns up my arms from getting splashed by doughnut grease, and my shoulders ached from the heavy lifting. As I examined my logbook, I felt my eyes grow heavy. I was falling asleep right there in my uniform.

A loud knock on our bedroom door startled me and woke me up. I told whoever it was to come in, and there was Blanche, blonde curls tucked under her Red Cross cap.

"Hello, friend," I said, giving her a tight hug.

"You reek of doughnuts, Fi," she said, smiling.

"Ha, so do you," I said.

"Also, there's a brown baby goat wandering around the sitting room downstairs. Pretty sure she just ate a book."

"Mrs. Tibbetts loves her animals," I said, laughing as I tidied up the paperwork on my bed. "They've been her only company out here for a long time, so they have the run of the place."

"Ew," Blanche said, making a face. "You ready to go? The girls are waiting for us downstairs. Mrs. Tibbetts is pouring rum and Cokes— excuse me, *Cuba libres*—but not really, because no limes to speak of around here."

We went downstairs to join the party. Frankie and Martha gave me hugs as Mrs. Tibbetts handed me a rum and Coke in a teacup. Benny Goodman was playing on the record player, and the windows were open, letting in an evening breeze that smelled of garden flowers with a touch of manure. Blanche had been right, the brown baby goat that Mrs. Tibbetts simply called "Baby" was roaming around the house, and two skinny chickens had wandered in from the garden.

"Mrs. Tibbetts, are you coming to the dances tonight?" Frankie said, putting her arm around the woman's shoulder. "You're welcome to join us."

"Oh no," Mrs. Tibbetts said, finally making a drink for herself, her cheeks glowing. "My dancing days are over, but I love having a house full again. It makes me miss my boys a little less."

"I thought we were only going to one dance?" I said, frowning.

"Well, we were thinking of stopping by a GI dance first," Martha said. "Then we can go to the officers' dance at the golf club. One of the majors told us we need to socialize with the GIs sometimes too. They get jealous, there's so few American girls here."

"But most of the GIs are so young," Viv said, pouting. "It's like going to a high school dance. They're nice kids, but some of them are kind of rough."

We sat around, sharing stories of our first week. All of us had the same complaints of aches and pains but also some funny stories of doughnut making gone wrong and overenthusiastic soldiers trying to help out.

"And that damn doughnut machine is the devil," said Blanche. "It makes a total mess and only seems to work well half of the time."

I heard the sounds of a jeep through the open window.

"I think Jimmy's here; he's offered to be our chauffeur for the night," I said, getting up to open the door.

"Can he stay sober enough all night to do that?" Dottie asked, echoing my own thoughts. "If he passes out, you're driving." She pointed at me.

Mrs. Tibbetts got up to open the door, but it wasn't Jimmy, it was Liz.

"Oh, I have the log for the week upstairs," I said, getting up.

"You can give that to me Monday," Liz said, smiling. "I just know you've all been eagerly waiting for mail, and the first batch finally came in."

She held up a bunch of letters, and I felt anxious at the sight of them.

Dottie had a letter from her younger brother, Richie, and some students from her class had sent her adorable letters with childish scrawl and drawings on the envelopes.

Both of Viv's sisters and her parents had written her, and she also received a couple of amorous letters from two fellas from the *Queen Elizabeth* she couldn't even recall meeting.

"Finally, here's some for you, Fiona," Liz said, holding the last few letters in her hand. I had been standing there barely breathing, praying I had mail too. "There's one here from your sisters, one from your parents, and one from an Evelyn Barker. Is that a friend?"

I saw Dottie and Viv give each other a look, and I felt myself get woozy, so I grabbed on to one of the chairs.

"Oh God," I whispered, gripping the arm of the chair for support. "It's Danny's mother." I had that floating feeling, like right before you're going to faint. "It's got to be news; she said she would only write if there was news. What do you think it is?"

"Oh, Fiona. I had no idea that your fiancé's last name was Barker. Shame on me, I'm so sorry," Liz said, looking distraught.

"It's okay," I said.

Everyone sat down, waiting on me.

"I can read it," Frankie said, holding her hand out.

I gave her the envelope, and Dottie and Viv came over and sat on either side of me. Blanche and Martha inched over too. Mrs. Tibbetts got up and went to fetch us more drinks.

"You ready?" Frankie said, carefully opening the envelope so as not to rip the letter inside.

"Not really," I said. There was no need to lie about it. "Just read it. Don't skim it first, just out with it."

Frankie took a deep breath and started,

> *Dear Fiona,*
> *I struggled to write this letter, mostly because I picture you*
> *somewhere in Europe when it arrives—and I know seeing*
> *my name will fill you with dread about possible news. I*
> *received the enclosed telegram two days ago:*

Frankie quickly flipped to the Western Union telegram, looked up at me, and said, "It's stamped June 30, 1944." She continued to read.

An intercepted unofficial shortwave broadcast from Germany mentioned the name of 2nd LT. Daniel Barker as a prisoner of war **STOP** No personal message **STOP** Pending further confirmation, this report does not establish his status to be a prisoner of war **STOP** Any additional information received will be furnished. **STOP**

So now you know this new information too, which raises more questions than answers. I have prayed that Danny was still alive, and this is the first glimmer of hope that he might be. But I am sure you feel the agony and frustration that I feel right now. Is the intercepted report accurate? If he's alive and captured, where is he? What condition is he in? When will they tell us more?

The International Red Cross in Geneva, Switzerland, keeps track of prisoners of war across the globe and reports back to the US regarding the location and status of its citizens. Families are supposed to be notified right away of any details, so I'm hoping we hear more soon.

I'm sorry to be the bearer of this news. Joseph and the girls are more hopeful and optimistic than I am. They all send their love. I hope your work with the Red Cross is going well so far. I envy you, as I'm sure you're kept quite busy without as much time to dwell on Danny's whereabouts.

I will write as soon as I learn anything more. If by chance you find anything out in the meantime, please let me know.

Love,
Evelyn Barker

Frankie put down the letter, and the room was quiet. Everyone was waiting for me to say something. To cry or scream. To react.

"Thank you for reading it," I said. "I feel numb." I was still light-headed, and my hands felt clammy. "It's hard to know how to feel. She's right—all the telegram says is he *might* be alive and a POW. It's news, but it's not very precise news."

"I can ask Judith if we can find out anything from the IRC," Liz said. She was standing near the door, and I had forgotten she was there. "Harvey Gibson must have connections there; he has connections everywhere."

"I'm not sure if Miss Chambers wants to do me any favors," I said.

"I'm not sure Miss Chambers wants to do *anyone* any favors," Viv said.

"Well, we'll see; it's worth asking," Liz said. "In any case, I'm truly sorry, Fiona."

"Thank you, and thank you for trying with Miss Chambers," I said.

"Of course. Let me know if there's anything else I can do," she said, and we said our good-byes.

"I still want to go out," I said. "Jimmy should be here soon. It beats sitting here reading this telegram a hundred more times to try to pull some other clue from it."

"Are you sure you're up for it?" Dottie asked, eyeing me critically. "I could stay back with you and Mrs. Tibbetts."

"I could make us some more drinks," Mrs. Tibbetts called out from the kitchen.

"I'm happy to do that too, but I think Mrs. Tibbetts might not need any more drinks," Viv said, eyes wide with amusement.

"No, I'm okay, I just need to get some air," I said, standing up, straightening out my uniform. "Martha, you said you'd give me some dance tips?"

"Sure," Martha said, reaching over to squeeze my hand. "Happy to."

"Well, let's go, then," Blanche said. "The boys await!" As if on cue, we heard Jimmy honking his horn outside, which sent the skinny chickens in the living room bolting, their feathers flying as they hid from the noise.

Everyone headed out to the car as I reapplied my lipstick. I picked up my change purse off the end table and stood for a moment in the sitting room. I was heading out to a dance, and somewhere out there Danny was sitting in a prison cell or worse. Part of me wanted to crawl into bed and ruminate about this news until I cried myself to sleep. Smiling and dancing with strangers felt like an odd thing to do now that I had another clue to his whereabouts.

"Fi, are you doing okay?" Frankie opened the front door and peeked back inside.

"No," I said, giving her a sad smile. "I was just thinking about his last letter to me, before he went missing. I lost it in London, and I looked everywhere, but it never turned up. And this news, if it's true, means he made it out of the crash alive. He's been alive this whole time, and yet I haven't received a single letter from him. Where the heck *is* he right now? What shape is he in? I can't . . ." My voice cracked, and I stopped talking, putting my hands up to my mouth. I closed my eyes and took a long, slow breath.

"I know it's hard, trust me, I know more than anyone," she said with a nod, sympathy in her eyes. "But I promise you, you're better off if you don't sit here and wallow."

"Thank you," I said. "Thank you for reading it for me. And for understanding. And I know you're right. I can't sit around here and feel sorry for myself. If I do that, I might as well not have come here at all. No matter what I learn about Danny's fate."

"That's right," she said. "So let's go dance; you can at least pretend to forget about it all for a while. I promise you it will help."

We heard the sound of the jeep's horn again.

"All right," I said. "I'll take your word for it. Let's go."

She grabbed my hand and pulled me outside.

Chapter Thirteen

August 23, 1944

As our days in the English countryside went by, we got more comfortable with our daily routine. Jimmy would pick us up in his jeep at dawn, then we would go get the Cheyenne in Doughnut Alley behind Red Cross headquarters. When we arrived, we'd pray the British baking ladies that worked the night shift in the doughnut kitchen had baked enough to get us through most of the day, because the doughnut machine continued to be an instrument of the devil.

We hit eight or nine camps each week, usually at least two a day, sometimes three if one of the other Clubmobiles was out of commission. Our faces ached from smiling, our throats hurt from talking, and our muscles were sore from everything else.

Quite a few of the GIs we came in contact with were from the Eighty-Second Airborne, and though many of them were young, they had the eyes of old souls, their invisible battle scars apparent after all they had endured in Africa and Normandy. They didn't speak of it, but you could see it in the way their hands shook when they were smoking a cigarette, or in the moments of grief revealed in their faces when they didn't think anyone was watching.

Viv, Dottie, and I grew fond of "our boys in the Eighty-Second," and though it took some of them time to relax and trust us, eventually they accepted us.

"There's this fierce, quiet pride about these men," Dottie said as we loaded trays of doughnuts onto the Cheyenne that morning behind headquarters. "I think they're finally warming up to us, though."

"I agree," I said. "They never complain, and they'd never, ever say they're sick of training in the countryside and need us to cheer them up, but something has changed in the last week or so. They don't treat us like visitors anymore."

"Well, I think they've adored us from the start," Viv said, coming out of the doughnut kitchen, struggling as she carried one of the huge tin cans of lard. "Where's Jimmy? Can we get on the road? I want to decorate the outside of this thing now that I've finally got paints."

"He went to the loo," I said. "And he stinks of booze. Again."

"Ain't had one drop to drink," Jimmy said, looking defensive, not to mention very pale and sweaty as he ran over to help Viv load the lard. "Are we ready to go, then?"

"Yes. Later today I need to recruit some GIs to help us scour the Clubmobile from top to bottom before Miss Chambers's visit tomorrow," I said. "We're going to be so great, she'll want to ship us to Southampton by the end of the week. We could be in Normandy by the weekend. You're going to play some songs, right, Dottie?"

"Yes, I'll play a couple," Dottie said. She had remained shy about playing in front of the troops, despite the overwhelmingly positive reception she had received the few times she'd done it so far.

Just as we were about to pull out of the alley, we spotted Liz Anderson waving at us from the back door of headquarters, and she came over.

"I'll be escorting Miss Chambers tomorrow, and we'll most likely see you midmorning," she said. "And remember: no ribbons or jewelry or anything nonregulation—she's a stickler. Go easy on the lipstick too—no bright red, Viv."

"Yeah, yeah," Viv said, rolling her eyes, and then added, "but thank you for the reminder. I know it's not you, Liz."

"And Fiona, I did send her a note about your fiancé right after I left Mrs. Tibbetts's that night, but she still hasn't responded," Liz said.

"I know you did," I said. "Thank you for trying."

For some reason, I doubted Miss Chambers would ever make my search for Danny a priority.

⁓

The last camp of the day was the very first one we had visited on the job, and the men there were some of my favorites. Viv and I recruited Tommy Doyle, Patrick Halloran, shy Sam Katz from Pennsylvania, and a few other GIs to help us clean the inside and outside of the Cheyenne until it shined. After the army green was as sparkling as the color army green could be, Viv got out the paints Liz had procured for her and went to work. Dottie was helping Eddie from Mesa write a letter home, and a few other GIs were waiting in line after him, so we told her to keep at it.

As I scrubbed the counters inside the Clubmobile, the Victrola was playing an Andrews Sisters record. I was surrounded by soldiers armed with brushes, cloths, and sponges as they helped me clean every inch of the Cheyenne's interior. Vera Lynn was sitting next to the Victrola like a queen on a small dusty-pink-and-white-checkered pillow Sam had found for her. The smell of cleaning agents and doughnut grease almost overpowered the odor of sweaty soldiers, but not quite.

"Looking good, Viv," I heard Patrick say. He was outside cleaning the windows.

"Are you talking about me or the Cheyenne?"

"Both," he said with a laugh. "Seriously though, that's some nice painting."

I leaned out to take a look at what she was doing. She had painted a delicate bright-green vine with red, white, and blue flowers framing the Clubmobile window. In the left-hand corner near the door to the front cab, she had added our names in bright red with a flourish:

Viv   Dottie   Fiona

THE BEANTOWN GIRLS

"Nice, Viv," I said. "Although I suspect you're painting today just to get out of cleaning in here."

"Me? Never," she said with a wink. She stepped back and admired her work. "I was supposed to be designing advertising campaigns by now. Instead, I'm standing in a muddy field in England, stinking of doughnut grease and trying to make this jalopy less ugly."

"Do you think you'll go back to your job after this?" I asked.

Viv sighed. "I don't know. They said I could have it back. But I didn't get to actually do anything beyond secretarial work, despite their promises. None of the women at Woodall and Young were allowed to manage any of the accounts—even the Kotex account, for Christ's sake. What the heck do men know about *Kotex*?"

"Hey, keep it down; you sound like my sistah," Tommy said from behind me, frowning in disgust, revealing his Boston accent. "We don't need to hear about that girl stuff."

"Sorry," I said, and we both started giggling.

Just then a truck pulled up and parked about twenty feet away. Captain Peter Moretti got out, along with another officer.

The young GIs fell over themselves to greet the two officers. Even though they weren't required to salute, all of them did.

"Please keep working, soldiers. I don't want to interrupt," Moretti said as he walked over. His cheeks were sunburned, and I had forgotten how tall he was. I hadn't run into him since the night we left London. I hardly knew the gruff captain at all, so I wasn't sure why the sight of him was like seeing an old friend.

"Good to see you, Captain Moretti," I said, smiling. "We've still got a few doughnuts left. Would you like one?"

"No, thank you, but maybe Lieutenant Lewis would like one or two?" he said, nodding to the thin man beside him with the sandy brown hair. Then he added, in a softer voice, "It's good to see you too, Fiona."

We made introductions all around. Lieutenant Lewis happily took three doughnuts and some lukewarm coffee and started talking with the GIs, teasing them about doing women's work.

"All spiffed up for tomorrow, *Beantown Girls*?" Moretti said to me as I jumped down to admire Viv's artwork.

"Oh, so you've heard? Yes, our director is coming from London."

"Not just your director. All the top Red Cross officials, including Harvey Gibson. And I heard some photographers too," he said.

"Oh no, please tell me you're joking," I said, feeling my stomach turn at the thought. "Do you know for sure?"

"Yes, a couple of my superiors are going to be giving them the tour," Moretti said.

"Hey, Fi, maybe you can bypass Miss Chambers altogether and just ask Mr. Gibson himself, see if he knows someone at the International Red Cross that can help," Viv said. She was now painting the silhouettes of three women wearing Red Cross uniforms under the Beantown Girls lettering.

"What do you need from the International Red Cross?" Moretti asked, frowning.

I looked away and bit my lip. There it was. The question. Here was another person who didn't know about Danny. I had to explain again, see the look of pity again, or hear another person stumble over their words. Again. Or did I?

"I had a question about a . . . um . . . a neighbor from home who might be a POW here. I know the IRC keeps track of those things; we thought Gibson might have a contact at the IRC," I said, realizing I was talking too quickly but not able to help myself. I wasn't a natural liar. "Although my neighbor's family may have heard more by now. The letter they sent was dated almost a month ago."

Viv flashed me a questioning look, but I ignored her.

Moretti tilted his head and examined my face. I self-consciously smoothed my hair, tucking the blonde strands in front under my cap. I couldn't remember the last time I'd brushed it or put on fresh lipstick.

"Look, if you don't have any luck with Gibson, I might be able to get some information for you," he said. "I have an old friend from New York who works for them. Tracking Allied POWs is part of his job."

"That's very kind of you. Thank you, um . . . I'll let you know."

Now Viv was glaring at me, mouthing, "Tell him," behind his back.

"Lewis, we've got to go," Moretti said and smiled. "It was his idea to stop; he was hoping for doughnuts. Good luck tomorrow."

"Thanks, Captain," I said, noticing that his smiles came easier now than when we first met. "We'll need it."

"Did you know Captain Moretti's a boxer? Like a top-ranked boxer?" Tommy said after they headed to their truck.

"I think everyone in England knows by now," I said, amused at their adoration.

"He's an even better soldier and captain," Sam Katz said in his quiet voice.

I looked up at Sam. "Really?"

Tommy, Sam, and the other guys started nodding, their faces solemn. "*Really.*"

The GIs got back to work. Viv came and stood next to me, watching the truck kick up dirt as it drove away.

"You've always been the worst liar," she said in a quiet voice.

"I know," I said. "Do you think he bought it?"

"Who knows," she said with a shrug. "But why wouldn't you just tell him?"

"Because I'm tired of telling my sad story?" I said with a sigh. "I don't know."

"He has to contact his friend for you," she said. "I think he's a much better bet than Gibson. You've got to track him down, ask him to do that, and tell him the truth."

"You're right," I said. "God, why the heck did I lie to him? I never do things like that."

Viv looked at me, and I couldn't quite read her expression. "No, you don't," she said. "But I think I get why."

"Oh, really? Why?"

"I'll tell you later. Let's finish up. Mrs. Tibbetts promised a surprise for dinner."

"Oh no, I really hope she doesn't cook that black-and-white-speckled chicken for us; she's become my favorite pet," I said, and we both started laughing as we went back to finishing our chores.

～

It was drizzling when we pulled into the camp the next morning. My eyes were puffy, and I was a bundle of nerves. I had woken up with the roosters, going over everything in my head, praying that we could wow Judith Chambers and Harvey Gibson with our skills and charisma.

"Why does it have to be raining this morning?" I said as we opened up the side of the truck and pushed down the counter. Jimmy jumped out and hooked us up to the water.

"Because it's England," Viv said.

"It's hardly rain at all," Jimmy said. "Just a sprinkle trickling down; ain't nothing to it, really."

"Okay, Dottie, you're going to play at least three songs today, yes?" I said. "'Don't Sit Under the Apple Tree'—they all love that one. And have you decided on the other two? Oh, Viv—don't forget to put the scales on the counter today. We actually have to weigh the water and the flour."

"Fiona, honey, you told us that three times on the way here this morning and at least another ten last night," Viv said, slamming the scale on the counter next to the doughnut machine. "And if you ask Dottie what songs she's playing again, I'm going to smack you."

"And I'm going to let her," Dottie said. "You need to relax, Fiona; it's going to be fine."

I looked at both of them, knowing they were right, but it didn't calm my nerves one bit.

"I'm sorry," I said, taking a deep breath and gripping the counter. "You're right, and I'll try not to be such a nag. Let's get ready."

We were setting up the counter with our guest log, cigarettes, gum, and Life Savers. It was our second time at this particular camp, and the welcome back made me feel better about the day ahead. Lots of greetings of "Hey, Boston!" as the GIs started to line up with their canteen cups.

Nelson Carmichael, a young, energetic dark-haired private from West Virginia, came running up to the Clubmobile. "Oh, hey, can me and a couple of my buddies help you girls make the doughnuts? Please?"

"I don't know, Nelson. It's a big day; Red Cross brass are coming," I said, biting my lip. "They'll be here in an hour or so."

"But last time you said I could help *this* time," he said. I had completely forgotten.

"Aw, let him help," Viv said. "It'll make us look good, having soldiers happily helping us. And we need to make at least one batch while we're here."

"Please?" he said again, holding his hands in prayer and batting his blue eyes at me.

"All right," I said, shaking my head, laughing despite myself.

"Hey, that's swell, thanks so much," he said, flashing a huge smile. "I'll be right back."

A few minutes later, Nelson came back with his two friends, George, a tall, skinny Southerner with bad teeth, and Alan, a slight young man with unusually large ears.

The coffee urns were on the counter, and the already-made doughnuts were stacked neatly in their trays. But with the six of us inside, we could barely turn around. We had a long line of hungry soldiers waiting, and I started to panic.

"Okay, everyone, listen up. We need to have a system," I said. "Dottie, you and Nelson mix the next batch of dough for the doughnuts. George, you grab soldiers' cups and squirt milk in them, and hand them to Viv to pour the coffee. Alan, you help me hand out the doughnuts. And someone start the Victrola. I almost forgot—put a record on and blast it, something fun. Don't let us down, boys; it's a big day."

"Pistol Packin' Mama" by Bing Crosby and the Andrews Sisters played over the loudspeakers, and the soldiers waiting in line cheered as we poured the first cups of coffee.

We were working like a well-oiled machine as the jeeps carrying the Red Cross officials and press drove up. I spotted Major Bill driving Harvey Gibson, Liz, and Miss Chambers. Talking and laughing with our boys, Viv and I smiled our biggest Red Cross smiles as the photographer ran over and started snapping photos.

I was beginning to relax, feeling like this day might go just fine, when I heard Dottie let out a cry of pain.

"Oh no. Oh no, this isn't good," Nelson said behind me. "Fiona!"

I whipped around to see Dottie with a huge gash down her forearm. Nelson grabbed a cloth and started to wrap it.

"Oh my God, Dottie," I said, putting my arm around her. "Are you okay? What happened?"

"I was getting some lard out of the damn can and I sliced my arm. I was trying to hurry, and I didn't remove the lid all the way; it's my own damn fault."

The cloth that her arm was wrapped in was already soaked with blood, so Viv grabbed some more cloths from one of the upper cabinets and shoved them at us.

"It's pretty deep; she's going to need to go to the hospital to get this stitched up," Nelson said. "Alan, tell someone to call for the ambulance."

The color had drained from Dottie's face, and she listed into me.

"Oh Jesus," I said, patting her face. "Someone get me a cup of water. Stay with us, Dottie. Viv, you and the boys take over. Nelson, help me get her out of here."

We stepped out of the Clubmobile, and a number of the GIs descended upon us. Someone handed us a blanket, and a medic came over with first aid supplies. They cleared a place for us to sit until the ambulance came. Dottie was still pale as she sipped water. Her injured arm was wrapped tight, but the blood was seeping through again. Liz came running over, and I explained what happened.

Somewhere behind her, Miss Chambers, Harvey Gibson, and the rest of the Red Cross administrators were in the crowd, shaking hands and talking with the soldiers. "Pistol Packin' Mama" was on its fourth loop.

"Nelson, can you please go help Viv, and maybe change the record too?" I said. Sweat was dripping down his face, and he looked crestfallen. "It's okay, hon, she'll be all right."

"Liz, could you go with Dottie to the hospital?" I asked. "I need to go help Viv; she'll never be able to serve all these soldiers alone."

"I can go with her too." I looked up at the sound of Joe Brandon's voice. He was gazing at Dottie with genuine concern and definitely something more. Dottie gave him a weak smile.

"The Twenty-Eighth's band is performing here later, so I have a few hours to spare," he said. "I just heard you were here, so I thought I'd come over to catch up with my favorite Red Cross girls."

"That would be great actually," Liz said to him. "After I see she's settled at the hospital, I really should head out to meet Gibson's group at the next camp."

"Come on, Dottie, let me help you," Joe said, reaching down to put her good arm around his shoulder.

"You'll be stitched up in no time," I said, giving her a kiss on the cheek when she got up.

"Thanks, Fi, I'm sorry . . ." She dropped the cup of water she was holding, and her glasses slipped off her face as she passed out against Joe Brandon. He scooped her up in both arms, carrying her against his chest.

The medics from the ambulance came running over with a stretcher and helped Joe get her on it and into the back of the ambulance. I handed Dottie's glasses to Liz, and she promised one of them would give us an update as soon as they could. I felt sick to my stomach, watching them drive away.

Poor Viv—the crowd of men had tripled in size since Dottie had cut her arm. I rushed inside the Clubmobile, and my feet made a splash on the floor as I stepped into a puddle of coffee at least three inches deep.

"What the . . . ?"

Viv looked over at me. Her lipstick had worn off, her hair was frizzy under her hat, and strands of it were sticking to the sweat on her face. She was passing out doughnuts with two hands.

"Alan was talking to one of his buddies and left the spigot on the coffee urn open."

"I'm so sorry, Fiona," Alan said. "I thought I had shut it off; I didn't even realize."

Nelson was back at work making the doughnuts, doing an adequate job at it except for the doughnut mix that seemed to have exploded all over the counters and the floor. He was standing in a gooey paste of flour and coffee and doughnut grease drippings.

"Alan, it's fine, but why don't I take over coffee? You can take charge of the record player and start passing out candy and cigarettes," I said.

"Good idea, because if I hear that song one more time, I'm going to kill myself," Viv said through her teeth as she smiled and leaned out the side to pass coffee to the front of the line. "How's our poor Dots?"

"She'll be okay," I said. "Joe Brandon just showed up like a knight in shining armor."

"Well, that was convenient," Viv said. "I still think he's a wolf."

"So do I," I said with a sigh.

I started handing out cups of coffee with her, forcing myself to smile and make small talk as I tried not to think about Dottie or how this day had turned out.

"I don't need any sugar, sweetheart; just stick your finger in the coffee—that will sweeten it up," said a soldier with a very dirty beard.

"You think I haven't heard that line before, honey?" I said, giving him a smile and a wink. "You've got to do better than that." His friends started to laugh.

"Hey, girls, good to see you again. Smile for the cameras." Mr. Gibson walked up to the window with Miss Chambers and a photographer. Gibson was wearing a suit, tie, and fedora, but he didn't seem the least bit bothered by the heat.

"Hello, Viv, Fiona," Miss Chambers said to us. "Mr. Gibson would like to come in and serve up some doughnuts with you girls. Take some pictures."

"Do you have an apron that's big enough to fit around me?" he asked, laughing.

"I'm sure we do," Viv said.

Viv took a quick look at the gooey floor and then back at me, raising her eyebrows. I shrugged. We had to let him come in; there was no getting out of it.

"Come on in, Mr. Gibson," I said. "But please watch your step. Things got a little messy when Dottie got hurt, and we haven't had a chance to clean up yet."

"Let me make a quick inspection before you head in, Mr. Gibson," Miss Chambers said, shooting me a look as she headed toward the door of the Cheyenne.

"I'll grab you an apron, Mr. Gibson," I said, turning around to get one out of the cabinet just as Miss Chambers walked in and gasped at the state of our kitchen.

Nelson looked up at her. He was covered head to toe in flour— even his hair was dusted with it. The goo on the floor had turned even thicker, and I had no idea how we were going to clean it all up.

Mercifully, Alan had just left to hand out cigarettes, but he'd forgotten to change the record on the record player like I asked, so the same damn song started for at least the twentieth time. I saw it all through Miss Chambers's eyes and cringed at what she was probably thinking.

She was about to speak, but instead she jumped back and screamed as Vera Lynn sprang down from the top shelf onto the floor, meowing loudly at the realization she was up to her paws in stickiness.

"Oh God, Vera, no," I said, grabbing Vera around her waist with both hands and shoving her back up on the top shelf, adding "cat" to the list of things we had to clean that night.

"Congratulations," Miss Chambers said. She crossed her arms and shook her head, giving her best condescending schoolteacher look. "This is by far the messiest Clubmobile I have ever seen."

Nelson started to laugh, but I gave him a look that shut him up fast.

"You don't have to tell us," Viv said, still pouring coffees and handing them out to soldiers with a smile as Miss Chambers stood there in judgment.

"Yes, it's a mess," I said with a sigh as I grabbed another tray of doughnuts to serve. "And I'm sorry for that, and we will scour it tonight. It's only when Dottie—"

"I know, the accident—that was unfortunate," Miss Chambers said, interrupting me. "But it also doesn't really reflect well on you. You've got men to serve, and Mr. Gibson is coming in for a photo op, so I will be brief. Bottom line is, I still have my doubts about you three. I was hoping you would change my mind today. But you didn't." She lifted one of her feet off the floor and examined the greasy goo dripping off it. "Anyway, we've got to send a few more Clubmobiles over to France in a little over a week. The Cheyenne definitely won't be in that group."

I felt my cheeks start to burn, devastated that we wouldn't be going with the first group from our Clubmobile class. I wanted to go for Danny, but at this point, I also wanted to go for myself. I knew we were up to the job, and I was angry that Judith Chambers still didn't think so. I was furious, but I blinked back my tears of frustration quickly so she wouldn't see.

"Honestly, things have been going really well overall," I said. "You can ask Liz. Just today wasn't—"

"Yes, but this was your *observation* day, your day to shine," she said. "And you didn't."

She paused, stepping back toward the door, taking one more look around at the mess. "Now I've got to bring Mr. Gibson in and warn him he might ruin his shoes. Get ready for the pictures. Put on some lipstick, but no bright red, Viviana."

She opened the door to step out but turned back, looking Viv and me in the eye.

"One other thing: I haven't forgotten—one of you has *got* to learn how to really drive."

With that, she stepped out and the Clubmobile door slammed shut behind her.

Chapter Fourteen

That evening, after what was by far our longest day yet, Liz brought a very pale Dottie home, and we settled her in with a blanket on the sofa in the sitting room.

"She has fifteen stitches up her forearm," Liz said. "The doctors told her to take a day off to rest and recover before she's back at it."

"I am more than happy to nurse her back to health," said Mrs. Tibbetts, tucking the blanket around Dottie.

"I've got to run, but Fiona, I need to ask you a big favor," Liz said.

"Sure, what do you need?" I asked.

"I'm sorry to ask this, because I know it's been a long day already," Liz said, "but I was wondering if you and Jimmy could make a late-night run, bring coffee and doughnuts to some men that are working overtime at a cement mixer. It broke down yesterday, and now that it's fixed, they're making up for lost time by working all night. One of the officers requested it, thought it would really lift their spirits."

My back ached from scrubbing down the Clubmobile, and I was in such a sullen mood I doubted I could lift anyone's spirits. But after the day we'd had, I felt I needed to redeem myself.

"Yes, happy to do that," I said, trying to smile.

"Thank you," Liz said, visibly relieved. "Jimmy will pick you up in the jeep in about an hour with all the supplies you need; no need to bring the Clubmobile."

We said good-bye to Liz, and Mrs. Tibbetts brought out some berry tarts and tea as we filled Dottie in regarding our conversation with Miss Chambers.

"I'm so sorry," Dottie said. "I feel like it's completely my fault that this happened."

"Nonsense, Dottie," I said. "Those huge tins of lard are a pain in the neck to open; it could have happened to any of us."

"It's true," Viv said, lighting up a cigarette. "And honestly? I don't think she was going to send us to the Continent no matter what happened today."

"Did you at least get to ask Mr. Gibson anything about the IRC tracking down Danny?" Dottie said.

"No," I said. That was another reason for my low mood. I was aggravated with myself for not asking when I had the chance. "We were so busy, I swear every soldier in camp turned out for doughnuts, and then the photographer kept taking pictures, and when I finally had a quiet moment to ask Mr. Gibson, he was gone."

"So now you've *got* to ask Captain Moretti to see what he can find out," Viv said, pointing at me with her cigarette. "And maybe don't *lie* to him this time about Danny being your fiancé?"

"I know, I know," I said. "I will. Although, now it's going to be awkward because I lied."

"Why exactly did you lie?" Dottie asked, frowning at me. "That's not like you."

"No kidding," I said. "I don't know. I didn't want him to look at me differently? It was an impulsive thing to do, and now I feel foolish. Anyway, how was Joe?"

"Yeah, how *was* the piano man? Still got the girl at home?" Viv said.

"Joe was very chivalrous and as handsome as ever," Dottie said, the color returning to her cheeks at the sound of his name. "I can still smell his Old Spice from when he carried me, which is driving me crazy. And he stayed with me for as long as he could. But yes, he's still got

Mary Jane. I asked him when he tried to hold my hand and kiss me on the cheek. He was *almost* apologetic about it, but again no mention of breaking it off with her, so I have to tell you, I was in such a bad mood from the day, and my arm was hurting so much, I just let him have it."

"Really?" I said. "What did you say?"

"Oh, I wish we had been there," Viv said. "Tell us."

"I said what kind of guy has a girl at home that he's supposedly in love with, while trying to kiss another one over here? And what kind of girl does he think I am? I told him I liked him, but I deserve better, and that we could still be friends, but absolutely nothing more unless he breaks it off with Mary Jane."

"Of course you deserve better," I said.

"Good for you, Dots. So how'd you leave it?" Viv asked.

"He apologized," Dottie said, with a sad smile. "Multiple times. He said he was confused, that he had feelings for me, and he hadn't expected that to happen. He said part of him just wants to live for the moment because, after all, we're *living* in the war, but he agreed, I deserve better. And he needed to figure things out."

"Figure things out how?" I asked.

A knock at the front door interrupted our conversation, and I could hear Martha's voice from the other side. Mrs. Tibbetts hurried over to let our friends in. "We heard you gals had a rough day and came over with a bouquet of freshly picked flowers and a chocolate cake that one of the mess hall cooks baked us," Martha said, handing Dottie the flowers.

"And some of our liquor rations to cheer you up," Blanche said, smiling as she took two bottles of wine out of a paper bag.

"I'll fetch us some cups," Mrs. Tibbetts said, clapping her hands together, happy for our small party.

"Only a half glass for me," I said. "I've got a date with six men and a cement mixer."

"What?" Blanche said, pouring glasses as quickly as Mrs. Tibbetts handed them to her. "You're kidding? Liz can't find someone else?"

"I'm sure she could, but after today, we've got to do all we can to stay on her good side," I said. We filled our friends in on our disastrous observation day, and after some cake and wine, we were feeling a bit less glum about it all.

"And then at the end of the day, when we had no mop, nothing to clean up that absolutely nasty pond of coffee, flour, and grease, Norman felt so guilty. So he went and grabbed a brace and bit, and we actually had him drill holes in the floor of the Clubmobile to drain it," I said, shaking my head laughing.

"We had to—nothing else was going to get rid of it completely," Viv said.

"And we've got holes in the floor now?" Dottie asked, cringing.

"We do, but it worked," I said. "We'll have to get a little rug or something to hide them next time Miss Chambers comes around."

"We might have to try that. We had a huge spill the other day and it was nasty," Frankie said, reaching for a second piece of chocolate cake.

"Hey, so Miss Chambers isn't sending you gals to France, is she?" Viv asked.

The room got quiet, and Frankie, Blanche, and Martha all looked at each other.

"You're going, aren't you?" I said, the ache in my stomach returning. Our friends were leaving us behind. Viv swore softly as she lit another cigarette. Dottie was on the verge of tears.

"We are going," Martha said quietly, putting an arm around Dottie. "And I'm so sorry you girls aren't coming with us. I'm sure we'll reunite soon."

"When do you leave?" I asked.

"We head to London in a few days to regroup, and then we go to Southampton from there," Martha said.

"We will definitely reunite soon," Frankie said, nodding. "One of the things that helped our cause is that Martha and I are both great drivers."

"Uh, no," Blanche said. "*Martha* is a fantastic driver. Frankie, you drive like a crazy person."

"I prefer the term *fearless*," Frankie said, giving Blanche a fake scowl.

"Uh-huh," Blanche said, rolling her eyes. "Anyway, you have to make the next group, you just have to. But who's going to drive? No offense, but I've seen you all in action, and you couldn't be worse."

"Only driver here is *me*," Jimmy said, pointing to himself as he walked in from the front hallway.

"Oh, Jimmy, I didn't even hear you knock." Mrs. Tibbetts came in from the kitchen, wiping her hands with a bright-blue tea towel. She raised her eyebrows at the sight of him.

He stumbled into the sofa and nearly fell on Dottie. And he stank of whiskey.

"Jimmy, any chance you've been at the pub?" I said, frowning.

"There's a chicken," Jimmy said, ignoring my question and pointing to the bird we had named Speckles, who was sleeping in the corner of the room. "What's a bloody chicken doing in 'ere?" His words slurred together.

"Swell," I said, rubbing my hands over my face. "Jimmy, you're supposed to be driving me to this cement mixer crew. Did you pick up the supplies? Did Liz see you like this?"

"Picked 'em up. Wasn't no sign of Miss Liz," Jimmy said with a shrug. "And I'm fine. Just had me some strong tea—I'm good." He patted his chest.

"I think tonight might be the night for a driving lesson for Fiona," Frankie said, giving me a pointed look.

"In the pitch black with only cat-eye lights?" I said, cracking my knuckles.

"Frankie's right," Viv said, eyeing Jimmy warily as he tried to stay upright. "Take your flashlight, and have Jimmy give you the directions, if he can remember them." She stood up and whispered in my ear. "It's safer with you at the wheel, don't you think?"

We both looked at Jimmy, swaying next to the sofa.

"All right," I said with a sigh. "Time for my driving lesson, Jimmy. Let's go."

~

The temperature had dropped at least thirty degrees since the afternoon, a sign that fall was on its way. The rain clouds had cleared, and the lack of artificial light anywhere revealed a brilliant star-filled sky and a nearly full moon. Despite the cool night air, I was sweating as I drove down the country roads with Jimmy as my questionable teacher and navigator. I gripped the steering wheel so hard, my hands hurt as I tried to remember everything I had learned in London.

My mood was still low, but if nothing else, driving offered me a distraction. I couldn't concentrate on anything other than not getting the two of us killed.

"How am I doing, Jimmy?" I asked, making sure he was still awake next to me.

"Goin' a bit slow, but you're all right," he said. "Just a few more miles 'til the turn."

He seemed to be sobering up. Mrs. Tibbetts had given him another strong cup of tea on our way out the door.

"You're stuck with us for a while longer, you know," I said. "We found out today we're not going to the Continent yet."

"Don't mind at all. Like you loads better than the last crew I drove. Your lot are more fun," he said. I looked over, and he was smiling. "More up for a laugh."

"Really?" I said. I couldn't tell if he was joking or not. "Thanks."

"Really. Dottie reminds me of me own daughter—small and dark like she was, loved music," he said quietly. "I loved listenin' to her play the guitar."

"Jimmy, you didn't tell us you have a daughter," I said.

He didn't say anything for a few moments. I glanced over at him, and he was staring into the darkness.

"Had a daughter named Anne," he said. "And a wife, me Shirley. Lost 'em both in the Blitz in September of '40."

For a few seconds, I was speechless, stunned by this fact about our driver, whom I realized I didn't know that well at all.

"Jimmy, I'm so sorry," I said, feeling physically ill. "I had no idea . . ."

"Don't talk much about it," he said, his voice sounding thick. "Ain't much to say. I was comin' home from work, missed the blast. Finally got there; there was nothing left. Me darlin' girls were gone. Whole city was on fire. Don't know how I survived it really." He paused before adding, "Sometimes wish I hadn't."

"I'm so sorry," I said, swallowing hard. I reached across to squeeze his hand, unable to wipe the tear running down my face. "So incredibly sorry."

"Yeah, well," he said, glancing over at me in the dark, squeezing my hand back. "I know you've got troubles of your own. I hope you find him." He looked up and added, "Oh blimey, here's the turn." He pointed to a road with no sign that I had nearly missed.

I took a sharp swing to the left almost on two wheels as we turned onto a narrow country lane. In the moonlight, you could see the outline of a cement mixer housed in a huge framework, and at the far edge of the field was a low, thatched-roof cottage snuggled into a hollow, an odd contrast to the modern machinery.

I wiped my face, pinched my cheeks, and even put on some lipstick in the rearview mirror. Jumping out of the jeep, I forced myself to smile as the men looked up from their work.

"Hey, fellas!" I said over the noise of the mixer. "Anyone up for a coffee break?"

They started walking over as I opened the back of the jeep to get out the coffee urn and trays of doughnuts. Jimmy started pouring them all cups.

"It's like a mirage," the first man to reach the jeep said to me, an enormous smile on his face as he took a cup from Jimmy.

"Nope, not a mirage, just a Red Cross girl and her driver on the job," I said, handing him two doughnuts. The others started coming over, all expressing surprise and gratitude that we had shown up at their tedious all-night job.

"I cannot believe you came out here," said another GI, his long face covered with dust and grime. "My name's Paul Coogan. Where are you from, Miss Red Cross?"

"Boston," I said, ready to play the geography game that we played at every camp.

"You're kidding?" Paul said, nearly spitting out his coffee.

"No, why?" I said.

"I'm from Burlington, Vermont," he said, pointing to himself. "I mean, we're basically neighbors."

"Okay, I guess you could say that," I said, laughing.

"Hey, wait, the two girls you work with are from Boston too, right?" he asked.

"Yes, but how do you know that?" I said, curious now.

"I've heard of you," he said. "Everyone says you three are the prettiest Red Cross girls in England."

"Well, thank you, Paul, that's awfully flattering, although I really doubt it's true," I said.

"I think it's true," he said, taking a sip of his coffee, and a couple of the other men started nodding. I felt my cheeks turn red.

"Well, jeez, you guys have made my night. I needed that today, thank you."

We sat under the stars and kept the conversation light, talking about the Red Sox, movies we had seen or wanted to see, and which big band we'd prefer to hear live.

The guys rarely wanted to talk about the war, but on this particular night we spoke about the possibility of Paris being liberated soon. It was the type of good news everyone craved. A sign that things were turning.

The men told funny stories of military life in Leicester, trying to outdo each other to make me laugh. When it was time to go, I promised to stop by their camp with the Cheyenne soon, and I realized I was in a much better mood than when I arrived. I was supposed to be the one boosting their spirits, but instead that's exactly what these men had done for me. Sometimes morale was a two-way street.

After Jimmy and I packed up, I started to get into the passenger seat, but Jimmy shook his head and pointed at the steering wheel.

"Behind the wheel again, Miss Fiona," he said. "You ain't never gonna be a good driver unless you get more practice."

I groaned and slid behind the wheel. After we turned onto the main road, it was a pretty straight shot back to Mrs. Tibbetts's, and I was feeling more comfortable driving, which was a good thing, because Jimmy fell dead asleep beside me. We were more than halfway home when the engine started to sputter and make a whooshing sound.

"No. No, no, no, this isn't happening. Come on!" I said, slamming the wheel as I stepped hard on the accelerator. Instead of speeding up, the jeep stalled out right in the middle of the road.

"Jimmy, Jimmy, wake up," I said, shaking him on the shoulder. "I think we've run out of gas, I mean petrol. Do you have any reserve petrol in here?"

"Nah. No petrol," he grumbled and rolled over, pulling his cap down low.

I got out of the car and looked up. Next to the road, there was a small herd of cows sleeping. They were black, but their farmer had painted white stripes on their bellies, to make sure they could be seen at night during the blackouts. It was at least a few miles until the next village, and it had to be after midnight.

I poured myself one of the last cups of coffee left in the urn and sat down on the back of the jeep. I was bone-tired, everything ached, and I longed for my bed at Mrs. Tibbetts's. After an hour or so, just as I was about to fall asleep in the jeep, I heard the sound of a truck and spotted its lights heading in our direction. As it got closer, I shined my flashlight into the darkness and got out of the jeep, jumping up and down, waving my arms to get their attention before they crashed straight into us.

The truck pulled over, and the driver jumped out, but I didn't know whether to laugh or cry when I recognized the officer.

"Of course. Of course it's you, Captain Moretti," I said.

"What do you mean *of course*?" he asked, amused when he saw it was me.

"You question me about why the Red Cross Clubmobile girls are even here. You think we're these damsels in distress that are a nuisance you have to protect. So it's absolutely perfect that you find me here, out of petrol, in the middle of nowhere. Basically . . . a damsel in distress."

"You're out of petrol?" he said with a sly smile, eyebrows raised. "You didn't think to bring any extra?"

"No, I didn't think to bring any extra. This is my first time driving here since London for God's sake," I said, annoyed at how much he was enjoying this. "And Jimmy didn't think of it because, well, he's Jimmy." I nodded at Jimmy sleeping. "Please tell me you have some?"

"You're in luck. I might have just enough in the back to get you home," he said. "Do you have any more coffee?"

"Probably. I'll dig out a clean cup," I said.

He went to his truck and brought back a small canister. "Do you want to do it, or will you let me?" he said.

"Oh, I can, I mean . . . oh God, will you please do it?" I said. It killed me to ask. "I'm afraid I'll spill it all over the ground . . ."

He was already filling the tank.

"What are you doing here anyway?" I asked when he finished and I handed him his promised cup of coffee.

"Checking on the fellas out at the cement mixer," he said. "They've had a hell of a time."

"Wait. Were you the one who requested a visit from the Clubmobile girls?" I said, smirking.

"I was," he said, smiling and raising his cup in a toast.

"You're changing your mind about us, then?"

"Well, let's just say you've definitely lifted the spirits of the men in the Eighty-Second, so that's something. Especially after what some of them have been through, it's . . . some of them are still in pretty rough shape."

He leaned against the truck next to me. He smelled woodsy with a hint of gasoline.

"Will you put in a good word with my supervisor, then? She's not a huge fan of me and my friends," I said. I told him about my day, and by the end we were both laughing about it.

"I was kidding about putting in a good word. But I do have to ask you something before you go."

"What's that?" he said. I still had the flashlight on. His face, with its rebuilt nose, wasn't classically handsome, but there was a ruggedness about him that was undeniably attractive. And tonight he didn't have the hardened look in his eyes that I'd seen there in the past, like he was waiting for the next shot to be fired.

"You mentioned that friend at the IRC. I was wondering if you could find out about my neighbor," I said. "His name is Danny Barker. He was reported missing last fall after his plane was shot down in Germany. He was in the air force, second lieutenant in the 338th Bombardment Squadron."

Why couldn't I just say it? *Fiancé, not neighbor.* I was so embarrassed I had lied in the first place, it was hard to come out with the truth now.

"Yes, my old friend Hank Miller, from New York, he works for the IRC now. He moved to Switzerland a couple of years ago to work with the Central Information Agency on Prisoners of War. His father was a POW in World War I—that's how he got interested. I can't make any promises, but if anyone knows anything, he will," he said, tracing his finger on the hood of the jeep.

"Thank you. Thanks so much," I said.

He looked at me, tilting his head, like he had more he wanted to say, but instead he just said, "No problem." His hand was right next to mine on the hood of the jeep. I blushed and stepped away.

"Anything else?" he asked.

I considered for a few seconds. *Tell him. Tell him now, Fiona. Out with it.*

"Only that I owe you one. Maybe two favors now—for the petrol . . . and for asking about my neighbor," I said. "I better go. Mrs. Tibbetts will be a nervous wreck that I'm still not back."

"Okay, you owe me." He nodded with that amused look again, but he had stepped away too. "I'll be in touch if I hear anything. And I'll make sure you get out of here okay before I leave."

I opened the driver's side door and climbed in as he shut it for me. Our faces were only inches from each other now as I started up the jeep and the engine roared to life. His breath smelled like coffee and peppermint gum. A quiet pause. I was barely breathing.

"You're good to go," he said, his voice quiet as he patted the door.

"Thanks again," I said, feeling flushed. "Good night."

"Good night, and drive safe," he said.

Heading off into the night with Jimmy softly snoring beside me, I saw Captain Moretti wave good-bye in my rearview mirror.

Chapter Fifteen

September 9, 1944

A few days after our disastrous observation, we said our sad good-byes to Frankie, Blanche, and Martha before they left for their journey to France. Frustrated and more than a little envious, I was even more determined now to get to the Continent. Jimmy had started giving me driving lessons in the evenings whenever he was sober and able. I kept managing our supplies and keeping meticulous paperwork and logs. I had even taken on some of Liz's work—compiling reports regarding output and productivity for London headquarters.

Viv and Dottie shared my frustration and had also begun doing everything they could to change Miss Chambers's perception of us. Viv was working harder than she ever had, no longer handing off all of her chores to any adoring GI nearby. And the way she could charm the most downtrodden soldiers with her teasing and banter was truly something to behold.

To everyone's relief, Dottie's arm was healing quickly, and she had finally come out of her shell, playing guitar and leading sing-alongs more often, delighting the men with her large repertoire of songs. Despite their begging and pleading, she had yet to sing a solo for anyone, but we were hopeful she was working up the courage.

"So are you going to even give us a hint about who's coming tonight?" Viv asked Dottie as she sat down at the mirror in our room, styling her curls into perfect victory rolls.

We were getting ready for a night out, a private concert at Leicester's De Montfort Hall for all of the soon-to-be-departing US troops. It was the biggest venue in the city and could hold up to three thousand people. The most curious thing about the concert was that nobody knew who was performing—the army had kept it top secret. Nobody, that is, except for key personnel, including one army bandleader named Joe Brandon. And he had shared the secret with Dottie, who refused to tell us.

"Is it an American band or a British one?" I asked. "Or maybe it's not even a band, just a singer? Vera Lynn? Or Bing Crosby?"

"I told you, I am absolutely sworn to secrecy by Joe," Dottie said with a mischievous grin. She was enjoying our curiosity far too much. "It's the best surprise. The army wants to keep it under wraps because most of the Eighty-Second is heading out in a few days, and, well, it's *that big.*" She clapped her hands.

"Oh come on, you can't even give us a little hint?" I asked, applying my lipstick and trying to get my own hair to behave.

"Not even a little one," she said. "I promised Joe. He's helping with the setup right now, might even be playing tonight. Who knows?"

"Speaking of playing, when is he going to dump his hometown girl for you?" Viv said.

"Maybe never," Dottie said with a shrug. "I can't lie to you two, I've still got a crush, but we're *just* friends. And he has been a perfect gentleman since our conversation the day I cut my arm."

"He better be," I said. "Or we'll sic Vera Lynn on him."

"He really has," Dottie said. "Talking to him is like talking to a friend I've known forever. But I keep reminding myself that he's leaving soon for God knows where. I may never see him again. This war is crazy, and it makes it hard to plan for anything. Or anybody."

"Has he even mentioned Mary Jane lately?" I asked.

"He hasn't, and I haven't asked. I honestly don't really want to know," Dottie said, shaking her head.

There was a knock at the door, and Mrs. Tibbetts peeked in on us.

"I know you're getting ready for the concert—oh! Look at you— you all look beautiful in your dresses. Just gorgeous," Mrs. Tibbetts said, smiling.

For the first time in weeks, we were allowed to don civilian clothes, so we were wearing the dresses we had worn to the Paramount our last night in London, the only ones we had with us.

"I forgot to give you these letters Liz dropped off earlier. I knew you'd want to read them straightaway," she added, passing them out to us. We ripped them open like Christmas presents. I still had that anxiety in the pit of my stomach, fearing bad news, but I was feeling so homesick I tore into the letters from my parents and my sisters anyway.

"Any news about Danny, Fi?" I looked up to see that Dottie and Viv were watching me, their own letters open in their laps.

"Nothing, thanks for asking," I said. "I scanned them quickly, and now I'm going to take my time and enjoy reading them."

After we read in quiet for a few moments, Dottie broke the silence. "Well, Richie says he may never forgive me for the fact that I'm going to miss his entire high school football season. And my mother said cooking Sunday dinner is no fun without me." She looked up at us, her eyes watering.

"I know I complain about my sisters, but I adore them, even though they drive me crazy. It's just hitting me that I might not see Aria's new baby, Gianna, until she's almost a year old," Viv said with a sad smile. "My first niece."

"The twins are making me feel guilty about missing their last high school play," I said as I traced the silly pictures they had drawn on the sides of their letter. "They're doing *You Can't Take It with You*, and Darcy is playing one of the leads."

The three of us sat there, rereading our letters, each of us aching for home in our own way.

"All right, girls, enough; this is too depressing," Viv said, waving her hands in the air and standing up. "We're going to go out and have some fun; we deserve it." She faced the mirror to apply one more coat of lipstick.

"You're right," I said, putting the letters aside and standing behind her, fussing with the flower in my hair one last time. "It's Saturday night; no use sitting here feeling miserable."

"And I promise you, this concert is going to be just the best," Dottie said, standing up and smoothing out her dress. "I was about to start crying, and I would have ruined my makeup, so let's go. Are you girls ready? I think I just heard Jimmy pull up out front."

We headed downstairs to catch our ride.

"I love that we can wear actual dresses for a change," Viv said, twirling around in hers. "I'm so tired of wearing that scratchy blue clown suit every damn day."

We gave Mrs. Tibbetts kisses on the cheek as we were leaving, promising to tell her all the details when we got home. Jimmy let out a long whistle when we walked out front to meet him.

"You girls look brilliant," Jimmy said, opening the door to the jeep with a bow. "You're also looking very well this evenin', Mrs. Tibbetts."

"Why, thank you, Jimmy, please come early for tea next time you pick up the girls," she said.

I noticed Jimmy had taken more care tonight. His hair was slicked back, and his Red Cross uniform was neatly pressed. The biggest surprise was that he appeared to be completely sober. Dottie gave me a wink when we got in the car. Now that we knew about Jimmy's family, we had a newfound perspective on our often-drunk driver. And we had been trying to do things to boost his spirits, like convince Joe Brandon to get him a ticket for the concert tonight.

"Off we go, then," he said. "There's cups and an open bottle of champagne back there for ya. One of the fellas gave it to me; ain't got a taste for the stuff."

Viv poured us each a cup and we toasted as Jimmy pulled away from Mrs. Tibbetts's.

"I cannot wait to see your faces when you find out the surprise," Dottie said as she took a sip of champagne. "This is going to be such a great night."

~

De Montfort Hall was a mile outside the center of Leicester on the edge of Victoria Park and the university. It was a beautiful old white stone building, with a low peaked roof and an impressive entryway flanked by large white columns on either side.

Jimmy dropped us as close as he could to the front and then went to park the jeep. We joined the line of hundreds of soldiers and US Red Cross personnel flowing inside. The excitement and anticipation of the crowd wafted through the chilly autumn air.

"Excuse me, I say, is that Miss Viviana Occhipinti?" said Harry Westwood, who had somehow materialized behind us in line, tapping Viv on the shoulder. "You won't reply to my letters, so the very least you can do is dance with me tonight."

"I thought this was US troops only," she said, teasing him. "What are you doing here?"

"As I have told you before, I have friends in very high places." He shrugged and pulled out a lighter for her cigarette.

Dottie looked at me, eyebrows raised.

"So you will dance with me, then, won't you?" he said, looking into her eyes.

"Harry Westwood, I do not even *know* you," she said, feigning annoyance, though she was enjoying every minute.

"That's why I sent you the letters, darling," he said. "So you could get to know me and I can get to know you. Did you even take a moment to read them?"

"I was too busy," she said, winking at him.

"Ah, now you definitely owe me a dance. I'm hurt," he said, clearly amused.

"Is there even a dance floor tonight, Dottie?" I asked. We were finally through the front doors and headed to the main auditorium.

"Oh yes, right in front of the stage," she said. "We're sitting on the right-hand side of it."

"Brilliant," Harry said, flashing a beautiful smile. "Very well, then, I will come find you, Viviana." And then he disappeared into the crowd.

"He is really gorgeous, honestly," Dottie said. "At least dance with him, Viv."

"You've got to admire his persistence," I said to Viv. "And why didn't you read his letters?"

"Because I knew it would drive him mad," she said with a self-satisfied grin "Because look at him. I'm sure he has women all over the UK falling all over themselves to get his attention."

"But why don't you at least give him a chance?" I said.

"Maybe I will," Viv said, and I noticed she looked like she was actually blushing. "It's that accent that gets me every time he opens his mouth. But then, like Dottie said, everyone is always leaving. What's the point really?"

"I think the point is to dance with a handsome Englishman and have fun," I said. "Maybe there doesn't need to be any other point."

"Maybe," Viv said, looking at me, seriously now. "And maybe, Fi? You should think about taking your own advice on that front."

I was about to ask what exactly she meant by that when we entered the auditorium and let out a collective gasp. It was a gorgeous space, with a curved, wood-paneled ceiling several hundred feet above us and burgundy seats on tiered balconies up to the rafters.

A red velvet curtain hung in front of the enormous stage. At the orchestra level, in front of the stage, was a dance floor with several more rows of seats on either side of it.

I barely recognized Liz Anderson waving us over to our seats. She looked so pretty, wearing a conservative eggplant-colored dress, her bobbed hair styled in shiny curls. We sat down with her and several teams of Clubmobile girls that we hadn't seen in a while, including Ruthie and Helen, the talkers from North Dakota, and Doris, ChiChi, and Rosie—a notoriously funny Clubmobile crew that we hadn't seen since London. We all shared stories of our adventures over the past several weeks. I wished once again that Blanche, Frankie, and Martha were still here with us. I missed our happy group of six.

When it looked like the auditorium was nearly filled to capacity, the lights flashed three times and people started clapping and whistling. Dottie was laughing and smiling a huge dimpled smile.

"Dottie, I can't wait," I said, hooking arms with her. "This is so exciting."

The lights in the hallway dimmed, and the audience started clapping as a slight man in a dark-brown suit and bow tie walked in front of the velvet curtain to the center of the stage in front of a large microphone.

"To all of the American soldiers and US Red Cross personnel here tonight, good evening and welcome to De Montfort Hall," he said. He sounded like one of the broadcasters we listened to on Mrs. Tibbetts's wireless. "My name is Arthur Kimball, and here in Leicester I'm known as 'the promoter who brings you the stars.'" He grinned and waited a beat as the audience started clapping again.

"In the interest of military security, we had to keep this concert top secret. Now . . . are you ready to see who's here to perform a concert tonight in your honor?"

The GIs in the audience started cheering and clapping. "Let's go!" someone yelled.

"All right, all right!" Arthur Kimball laughed. "Without further ado, introducing Major Glenn Miller and the American Band of the Allied Expeditionary Forces!"

Collective gasps could be heard throughout the hall. A couple of the Clubmobile girls near us actually started to cry tears of joy. Viv and I had our mouths hanging open; we could not believe the most popular bandleader in America had come all the way to Leicester. Dottie looked at us, laughing, enjoying our reaction.

"I told you!" she said. "Amazing, isn't it? The *best* surprise. Can you believe he's actually here?"

The velvet curtain started to rise as the first notes of Miller's signature hit, "Moonlight Serenade," rang out. By the time the curtain revealed Miller's forty-five-piece orchestra, the energy in the auditorium was pure electricity, and the entire audience was on its feet in a standing ovation, clapping and cheering.

Glenn Miller was standing in the middle of the stage, playing his trombone and looking very serious. A good-looking man in his late thirties, he was dressed in his military uniform and wearing the signature round, metal-framed glasses that made him look professorial.

The rest of the band couldn't hide how delighted they were at the crowd's reaction. When the song ended, we were all still on our feet, and I could barely hear myself think over the thundering applause.

"It's an honor to be here to play for you tonight. Thank you for your service," Glenn Miller said into the microphone at the front of the stage. "As I've said before, America means freedom, and there's no expression of freedom quite so sincere as music."

The soldiers were swelling with patriotic enthusiasm as they cheered for the American icon. "Now we're going to turn it up a notch. Does anyone here know how to jitterbug?"

The crowd roared as the band started to play "One O'Clock Jump." Soldiers started coming over to our group, asking us to dance, and though I couldn't jitterbug as well as some of the eighteen-year-old GIs,

I had improved thanks to all the dancing I'd done at the camps and some lessons from Martha.

"Come on, Fiona. I know you want to dance." Tommy Doyle held out his hand to me, and I couldn't say no.

The dance floor in front of the stage filled up with couples fast, and the celebratory, party atmosphere continued as the band played more of their hit songs.

After dancing with several eager partners, I had to take a break from the hot, crowded dance floor and get a drink at one of the bars just outside the main hall. I noticed Viv was dancing and laughing with Harry Westwood, but I didn't see Dottie anywhere. I got three cold Cokes and started to make my way back to my seat, where Viv met me and accepted one with gratitude.

"We're going to take a quick break. Glenn Miller and his band will be back in fifteen," the emcee said at the end of "In the Mood" as the curtain closed.

"How's Harry Westwood?" I asked.

"Handsome," she said. "Can't deny that. And he has nice hands." Sweat was dripping down the side of her face, and she was breathless. "And he's smart, interesting, was a lawyer before the war. Maybe he's not the wolf I thought he was. Where the heck is Dottie?"

"No idea," I said, scanning the hall. We drank our Cokes and chatted with some of the girls sitting near us. And then the lights flashed three times, and people started to settle down into their seats.

Arthur Kimball took center stage again and tapped the microphone.

"For our first song in the second half of the show, we've got a special treat for you," he said. "We have a very talented female vocalist who is going to perform. She's working here as a Red Cross Doughnut Dolly, but once you hear her, I think you'll agree that she has a music career in her future."

All the Clubmobile girls were giving each other looks, whispering about who it could possibly be. I clutched Viv's hand and looked at her.

"Absolutely not possible," she said, shaking her head.

"No. No way. She would never," I said.

"A music teacher from her hometown of Boston, Massachusetts," said emcee Arthur, "introducing . . . Miss Dottie Sousa!"

Our whole Red Cross section jumped out of their seats and started to cheer and clap wildly. Viv and I stood there, staring at the stage and holding on to each other as the curtain rose to reveal our dear, sweet, shy Dottie, looking beautiful in her cream-colored dress, standing in front of a microphone with Glenn Miller's band.

"What the hell is happening?" I said in Viv's ear. "And why isn't she wearing her glasses?"

"Oh my God. Is she drunk? What if she's drunk?" Viv asked. "I think she had more champagne than we did. Fi, I'm about to throw up."

"Me too."

We didn't even sit down when everyone around us did. We couldn't. We stood there, paralyzed with worry about what our friend was about to do. I pictured her running off the stage in tears or fainting, and I prayed that she would make it through whatever the heck she was going to do up there.

The audience got quiet, and I saw Joe Brandon, at the piano, give a signal to the band to start. The first notes of the song started up, and Dottie's cheeks were scarlet as she blinked a couple of times. She looked in the direction of Joe, and he was smiling at her and nodding in encouragement.

"Can she even see him without her glasses?" Viv whispered.

I shook my head.

Dottie began to sing the first few lines of "Someone to Watch Over Me," and Viv and I, still holding hands, looked at each other in shock. I was dumbfounded. I always knew she had a pretty voice. I heard it when she sang next to me during the sing-alongs. She had sung in the church choir, and she sang for her students all the time. But in all the years we had been friends, I had never heard Dottie *really* sing, all by herself. As the song continued, her singing got stronger, more confident, less self-conscious. And it took my breath away.

I wasn't the only one that was awestruck. The audience was enchanted. I glanced at a few of the soldiers sitting near us, and the light from the stage reflected off the tears glistening in their eyes. Her voice was sweet and clear and beautiful, and something about it seemed to take them back home.

Liz and the rest of the Clubmobile girls looked as shocked and as proud as I felt. And Jimmy, who was a few rows behind us, was beaming from ear to ear.

She finished singing, and this time the standing ovation was all for Dottie as the audience, starting with our Clubmobile section, leaped to their feet. Dottie stood there with her hands clasped in front of her mouth, an expression of pure joy and surprise on her face. She couldn't believe what she had just done. Glenn Miller walked over to her, said a few words, and kissed her hand. Then, holding it up to the audience, he signaled us to give her one more round of applause.

I swallowed the lump in my throat and wiped my eyes. Viv pulled out her handkerchief, crying and laughing.

"Jesus Christ," Viv said, shaking her head. "I had no idea, did you?"

"I knew she could sing, but not like *that*."

"And she's so damn good, Fiona," Viv said. "That was amazing."

"I agree," I said.

"Thank you to Dottie Sousa for that beautiful performance," said Arthur the emcee. "Remember that name, folks. Remember that *voice*. Now we'll hear from the Army Air Force Band's male vocalist, Dennis Goodwin."

Viv and I rushed out of the auditorium and down the hall that ran parallel to it until we finally found the backstage door. Dottie walked out just as we were about to open it. We screamed when we saw her, our voices echoing in the empty hallway as we collapsed into a group hug, jumping up and down. A military policeman was standing nearby, looking annoyed yet amused.

"That was incredible," I said, when we finally broke away. "Dottie, all these years, I had no idea you could sing like that. I'm so proud of you I could burst."

"Honey, you are *really* talented," Viv said. "I'm not just saying this because you're one of my best friends. You're not like local-church-talent-show good; you're more like Andrews Sisters good. Maybe even better."

"Thank you," Dottie said, her cheeks flushed. She was still glistening with sweat from the stage lights. "I was so nervous that I thought I might be sick; the extra glass of champagne helped calm me a little."

"How did you ever get up the courage to do it?" I said.

"My whole life, I've dreamed of doing something like that," she said. "My students always told me I should. But you know me. I just never thought I'd have the nerve. Then when I cut my hand and messed up observation day . . ."

I started to protest, but she kept talking.

"I know it wasn't entirely my fault, but it didn't help, did it?" she said. "Anyway, I've been trying to play for the troops more, do things that will improve our standing in Miss Chambers's eyes. And when Joe told me there was going to be a secret concert with a big band, I got the idea. I sang for him with my guitar, and he was blown away when he heard me. He helped me make it happen. And something like this has to get back to Miss Chambers in London, right? Nothing improves soldiers' morale like music from home."

"So, wait, Joe convinced the Glenn Miller Band to let you sing?" I said.

"He did," she said. "He said with a voice like mine it wouldn't take much convincing. So, when they got here I sang for the band, and the guys went crazy. Glenn Miller is a serious man, very hardworking. But he was really happy to have me. Just now onstage, he said I have a future in music if I want it. I'm sorry, I don't mean to brag."

"You sang with *Glenn Miller*—brag all you want, my friend," Viv said, putting her arm around Dottie.

We headed to one of the bars to get drinks and celebrate Dottie's solo singing debut. The band started playing a slow song, and Harry Westwood came out of the auditorium, his eyes scanning the bar area for Viv. When he spotted her, he came over and offered her his hand.

"Night's almost over. I think we should have at least one more dance, don't you?" he said to her.

"Do you?" she said, looking at his hand like she might say no. But then she put down her glass of Coke and took it. He looked relieved.

"You were marvelous, Dottie," he said, and she thanked him before they walked away.

"What's going on with him now?" she said.

"With Viv, who knows?" I said. "She likes the attention, not to mention the British accent."

"Speaking of attention," Dottie whispered, taking a sip from her straw and signaling with her eyes that there was someone behind me.

I turned around and nearly bumped into Peter Moretti.

"Oh," I said, startled. It was the first time I had seen him since the night I ran out of petrol. "Hi."

"Hi," he said in a quiet voice, no smile. His hair had been recently cut, and I could smell his cologne, the same one he'd been wearing the last time I saw him. Pine trees and cedarwood.

"Would you like to dance?" he said.

"I thought you didn't dance."

"I don't," he said. "But it's my favorite song, and it's Glenn Miller live, so I thought—" He now looked like he regretted asking me, so I interrupted him.

"You're right," I said with a nod. "Let's dance."

Peter congratulated Dottie, and I kissed her on the cheek. She gave me a curious look, just as Liz and some of the other Clubmobile girls came over and mobbed her with hugs.

I was flustered, so I'm not sure who took whose hand first, but we were holding hands as we walked onto the dance floor. I couldn't deny that warm butterfly feeling in my chest and the thrill I felt that my hand was in his. And then almost at the same time came the crush of guilt.

You're still engaged. He's missing, but as long as he might be alive, you're still engaged to the only guy you've ever loved.

I'd had crushes in high school, but Danny was the only man that I had ever been truly in love with. I didn't know it was possible that your heart could ache for one person and feel something toward another. My life had never been that complicated.

We faced each other to dance, and he noticed my far-off look as he put his arms around my waist.

"Are you okay?" he asked, as I put my arms around his neck.

"Yes, of course," I said, giving him a small smile, and I felt him relax. I prayed he couldn't hear my heart beating. "I wouldn't have guessed 'A Nightingale Sang in Berkeley Square' as your favorite song."

"There's a lot of things you don't know about me," he said, flashing his crooked smile.

"That is true," I said. "Maybe I should learn more. After the war is over, are you going to go back to boxing?"

"'After the war is over' is a lifetime away," he said. "But no, I won't go back to boxing. I went into boxing because I was a poor kid from the Bronx, and I was good at it and could make good money. Now I'm twenty-seven years old, and it's a young man's sport. I'll finish my degree if this war ever ends—for free, thanks to the army."

"What degree is that?"

"Mechanical engineering," he said, watching me for a reaction.

"You're right," I said, a little surprised. "I don't know much about you at all."

He was gazing into my eyes. It was that feeling I thought I might never feel again. A feeling like you're the only two people in the room. I looked away first, feeling guilt over what I wanted to happen next between us.

"What about you, what are you going to do after?" he said.

"I have no idea." I sighed. "I feel uneasy, not knowing."

"I think we're all feeling that way," he said.

We stopped talking but kept dancing, and then relaxed into each other. I tried not to think and to just enjoy the moment, but my thoughts kept getting in the way.

"Do you know when you ship out?" I asked.

"I do, but I can't say," he said. The song was almost over, and he grabbed my hand and started pulling me off the dance floor.

"Wait, where are we going?" I asked.

"For a walk," he said. "To get some fresh air. And talk."

I saw Viv with Harry, and she gave me a look that said there would be questions later.

Victoria Park was quiet and chilly, and a few other couples were walking the grounds or sitting on park benches. But we were just two people; we weren't a couple at all.

We walked side by side. He took his jacket off and put it around my shoulders, his arms lingering around me for a few seconds.

"That night at the Paramount?" he said, his voice quiet. "When you waved at me across the hall? I did see you. You looked so beautiful. Just like tonight, your hair with the flower in it, that dress. I couldn't take my eyes off you. And when you caught me, I was so embarrassed I pretended not to see you. It was stupid. I'm sorry."

"Thank you," I said. *He thinks I'm beautiful.*

"I did send a note to my friend in the IRC," he said, pausing before adding, "I haven't heard anything back yet."

"Thank you for doing that," I said, feeling several kinds of guilty now, so much so that my stomach was churning. He was quiet for a minute as we continued to walk. He went to reach for my hand, but then he hesitated.

"Fiona, why didn't you tell me that Danny Barker is your fiancé?" I stopped walking and faced him. He leaned into me and looked into my eyes again. "Why?"

I wasn't sure how he'd found out. It could have been from anyone. The only person I had kept it a secret from was him.

"I'm sorry. I've asked myself that same question, because I never lie," I said. "I think it's because I just wanted to be Fiona Denning to you. I didn't want to tell you my sad story because I didn't want you to look at me with pity. I'm so sorry."

"Is that the only reason?" he said, grabbing the tips of my fingers.

"Peter," I said, taking his other hand before I even knew what I was doing. "You have to understand, I had my whole life planned . . . If someone had told me a year ago that tonight I'd be dancing with an army captain at a secret Glenn Miller concert in the middle of England, I would have said they were insane.

"I came here after I found out Danny was missing, because all I knew was that I had to get out of town and do something. People looked at me like my life was over at twenty-five years old. I know my fiancé is either in a POW camp or . . . or dead. I need to try to find out what happened to him, and I will accept and deal with the news when I get it. But no matter what happens, *my* life isn't over. And . . . that's my story of how I ended up here."

"Okay," he said. "But you still didn't answer my question. Did you not tell me Danny Barker was your fiancé because you didn't want my pity, or because of the way you're feeling, standing here, holding my hands right now?"

I started to speak, but I couldn't get the words out. To admit I had feelings for him was to betray Danny, or the idea of Danny at least. I was beginning to have trouble remembering Danny the person.

Peter was watching the emotions cross my face as he put his hand on my cheek. He leaned down like he might kiss me on the lips. And I found myself wanting to kiss him back so much that it hurt. I wanted to surrender to that dizzy, elated first-kiss feeling, the kind that you relive for days after it happens. But instead I pulled away from him and took a small step back.

"I'm a mess," I said, looking up at him. "I'm so sorry. You're not wrong. About why I didn't tell you. But . . ."

"That's all I need to know. Please don't apologize," he said, a small smile on his face now, but there was disappointment in his eyes as he reached out and put his hand on my cheek again. It would have been so easy to just melt into him then. But it didn't feel right, even if I was only being loyal to a ghost.

"Thank you for asking your friend," I said. "I feel an obligation to find out what happened. If he's alive? I need to find him. I owe him that. I hope you understand."

"I do," he said. "I would do the same thing."

"I think you would," I said.

"And I promise I will send you a letter if I hear anything at all from my friend about what POW camp he's in, or anything else."

"Thank you so much," I said.

"Thank *you*," he said, "for saying yes when I asked you to dance. The memory of this night? It's going to help me get through all the dark nights that are coming."

He reached out and put his arm around my shoulders, and it made me feel so warm and content I couldn't even pretend to protest. We walked back to De Montfort Hall like that, and I knew that the memory of this night would stay with me too.

Chapter Sixteen

September 11, 1944

The Monday after the dance found us back at one of our favorite camps, the one we had visited on our very first day. As we served doughnuts and caught up with some of the soldiers we hadn't seen in a little while, you could feel a change in the atmosphere. Many of the men looked anxious, especially the younger ones, and the laughs didn't come as easily. There was a frenetic amount of activity as officers and GIs checked maps and equipment and rushed around attending briefings.

"Hey, Fiona, I need to ask you a favor," Boston Tommy said as I handed him a cup of coffee shortly after we arrived.

"Sure, hon, what can I do for you?" I asked.

He looked at the line of men behind him and said in a soft voice, "It's kinda personal. Can you take a minute?"

I nodded and told Viv and Dottie and our Victrola helper, Sam Katz, that I'd be right back.

"What is it?" I asked when I stepped outside the Clubmobile and we were out of earshot of his friends.

"This is the address for my mom and dad," he said, handing me an envelope. He looked so serious, which wasn't like him.

"Okay, do you need me to mail a letter for you? I'm happy to. Is that all?"

"Fiona, I want you to write my mom a letter if I don't make it," he said. "Tell her about our life here for me, because I'm not such a good writer. Her name's Eileen. She's a really good cook. And I should have told her that more, you know? I loved her stew and her breads, and I should have told her. I miss her and my pops. God, I miss them so much."

"Tommy I . . . ," I began. "You've got to think positive; you shouldn't be thinking like that."

"No, that's *exactly* the way I should be thinking," he said. "We're jumping straight into enemy territory, our fourth combat jump. I jumped into Normandy on June 5 and came out of there on a stretcher. I spent two days on one of those Red Cross boats and five in the hospital. It's a goddamn miracle I made it through."

He lowered his voice even more. "And this jump? It's going to be bad, I can tell. You can see it on the officers' faces. No time to plan. We're not ready."

I felt sick to my stomach and prayed he was wrong.

"I *will* keep the address, but I'm sure I won't have to send her a letter," I said, forcing myself to smile. "We'll see you over there soon."

"You girls are the best. It's like having older sisters around," he said with a smile. His Boston accent coming through strong at the end with "oldah sistahs."

I tucked the address in my pocket and gave him a tight hug. "I've got to help Viv and Dottie before they kill me. I hope I'll see you again this week before you all go."

When I got back into the Cheyenne, Sam was gone, but Liz was there with some additional supplies for us. Vera was already curled up, sleeping on the fifty-pound bag of doughnut flour that Liz had brought in.

"It's happening this weekend. They're sending thousands of troops into Holland, including the Eighty-Second," Liz said. "They're shipping out to the airfields on Friday, and I want the Cheyenne to follow them, go from field to field. I'll send a supply truck with you. You'll be sleeping in the Cheyenne, unless any of the RAF bases have beds. It's going to be a little rough, but if ever they needed some support, it would be now. You up for it?"

"Of course," I said, feeling sick again at her confirmation. I hoped that I would get to say good-bye to Peter before he left, and then I felt a pang of guilt for hoping.

"I can't believe they're all leaving," Dottie said after Liz left. She was checking her guitar, getting ready to play a few songs before we headed to the next camp. She had become a sensation since the concert. On Sunday, when we had taken a trip into Leicester, soldiers kept stopping her and begging her to sing for them right in the middle of the street.

"I can't believe that we're not," Viv said. "What are we going to do with so many of them gone? Sit around with Mrs. Tibbetts and her petting zoo, twiddling our thumbs?"

"Is Joe shipping out, Dottie?" I asked.

"Yes, to join the rest of the Twenty-Eighth on the Continent," she said. "Though he couldn't tell me details. What he did for me on Saturday night? I'll never be able to thank him enough for that, and for his friendship," she said, still trying to convince herself that was enough.

"Now, while we're cleaning up this mess and don't have soldiers crawling all over this thing, *you* need to come clean, Fiona," Viv said. "What happened with Peter Moretti Saturday night?"

I had been dodging their questions, not ready to talk about it, though I had been thinking about him ever since. I wanted to tell my friends, but I had been almost afraid to acknowledge how I felt, even to them.

"All right, here's what happened . . . ," I said, and I told them every single detail of the evening, including how I felt then, how I was still feeling. When I was finished, I looked up at Viv and then at Dottie. My face was red from talking about it all. I realized they had both stopped what they were doing and were just looking at me.

"For the record, I didn't tell him about the fiancé part," Viv said. "I swear."

"Me either," said Dottie.

"I didn't think you did. It could have been anyone," I said.

"Fiona, it's okay, you know," Dottie said, coming over and sitting next to me on the floor where I had been scrubbing grease from it. "You need to forgive yourself for having feelings for him. You're human, and let's face it, we're surrounded by men *all the time* in this odd life we're living here. Also, Peter Moretti seems like a very decent guy."

"I agree with Dots, one hundred percent," said Viv. "As I've said, everyone is coming and going over here; no one knows what's going to happen after all this. Don't be so hard on yourself for *having a life.* Frankly, I think it's about time."

"Yes, but I keep thinking, what if Danny's still alive? I feel like it's such a betrayal."

"If he's still alive, he would understand," Dottie said, patting my arm.

"The Danny Barker I know definitely would," Viv said. "Please stop beating yourself up, for the love of God."

"Hey, where's the famous singer Dottie Sousa?" Eddie Landon banged on the Cheyenne's window and made us all jump. "We're ready for some singing."

"Showtime," I said, as I helped her off the floor.

Dottie grabbed her guitar and started to play to loud cheers as I began cleaning again, thinking about the conversation, relieved that it was over. I wanted to accept what they were telling me so badly, that Danny would understand, that it was okay to have feelings for someone else. But then I would think of the possibility that he was in a POW camp somewhere, depressed and miserable, and the feelings of guilt and betrayal would bubble up all over again.

Maybe it was better if I didn't say good-bye to Peter Moretti. Maybe it was for the best if I never saw him again. It would make things simpler. Wouldn't it? But just the thought of never seeing him again made my heart ache. I knew, almost despite myself, that I would do everything I could to try to find him that weekend, to at least say good-bye, possibly for the last time.

~

On the following Saturday afternoon, we were sitting outside enjoying the sun and a cup of tea in Mrs. Tibbetts's garden as we waited for Jimmy to pick us up for our long stretch of work, hitting all the air bases before the troops took off for Holland. We heard a jeep coming down the road and thought it was him, but Mrs. Tibbetts came back into the garden with Joe instead. Baby the goat followed behind them, bleating at Joe in judgment.

"I'll go get the teapot," Mrs. Tibbetts said, taking her time on her walk to the kitchen.

Joe looked disheveled with dark circles under his eyes. He was gripping an unsealed envelope. Dottie put her cup down and stood up, looking at the envelope in his hand. Viv glanced at me with raised eyebrows and kept sipping her tea.

"Dottie," he said. "Can we talk?"

"Yes, we can talk right here," Dottie said. "We're leaving any second. Jimmy is picking us up. We'll be gone for a couple days."

"I know. I'm leaving today for the Continent, heading to Southampton in a little while. And I had to show you this before I left. It's a letter to Mary Jane. You can read it if you want. It's the one . . . it's the one that I should have written the moment Fiona introduced us in London. And I'm sorry it took me so long to realize that. I've been so stupid. I told Fiona on the ship, all this time I expected to get a Dear John letter from *her*, breaking up with *me*. The truth is, we'd been growing apart even before I left. And I've been waiting for that letter to

180

come. And I don't know why I've been waiting for it, because I've been wanting to end it since the day I met you.

"I'm in love with you, Dottie. I'm not sure how you feel now, after I behaved so disrespectfully at first but . . . oh, no, don't cry . . ."

He walked over and put his arms around her in a hug, leaning down to kiss her on the lips. I caught Mrs. Tibbetts watching from the kitchen window, smiling and clasping her hands together. I grabbed Viv by the elbow and pulled her up.

"We'll give you two a moment alone," I said, giving Viv a look. As a reminder to Dottie, I added, "Jimmy will be here soon."

They didn't hear a word.

A short while after Dottie bid a sad good-bye to Joe, Jimmy picked us up in the Cheyenne. We were accompanied by a military police escort and Major Bill, who was driving a two-ton truck of supplies behind us. Our caravan drove all night through the silent villages of Lincolnshire, trying to reach as many soldiers in as many airfields as we could before they all departed. We had decided that we could sleep when they were gone.

Just before sunrise, we reached the airfield at Folkingham and parked right near the hangars where the C-47s, the military transport planes, were warming up. It was that pitch darkness right before any hint of dawn, and a cold wind was whipping across the field.

The soldiers were walking around loaded down with their equipment. Some of them were jumping or jogging, trying to stay warm and psych themselves up. I saw Patrick Halloran holding tight to the Saint Christopher medal around his neck and quietly praying. Many guys came over to the Cheyenne, laughing and joking with us, trying to keep their mind off the obvious. More than a few were drenched with sweat despite the chill in the air.

"Fiona, Viv, thank God you're here. I need a huge favor," Nelson, our eager helper from observation day, said as he came running over with something wrapped in a blanket.

"Sure, Nelson, what can I do for you?" I said. I offered him a doughnut, but he shook his head and unwrapped the blanket.

Inside was one of the ugliest little dogs I'd ever seen. She couldn't have been more than seven pounds, with black and brown hair that was either matted with dirt or sticking out straight. Her pink tongue was dangling halfway out of her mouth, and she had enormous bulging black eyes that looked too big for her head.

"I need you to take Barbara," he said, pleading.

"Oh my God, is that a *dog*?" Viv said, leaning out the window to get a better look.

"Yeah, she's a mutt. She's the best—a sweetheart, right, Barb?" he said, hugging her while giving us the hard sell. "She'll love Vera, I promise. She *loves* cats. Will you take her?"

"Who names a dog Barbara?" Dottie asked, smiling while she patted the poor thing.

"Hey, it's after a girl from home," Nelson said. "It's a great name."

"Nelson, how did you even get her to the airfield?" I said.

"Don't ask." He gave me a mischievous look. "So, will you girls take her?"

I looked at Dottie and Viv, and they both gave me slight nods. How could we say no?

"Only if you come get her back from us someday," I said.

"I promise." He smiled. "She'll eat anything; she's easy, you'll see," he said, looking over his shoulder. Then he added, "I've got to go. One last hug."

He hugged the scruffy dog so tight it broke my heart. "Good-bye, Barbie girl, see you soon," he whispered.

He handed her to me, trying to blink away the tears in his eyes.

"Okay, gotta go. Thanks, girls. Bye, Barbara!" He ran off to hide his tears, and Barbara started to whimper.

I heard a hiss behind me and looked up to see Vera Lynn standing on the top shelf looking down, her back arched and her orange tail puffed up. Barbara peered up at her and barked in greeting.

"Oh, this is going to be fabulous," Viv said, rolling her eyes. "Also, *Vera Lynn* and *Barbara* are definitely the stupidest pet names in the entire ETO."

"Here, give her to me," Dottie said. "I think you'll be a great addition to the team, Barbara." She gave the dog a hug and arranged the blanket on one of the shelves on the opposite side of the Clubmobile from Vera.

We had said good-bye to so many friends that morning, and we were so tired it was impossible to hide our emotions. The three of us had to step away from the Cheyenne's window at different times so they wouldn't see us cry: Eddie from Arizona, George and Alan—our other observation day helpers, Patrick Halloran, Sam Katz, Nelson, and way too many others to name.

We blared records over the PA, playing the cheery songs from home that they loved, and the soldiers continued to line up for coffee and conversation to distract them from what they were about to do. At every airfield, I kept searching through the sea of men for the one soldier I had yet to say good-bye to but desperately wanted to see. I was starting to lose hope. Finally, I spotted him before he saw me.

Peter was standing with some of his men, and they gravitated around him like he was the sun, a strong and steady light in the darkness.

"I'll be right back," I said, taking off my apron.

"Do you see the line, Fi?" Viv asked, annoyed. But I was already out of the truck, running over to him.

"Hi," I said, trying to smooth down my hair, but the wind kept whipping it around.

"Give me a minute, fellas," he said. They didn't whistle or crack jokes; they just nodded and respectfully walked away. Except one.

"Fiona, I didn't realize that was you," Tommy Doyle said.

"Tommy, is that you under all that equipment? So happy I got to say good-bye to you, my dear friend," I said, giving him a hug. "I still have the address. But I won't need it. Stay safe, and I'll see you soon."

"Sounds good," he said and then whispered, "Captain Moretti is a really good man. A soldier's soldier. I approve."

I just nodded and smiled, kissing him on the cheek, and then he ran off to join the rest of his friends.

Peter had watched this exchange, amused. "Hi," he said, giving me a small smile.

"Hi," I said, and at the same time we stepped closer to each other and then both laughed, a little embarrassed.

The sun was just beginning to rise. Tommy had joined the groups of soldiers heading toward the planes now, dark silhouettes against the orange and pink colors of the horizon, like a scene from a movie. An icy breeze blew up again, and I put my arms around myself and shivered.

"I'd give you my jacket if I could," he said. "But I'm loaded down at the moment."

"It's okay, I'm just glad I got to see you."

"Me too."

We stood there for a few seconds looking at each other, and he stepped even closer still.

"Thank you again for last Saturday night," he said into my ear. "I have something I want to give you."

"Peter, I . . ." But he raised one hand while he reached into his pocket with the other and pulled out a little plastic box. He handed it to me, and I opened it. It was his Purple Heart.

"Like a lot of our guys, I was injured landing at Utah Beach," he said. "I want you to have it."

"Peter, I can't—" I started to protest and give it back to him, but he interrupted, placing his hand on mine, over the box.

"Take it. As a token of friendship and admiration, nothing more," he said, but he looked in my eyes and we both knew he was lying.

"I . . . thank you," I said as he took his hand away.

"Be safe," I said. "I'll see you on the Continent."

"I hope you don't," he said, his expression serious, and I was stung by his words. "It's just that you're so much safer over here. You have no idea. And you know how I hate having to worry about you doughnut girls."

"That's true," I said with a small laugh.

"Things are going to be hot over there at first, but when I finally get my next batch of mail, I'll get word to you if I hear anything from Hank at the IRC. I promise you that."

"Thank you," I said, looking at his face and trying to memorize it—the scar on his brow, his large dark eyes. I had tried to memorize Danny's too, and my heart was aching in ways that felt very familiar and yet so different. It turns out you can care for two men at the same time, but you never care for them in the exact same way.

Someone yelled, "Captain Moretti!"

"Time to go. Take care of yourself," he said.

"You too."

"Remember, you're no use to these guys if you're crying," he said as he wiped a tear from my cheek.

"I know," I said, nodding and smiling through the tears. "Good-bye."

He looked around quickly to see if anyone was watching, and then he pulled me into his arms, kissing my forehead, letting his lips linger there for a moment.

"Good-bye, sweetheart," he whispered, and with a nod, he walked toward the line of C-47s. As I watched him walk away, I bit my lip to keep from crying more.

"You okay?" Viv asked when I stepped into the Cheyenne and grabbed my apron.

"Yeah," I said with a deep breath. "I am. The hardest part of this job are these damn good-byes."

After we had served everyone we could, Jimmy started up the Cheyenne and we headed to the middle of the field with all the others that were left behind. I sat on the hood of Major Bill's jeep, between Dottie and Viv. Dottie kept nodding off on my shoulder. Hundreds of C-47s, carrying our brave friends, wheeled around the field and then struck off, heading for the channel in a steady stream, until there were so many planes in the sky they nearly blocked the early morning sun.

~

We arrived back at Mrs. Tibbetts's a little while later and stumbled into the cottage, where our dear billeter was waiting for us with a warm meal of fried tomatoes, eggs, toast, and hot tea. I didn't realize how ravenous I was until we sat down at the kitchen table.

"Liz was here waiting for you," she said. "She thought you'd be home earlier, so we sat and had tea, and she waited for about an hour. She's a lovely girl."

"What did Liz want?" I asked, frowning. We were supposed to see her the next day at headquarters.

"She didn't say, but she left you this note," she said with a nod.

She handed me a cream-colored envelope. I opened it and read out loud:

> *Fiona, Dottie, and Viv—*
> *Please take the next two days off to recover from your marathon thirty-six-hour shift. Well done, you!*
> *I came by because I have news I couldn't wait to share. Miss Chambers has recently been inundated with letters from a number of the officers that have been stationed in the Midlands, all of them singing your praises. We'll talk more when we meet this week, but, long story*

short, it's time to start packing your bags. We'll all be heading to Zone V in less than two weeks.

I couldn't be prouder of you three and the work that you've done here. You've all come a long way. Get some sleep, and I'll see you soon to make plans.

Warmest—

Liz

I looked up at the faces around the table. My brain was hazy from lack of sleep, and I was almost too tired to process the news. We were going to the Continent—we were finally going to France.

"Wow, that's not what I expected," Viv said, stifling a yawn.

"Do you think we can take Barbara?" Dottie asked. She had prominent circles under her eyes and was nearly asleep in her tea.

We were all quiet for a moment, absorbing the impact of this news.

"Do you think you might be able to take me?" said Mrs. Tibbetts, giving us a sad smile, her eyes shiny with tears. Dottie squeezed her hand, and I leaned over and gave her a kiss on the cheek.

Chapter Seventeen

September 23, 1944

Less than a week later, Jimmy arrived at Mrs. Tibbetts's at 6:00 a.m. to take us back to 12 Grosvenor Square, Red Cross headquarters in London, to gather with other Clubmobile groups. After meeting there, we would join a caravan heading for Southampton and ultimately cross the channel to France on one of the Liberty transport ships.

The days had blurred into a whirlwind of laundry, packing, writing letters home, and saying good-byes to the remaining troops that were still in the area. I took one last look out our bedroom window, our fairy-tale view of the enchanting English garden and the sheep in the meadow. I would miss this place. I had taken for granted how lucky we had been to have such a perfect billet and a gracious host with a beautiful cottage, fresh vegetables, eggs, and running water.

And while the work hadn't been easy or perfect, this place, this job, had taken me out of my grief-stricken rut. It had forced me to focus less on myself and more on helping the men that were here, doing the best that they could, sometimes under unimaginable circumstances.

Viv, Dottie, and I had barely absorbed the fact we were going to the Continent. I was thrilled and nervous and, in quiet moments, a little scared.

"Fiona!" Mrs. Tibbetts yelled from downstairs. "Are you ready?"

"Yes," I called, trying to memorize the view before I hurried down.

"We're all packed," Jimmy said. "It's time."

The Cheyenne had a small trailer attached, which included necessary equipment like a back-up generator, water tanks, tents, and other supplies. Jimmy would be accompanying us all the way to Southampton, but then heading back to London to become the driver for a Clubmobile group arriving after we left.

Mrs. Tibbetts walked us outside, blotting her eyes with her blue tea towel, which of course made us all get misty-eyed.

"Please promise me you'll write, so I know you're safe?"

"Of course we will," I said as the three of us leaned in and gave her a hug.

"And you'll come back and visit?" she asked. "Someday after all this nonsense is over. You can meet my boys when they come home."

If they come home, hung in the air around us like a dark cloud. I knew we had been a distraction from her worries; now she would be alone with them once again.

"We would love that," Dottie said.

"Definitely," added Viv.

"Be back soon, Mrs. Tibbetts," Jimmy said, tipping his hat to her.

"Please come by for tea, Jimmy," she said, giving him a warm smile. "And as I've told you, you may call me Ginny."

Jimmy started the Cheyenne, and we all settled in, Viv in the front, Dottie and I in the back. Vera was on my lap, and Barbara was on Dottie's. We had given Barbara a few baths and a trim since Nelson had given her to us, but with her bulging black eyes and weird tongue, she would never be considered a good-looking dog.

As we drove down the road, we kept on waving good-bye to Mrs. Tibbetts until we could no longer see her.

"I don't think I even knew that Mrs. Tibbetts's first name was Ginny," Viv said, giving Jimmy a sidelong glance. "I'm going to miss her. She's so lovely, and very pretty, don't you think so, Jimmy?"

"Aye, she's a fine, fine lady," Jimmy said. If he was still drinking, he wasn't doing it around us anymore. And he looked better, healthier. His cheeks were ruddy, and his hair was always slicked back now. He looked ten years younger than when we had first met him. "Was thinkin' she might like to go to the pub with me some night, when I'm back."

Viv gave a quick look back at us through the little window and winked.

"And *I* was thinking that would be a terrific idea. Don't you agree, girls?"

"Yes, great idea," Dottie and I said, with way more enthusiasm than necessary.

Jimmy dropped us off at Red Cross headquarters a little after 9:00 a.m. An older woman was sitting at the front reception desk when we walked in, and she looked up our names.

"You three are part of the group headed to France," she said, reaching into her drawer. With a flourish, she presented us all with circular patches with a red five in the center, our Zone V patches.

"These are to be worn on your left sleeve from now on," she said. "A meeting is being held for you in a room at the end of the hall—second-to-last door on the right."

Thanking her, we took the patches and headed toward our meeting. Smiling ear to ear, I felt a surge of pride and gave Dottie and Viv the thumbs-up. We had made it—we were going to the Continent.

We walked into the large lecture hall, greeting some girls we hadn't seen since training because they had been stationed in other areas across the United Kingdom. I spotted ChiChi from the Dixie Queen, along with Doris and Rosie. Helen and Ruthie from North Dakota were also there and waved us over to a row of seats in front of them. Just as we sat down, Miss Chambers and Liz entered the room, and everyone stopped talking.

"Good morning, ladies," Miss Chambers began. "Welcome back to London. You are the latest group of Clubmobiles to be heading to the Continent."

"Your life changed when you joined the Red Cross," she said. "Now that you are heading to France, it is about to dramatically change again. Here in England, you have lived as civilians in a civilian setting. While you're familiar with the threat of air raids and buzz bombs, this is a friendly, unoccupied country.

"On the Continent, you'll be living and working as part of a military unit in a combat zone, sometimes very close to the front lines," she said. "You'll spend much of your time on the road and camping out. K rations may become your most frequent meal, and running water will be a luxury. It's going to be an adjustment, but you're here because we think you're up to the challenge."

"She's always such a ray of sunshine," Viv whispered, and Dottie and I both shushed her.

"If for some reason you're not up to the job, you will be pulled back," Miss Chambers said. This time she was looking right at us, as if she'd heard Viv. "But I've only had to do that once so far. Now Miss Anderson is going to go over the logistics of what needs to get done before you leave this evening."

Liz Anderson discussed converting our pounds and shillings to francs, and where in the building we would find our K rations, water tablets, and seasick bags. She also handed us little *So Now You Are Going to France* booklets with information about the language and customs.

When the meeting was finished and we got up to leave, I was not surprised to hear Miss Chambers behind us saying, "Fiona, Dottie, and Viviana, could you come here, please?"

We walked over to where she was standing at the front of the room.

"As you know, I wasn't sure I'd ever be sending you three to the Continent," she said. She was so tall, she always seemed to be looking down at you. In our case, I was pretty sure she always was.

"Oh yes, we're *well* aware," Viv said in a tone I thought was perhaps a bit too salty, so I gave her a little kick. No need to mess up our plans now.

"My original plan was to keep you in Leicester with the remaining troops, but a few things changed my mind," she said. "One was that I received letters from the officers there about what a commendable job you were doing. The other thing was how highly Liz Anderson speaks of you. She wants you three with her on the Continent. Liz and these officers have clearly seen a side of you that I haven't witnessed."

She paused for a second. "And finally, there is the now-legendary tale of Dottie Sousa's singing debut at the secret Glenn Miller concert. That is one heck of a way to come out of your shell, Miss Sousa. I had no idea you had it in you."

"Me neither to be honest," Dottie said, blushing deeply. "Thank you."

"One more thing: Fiona, I wanted you to know that, after Liz told me, I did write the IRC on your behalf about your missing fiancé," Miss Chambers said. I was surprised and touched that she had taken the time. "Nothing back from them yet, but I'll try to get word to you if I hear anything."

"Wow," I said, not able to hide my surprise. "Thank you."

"Of course, dear," Miss Chambers said. "I know I'm tough on you three, but I do have a heart." She gave us a small smile. "That said, safe travels and please prove yourselves worthy of Liz's recommendation. Do not let her down."

The three of us all promised we wouldn't, and after more thank-yous and farewells, we sprinted out of the hall, still worried that she might change her mind at the last minute.

∼

That afternoon we headed to Wimbledon Park to rendezvous with the group going to Southampton. Liz came over to us as soon as we arrived, looking worried and frazzled, which was very unlike her. And then the air raid sirens started.

"That's a sound I haven't missed," Dottie said. We had been lucky in the Midlands not to have any close calls with buzz bombs the entire time we were there.

"Helmets on. Jimmy, you too. Word is there's a large number of V-1s incoming," Liz said, looking around, silently counting heads. "I think we've got everyone, so we'll be getting on the road to Southampton any minute. I want to get out of here before the brass change their minds and tell us we have to take shelter and wait. That will screw up our crossing; it will screw up everything."

With our helmets on, and the sound of explosions in the distance, we drove out of the city in an enormous caravan of eight Clubmobiles, four supply trucks, five Hillmans, twenty jeeps, and twelve trailers. Escorted by motorcycles, we made a grand exit out of London, waving good-bye to everyone we passed.

The trip took longer than we expected because, despite the impressive look of the caravan, a number of things went wrong as soon as we left the city. Two of the trucks' batteries died, a few vehicles ended up with flat tires, and the Clubmobile Dixie Queen ran out of petrol.

We pulled into the staging area in Southampton later that evening and awaited word from Liz as to whether we would be shipping out or would have to camp overnight. Jimmy had been particularly quiet on the trip.

"Jimmy, you okay?" I said, as we all got out to stretch our legs, eat our K rations, and socialize.

"Better than I've been in a long time." He looked at me and smiled. "Just sad to be sayin' good-bye."

"Now?" I said. "You're not going to drive us to the docks?" I felt panicked as it occurred to me that I was going to be our driver from this moment on.

"It ain't that far," Jimmy said with a laugh. "You'll be all right. Last time you'll have to drive on the left side for a long time."

"But how are you getting back?" Dottie asked. She was holding her helmet on her hip, and Barbara was curled up in it, fast asleep.

"Got a ride arranged with one of them Red Cross service trucks," he said. "Headin' back to London, then Leicester in a few days."

"Now don't forget to take Mrs. Tibbetts to the pub," Viv said. She kissed him on the cheek and gave him a huge hug. Dottie and I followed suit. He turned red from all the affection, and his eyes welled up.

"Will you fetch me Vera Lynn? Think it's for the best that she and Barbara are goin' their separate ways," he said. He looked at Barbara; her poor nose was covered in scratches from her failed attempts at feline friendship.

"Oh, you can't forget Vera Lynn." Viv nodded. "I'll go get her."

Liz came over with a clipboard, looking happy and relieved.

"Huge luck: they can get us on the ship tonight," she said. "We're heading to the docks now. I thought we might be stuck here for days. Fire up the Cheyenne, ladies."

Viv handed Vera off to Jimmy, and the four of us stood there for a quiet moment, sad but not sure what else to say.

"Fiona, remember everythin' I taught ya now. Don't forget to double clutch to—"

"Climb the steep hills," I said, interrupting him. My heart ached. Another good-bye to add to the chain of them in this war.

"You girls have been me favorites," he said, shaking his head and showing no embarrassment at the tear sliding down his cheek.

"Jimmy, you've lost so much in this war that I can't even imagine," I said. "I hope you find love and happiness again. I wish that for you more than anything."

"Wish the same for you, my girl," he said in a whisper, his hand on my shoulder. "Be safe and remember everythin' I taught ya."

I gave him a final hug and climbed into the Cheyenne.

Chapter Eighteen

September 24, 1944

"Fiona, wake up. You can see Utah Beach."

Dottie was nudging me awake, and it took me a few seconds to remember where we were. The night before, the three of us had waited on the docks at Southampton for a few hours until they finally lifted the Cheyenne onto the deck of a sparkling new Liberty ship dubbed the *Famous Amos*. It had been a long process, and we sat around and watched as a machine wrapped it in a huge net like it was a big army-green elephant, and then a crane had to lift and lower it, ever so carefully, into the hold of the ship.

After it was loaded, the captain had invited us on board, where we had received a friendly welcome by the crew. Many of them looked freshly shaven; some even had flowers in their lapels. The three of us and the other twenty-two Clubmobile girls on board were all wiped out after our long day of travel. Viv, Dottie, and I had found a spot on deck to lay out our bedrolls, and I had fallen asleep in seconds.

"Viv, come see," I said in her ear. "It's our first morning in *France*. And I smell coffee—we need to go find it."

In the light of day, I realized the *Famous Amos* was part of a huge convoy of Liberty ships and other landing craft that had been escorted by minesweepers and destroyers. We stood at the ship's rail under the splendid September sun and looked at the vastness of Utah Beach. Wrecked military vehicles had been abandoned on the sand, and battleships destroyed by German artillery jutted out of the water at frightening angles. I tried to comprehend the massive invasion that had happened just months before.

"Say a prayer for the souls lost, girls. This is hallowed ground now." The ship's captain came up next to us. He was a little under six feet tall, with salt-and-pepper hair. He gripped the railing and gazed out onto the beach, his face solemn.

"How many souls?" I asked.

"Don't know for sure yet," he said. "In the thousands. And every time I'm back here, I'm moved by the scene. I feel their ghosts."

I shivered, feeling goose pimples as I made the sign of the cross and said a silent prayer. Viv and Dottie did the same.

"Thousands," Dottie whispered after a moment, her voice thick with emotion. "Good God."

"I still don't know how any of them do it," Viv said in awe. "Running straight into danger like they do. I've been thinking of the Eighty-Second leaving."

"Me too," I said.

"They went to Holland most recently, yes?" the captain asked. "Operation Market Garden?"

"Yes, do you know anything?" I asked, aware of the urgency in my voice. "We were with them before they left. We've been listening for reports on the wireless and asking—"

"Ah, it didn't go well," he said, shaking his head in disgust. "They were trying to secure some major bridges and roads deep behind German lines, but the German counterattack was ferocious. They were ordered back to France."

"Do you know if there were many casualties?" It hurt to even ask.

He looked at me, furrowing his brow, like he was surprised at the question.

"Of course there were, dear," he said. "There always are."

"Goddamn it," Viv said.

I felt sick to my stomach. Dottie squeezed my hand. We were all thinking the same thing. These were our friends. Our boys. Tommy. Patrick. Nelson. And Peter. And too many more to comprehend.

"Fiona, you look like you could use some breakfast, and I desperately need some coffee," Viv said. "Please, do you know where we might find some, Captain . . . I'm sorry, sir, what is your name?"

"Captain Fisher," he said, and we all introduced ourselves.

"I'll be honest, I was expecting *tanks*, not dames," he added with a smile. "But all these women on board have done wonders for my crew's morale, and the ship's never been so clean. You're welcome to the mess hall for coffee and some decent navy food, and we have two showers on the second deck. We're arranging times for you all to use those at a certain hour."

"But when are we going ashore?" I said. We were so close.

"Oh, not for at least a few hours, if not days," he said. "The seas are too rough. If we try to get your vehicle on a landing craft barge right now? Well, we could hit a rogue wave, and you'd never see it again."

"*Days?*" I said.

"We'll just have to see," he said. "Go get some breakfast. And how about this? When it's time to go, you three will be the first off, I promise you."

∿

Eggs, coffee, and a fresh shower made me feel human again, and while the waters were a little rough, the sun was strong, so we spent most of the day on the deck, waiting. Dottie even got someone to hook up the Victrola to a loudspeaker for an impromptu dance.

"This is the best time I've had in months," a young redheaded crew member said, as he patiently dealt with my mediocre jitterbugging.

When there was a break in the dancing, Dottie went with one of the men to find us all some Cokes, and we sat down and enjoyed the feel of the sun on our faces. Someone brought out cards to play pinochle, and Viv pulled out a sketchbook she had bought in London. I sat next to her as she sketched a picture of the shore.

"We're off the coast of a place where thousands of American men died. And we're dancing," she said, squinting and tilting her head, looking out across the water. "It feels a little off, don't you think?"

"I've thought about that," I said, nodding, leaning over the railing. "But honestly? I think any of the men killed here would say, *Damn Hitler! Play that American music and dance.* It gives these men some hope and cheers them up. Helps them fight another day."

Viv was about to say more, but we were interrupted.

"Say, you're really talented," the redhead, whose name was Phillip, said as he came up behind us. He was looking over Viv's shoulder at her drawing. "Do you think you could sketch a picture of me to send my mom?"

Viv glanced over at me, annoyed at the request, but I just mouthed, "It's for his *mom.*" How could she refuse?

"Sure, Phil," she said with a sigh. "Why don't you stand against the rails here where the light is good?"

When she was almost finished with his picture, a few other crew members came up behind her to watch.

"Wow, are you a professional artist? That's swell!" one of them said.

"No, I'm an underpaid advertising secretary," Viv said with sarcasm. I walked over to get a better look. It was a beautiful sketch; it captured the soldier perfectly without being cartoonish or overdone.

"Underutilized secretary too," I said. "Viv, you really are so good."

"Thanks." She sighed. "Be nice if I could actually do something with it someday."

More men started coming over, to admire both Viv and her sketches, and many of them also asked for portraits to send to their loved ones. Soon there was a line of them waiting their turn.

Dottie and her new friend returned with cold drinks and chocolate cake, and after the refreshments were passed out, she went to the Clubmobile and came back carrying Barbara, with her guitar over her shoulders.

A few more Clubmobilers, including ChiChi, Rosie, and Doris from the Dixie Queen, joined us as Dottie played some songs, and soon everyone on deck was sitting around us singing along.

I was on a blanket toward the back of the crowd, near Viv, who was still sketching portraits as fast as she could, when I spotted Liz and waved her over.

"Any news?" I asked, handing her a Coke.

"It looks like the seas have settled down enough that we'll be getting on the barges in about an hour. Could you help me spread the word to the rest of the girls?" she asked.

"Of course," I said. "Anything else I can do?"

"No," she said.

"Liz, I wanted to say thank you for putting in a good word for us with Miss Chambers," I said. "I know we're here because of you."

"You're all here because of *you*," Liz said, taking a sip of Coke and looking out at the water. "I've been meaning to ask, do you know what you're going to do after the war? Have you thought about it at all?"

"Honestly, I have no idea," I said. "It depends on so much." Mostly on whether Danny was dead or alive. The grief was still always there for me, in the background, like an enemy I'd made a truce with. I'd never like it, but I had grown accustomed to it.

Liz nodded; she knew exactly what I meant.

"I just wanted to tell you that whatever happens, the Red Cross is going to be here even after this war is finally over. In London, Paris, Berlin. There'd be a job for you if you're interested. You're even better at some of the management aspects of this work than I am."

"I'm flattered," I said, smiling at her. "Thank you. I'll think about that." I felt a glow of pride, diminished only by the queasy feeling about my future.

"Oh, before I forget, you must have charmed Captain Fisher, because he said you three have to be the first Clubmobile ashore. Are you okay with that?"

"Absolutely."

I smiled and went to spread the word that it was almost time to go.

≈

"Why won't it start?" I said, feeling panicked, my palms sweaty on the steering wheel. "I can't get it into low gear; nothing's moving."

The seas had calmed, the tide was in, and the Cheyenne had been moved onto one of the barges. Now the three of us were sitting in the front seat, ready to be the first Clubmobile of our group to drive onto French soil. The only problem was, the truck wouldn't start.

"I don't know, did you do anything differently?" Viv asked.

"Did we run out of petrol?" Dottie asked.

"Nothing different, and I just filled the tank," I said. We were surrounded by Liberty ships, barges, and the amphibious jeeps known as ducks. Many of the barges were queued up to land right after us.

"This is a nightmare," I said. I looked up at the sky and tried to think what to do next. It was filled with Allied fighters and bombers headed for the Continent, and you could hear the echo of artillery fire in the distance. "My God, I am holding up the entire *war*."

"What's the problem?" The young GI who had helped get the Cheyenne on the barge came over.

"I'm sorry, I've done everything I can think of, and I can't get this thing started," I said.

"Oh, wait," he said, laughing. "It's not your fault. We immobilized it in case we hit rough seas."

He showed me what he did, I got the Cheyenne into gear, and we couldn't help but cheer when we drove down the ramp and our wheels hit the sand.

The beach was a haunted obstacle course of foxholes, concrete pill-boxes, and debris. It was by far the most treacherous terrain I had ever driven on, and I gripped the wheel tightly, sitting up straight and keeping my eyes on the beach. The enormous craters left over from bursting mortar shells were the hardest to navigate around. At one point my left front wheel slipped into one, and I swore as the steering wheel jerked out of my hand for a moment. I also had to keep turning on the windshield wipers to see because there was so much dirt and dust in the air.

"The captain was right," Viv said.

"About what?" Dottie asked.

"You can feel the ghosts."

I got goose pimples on my arms again when she said it, because it was true. There was a heaviness to the air that had nothing to do with the dust.

We found the road to Transit Area B, which was just a nearby field with a few army tents. We'd be camping with the rest of the caravan before heading to the new Red Cross club in Cherbourg the next day.

"Well, I'll be damned—real live American girls." A private with a thick Southern accent came out of one of the tents to greet us. He spread his arms wide. He was very thin with dirty-blond hair and at least a few days' worth of stubble on his face. "Welcome to the Continent."

"Thanks, soldier. How long have you been here?" I asked.

"In France? D plus 114," he said with pride. On the ship, I had learned the D was for D-Day. "I'm an engineer, was in Africa, Sicily, and Italy. Come on, I've got a jeep. I'll give you a quick tour before the rest of your group gets here."

We rode along the beach and then inland, covering our mouths to keep from inhaling the dust, as Dick, our GI host from Tennessee, started talking about his experience on D-Day.

"It was miserable and cold, and we had to climb out of the boats, neck deep in water," he said. "There were bodies floating all around me. And then when we got to shore, there were mines everywhere—the air corps had totally missed them! My buddy Butch was hit by a sniper and killed right in front of me. His head was just gone . . ."

Dick kept talking as we drove, in a trance, giving us the play-by-play of all that had happened to him, like a confessional. We couldn't have stopped him if we had tried. And from the way he was going on, I knew that he would be haunted by the images of that day until he was an old man.

We pulled up to the first American cemetery, lines and lines of plain white wooden crosses. Soldiers were walking along the rows slowly, stopping to examine the dog tags draped over the crosses, reading the names, looking for their friends. I bit my lip and said some silent prayers as we got out of the jeep and started walking through.

"I'll show you Butchy's cross; it's a couple of rows over," Dick said, tromping through the cemetery, leading the way. "Will you look at that?" Dick stopped and pointed. "The French people who live near here? They put a rose on every single grave. *Every single one*. Can you believe it?"

There was something about this kind gesture that broke an emotional dam in Dick, and he kneeled down in front of one of the crosses and began to weep, and my heart ached at his raw grief. I kneeled down next to him and put my arm over his shoulder, which made him sob even more. I looked up at Viv and Dottie, and we were all trying our best not to cry. We didn't want to make it worse for him or any of the other soldiers searching for their friends among the crosses. We walked Dick back to the jeep, where, once he composed himself, he started apologizing profusely.

"I'm so sorry, I don't know what came over me," he said, taking a deep breath and starting the car. He rubbed his hands over his face. "Just the rose on every grave . . . and then being with you three makes me think of home and . . ."

This time Dottie leaned over and put her hand on his back. "It's okay," she said. "Thank you for showing us." We drove back to the camp in silence.

By the time we got there, the rest of our group had arrived at the camp, and we focused on setting up our gear for the evening. We also tried to sponge some of the dust and dirt off ourselves, using our helmets as tiny sinks.

That night after dinner and another sing-along with the soldiers, we sat on our bedrolls and sleeping bags next to the Cheyenne, listening to the sounds of battle that were all around us, seeing flashes in the sky. Right as we were settling in, one of the soldiers came over and handed us a bottle of wine to thank us "just for being here."

We dug the cork out with a knife, and I retrieved three coffee cups from the Cheyenne.

"You okay, Fiona?" Viv asked. She was sitting up, her legs tucked under her as she smoked a Chesterfield.

"Yeah," I said. "That kid today? Dick? That was tough. That poor guy."

"I've been thinking about him all day," Dottie said. "And I've been thinking about Joe, of course, and my brother, who's still somewhere in the Pacific. And the Eighty-Second. Too many guys to worry about."

"I know, poor Dick. Jesus," Viv said. "And I've been praying for our friends from Leicester too and, believe it or not, Harry Westwood."

"Oh?" Dottie said in a teasing voice.

"Yeah." Viv shrugged. "I think I might actually have a thing for him."

"Good," I said. "I think he's good for you."

"You haven't said much about saying good-bye to Peter, Fi," Viv said. "What are you going to do if you see him again?"

"If he survived Holland?" I said, thinking about the captain's words and feeling sick all over again. "I don't know. Don't get me wrong. I still love Danny with all my heart. But then the war happened, and he went missing, and here I am now, in this place, where I care about Peter too. And what do I do with that? What do I do if I see him again?"

"Here's what I think you should do, Fi," Viv said, sitting up and looking at me, her face serious. "Stop thinking so damn much. Stop trying to control what you can't. This life over here is a world all its own. None of us knows what the hell is going to happen in the next hour, never mind months from now. Focus on one day at a time. And if one of these days you happen to reunite with Peter? Simply enjoy that day for what it is."

We were all quiet for a moment as we sipped red wine, and I thought about Viv's words. The truth was that living for the moment had occurred to me too. It was impossible to plan for anything or anyone when your future could be shot out of the sky tomorrow.

"You're right," I said. "But you both know how much I like to plan."

"No, really? You?" Dottie and Viv almost said these things in unison, full of so much sarcasm that I kicked both of their feet across our bedrolls.

"All right, point taken." I sighed.

After we stopped talking and settled down to sleep, I stayed up for a long time watching the horrible, fascinating flashes of shell fire in the distance against the black sky. It was still hard to believe I was camping on a beach in France in the middle of the war.

I thought about my last days with Danny and kissing him on our checkered blanket on Bunker Hill. And I thought about the feel of Peter's lips on my forehead before he left for Holland. Viv was right: living in the midst of war was its own reality. And all of us that were living in it longed for intimacy and connection, however fleeting, because it reminded us of what mattered most.

Chapter Nineteen

September 25, 1944

After a fitful sleep, we woke up caked in more "Normandy dust," as the soldiers called it, and I was desperate to get to Cherbourg so we could take a real shower at the Red Cross Club Victoire.

We followed Liz's jeep in a convoy and made the thirty-mile trek to the newly liberated city. England had barely prepared us for the devastation of the battle-scarred Normandy countryside. And though Jimmy had tried to teach me well, my just passable driving skills were not quite up to the task of navigating the near-demolished roads.

There were enormous bomb craters everywhere. Sheep, cows, and horses lay dead, pushed off to the side of the road or in pastures. Hundreds of flies buzzed around them, and the stench made you cover your face as you passed. There were trees that had fallen in the road as well as others with sheared limbs dangling dangerously above us. We saw newly erected signs in English with notices such as "Mines Cleared to Hedges." One sprawling field was littered with the helmets of German soldiers that had been taken prisoner by the Allies.

The road was also congested with heavy traffic going in both directions. Allied army vehicles of every type, including large convoys like ours, shared the road with haggard French villagers that were finally returning to their homes, many of them with only a baby carriage or cart full of their possessions.

But amid all this devastation, there was also a feeling of goodwill and genuine happiness among the Allied soldiers and the French. Now that Paris was liberated and the D-Day invasion successful, it felt like everyone was exhaling for the first time since the war started. There was a palpable degree of hope in the air.

As we drove, our Clubmobiles were greeted with whistles and whoops from the hundreds of soldiers we passed. Some were walking, weighted down by their battle gear, their faces streaked with dirt under mud-crusted helmets. When they spotted us, they broke out into smiles and shouted familiar questions like, "What state are you girls from?"

French men, women, and children stood in front of their destroyed homes and still managed to smile and wave at us as they watched us go by. Some gave us the *V* for victory sign, and we heard yells of *"Vive la France!"*

One little dark-haired girl in a tattered pale-blue dress came running up to the Cheyenne to toss us a bouquet of pink roses. Hers would be the first of several baskets and bouquets of flowers we would receive along the way, and we decorated the Clubmobile with them inside and out.

Halfway to Cherbourg, we reached the town of Valognes, which was decimated to the point that it was no longer a town at all. There were gigantic heaps of rubble where buildings had once stood. Any structures that were still standing had been hollowed out, some stripped down to their frames, a phantom of what they used to be. A couple of buildings resembled oversized dollhouses, the facade blown off, but the broken stairs and shattered, furnished rooms inside fully visible.

"That was the longest thirty-mile drive I've ever taken," Viv said as we finally arrived outside the city of Cherbourg hours later. Liz was parked on the side of the road near the entrance to the city. She waved us down.

"Park here. I'll drive you to the club in the jeep like I did the other two groups," she said. "Some of the streets are too narrow to maneuver the big vehicles through."

Dottie had fallen asleep with her head against the door of the truck, Barbara softly snoring in her lap. Viv elbowed her awake.

"My arm aches from waving at people so much," Dottie said stretching, much to Barbara's annoyance. She put her hand to her head and added, "Oh, and my hair feels awful, so stiff, like it's plastered with dust."

"Uh, yeah, it is, and it looks disgusting," Viv said. "As does mine. But Fiona, I think yours might be the worst."

"Hey thanks, Viv," I said. "Pray the showers at the club are working."

The city of Cherbourg also had areas that were destroyed, though some streets had fared better than others. On the less damaged passageways there were beautiful, unscathed gray stone buildings with chocolate-brown storefront signs advertising various *pâtisseries, boulangeries*, and *boucheries*. I finally felt the first thrills of being in France, a place I had only dreamed about visiting. We had made it at last.

The enormous American flag in front of Club Victoire made it easy to spot. Liz dropped us at the door, and we were greeted by the club director, Marion Hill, and her staff. They were dressed in fresh uniforms and white shirts, which made me feel even worse about how grimy we were.

Marion led us into a large lounge where a number of soldiers and Red Cross personnel were having coffee, sodas, and cigarettes. The walls were freshly painted battleship gray and decorated with numerous army division emblems and American flags.

"*Holy cow!* Is that who I think it is under all that dirt?" Then I heard someone scream my name before we were tackled by Blanche, Martha, and Frankie. The six of us hugged and laughed, and Dottie and Martha shed some joyful tears. A few of the soldiers started clapping for us, enjoying our reunion scene.

"Viv, how's that manicure holding up now?" Frankie said, laughing.

Viv held up her short, polish-free, chipped fingernails and smirked. "You're hilarious, Frankie."

"Follow me, I'll show you where you'll be sleeping tonight as well as where the showers, toiletries, and towels are upstairs," the club director said. "No hot water, but at this point, I'm sure you just want to be clean. Oh, and I have some fresh white shirts you're welcome to have if they fit you."

We told our friends we'd be right back and went to scrub up, wash our hair, and feel human again.

When we emerged downstairs an hour later, Martha, Frankie, and Blanche applauded as we twirled around and showed them our newly clean selves. They had saved us some seats around a scratched-up wooden coffee table in the corner of the lounge.

"Okay, Liz is running around like a chicken with her head cut off; I see that hasn't changed," Blanche said, taking a cigarette from Viv. "She came and told us that she'll be back to talk to us about our first assignments in a little while. And then we'll take you to a café down the street we've been to a few times. There isn't much food available, but there's tons of wine and liquor, and, between the French and American soldiers, we've never had to pay for it. We're staying here tonight too—cold showers or not, it's a nice break after living like gypsies for the last two weeks."

"Girls, it is *crazy* over here," Frankie said, coming back from the little bar with a Coke. She took a sip and just paced back and forth in front of us. "Leicester was a picnic in the park compared to this. But it's thrilling to finally be right in the thick of the action . . ."

"It's also sometimes horrific and traumatizing—don't forget to mention that," Martha added, raising her eyebrows at Frankie.

"Really?" I said. "How's that been, getting used to it, I mean?"

Martha paused for a second before answering. Some of the fullness had gone out of her round face, probably from too many K ration meals.

"On my farm back in Iowa, we have to slaughter animals some-times, and it's absolutely awful. The first time I saw my father slaughter a pig? I was probably nine years old. I'll never forget it—the sounds, the smell. I cried all night long. I never got numb to the horror, but over time, I got used to it. I think that's what witnessing a war is like—what you see is still so terrible, but you soon realize it's part of life here and you have to deal with it."

"Martha's right," Blanche said. "We've seen some horrible stuff: soldiers wounded like you wouldn't believe, dead Germans, just . . ." She shuddered. "But you've *got* to get used to it, or you might as well go home, right? They don't need Red Cross girls that are blubbering messes, falling apart all the time. We'd be useless to them."

There was a pause in conversation as we all pondered this. Blanche put out her cigarette in the tin ashtray on the coffee table and said, "Enough grim talk. Who's in love? Got any scandals?"

"Martha's in love," Frankie said with a mischievous grin, taking a cigarette from Viv. She was still standing, tapping her foot and leaning against Dottie's chair. "He's an *undertaker* from Topeka, Kansas. Isn't that amazing?"

"Seriously?" I said, trying not to laugh. The color in Martha's cheeks grew deeper by the second.

"Oh, be quiet, Frankie," Martha said. "His name is Arthur. And yes, that is his job back home."

"He's a very nice undertaker," Blanche said, nodding, her expression serious, but then she covered her mouth and started giggling, waving her hand in front of her face. "I'm sorry, Martha, I know we tease you about him way too much."

"*Way* too much," said Martha, kicking her foot.

"We can't wait to meet him," Dottie said, trying to make Martha feel better.

"Any word about Danny, Fiona?" Frankie asked, sounding hopeful.

"Nothing since you left," I said, and all of my mixed feelings came bubbling up. "No mail from home at all since you left. No news from the IRC. Nothing."

I didn't want to dwell on it or get into anything else, so I said, "Viv, you have to tell them about running into Harry Westwood again."

"Where and when?" Blanche asked Viv. "Spill the beans, Viv. He is gorgeous. We want all the dirt."

"I saw him the night of the Glenn Miller concert a couple of weeks ago," Viv said. "Oh girls, I wish you had been there, because *that* was a pretty fantastic night."

Our three friends gasped at the mention of Glenn Miller. Blanche and Martha could not get their questions out fast enough as we proceeded to tell them all about the secret concert, including Dottie's big singing debut, which made Frankie spit out her Coke.

That led to the story about Joe Brandon professing his love for Dottie. And I could tell Viv was itching to say something about Peter Moretti. I was silently warning her not to with my eyes, when Liz walked into the lounge, files and clipboard in hand.

"Ladies, you're the last Clubmobile group I'm meeting with today," she said. "Are you ready to hear what's next?"

"Yes, please, Liz, let's get this show on the road. We want to go drink champagne," Blanche said.

Liz rolled her eyes, pulled up a chair to sit with us, and opened one of the file folders.

"Even with eight more Clubmobiles since yesterday, we still have a huge number of troops to cover, so I've mapped out a way to reach as many units as possible."

She showed us a map with pinpoints marking the different camps in this part of France as well as some lists of different groups that I couldn't read from where I was sitting.

"I'm splitting the Clubmobiles over here into groups of two and three," she said, pausing for dramatic effect before continuing. "I'm not sure Miss Chambers would approve of this decision, but the Uncle Sam and Cheyenne are going to be together moving forward."

The six of us caused a small scene, again, and soldiers and Red Cross workers looked over with curiosity as we all cheered at this news.

"So, good decision?" Liz said, clearly pleased with herself.

"*Such* a good decision," I said. "Thank you so much."

"Don't let me down, girls," she said, getting serious again. "You all are going to be out in the field with not much contact with me or any other Red Cross personnel. For that reason, you'll have an army liaison assigned to you at all times. He'll be your mother superior over here. He'll drive the supply truck, take you to the different camps, and help you navigate the often-insane routes. Of course, he'll also help keep you safe, get you out when you're too close to the action."

"Who is this liaison? Do we know him?" Frankie asked, looking skeptical.

"No, you'll meet him first thing in the morning," Liz said, distracted and shuffling through her files. "Finally, I'm going to designate Fiona as the captain of your group. She's great with keeping things organized and paying attention to the important details of life on the road. Are you all okay with that?"

My five friends nodded in agreement, and I looked around at all of them with gratitude.

"Told you she'd be the best," Viv said to Liz.

"Aw, thanks, Viv. And everyone," I said, feeling my face grow warm.

"Happy to be your second-in-command," Frankie said. "Only if you need one."

"Okay, *now* can we go have champagne?" Blanche said. "Liz, you're welcome to come with us."

"Now you may go. I'll go over the rest of the details in the morning when we meet down here at six a.m.," Liz said. "I'm finally going to shower myself. Maybe I'll join you for a glass later."

❧

Our friends took us to a café next to Cherbourg's city hall that had some minor shell damage, but by some miracle it had been spared the devastation of some of the surrounding buildings. The owner, a slight gray-haired man in his sixties wearing a black apron, had done his best to clean up the rubble on the street outside to make room for the café's rickety wooden tables and chairs. He pushed a couple of them together for us, threw a few ashtrays on them, and made a gesture for us to sit.

"Filles américaines," a French soldier sitting at the table across from the front door called over to us as he nodded. *"Bonsoir.* You like champagne?"

"Blanche wasn't wrong," Frankie said. "It happens every time we come here."

"Non, merci," Martha said, giving the man a shy smile and waving her hand, signaling no thank you.

"The trick is to refuse once or twice, and then they will *insist,*" Blanche whispered to us.

Just then the old man came back with a younger woman wearing a simple floral dress, her hair tied with a red bow. She had a tray of six glasses, and he had two bottles of uncorked champagne. We looked over at the table of the French soldiers as the two employees served us, but they shrugged.

"Pas nous," the one who had offered champagne said, raising his hands, making it clear it wasn't them.

The young woman pointed behind us, to the table farthest away, on the corner of the street. The four American officers sitting there raised their glasses to us and smiled.

"Vive la France!" one of them said, and the whole café shouted, *"Vive la France!"* in return.

"Does anyone know any of those officers?" I asked.

"Never seen them," Blanche said as Viv lit her cigarette. "But that one with the mustache is a looker. I'd consider burning toast for him in the morning."

"So, Martha's in love with the undertaker," I said.

"His name is Arthur, Fi," Dottie said, kicking me.

"Yes, sorry, Martha," I said. "But what about you, Blanche? Frankie? No romantic interests?"

"No, nobody that's really caught my eye. Well, except for Mustache over there," Blanche said. "You know what it's like. So many of these fellas are so damn young, and some of the officers are charming, but it's not like there's much time for real dates, and certainly no privacy for . . . well . . . *anything*, not even a kiss."

"And I'm not interested," Frankie said, taking a sip of champagne. "Too much to do over here. Besides, I had one love of my life—no one else could come close. I'm sure you understand that, Fiona."

"Um . . . yeah. Of course," I said, my face growing warm, that uneasy feeling in my stomach. What was wrong with me that I had been able to let someone else into my heart? I saw Dottie and Viv watching my reaction.

"Are you enjoying the champagne?" The mustached officer was standing next to our table. He was very handsome with thick dark hair, gray-green eyes, and prominent cheekbones.

"We are, sugar, thank you," Blanche said. The officer put his hands to his heart.

"Do I detect a New Orleans accent?" he said.

"Yes, you do," Blanche said, clearly pleased. "Where are you from?"

"I'm from Portland, Maine," he said.

"Oh," Blanche said, frowning.

"But I love New Orleans," he said. "My friends and I just wanted to send over the bottles as a thank-you to you girls for doing what you do over here."

"Well, you don't have to go anywhere yet. Why don't you pull up a chair?" Blanche said. "What's your name?"

"I'm Captain Guy Sherry." He grabbed a chair and pulled it up next to her. As Blanche was doing the introductions, I watched two GIs come down the street toward the café. One was shorter and stocky, the other lanky, and they both looked pretty beat up—the stocky one had a large white bandage on his forehead, and the other was walking with a small limp.

"Patrick Halloran!?" I said, jumping up and running over to give the limping GI a hug. "And Eddie Landon, is that you under that bandage? My God, it's good to see you boys. I cannot believe it." Dottie and Viv ran over to greet them too, and we stood in front of the café, hugging and laughing.

"Where's the rest of the Eighty-Second?" I asked.

"The operation didn't go well. We lost some guys," Patrick said, looking away from us, focusing on something only he could see. "Some are in France. Eddie and I were injured, so we ended up on a Red Cross boat, and they brought us to a tent hospital here. We've got to catch up to them. We volunteered to drive a supply truck on the Red Ball Express, so we'll get there fast."

He paused for a moment.

"Fiona," he said, looking at me, his big eyes full of sadness as he searched for words. I felt like I might be sick. "Tommy . . . Tommy didn't make it."

"Oh no, Patrick. *No*," I said, putting my hand up to my mouth.

The address I had for his mom was packed away. That night, I would stay up and write the letter I had hoped I would never have to send. I bit my lip so I wouldn't burst into tears. Dottie was already welling up; Viv was trying to hold it in like me.

I wrapped Patrick in a tight hug. He sobbed into my shoulder, trying to hide his emotions so nobody in the café would notice.

I felt a tap on my back, and the old man who owned the café handed me a small shot glass of Cognac and pointed to Patrick with a sympathetic smile. I pulled out of our embrace and handed the drink to Patrick, shielding him from the rest of the café while he composed himself and took the shot.

"I'm going to pull over another little table," Viv declared, kissing Patrick and Eddie on the cheeks and grabbing Patrick by the elbow. "Let's make this a reunion party, boys; I think you need it."

The American officers had also moved to a table closer to us, and soon the air did start to feel festive. We shared stories and tried to keep the conversation light as the sun went down and the café owners put candles on all the tables. The boys told us that our other friends, our doughnut helpers from Leicester, were all okay, and they couldn't wait to tell Nelson that Barbara the dog had made it to France.

"Is Captain Moretti in France too?" I almost jumped when Viv asked the question. She glanced at me and mouthed, "You're welcome." I had been trying to get up the nerve, but I was terrified of the answer. Patrick paused and took a sip of his Cognac. The owner had been spoiling him and Eddie with unlimited drinks and small plates of food—fried potatoes and cold beets and olives.

Please be okay. Please be okay. I couldn't breathe while I waited for his answer. His Purple Heart was in my pocket as we spoke.

"Of course," Patrick said in a matter-of-fact tone. I exhaled and looked away so they wouldn't see my tears of relief shining in the candlelight.

"I know some GIs hate their officers, but Captain Moretti?" Patrick shook his head. "Nobody feels that way. He's the type of soldier that everyone wants to *be*. Never loses his cool under pressure. Never screams like some of the other officers. So brave every goddamn time."

"Yeah, but as I've said before, cowards don't become nationally ranked boxers," said Eddie.

"When you see him, please tell him I said hello," I said. "And that I'm glad he's okay."

"Of course," Patrick said, giving me a knowing look. "I'm pretty sure he'll be happy to know *you're* over here."

"Can you squeeze in another seat?" Liz was standing next to the table, and it took her a second to recognize the boys from the Eighty-Second as they both leaped from their seats and gave her a hug.

"I see you've met Captain Guy Sherry," Liz said. She squeezed in between Frankie and Dottie, and the little old man appeared out of nowhere and handed her a glass. "Or at least *Blanche* has met Captain Guy Sherry."

"Who is he?" I asked, frowning.

"He happens to be the liaison I told you about this morning," she said. At some point, Blanche and the captain had moved to a table away from the crowd, up against the café's facade. Their faces were almost touching as he whispered into her ear, his hand grazing hers on the table. They were sharing a cigarette.

"Wait—*he's* going to be traveling with us?" Martha said, eyes wide.

"Yes, he is," Liz said, laughing a little. "To be fair, he has no idea what Clubmobile group he's been assigned to."

We all looked around at each other, amused and unsure of what to do next.

"Who's going to tell Blanche?" Viv asked.

"She'll find out soon enough," Frankie said, rubbing her hands together. "This is fantastic—Blanche is the star of her own scandal. We're going to need more champagne."

Chapter Twenty

September 26, 1944

Dear Mrs. Doyle,

I'm struggling to find words to convey how sorry I am for the loss of your son, Tommy. My name is Fiona Denning, and I'm a Red Cross Clubmobile girl from Boston, currently stationed in Europe. Your son became a dear friend of mine here; we met while he was stationed in England. I loved Tommy like a little brother, as did my friends Viv and Dottie.

Tommy often helped us make doughnuts and coffee for his fellow soldiers. He always said how proud you would be that he finally learned how to cook something. He often bragged about your cooking and talked about how much he loved and missed his family in Southie.

Tommy was an amazing young man, and to know him was to love him. Life here can be so hard, but he was always able to cheer people up, to get them to smile or laugh for a little while, no matter the circumstances.

And he was always looking out for his friends. You must know he had so many friends here who loved him dearly and mourn his loss. His best friends, Patrick

Halloran and Eddie Landon, are planning on visiting you when this horrible war is over. We all want you to know how much Tommy meant to everyone over here.

I will miss his deep belly laugh and his proud Boston accent. I will miss dancing the jitterbug with him in muddy fields in the British countryside and drinking coffee and talking to him about the Red Sox and all of the things we loved about our hometown. I will miss my dear friend so much.

Again, I am so incredibly sorry for your loss, Mrs. Doyle. I just hope that this letter offers you a little solace knowing that your beautiful son had such a positive impact on those around him here, and that he was loved and adored by many.

Warmest regards,

Fiona

I had woken up at five and rewritten the letter for the tenth time before putting it in the addressed envelope and sealing it so I wouldn't have the opportunity to rewrite it again.

What do you say to a mother who has just lost her son? No matter how I rearranged the words, they would never be good or meaningful enough. The draft sealed in the envelope was the best I could do. I hoped it offered her a small amount of comfort.

At six, we all met downstairs to wait in front of Club Victoire with our musettes. We hadn't even told Blanche about the captain before we left the café; we had just dragged her out of there at eleven so that she wouldn't do anything she'd regret, and so that the rest of us wouldn't be completely exhausted in the morning.

The six of us stood in front of the club, still yawning and rubbing our eyes as two jeeps came around the corner and pulled up. Liz was driving the first one, Captain Sherry the second.

"Good morning," Liz said, a huge smile on her face. "I think you've all met Captain Sherry. He's going to be your liaison for the next eight weeks."

"Yes, good morning, we, uh . . . met briefly last night," Captain Sherry said, his feelings of awkwardness about the situation apparent. His face was several shades of scarlet, and he could not even look in Blanche's direction. "And no need to be formal. Please call me Guy, or Captain Guy, or whatever you like."

We said our hellos, and Blanche's jaw dropped open as she absorbed the news. Her blonde curls were disheveled, and she turned a shade of green, either from too much champagne or the shock of discovering her flirtation from the night before was going to be our new constant traveling companion. Frankie was so entertained by the whole situation that I elbowed her to tone it down a little. "Who's riding with me?" Liz asked.

"Me," Blanche said, raising her hand, throwing her gear in the back and jumping into the front seat of Liz's jeep before anyone else had moved. Viv and I joined her.

As soon as we pulled far enough away that we were out of earshot, Blanche burst out, "For Christ's sake, why didn't anyone tell me this *last night*? This is mortifying. Did all of you know?" She hung her head in her hands.

"I told them when I got there," Liz said, trying not to smile.

"Why didn't you tell *me* when you got there?" Blanche said.

"After that much champagne, would it have done any good?" Viv asked her. "Honestly?"

Blanche gave Viv a look, then she eyed me. Her face had gone from green to flaming red, and she buried her face in her hands again. She started to shake like she was sobbing, and Liz and Viv looked at me, eyes wide, not sure what to do. But then Blanche raised her head, and we could see that she was laughing so hard she was crying. And then we all started roaring too, relieved that she had taken it so well.

"I mean, I'm still embarrassed, but you have to admit, it's pretty hilarious," Blanche said. "What are the odds? I haven't flirted like that with anyone since London, and then to find out 'Captain Guy whatever' is coming *with us*? Are you joking? You can't even make it up."

"I'm so glad you aren't crying," I said, still laughing.

"Phew, thank God I was a good Catholic girl," Blanche said. "One more glass of champagne and I might not have been. *That* would have been a reason to cry."

"*That's* why we dragged you out of there," I said.

"Are you going to talk to him about it?" Viv asked.

"I don't really have a choice, do I?" she said. "We're going to be stuck with him; I'll have to."

"I'm sure if you make light of it, it'll be fine. I already talked to Captain Sherry about keeping things proper," Liz said. She paused before adding, "Please tell me it was nothing more than just a night of flirting."

"Ha! No, honestly, that's all it was," Blanche said, a little too forcefully. "Don't get me wrong; he's handsome as hell. A total ringer for Clark Gable. But I never thought I'd see him again."

"Uh-huh," Viv said, elbowing me in the back seat, clearly unconvinced.

"Oh, be quiet, Viv," Blanche said, annoyed but laughing again.

When we arrived at our Clubmobiles outside the city center, Blanche darted into the Uncle Sam without even looking Captain Guy's way. Martha, Frankie, and Dottie, who was carrying Barbara in her helmet again, climbed out of his jeep, trying not to giggle too much.

"All right, Captain, you've got the itinerary. As I said, Fiona will be your right-hand woman as head of this crew," Liz said. "I'm going to be trying to check in with different groups throughout the journey. But if I don't get to you, I'll see you in Paris in early December."

"Sounds good," Captain Guy said. "Fiona, I'm sure you'll help me make peace with the group." He gave me a pleading look with his eyes.

Blanche wasn't wrong about him being a Clark Gable look-alike. He had probably already broken more than a few hearts in the war.

"I'll do my best," I said. "Liz, why Paris in December?" I couldn't believe we would actually get to see Paris.

"We'll be reuniting there with all of the Clubmobiles that came over together," Liz said. "There'll be a new plan from there."

All of us said our good-byes, and the Cheyenne and Uncle Sam followed Captain Guy's supply truck to set off on the road.

~

Planes flew over, tanks roared past us, and soldiers whistled and waved as we once again navigated the crowded, debris-strewn roads. We saw more utter devastation, rotting animals and blown-out villages with mountains of rubble that made you catch your breath and wonder how they would ever rebuild.

But there were hopeful signs too, signs of life returning, and of France's resilience. Gnarled old men wearing sabots walked down the sides of the road, seemingly complaining to one another and shouting flirtatious things to us in French when we passed by.

We drove by a cottage, and although its roof had been nearly shelled off, it had freshly painted pale-yellow shutters and pink geraniums in its window boxes. A tiny boy in a checkered smock tumbled out the front door and yelled *bonjour* to us.

At one point, I had to maneuver around a group of young nuns in full habits, laughing as they rode bicycles in a way that managed to look both dignified and silly.

We finally arrived at our first campsite in the middle of the countryside on the outskirts of a tiny village. There we encountered a group of combat engineers that had never even seen a Clubmobile before. They had just arrived there the day before, and you would have thought we were the Andrews Sisters the way the men cheered as we drove up. They rolled out the red carpet, setting up our two pyramid-style tents under some apple trees a little apart from the main camp so we'd have some privacy. They even dug us our latrine.

"All right, ladies, this will be our base for the next few weeks," Captain Guy said after our living quarters were nearly set up. "Every day you'll be split up and will drive out to serve some of the remotely stationed ack-ack, infantry, tank, and artillery units in the area."

"Captain, these soldiers have been so kind in helping us get settled, I thought we'd start making doughnuts and coffee right away if that's all right with you," I said. All the girls seemed in agreement, except for Viv, who looked at me like she would have preferred a nap.

"Of course," he said. "Before you do, though . . . uh, Blanche, could I have a word, alone?"

Blanche turned a deep pink and nodded, and the two of them walked away to talk under the apple trees.

We all gave each other looks and tried not to giggle too much as we headed over to the Clubmobiles. A GI named Monty volunteered to help set up the generators.

"Hey, I'm from Portsmouth, New Hampshire," he said. He noticed the *Beantown Girls* painted on the Cheyenne and nodded to it. "You're from Boston?"

"We are," I said. "You a Red Sox fan?"

"Oh yeah," he said. "Too many Yankee fans around here. I really can't believe you girls came all the way out here for us."

"How long you been here, soldier?"

"D plus 116," he said. "Who's this?" Monty pointed to Barbara, who was sleeping in the helmet on the counter next to the Life Savers and Lucky Strikes.

"Oh, that's Barbara. We're taking care of her for her owner in the Eighty-Second Airborne," Dottie said. "Want to hold her?"

"Barbara the dog." Monty laughed as he picked her up. "Great name."

After we had the doughnut machines going and the coffee brewed, we let Monty pick out the first record for the record player. The actual Andrews Sisters started playing over our speakers but softly, per the commanding officer's request. A couple of nearby GIs were shaving in front of tiny mirrors, using their helmets as sinks, but they immediately dropped their razors and came running over, smiling at the sound of music. Others followed from all over the camp, leaving whatever they were doing behind to listen to the sounds of home. We had long lines in front of both Clubmobiles until the end of the day, and though we were exhausted, the gratitude from the men made it all worthwhile.

Monty sat with us under the apple trees in the afternoon sun, telling us all about his plans to marry his high school sweetheart when he got home.

"Thelma's waiting for me to come back," he said, sipping coffee. "Such a great gal; you'd love her. We want to move to Boston or a bigger city; New Hampshire's kind of a snore."

We heard some noises in the field about a couple hundred yards beyond the apple orchard, and Monty stood up. He dropped his coffee cup on the ground, and his whole demeanor changed.

I caught sight of some children playing in the field.

"Nothing to worry about," I said. "Just a couple kids."

"No. They shouldn't be over there. It hasn't been cleared. It hasn't been swept yet." Monty dropped his doughnut on the ground. "Why don't they know that? There might be mines; they could get killed." He ran to the field.

"Hey, hey!" Monty yelled, waving frantically at the children as he approached them. "Danger! Run away! Danger!"

The first mine went off, the blast so loud it shook the ground underneath us. In that instant, I saw Monty grab one of the kids and throw him as a second mine exploded. The boy Monty had thrown was badly injured and started shrieking, the lower part of his right leg shredded. In one horrible moment, Monty was there and then he was gone. Through the ringing in my ears, I heard people around me start screaming too, and soldiers came from all directions trying to save Monty and the injured children.

I looked down at Monty's coffee cup and half-eaten doughnut on the ground, ran behind the Clubmobile, and threw up. Then I wiped my face and rushed over to see how I could help. Martha had already commandeered a jeep, and Frankie was carrying a little girl with long black hair. I went into the Clubmobile and grabbed a bunch of clean rags to help Frankie wrap the little girl's arm. A soldier was carrying the little boy with the injured leg, which was now in a tight tourniquet. There was a third boy with white-blond hair who was not hurt but still in shock. Blanche had taken a blanket and wrapped it around him.

A group that included Frankie and Martha sped off to bring the children to a nearby field hospital. Captain Guy, who spoke French, walked over to the village to find the children's parents.

Several soldiers surrounded Monty's body. He wouldn't be going to the hospital. I felt like I might be sick again. His girlfriend, Thelma, would get the news that nobody ever wanted.

"Uh, Fiona?" Blanche called to me, as she sat next to the blond boy. I looked up, and she pointed to Dottie, who was sitting on the ground, her arms wrapped around her knees. "It happened to Martha too, the first time we . . . the first time something like this happened."

"Dottie?" I said. Dottie was staring into space, her teeth chattering, her skin ashen. I called for Viv to bring me a blanket.

"Honey." I patted her face. "Let's get you some coffee; you've had a shock, we all have. For the sake of the soldiers here, we've got to pull it together. Remember we're no use to them if we don't." I echoed Peter's words to me before he left.

"He was just here," Dottie said in a whisper. "Jesus Christ, he was *just here* with us. And those poor children."

"The kids are going to be okay," I said. "Monty saved them. He saved their lives."

I gave her a hug as Viv came over with a blanket and handed her Barbara, who instinctively snuggled into her arms. Viv sat down next to us and lit a Lucky Strike, and I noticed her hands were shaking uncontrollably.

"We've got to stay strong," I said. "That really dark place in your mind? Don't go there, Dottie. That's one thing I learned when Danny first went missing. If you go there, you might not come back."

Dottie took some deep breaths, and we sat there in silence for a time. I looked over, and Blanche had her arm around the little boy, who was still crying and nibbling on a doughnut.

A group of five soldiers had wrapped Monty's body up. Their faces were dirty, their expressions resigned; some of them had his blood on their uniforms.

"I keep thinking about how he ran toward danger like that to save those kids," Dottie said as we watched them walk away. The color had returned to her cheeks. "He didn't even think. He just went. How the hell does someone become that brave?"

"I don't know," I said. "I think being here brings out strengths in people they never knew they had."

Chapter Twenty-One

December 1, 1944

I heard the sounds of mess kits rattling and a rooster crowing in the distance before I opened my eyes. Someone had already made coffee. It was a little before seven on a chilly December morning, and we were on a farm near a village twenty miles outside of Paris.

For eight weeks, we had traveled like nomads from camp to camp, serving grateful soldiers mountains of doughnuts and rivers of coffee as we camped all over the French countryside, in barns or bomb-damaged châteaus, but most of the time in our tents.

Planes continued to roar overhead, and tanks often barreled past us. More than once we had been forced to move because of nearby shelling. Every night, the sky was filled with the flashes of battle.

We had worked in the mud and the rain as temperatures got colder by the day. And the Cheyenne had gotten stuck in the muck on the roads at least once a week. Mercifully, there had been no accidents as horrific as our first day, but we had visited a few of the field hospitals and seen the injuries that these men endured. There were men with missing limbs, men who were blind, men on crutches and in wheelchairs, to say nothing of the psychological impact that you couldn't see at all.

We would be packing up and heading to Paris in the afternoon, staying in beds for the first time in forever, and I could hardly wait to take a real shower. Having to wash my hair using a water-filled helmet was something I would never really get used to.

In the dim light of the tent, I could see Dottie still asleep and was surprised to find Viv already up and out. I put my long johns on under my uniform, threw on a sweater and my field jacket, and peeked out of the tent. Viv was standing in front of the Clubmobile with her pad, sketching a young GI's portrait with her charcoal pencils. He was leaning against the Cheyenne with a nervous smile on his face. Our Clubmobile exterior now included the painted emblems of all the outfits we had visited. The Seventh Armored Division. The Eighty-Third Infantry Division. The Fifth Infantry. And the Eighty-Second and Twenty-Eighth, of course.

"You're up early," I said to Viv.

"I know, but I promised Ronald here that I'd sketch his portrait before we left for Paris," she said. Ronald nodded to me.

"Don't move, Ronny, I'm almost done," she said. "There's coffee in the truck, Fi. After you get some, I've got some gossip to go with it."

I quickly fixed myself a cup and sat down next to Viv. She handed Ronald his portrait.

"Thank you. My mom is going to love this," he said, giving her a huge smile before he headed off.

"Okay, spill it," I said.

"Guess," she said.

"Oh no, you can't do that. What is it?"

"Let's just say you won't be shocked."

"Blanche and the captain?"

Viv smiled, and I knew I was right.

"Yup," she said. "I was up extra early, too excited about Paris to sleep, which as you know never happens to me. I got up to make coffee, and that's when I spotted her sneaking out of his *tent*."

"Are you joking?" I said, nearly spitting out my coffee.

"No!" Viv said, laughing. "He's got to head back to London today."

"I say it's about damn time. Honestly, the way they've been pretending since Cherbourg?"

Blanche and Captain Guy had shared a laugh about their flirtation at the café in Cherbourg on our first day on the road, so there hadn't been any awkwardness between them. However, since then, it had become clear that they had real feelings for each other. The signs were obvious, like when we were all sitting around a fire with some of the guys, and you'd catch them gazing at each other, or during one of Dottie's evening concerts when the captain always ended up sitting next to Blanche.

"Are you going to tell her you saw?"

"Of course I am," Viv said with a wink.

"Did you ever hear from Harry Westwood?" I said. "Can he see you in Paris?"

"I sent that note a while ago, but haven't heard a thing back from him, damn mail here," Viv said.

"Tell me about it," I said. "Nothing from home, nothing from Peter about . . . anything."

"Do you regret not getting in touch with him, telling him we'll be in Paris for a couple days?" Viv asked after a moment. "You know, in case he could see you there?"

I paused before answering the question. I could feel the Purple Heart in the bottom of my pants pocket.

"*Yes*. No. I don't know, Viv. I guess. But then just the thought of seeing him stirs up so many emotions about Danny. It's probably better to just let things be . . ."

Viv opened her mouth to argue my point, but I started walking to the tent before she could. I wasn't in the mood.

"At least Dottie knows she's going to see Joe," I said over my shoulder. "I'm going to go get packed up. I can't wait for a couple days of civilization."

~

Dear Deidre, Darcy, and Niamh (and Mum and Dad!),

Hello, my dear family. We've been on the road in France for eight weeks, and I was beginning to think you all had forgotten me. But when we arrived in Paris (yes, Paris!) yesterday afternoon, I received a bundle of mail and packages, and it's like Christmas came early. That tends to happen with the mail here—nothing for weeks, and then it all catches up to us in a deluge.

Thank you so much for the care packages. It's getting colder, and I love the red wool scarf and mittens. I'm so glad you got my note about the fur-lined boots—they fit perfectly.

For two nights, we're staying at the Hôtel Normandy, which the Red Cross has turned into a women officers' club. I have my own wonderful room with a real bed, a bath, HOT water, and steam heat. You don't realize how much you miss the amenities of modern life until you don't have them. We've been living on the road like GIs and looking like GIs as a result—even Viv! It's nice to feel like a girl again, even if just for a little while.

Yesterday when we arrived, we borrowed a Red Cross jeep to tour the city. We drove around the place de la Concorde and down the Champs-Élysées and loved every minute. Despite the fact that it's still recovering from the Nazi occupation, Paris is breathtaking in all the ways that people describe. French flags fly everywhere, and the stores have beautiful red, white, and blue displays in their windows. The people are so happy, and so lovely to Americans. Parisian women are incredibly stylish; their

229

hairdos are very high, as are their wedged shoes, and they wear their purses on long straps.

 We spent today relaxing, having tea in the Tuileries Garden and exploring the city like true tourists. I haven't had anywhere to spend my money on the road, so I splurged on French perfume and a new dress. Tonight, we're going to a nightclub that's popular among the Americans here. Since we arrived in the city, we've already run into lots of our officer and GI friends from the road. We've also reunited with the other Clubmobile girls and shared our stories. It's been a nice hiatus from our work-days in the field.

 No more news about Danny from anyone's sources. Maybe you've heard from the Barkers?

I didn't know what to write next. I still thought of Danny daily; the grief of his absence had been a part of my life for over a year. But I couldn't deny that I missed and worried about Peter too, even if ours was just a war-time friendship. And what Viv had said had proved to be so true: being in the midst of this war was a world all its own.

I was so tired at the end of most days, I didn't even have time to grasp the devastation, the tales of horror coming from the front, the weight of what all this meant. Sometimes I imagined myself as a grand-mother, looking back on this time, studying old photos and thinking about it all with the gravity that it deserved. And then I would start to wonder if I would ever become a grandmother and who would be by my side if I did.

"Fiona! Fiona!" Frankie knocked loudly on my hotel room door. "Our ride to the club is here. Are you ready?"

"Yes, one minute."

I got up from the bed, smoothed out my new dress, and stood in front of the mirror. The dress was a silvery gray wrapped number with a draping scoop neckline and a flowy skirt. That afternoon, Viv and I had decided we were completely sick of the only dresses we had brought with us from home, so after asking a lovely Frenchwoman who spoke English, we discovered a boutique with reasonably priced dresses in Paris's Latin Quarter. It was more dramatic than my usual taste, but the boutique owner convinced me I was meant to have it.

I took a quick glance at myself in the mirror and swiped on some deep-red lipstick. I had twisted my hair up in front with a pretty new silvery purple dragonfly comb I had purchased, but the rest was down, and I had done my best to roll it so that it fell in waves.

I grabbed the black shawl I had borrowed from Viv and opened the door to see Frankie standing there smiling. She looked adorable, her dark curls bouncing, wearing a black dress that she had borrowed from ChiChi of the Dixie Queen, who was the same petite size.

"Oh, Fiona, you look absolutely stunning," Frankie said, giving me a hug just because.

"Thank you, and so do you," I said, taking another look and smoothing out the dress, a bit self-consciously. "You really think it's okay?"

"It's better than okay, it's gorgeous. Come on, you know it is," she said, grabbing my hand. "Let's go. Viv, Blanche, and Martha are waiting downstairs."

We walked into the hotel lobby, and I spotted Viv standing with Harry Westwood. He had obviously received her letter. They were standing next to the hotel entrance, leaning on a settee, and I was once again struck by how they looked like Hollywood come to life. Viv was wearing her new emerald-green V-neck dress with a narrow waist and flattering beaded peplum detail that tied in the back. Her auburn waves were styled in victory curls under a new black beret with a peacock feather in it. Harry Westwood was in his RAF dress uniform that emphasized his long, lean frame. Other guests in the lobby did a double take, and a few whispered to each other as they passed by.

Blanche and Martha were sitting at the bar opposite them, looking refreshed and beautiful themselves as they sipped red wine.

"Is Dots meeting us there?" Blanche asked, and I nodded. Dottie had spent the afternoon exploring the city with Joe and was meeting us at the club.

"Ladies." Harry swooped over when we arrived and kissed Frankie and me each on both cheeks. "Our chariots await."

"Wait, what chariots?" I said. "I thought we were getting picked up by a Red Cross truck?"

"Oh no, I made other plans," he said, grabbing Viv's hand as he led us all outside. There were two horse-drawn taxicabs.

"They have wool blankets in the back to keep you warm," Harry said. "It's a lovely way to see Paris. Viv and I are going to take the long way to the club; we will see you all there."

He had taken off his jacket and put it around Viv's shoulders. I watched her as she looked up at him, and her expression was one of unguarded joy. Viv, always a cynic about love, was falling for the dashing Englishman.

"Have fun, lovebirds." Blanche waved to them as they pulled away from the hotel.

The driver held our hands as we climbed into the carriage and settled in under a pile of wool blankets.

"Speaking of lovebirds," I said, looking at Blanche.

"Yeah, yeah," Blanche said, giving me an exaggerated scowl. "The worst-kept secret in France."

"So, you figured it out?" Martha said, giggling.

"Yeah, Blanche, and I think most of the GIs knew too; I heard them talking about it," Frankie said, biting her lip.

"Viv told me," I said. "But honestly? It wasn't a shock. And Viv, Dottie, and I all agreed, Captain Guy proved himself on the road; he's a good man. How'd you leave it with him?"

"I left it like nearly everyone does over here, I guess," Blanche said with a sigh. "We'll do our best to keep in touch, meet up in Paris or London or somewhere if we can ever take a leave. It stinks we're in the most romantic city in the world and he's not here, but that's life in the ETO."

"We'll find dance partners in no time, Blanche," Martha said. "Let's have a fun night. We deserve it after working nonstop for so long. *I* deserve it."

"You didn't even tell Fi about Arthur," Frankie said to Martha. "Speaking of *secrets*."

"Listen to this," Martha said, sitting up and slapping my knee, an angry scowl on her sweet face. She was wearing a new red flared shirtwaist dress, and her cheeks were rosy from the cold. "Blanche and I were sitting at a café this afternoon, and these soldiers at the next table started talking to us. Turns out one of them is from Topeka. So, of course, I ask if he knows Arthur Reed the undertaker."

"Yes, and did he know him?"

"He said, 'Yeah, yeah, I know him,'" Martha said, getting more animated. "And then he adds, 'My older sister plays bridge with his *wife*.'"

"What!?" I said, holding my hand to my mouth. "Oh no . . ."

"Oh *yes*," she said. "I was careful to make sure it was the same Arthur. But seriously, how many undertakers named Arthur could there be in Topeka anyway? It was him."

"I'm really sorry," I said.

"Aw thanks," she said. "I thought I would be totally heartbroken, and I am a little, but mostly I'm just furious. For me and his wife. What a wolf."

"And as I've said all along to her, you can do much better than an undertaker from Topeka," Blanche said with a nod, putting her arm around Martha.

"Yeah, you did," Martha said, leaning into her.

"I'm just going to miss teasing you about him, though," Frankie said, and Martha kicked her.

"Martha, you are beautiful and smart, and the best damn truck driver I've ever met," I said. "Did you really want to end up with a guy that deals with dead bodies for a living?"

"Honestly," Blanche said, eyebrows raised.

Martha started to laugh. "All right, girls, you made your point. Now I'm *really* ready for some dancing."

We pulled up to the club in the carriage, and we could hear the sounds of the swing band inside. Despite the chill in the air, people had spilled out onto the streets—Allied soldiers, Frenchwomen, and Red Cross personnel, all socializing, in no hurry to go inside. We made our way through the crowd into the club, ducking through a small black wooden door that revealed a much larger space than I'd expected. There was an elevated stage with a dance floor in front and tables and chairs all around the perimeter, reminiscent of the Paramount in London.

Dottie came running up to me as soon as we walked in.

"Did you see the band?" she asked me, pulling my arm. "Look—it's an *all-girl* orchestra. They're Americans, and they've been touring with the USO. Isn't that amazing? They're called the Starlettes. The leader's name is Joy Sanders, and she's fabulous."

I looked up, and sure enough the entire orchestra was composed of women in smart navy-blue suits, sounding as good as any orchestra I'd ever heard, except for maybe Glenn Miller's.

"Wow, they're so good," I said.

"Joe was telling me there's a few of them that have started around the country since the war," Dottie said. "He brought me here early to meet them, and I sang and played with them."

Joe came over then, gave me a hug hello, and grabbed Dottie's hand. "Dottie, they're asking if you want to sing tonight," he said.

"I think I do. I'll meet you backstage; let me go have a drink with the girls first," she said, kissing him on the cheek.

I was so happy for Dottie and Viv. But to see them both falling in love made me feel lonelier than I'd felt in a long time, even though I was surrounded by friends.

Blanche waved us over to a table she had found with Martha and Frankie, and they had somehow already wrangled a waiter to bring us drinks. Viv came over to join us too.

"Where's Harry?" I asked. "I want to thank him for the carriage ride."

"He's saying hello to some 'chaps' of his," Viv said.

"A toast, dear girls," Blanche said after the waiter had handed us our drinks. "To us and to Paris."

"To us and to Paris."

As the six of us clinked our glasses, a woman at a nearby table tapped Viv on the shoulder.

"Excuse me, but I have to ask, are you with Harold Westwood?" She spoke with a British accent and pointed across the club to Harry. The woman had sleek, jet-black hair and was sitting with two other young women. Frankie was eyeing them like she was ready for a fight if necessary.

"Yes, I suppose I am," Viv said, amused at the question. "Why do you ask?"

"And you're an *American*," the woman said, with a catty smile. "Fascinating."

"Why is it so fascinating?" I asked.

"We were wondering who you were, given that you're with one of the most eligible bachelors in England. I don't think his family will be happy to hear he's spending time with an American girl."

"I'm sorry, I don't know what you're talking about," Viv said, sitting up and frowning at them now.

"That's *Lord* Harold Westwood," the woman said. "He's a baron. His family is one of the wealthiest families in England."

"What?" I said, as I started to laugh. "You're kidding."

"No, I am definitely not kidding," the woman said, sounding haughtier by the minute. "I'd be careful if I were you; the British upper class can be *vicious* to outsiders."

"Thanks for the tip, but I'll be fine," Viv said, her voice cold as she turned her back on them, her cheeks a deep red.

Princess Viv was seeing a British aristocrat. Of course she was.

I gave her a sidelong glance. "You didn't know?" I said.

"No," she said. "I'm wondering if they have the right Harry Westwood; he's never said a word."

"Viviana Occhipinti, you just made my night," Blanche said, passing her a cigarette. "This might be the best gossip we've had in the war."

"I agree, but what are you going to do?" Frankie said.

"Calm down, girls," Viv said, scanning the crowd for Harry now. "I don't even know if it's true."

"Yeah, but they wouldn't really have a reason to lie about something like that," Martha said. "I mean—"

"Hey, Fiona," Dottie said, interrupting her. She was looking behind me at the entrance. She pointed, so I turned to look.

A group of officers had just walked in. My gaze drifted to the tall, broad one standing in the middle. The one with the thick, dark hair and the smile I would know anywhere. *Peter.* I gasped and stood up as my cheeks grew warm and I felt butterflies in my stomach at the sight of him.

He had already spotted me and just mouthed a hello, raising his hand to wave.

"What? How did . . . wait." I whipped around to look at my friends, and they were all smiling.

"Viv and I wrote him a letter," Dottie said. She patted my hand.

"What are you waiting for? Go see him. Remember, have fun and don't overthink it." Viv gave me a shove.

I made my way over, through the crowds and tables and chairs, and it was almost impossible to get through the throngs of people. I finally reached the group, and his officer friends parted to make way for me so that we were standing face-to-face.

For just a second, we stood there awkwardly, but then I got on my tiptoes and threw my arms around him, and he pulled me up into a hug. I could feel his heart beating fast in his chest, and I heard one of his friends let out a whistle, while another whispered, "Moretti's a goner."

When we stepped apart, he was still holding on to my hand. I shook my head and smiled. "I can't believe they sent you a letter," I said.

"And I understand why *you* didn't," he said, leaning down and talking into my ear. "But you're okay that I'm here?"

"More than okay," I said, and he gave me a relieved smile.

"There's a café a few blocks down," he said. "I thought maybe we could go there, somewhere quieter than this?"

"Yes, perfect," I said. I went to grab my purse and shawl and say good-bye to my friends.

"Viv's right," Dottie said, giving me a hug good-bye. "Please let yourself have a little happiness *tonight* for God's sake. You deserve it, Fi."

There were still crowds of people milling around outside of the club. Now a hunched old man in a burgundy sweater was playing an accordion for francs across the street from the door, and there was a tipsy couple laughing and dancing to his song.

We walked down the street, and Peter held my hand. It felt small and warm in his, and there was an undeniable electricity between us. The cold December air smelled like snow, and the Paris street at night, with its ornate lampposts and beautiful trees, some glistening with ice, was almost too pretty for words.

I took a deep breath and closed my eyes. *Just live. Just live for this very brief, fragile moment in time.*

I opened them again, and Peter was watching me.

"Are you okay?" he asked.

"Yes," I said. "I think I'm better than I have been in a long time . . ."

He paused and then, in a whisper, said, "Me too."

"I was so heartbroken to hear about Tommy Doyle. About everything that happened in Holland. About everyone you . . . *we* . . . lost."

Peter didn't say anything; he just squeezed my hand tighter, looked up at the sky, and nodded as the snowflakes started coming down.

We turned a corner onto a street that was no more than an alleyway. On the right, there was a tiny sign above a door that said, *Chat Blanc, Chat Noir Bistro* with a painted picture of a black cat and a white cat intertwined. We ducked inside.

The café had a checkered tile floor and was sparse but clean, with several French, British, and American flags decorating the wall above the small bar. There were two men in uniform at the bar, and only one of the tables was occupied with two young couples chatting away in French. The owner was a hefty man with wild silver hair, and he welcomed us with an enormous smile.

"Américains? Bonsoir! Bonsoir, monsieur, madame." He held his arms out and led us to a table in the corner by the front window.

We hadn't even seen a menu when the owner's wife, a tall, thin, elegant-looking woman, brought over a bottle of red wine and some small plates of olives and nuts.

"From the bar," she said in careful English, pointing to the two Allied soldiers sitting there. They held up their glasses to us and smiled, and we held ours up in return, saying our thank-yous in English and French.

"So much happiness in this city. It makes you feel like the war is already over," I said.

"I wish it was, but I know better," Peter said with a rueful smile. "We've got some work to do still."

I just looked at him. Up close, you could see that Holland had taken its toll. There were a few more grays in his dark hair.

"I don't know how you do it, how you keep going," I said. "I don't know how any of you do it."

He looked up at me, surprised. "Me? How do *you* do it?" he said. "I think about that; you didn't have to come, and yet here you are, helping us. I'm sorry that I ever doubted that. I'm in awe of the fact that you volunteered. I *had* to come, but you *chose* this."

"I did and I didn't," I said. "I feel in some ways like it chose me."

"Maybe it did," he said. He took a sip of wine and then grabbed my hand across the table and held it tight. We sat there looking out the window, enjoying the moment.

"I've missed you," he said, gazing into my eyes. "And I've worried about you. And being here with you tonight reminds me of what it is to actually have a life outside war."

"I've missed you too," I said. I pulled my hand away, so I could put my purse on the table. I pulled out his Purple Heart.

He stared at it for a long time, then took my hands in his.

"We're both leaving again tomorrow," he said. "Let's just try to enjoy this beautiful city for a few hours. Try to enjoy this?"

"My thoughts exactly," I said. I held up my glass. "To tonight."

"To tonight," he said, clinking it. "And now, Fiona Denning, I want to hear about you. Tell me more about Boston and your family, your sisters and your schools. Tell me about your favorite flavor of ice cream and that job with the mayor. Tell me everything."

"Oh well, if I'm going to do that, you've got to reciprocate," I said. "I want to hear all about the legendary boxing career that all your soldiers keep bragging about."

"Ha! Not exactly legendary, but yes, I will tell you," he said. "It's still early. We've got time."

We sat by the window at the little café table with the snow falling outside, and we talked and laughed for hours, the owner bringing over another bottle of wine and more small plates of food and even a basket with freshly sliced baguette, which felt like a luxury. I learned about Peter's life growing up in New York City, about his Italian parents and his younger brother Anthony and his little sister Danielle.

I told him about being the oldest of four sisters and what I loved about Boston, the neighborhoods and the Red Sox and the Common and the Charles. I talked about how Viv, Dottie, and I became friends at college and all the crazy issues I had to deal with at the mayor's office on a daily basis.

We were a couple. Except that we weren't at all. We were like so many others, Americans living together inside the war. We all used every mental trick and emotional stop valve we could muster to get through it, not unscathed, but at least in one piece. We used music and dancing, laughter and drinks, and if we were really lucky, we used a night like this to help us survive.

Right now, Peter and I were in our own separate space outside of everything, living for this brief time together because it made us feel hopeful and human. And tomorrow we would go back to the war and hope for another moment like this in the future, though there were no guarantees there would ever be one.

We stayed at the café until they started shutting off the lights, and then we found a horse-driven taxi to take us back to where we were staying—the Hôtel Normandy for me, Paris's new Red Cross Rainbow Corner for him. He put his arm around me protectively, and I closed my eyes and leaned against his chest, wishing the night didn't have to end.

"When I saw you in the club tonight wearing this dress?" he whispered in my ear. "I've never seen anyone look so beautiful."

"Thank you. I wanted so much for you to be there." I smiled. "I owe Dottie and Viv for sending you that letter. I'm sorry I didn't do it myself."

Our faces were so close I could feel his warm breath on my cheek. I lifted my head, and we were face-to-face, his look of longing mirroring mine. We both leaned in, but right before our lips touched, he pulled away, a tormented expression on his face.

"Fiona, I have to tell you something," he said. "I should have . . ."

"Shh . . . ," I said, putting my finger to his lips. "Not yet. Please. Kiss me."

He let out a sigh and took my face in his hands, and finally our lips touched, and we kissed. We kept kissing, long and slow, and I leaned into him as he pulled me in close. There is nothing like the euphoria of a first kiss, one that I hadn't even realized I'd been waiting for so desperately. It felt like my heart might burst from my chest.

The driver cleared his throat, and I realized that we were in front of the Hôtel Normandy far too soon. Peter helped me out of the cab and walked me inside the hotel. It was so late nobody was at the front desk.

"My carriage just turned into a pumpkin," I said as we walked inside. "I know you have something to tell me; I think I've known all night."

It was true. In our hours of talking about our lives at the café, I had purposely not mentioned Danny once, and neither had he. Danny had been there, though, as a shadow, a question left unanswered, a hole in my heart that hadn't yet healed.

"I . . . I just wanted this night for us," I said. "That's why I didn't ask sooner."

"That's why I didn't tell you earlier," he said. He put his forehead on mine before he pulled away and took a letter out of his pocket. He brought me over to one of the lobby sofas and sat me down.

"I finally got this letter from Hank at the IRC." Peter looked at me with compassion and so much more. I crossed my arms and braced myself. Here was news that was about to change my life. Again. "They found him, Fiona. Second Lieutenant Daniel Barker is at a POW camp in East Prussia for Allied airmen known as Stalag Luft IV. He's alive. At least he was alive as of this report two months ago."

"How many are at this camp?" I asked, simply because I didn't know what else to ask or how to process this information.

"Over six thousand," he said.

I sat there staring into space. Trying to remember Danny's voice, his face, the last words we said to each other. I put my head in my hands. Danny hadn't died a year ago like I thought he had. He was alive just two months ago. He might still be alive today.

I wanted to cry, but I knew if I did I wouldn't stop, because not only would I be crying for Danny, I would be crying for everything lost in this war. For Tommy Doyle and Monty and the rose on every grave and the thousands of families grieving. Selfishly, I would be crying for myself and Peter, caught in this purgatory between war and real life.

"You asked me to find out, and I did. I thought at least if I can't have you, I can do this one thing for you. You deserve to know where he is. To know he's alive."

I looked up at him and grabbed his hand.

"Thank you," I whispered. "Some men would have thrown the letter in the trash and not told me."

"I could never do that," Peter said, his expression pained.

"This war has changed my life forever, it's changed who I am," I said. "I was wrapped up in my grief at home, and then I came here and threw myself into this job, and it's turned out to be this crazy, fulfilling life that I wouldn't trade for anything. And it's led me to you. But before all this, Danny was the man I was going to marry, and I owe it to him to try to find him."

"I understand," he said, looking down at my hand, and we sat there in silence for a few moments.

"Do you . . . will you still marry him?" he asked, looking up at me. "You know what? Forget it, don't answer. If he was lucky enough to love you first, he's probably lucky enough to make it through this war."

To love you first. Those words hung in between us, and I knew they were true. Peter loved me. And now I knew that it was possible to be in love with two people at once.

"Peter, I need you to know, I feel . . ."

This time he put his finger to my lips and took my face in his hands once more and kissed me, a more desperate, passionate kiss as we pressed against each other, all of our emotions and questions wrapped up in it.

"In another life . . . ," I said.

"In another life, we would leave the Normandy and I would whisk you away to a romantic hotel with a view of the Eiffel Tower." He looked at me with an intensity that made me blush.

"And I wouldn't hesitate to go," I said, because I couldn't deny it.

We looked at each other, thinking of what that night would be like, until he broke the spell.

"But in another life," he said, letting out a deep breath, "you wouldn't have a fiancé who's in a POW camp, holding a black-and-white photo of you, the one thing that's kept him going all this time."

I had pictured that very scene in my mind. Poor Danny. What had he endured? And again, I was overcome with grief and guilt. If he knew what I was doing right now, it would devastate him. I nodded, feeling my eyes fill with tears.

"I know you're hurting, and I understand why. Just . . . thank you for tonight; it's the best night I've had in this war by far. No, not just in this war. It's one of the best nights of my life. I'll never forget it," Peter said, playing with the strands of hair that had fallen out of my comb.

"Write me? Please? I think we're heading in the same direction, yes?" I said.

"We are, and I wish you weren't," he said, helping me off the sofa, his expression serious as he pulled me into a last embrace. "You'll be closer than ever to German territory. Be safe, listen to the officers you're with. If they tell you things are getting hot, get your girls out. *Fast.* Don't do anything foolish. Keep yourself alive."

"You better do the same," I said. Then I added, "Can I keep your Purple Heart?"

He laughed and whispered into my hair, "Not just that one."

Chapter Twenty-Two

December 3, 1944

We left a cold gray Paris the next morning, a convoy of eight Clubmobiles and at least as many supply trucks and jeeps headed to Bastogne, Belgium. We drove in silence for the first hour, the three of us in melancholy moods after a night of too much fun and not enough sleep.

"I think having a break like that? It just makes it worse," Dottie said. Her eyes were puffy from crying, and Barbie kept licking her face to try to comfort her. "We're better off pushing through, working hard, forgetting what it's like to sleep in real beds and wear pretty dresses."

"And kiss handsome men," Viv said, smiling. "That's what you're really saying, Dots."

"True. Well, one handsome man anyway," Dottie said. "And ugh, the worry, the nervousness of what might happen to him."

"Isn't he pretty safe being the leader of a band?" Viv said, her question hovering between compassion and sarcasm.

"I thought so, but believe it or not, the band ends up on the line too, especially with all of the losses the Twenty-Eighth has suffered," she said. "Although I should consider myself lucky because they're so beat up and exhausted, they're heading to a rest center in Clervaux,

Luxembourg. It's quiet, a small town tucked safely in the mountains, not too far from us."

"So, you haven't even told us, is Harry a lord or a duke or whatever?" I asked Viv. "And where is he headed now?"

"Harry is here and there and everywhere," Viv said, a bitter edge to her voice. "But he won't be heading anywhere with me."

"What are you talking about?" Dottie asked. I glanced over, and Viv's face had turned grim.

"Harry is indeed a lord," she said. "I asked him. And then I told him what that nasty British girl said about his family, thinking he would find it funny."

"And . . . ?" Dottie asked.

"Instead he got very serious," Viv said. "He told me that he hoped I didn't expect to meet his parents. That they wouldn't understand and 'let's just have fun and enjoy the night, darling. It's the war, after all.' And I realized at that moment that I had started to think of him as something more than just a war fling. And what really stinks is, I thought he thought the same of me. But he didn't." Her eyes looked sad, but her expression was angry. "So I told him I didn't want to see him again. Because really, if that's what he thinks, why would I? There are plenty of other fellas here to go dancing with."

Dottie reached out and grabbed Viv's hand.

"I'm so sorry," I said. "From the way he acted, he certainly seemed like he was head over heels for you."

"Yeah, well, that's men for you sometimes. Most of the time," Viv said with a shrug, wiping her face. "Your turn, Fiona. You've barely said one word since we left Paris. Out with it. What the heck happened last night?"

I paused for a second, not knowing where to begin. So I blurted out the most important detail.

"Turns out Danny is alive at a POW camp in East Prussia," I said.

I could see both of their looks of shock out of the corner of my eye as I tried to keep my focus on the road and not get too emotional. I told them all the details of the romantic evening, the one that I was still reliving in my mind, despite my guilt. And how Peter and I didn't bring up Danny until we had to say good-bye.

"Jesus," Viv said.

"Were you angry that he hadn't told you the news earlier in the night?" Dottie asked.

"No," I said. "I took your advice, girls. I really just wanted to have a few hours being with him. Being happy. And I did. And now that I know? I'm sick over it, of course. I stayed up all night thinking about Danny in prison all of this time, of what shape he's in and what he's gone through."

"Oh, Fi, I'm so sorry," Dottie said. Viv put her arm around my shoulder.

"Do you want a cigarette?" Viv asked. "Spending an incredibly romantic evening with someone and then having them tell you that your dead fiancé's alive? That's kind of a lot to handle."

"For God's sake, Viv," Dottie said.

"What?" Viv said. "It's true."

"No kidding, Viv," I said. "It is a lot to handle. But no thank you. I'm not sure how or when it's going to happen, but I want to be one of the first in the Red Cross to help liberate the POWs, maybe even get all the way to Stalag Luft IV itself."

"I'll go with you," Dottie said.

"Ugh, then I suppose I have to go too," Viv said, and Dottie elbowed her. "I'm joking. Of course I'll go *if* we can get assigned, but that's a big if."

"And what are you going to do about Peter?" Dottie asked.

"Nothing," I said. "I may never see him again." The thought was hard to bear.

"I bet you'll see Peter again," Viv said. "But there's not much you need to *do* about it, really. I know you care about him, but it's not like you're in love with him or anything. Wait . . . are you?"

I just looked at her. I couldn't say the words out loud, but after last night, I couldn't deny it either.

"Oh God," Viv said, as we crossed over the border into Belgium. "Things just got way more complicated."

~

The small city of Bastogne was in the Wiltz valley in the Ardennes, a region of dense forest, meandering rivers, and rough terrain. Twenty-four of us were billeted in an abandoned château just outside of town. We were all relieved we didn't have to set up tents, as the snow had been falling almost daily, and it wasn't more than twenty degrees out. The château was unheated, but at least it was real shelter, and there was a large courtyard where we could park all of our trucks.

The six of us found a room where we could set up our cots, bedrolls, and sleeping bags next to a large woodstove. We had a dinner of K rations with the entire group in the large, unfurnished dining room that night.

"Okay, just a couple reminders before you head to bed," Liz said as we were wrapping up dinner. "Curfew here is eight p.m., because our guys are still finding Nazis hiding in the woods. Also, there are liable to be mines anywhere, so stay on the roads at all times. In fact, we don't even want any of you turning around on the roads because the shoulders haven't been cleared of mines yet."

A couple of girls groaned at this.

"I know it's a pain," Liz said. "But the danger is real. And speaking of driving, pay attention to whoever is guiding you; one wrong turn could land you in enemy territory. The 'front' is all around us; it's not one straight line marked by barbed wire and a big sign."

She picked up her files and added, "Okay, that's all; please be ready bright and early tomorrow morning, ladies. I'll come around with your assignments."

"Fiona, can you six set up in Bastogne's town square at six thirty tomorrow morning?" Liz tapped me as I was getting up from the table. "It's the perfect crossroads, the infantry heading to the front, medics coming back. And then in the afternoon I thought you could hit some of the engineering units repairing bridges. I'll have a GI in a jeep escort you."

"Of course," I said.

"Is everything okay?" Liz said, watching my face. "You all were in deep conversation at the end of the table."

After catching up with the girls from the Dixie Queen, I had huddled with Blanche, Martha, and Frankie to share the news about Danny. And Peter.

"I'll tell you about it tomorrow," I said with a yawn. "It's a long story."

"Okay," she said. "Get some sleep. Oh, and if you have any trouble with the woodstove in your room, there are some GIs that will be checking in on us to help. Just let one of them know."

❧

The first couple of weeks in Bastogne, we settled into a regular routine and were even busier than we had been in France, with everything made a hundred times more difficult because of the freezing-cold temperatures, ice, and snow. We'd get up in the morning, wolf down some K ration "dog biscuits" as Blanche called them, put our field jackets on over every piece of clothing we owned, and head to the courtyard to make doughnuts. And we would always run into some sort of delay because the tub of lard was frozen shut or the British generator wouldn't fire up.

Our teams from the Cheyenne and the Uncle Sam would open up shop in the square at Bastogne as hundreds of soldiers passed through, coming from all different directions. It was a seven-road junction in the middle of a dense forest where few roads existed.

In the afternoons, the trucks would split up for different assignments. For me, Dottie, and Viv, that usually meant nearly freezing to death as we followed a GI to one of the remote groups of engineers repairing bridges. The wind would whip through the unheated cab, chilling us right through our layers of clothes and the wool blankets on the seats.

On this particular afternoon, we had served some outfits that were part of the 106th Infantry Division near the village of Vielsalm. Most of the men were young and relatively green, having just arrived in the fall. From the moment we arrived, something felt off; the low morale hung in the air like a sickness. Men sat playing cards by small fires, but there were no easy smiles or laughs like we regularly saw at other camps.

We did all we could to lift their spirits and kept serving coffee and doughnuts, cigarettes and candy until we had nothing left. Poor Dottie played her guitar for them with nearly frozen fingers. Barbara even got in on the act as the men passed her around and unsuccessfully tried to get her to play fetch. As we were packing up, the commanding officer, Major General Andrew Jones, came up to us just before we were ready to leave.

"You girls made my men's day," he said. "It's been a rough run; many of these fellas are young—almost all of them are under twenty-two years old and new here. And this weather isn't helping their mood. God help the lot of them if we see any real action."

"This weather isn't good for anyone's mood," I said.

"I have to ask a favor," he said. "I know there's another mail delivery coming soon, several truckloads into Bastogne. When it arrives, is there a chance you could make a special delivery to us? It would be the boost they need. Serve 'em some more coffee, pass out the mail. You know how it is—mail's a lifeline to these men, especially before Christmas."

"Of course we can do that, sir. Happy to."

We got in the car and followed our GI driver back to our château. It was getting dark, and the snow was coming down, as it seemed to be every other hour. A couple of times one of us had to get out and fix the windshield wipers, which were barely adequate.

After one of these stops, I banged my hands on the steering wheel and rubbed them together to try to warm them up. The tips of my fingers were so icy cold, it was making it harder to drive.

"Fiona, I've been meaning to tell you: you've become quite the driver," Dottie said through chattering teeth. "You drive on these slippery, treacherous roads like it's nothing now."

"Thanks," I said. "I actually don't dread it like I used to. I kind of love it, even in this weather."

"I'm praying that the girls have the woodstove going already. I have three pairs of socks under these boots, and my toes are still numb," Viv said.

"I would pay a thousand dollars for a hot bath," Dottie said. "And a letter from Joe, or Christmas mail from home."

"You heard the major about mail delivery to the 106th?" I said as we headed up the drive toward the château.

"Yes," Viv said. "No way to say no to that really. Those boys were miserable."

Desperate to get warm, we ran into the château as soon as we got there, saying hello to a few Clubmobile girls as we climbed the stairs to our room.

We walked in, and Blanche was huddled on her cot, wrapped in her sleeping bag like a mummy; her face the only thing visible. Frankie and Martha were in front of the woodstove on the other side of the room, trying to get it going.

"Oh, hey, girls, don't mind me," Blanche said. "Not feeling so great, and I'm pretty sure my hands are almost frostbitten."

"We're all frozen," Frankie said as Martha continued to poke at the wood in the stove. "And this damn wood is so wet from the snow, we can't get it—"

The room lit up as the woodstove exploded. The sound was deafening, and then there was fire, some of it engulfing Martha and Frankie, who both let out the most horrific screams.

They were both on the ground, so I grabbed my sleeping bag, and Viv and Dottie did the same as we tried to pat down the flames scorching their clothes and bodies. Girls and GIs started running into the room, and someone doused them with water as one of the GIs tamed the flames still shooting out of the woodstove.

Martha's hands were burned beyond recognition, and she had another burn across her cheek. She was sobbing hysterically from the pain. The fire had scorched through Frankie's pants, and her right thigh was badly burned. Tears streamed down her face, which had turned gray and ashen.

"I'm a medic!" A soldier with dark-brown hair came running in with a first aid kit and kneeled down in between them. "We've got to get them to the nearest station hospital now."

"I'll drive if you can show me the way," I said. "We can take them in the Clubmobile."

"Good," the medic said. "The hospital is in Thionville, about an hour from here."

"I'll go with you," Blanche said, tears streaming down her face.

"Should Dottie and I come too?" Viv said, devastated as we watched the medic tend to our poor friends. Dottie was kneeling next to them, stroking Martha's hair, trying to comfort her, but she was still crying hysterically.

"No, it's a long drive, and the Cheyenne's going to be crowded as it is," I said to Viv, giving her a quick hug. "Clean up in here, try to get some sleep for both of us."

Some GIs came back with stretchers so they could carry the girls downstairs to the truck. The medic, named Wyatt, gave them both morphine for the pain.

We got them settled in the back with Wyatt, and Blanche sat up front with me. Wyatt gave me basic directions, and I put the cat-eye headlights on and started down the road to the field hospital.

"Blanche, what happened?" I said. We had been driving in silence for about a half hour. Martha and Frankie were quiet now, and Wyatt the medic was taking good care of them.

"I know exactly what happened," Blanche said. She had a mustard-colored military blanket wrapped around her. "We came in damn near frozen to death; I couldn't even help them, my hands hurt so bad from the cold. We were desperate to warm up, but the wood was so wet it wouldn't light for anything. Finally, Frankie and Martha decided to pour some gasoline on it, only a little at a time. I told them it was a bad idea. I should have insisted we call a GI to help." She started to sob. "This is my fault."

"No, it's not," I said. "This was an accident; you cannot blame yourself."

We arrived at the station hospital, which had the look of a small, well-kept medical clinic. They whisked Frankie and Martha inside to tend to their injuries, and Blanche and I thanked Wyatt and sat in the makeshift waiting room to wait for the doctor.

We had only been there an hour when casualties started coming in, first just a few and then one after another until the clinic went from calm and quiet to mass confusion.

"Why were these soldiers moved?" I heard one Red Cross nurse ask a doctor. "They should be at the field hospital near the front."

"Unless the field hospital is full," the doctor said, a grave look on his face.

The nurse looked up at him to see if he was serious.

"What in God's name is happening?" she asked him.

Those questions were echoed through the night as more injured kept coming in and the doctors and nurses worked at a feverish pace to try to keep up with the flow.

I walked outside for some air and heard the roar of military vehicles on the road in massive numbers.

"Do you know what's happening?" I asked a nurse who had stepped outside for a cigarette.

"No idea," she said. "Nothing good."

"Can we help somehow? My friend and I feel helpless in there."

"Follow me," she said.

Blanche and I spent the rest of the night taking orders from the incredible nurses, helping in any way we could, whether it was fetching bandages for them, holding the hand of a young man getting shrapnel removed, or helping a GI sip water from a straw. All the while, we anxiously waited to talk to the doctor tending to Martha and Frankie. He finally called us over around 3:00 a.m., when there was a lull in activity.

"Your friend Martha has third-degree burns on her hands. They're going to require skin grafts and plastic surgery," the doctor told us. "We've got to move her to London for that. Frankie's burns aren't as bad—first degree—but she'll be here at least for a couple of days."

Seeing our sadness, he gave us a sympathetic smile. "They're lucky to be alive. It could have been much worse. They're both sleeping now, and you should go get some rest yourselves."

They had Frankie and Martha in beds next to each other; they were sound asleep, with loose bandages on Martha's hands and face and on Frankie's leg. They looked younger, more vulnerable, sleeping in their hospital gowns. We left notes of encouragement on the table in between their beds and shed some tears as we kissed them both good-bye on their foreheads. Then Blanche and I found an urn of stale coffee and had a quick cup before we started the drive back to the château. Wyatt the medic had already hitched a ride back an hour before. It was well before dawn, but the roads were now even more crowded with convoys of vehicles, all headed in the same direction as us.

"What the hell is going on? I thought it was supposed to be quiet around here," Blanche said.

"My guess?" I said. "The Nazis decided this dense forest was the perfect place for a surprise attack."

"Just in time for Christmas," Blanche said, sounding tired and depressed.

"You should sleep. Who knows how long it's going to take us to get back?" I said. "And who knows what will be waiting for us when we do."

Chapter Twenty-Three

December 17, 1944

Blanche and I got back before dawn and filled everyone in about Martha and Frankie before passing out on our cots for a few hours. I slept in and hitched a ride to Bastogne town square to join Viv and Dottie at about ten. It was mayhem when we got there, so many more troops and tanks and vehicles. The younger soldiers looked panicked, and the older officers were trying to figure out exactly what was happening. Belgians were on the streets too, some on horses and bikes, some pushing carts with their belongings—all of them leaving the city in droves.

Through the chaos, we tried to serve coffee and doughnuts and remain calm, but there was high anxiety in the air. I spotted Liz through the crowds in the square around lunchtime, and she made her way over to us.

"How's Blanche doing?" she asked when I stepped out of the Clubmobile.

"Okay," I said. "She didn't look too good when she woke up this morning, so I told her to sleep in."

"Good," Liz said, nodding, looking up at the sky, distracted. "So, two things. First, we're moving out of the château tomorrow as early as possible. To Verdun, France, a couple hours south. Nobody knows what the hell is going on, but it's getting too hot here for us. Bastogne is a major crossroads; it would be a natural target for the Germans. Although if that's what's going on here, then they shocked everyone."

"Okay," I said. "We can help Blanche with the Uncle Sam and Frankie's and Martha's gear. What else?"

"Mail just arrived here for the military stationed in this area. Five whole truckloads, mostly Christmas letters and packages. The brass say if by some chance the Germans do take Bastogne, they'll burn it all as soon as they get their hands on it."

"So you want to get it out of here," I said.

"Yes," Liz said with a nod.

"Well, we could drive the trucks out of here ourselves when we evacuate," I said. "Or, if the trucks need to stay, we could have all the Clubmobiles meet here in the morning and load as much as we can into them. We won't be making doughnuts between here and Verdun, so we can stuff the back with mail sacks."

"The trucks will probably need to stay," Liz said.

"I'm sure we can get five truckloads' worth between all of the Clubmobiles," I said.

"I agree, we can do that first thing tomorrow," Liz said. She walked me back over to the Cheyenne because the line was now at least fifty deep, and Dottie and Viv were giving me dirty looks, signaling they needed help.

"Oh, and Liz!" I called to her as she was walking away.

"The 106th in Vielsalm. I promised the commanding officer that we'd deliver any mail that came in for them, at least to a few of the outfits," I said, squeezing into the window next to Viv to pass out doughnuts as we talked. "A lot of them are so new, so young. They could really use the morale boost."

"I'm not sure it's safe. And we're heading to Verdun at the crack of dawn tomorrow," Liz said, looking torn.

"We could go this afternoon. It's a quick trip; we'll be in and out," I said. "Just head up there, drop it off, turn around, and be back by tonight."

"They were pretty miserable," Viv said. "As much as I'm not really in the mood, I'd be thinking of those poor boys—not even a letter to open on Christmas."

"Me too," Dottie said, poking her head out the window above ours. "And Fiona's driving is seriously impressive now; we'll be back in no time."

Liz paused for a moment, considering.

"Okay, go," she said, still unsure. "But take more than the 106th's mail; load up as much as you can so you're good to go for tomorrow. And promise me you'll drop the mail to them and hurry back, no stops. Keep driving until you're back here safe with us. Don't make me regret this."

"I promise," I said. "We'll be fine."

~

Later that afternoon, Viv, Dottie, and I headed to Vielsalm in a thick, heavy fog. Though the roads were now covered with at least a foot of snow, the ground underneath hadn't frozen, so we had to drive through a sludgy mess several inches deep. I held tight to the steering wheel, swearing one minute, the next saying silent prayers that the Cheyenne wouldn't get stuck.

We were in another traffic jam of military vehicles heading north—armored tanks, Hillmans, jeeps with soldiers spilling out of the back. Some were better designed for the messy conditions than others. GIs dressed in full battle gear walked in single file down both sides of the roads. Some of them were wearing white camouflage suits over their uniforms. At one point, I was overcome with an uneasy feeling and considered turning around, but then I thought of the major's plea, and I took a deep breath and kept driving.

"I think that Major Jones owes each of us one of those snowsuits for making this drive," Viv said, shivering as she crossed her arms. "I could use another layer. I could use another *six* layers."

"Couldn't we all," I said. We had wrapped some more of the mustard-colored wool blankets from the field hospital around our legs, but it still wasn't enough.

"I thought this whole Ardennes region was supposed to be a quiet area where the soldiers could rest?" Dottie said. "This is anything but quiet. I hope Joe and his men are okay. I have a bad feeling about this."

"He's probably fine, playing with his band, drinking beers in some toasty warm café," I said.

"You haven't talked much about Danny. Are you doing okay?" Dottie asked.

"Yeah, I'm okay," I said. "Since Danny's mother's letter, I was almost prepared to hear that kind of news. Peter just filled in the blanks. And now I just have to figure out how to get to him."

The girls agreed, and we drove in silence for a stretch.

"And what about Peter?" Viv asked.

"He's here somewhere, not too far," I said, not admitting that I looked for him in the face of every officer. "I relive that night in Paris in my mind, and then I feel guilty for reliving it. And I worry about him as much as I agonize about Danny. I'm a mess."

"Honey, who isn't?" Viv said, patting my knee. "I'm so mad at myself for falling for Harry. Stupid Brit. It was that damn accent."

We pulled into the base in Vielsalm a half hour later, and it was even more frenzied and chaotic than Bastogne. The shelling and ack-ack fire that I was used to hearing in the distance sounded decidedly closer than normal. I had never seen as many armored tanks in one camp before, and the queasy feeling I had on the road returned. We drove past a group of soldiers smoking cigarettes around a bonfire, waving and beeping as we always did, but instead of the usual catcalls and cheers, they just gave us odd looks.

There was a pale blond soldier who, despite the cold, was shirtless, looking into a mirror as he shaved his face. Viv whistled as we drove by, and he dropped the razor when he saw her and just gaped back.

"Jeez, even tougher crowd than yesterday. He didn't even smile," Viv said.

We parked near the water supply as we did the day before and jumped out to hook up so we could at least make coffee. A number of GIs started walking over to the Cheyenne, looking at us with a mixture of awe and nervousness.

"What's the matter, sweetheart?" I said to the first soldier within earshot. "You look like you're seeing a ghost."

"Uh . . . I just can't believe you're here," he said.

"Jesus Christ, what on God's green earth are you gals doing here?" Major Jones came out of one of the field tents and stormed over to us, his face red, fists clenched.

"Fulfilling our promise to you, sir," I said, trying to keep my voice calm, though his anger had me shaking. "We brought you the mail like you requested."

At this, his whole demeanor softened. He shook his head, looked up to the sky, and swore to himself.

"Thank you. This is my fault," he said. "I'm so sorry, girls. Had I known . . . Our electricity has been cut off. We've lost all roads leading out of here, except of course the one you came in on, but it's only a matter of time."

"Sir, what are you saying?" I asked, frowning, afraid of the answer.

"I'm saying that yesterday it was safe here," he said. "But the lines changed overnight. The Germans have surprised us; we never thought they'd be crazy enough to attack us in this kind of terrain or weather."

"But they have," Viv said.

"They have," he said. "You're now at the front. This is a forward command post, and things aren't going well. Two of our regiments to the north have been captured, a few thousand men at least. And we've already suffered numerous casualties. There's a good chance that we'll be surrounded and trapped by morning."

"And we can't just leave now?" I said. "Back the way we came?"

"No," he said with a kind of finality that you don't question. "Too risky, way too dangerous. For all we know, we're already cut off."

"So what do we do now?" Dottie asked him in a soft voice. She looked as nervous as I felt.

"Make some coffee?" he said, giving her a smile, trying to calm her. "Pitch in at the dispensary? Lord knows the medics need the help."

We all looked at him in silence, trying to absorb what he was saying.

"Look, I'll try to get you out of here by tomorrow, but understand you may be walking out. Pack a musette bag, be ready to leave at a moment's notice. I'll have one of the guys bring over an incendiary device for your Clubmobile. If the Krauts do capture us, they're not getting any of your supplies."

An officer called out for him from the large tent that had been transformed into command post headquarters, and the major said good-bye and left.

"This can't be happening," Dottie said. She adjusted her scarf. Her hands were shaking, but this time not from the cold.

"Oh, it's happening," Viv said. She was pacing, swearing under her breath.

"Did he just say he wants us to bomb the Cheyenne?" I said with a groan, covering my face with my hands. "We've got all that mail for the other troops with us."

We sat in stunned silence for a few minutes, and then the cold started to seep into my bones.

"All right, we might as well make ourselves useful," I said, jumping up and down to warm myself up. "After we get our musette bags packed, let's make some coffee and see what we can do to help with the injured."

"But wait, what happens if we don't get out?" Dottie asked, still trying to understand what had just happened.

Viv looked at me and shrugged.

"You mean if we get captured too?" I said. "Don't even think about it. I promise you, we are getting the hell out of here one way or another."

Even as I said it out loud, I wasn't at all convinced it was true.

～

For the rest of the day, we did what the major suggested and pitched in, first making coffee for a few hundred soldiers coming back shaken and filthy from the line, and then helping the medics in the dispensary that evening. We were busy making soup for the wounded soldiers being brought in when we learned that we had been completely cut off, surrounded by the Germans on all sides. The news was expected at that point, and when it was announced, we just looked at each other with grim acceptance.

That night we brought our bedrolls into the mess hall and found a quiet corner to set up in. We settled into our sleeping bags, but I couldn't fall asleep. The reality of our situation seemed clearer in the darkness of the hall as I listened to the sounds of battle just outside the walls. We were in a camp surrounded by the Germans, and, based on reports, the front lines were barely keeping them at bay. We could be captured at any moment.

"I'm going to have to wash my hair in my helmet tomorrow; I'm feeling desperate," Viv whispered.

"Me too," Dottie said.

"Girls, I told you, we're going to get out of here," I said. "We'll figure it out."

"Oh, really?" Viv said, her voice angry. "It's time to stop lying to yourself, Fi. We could be wearing prison garb by tomorrow."

"Oh please, Viv, we're not going to be wearing prison garb," I said, annoyed.

"You don't know that," Viv said, sitting up now and raising her voice. "You don't know anything! We have as much chance of dying as we do of getting out of here."

"That's not true," I said.

"You don't really believe that, do you, Viv?" Dottie asked. We were all sitting up now, facing each other in the shadows of the mess hall.

"Oh, yes I do, and I think we all better come to terms with the fact," Viv said, still angry and emotional. "You saw the injuries today— they're not happening a hundred miles away. They're happening right down the goddamn road. So frankly, Fiona, I'm tired of your whole Pollyanna act, like you're going to figure it all out and get us out of here. The fact is, we have absolutely *no* control over what is happening right outside this mess hall, and we had better prepare for the worst."

"My whole Pollyanna act? Really?" I said, furious at her words. "Would you prefer I curl up in a ball and cry? We might not have control, but I prefer trying to figure out how to take action over feeling hopeless. I prefer trying to find a way to get the hell out of here so that we *won't* get killed. Maybe you should focus on that too, instead of being so negative and miserable."

"Stop. That's enough, both of you," Dottie said, in a voice that I imagined she used with her elementary school classes. "This conversation is over. It's only going to get uglier if it continues. We're all exhausted and scared about what's going to happen, but arguing about it won't help. Go to sleep. Not another word."

I started to open my mouth but thought better of it and just sighed, lay down, and rolled over so I didn't have to face Viv. I heard her huff and do the same. That was the last thing I remembered.

≈

The next morning, Viv and I still weren't talking as the three of us made more coffee for the men. Dottie was eyeing both of us with annoyance as we talked to the soldiers we were serving but not to each other. Before lunch, Stan, the mess sergeant, came by to see us.

"We've hardly got any food left. You gals have anything?" he asked. He had a shiny bald head and a frayed apron that barely fit around his chubby frame.

"We've got Red Cross doughnut flour and no electricity to make doughnuts. You can have it all," I said.

"Better than nothing. I guess we'll make pancakes," he said, as we helped him lug all of our bags of flour into the mess hall.

As the three of us helped him mix the doughnut flour into something resembling chunky pancake batter, I couldn't stand the tension between me and Viv anymore, so I was the first to speak.

"You're right, I might do the Pollyanna act sometimes, but it's only because I don't know what the hell else to do," I said, grabbing Viv's elbow as she passed by to get more flour. "I just feel desperate to get out of here. And if I don't stay positive, I might lose my mind. Or start crying and never stop."

"And I'm sorry I was acting nasty," Viv said. "Dottie was right. I'm just exhausted and worried and so sick of this weather, sick of everything."

"We all are," I said as we hugged.

"Thank God," Dottie said, watching as she mixed batter in a large metal bowl at the counter across from us. "Bad enough we're stuck here, I cannot deal with you two fighting."

"Enough with the hugging; where's that bag of flour?" Stan barked.

"Oh, getting it now," Viv said, as she hurried over to where we had stored them.

~

The next several days, all of them freezing cold and snowy, blurred together as we tried not to think about being captured and kept ourselves busy in any way we could—making coffee, assisting the medics, cooking hundreds of pancakes with the mess sergeant. And of course, we did everything we could to try and comfort the soldiers. We helped tend to the wounded and tried our best to lift the spirits of the tank men and the hundreds of soldiers coming back from the line, still shaky and dazed from combat.

On Sunday morning, we woke up in our corner of the mess hall after a fitful night listening to the fighting.

"Is it me, or does it sound like it's even closer today?" Dottie whispered.

"It's not you," Viv said.

"My God," I said, looking out the window at the whiteness. "It's snowing sideways. You can barely see anything."

"I have good news and bad news," Stan said, arriving just as we put the coffee on. "The good news is that an armored division and an airborne division arrived in the middle of the night. The place is thick with troops, and hopefully we'll break through soon, because these boys are sick of K rations and coffee, and so am I. They can't drop us any supplies by air until this goddamn weather clears."

"What's the bad news?" asked Dottie, eyebrows raised.

"The bad news is that German gunfire is getting closer by the hour." And just at that moment, we heard the sound of artillery shelling coming from somewhere on the north side of the building.

"Fantastic," Viv said.

"Maybe today will be the day we get out of here," I said.

"Yeah, you've been saying that all week, Pollyanna," said Viv.

"I know, I know," I said, elbowing her. "But I am going to track down Major Jones and talk to him, see if there are any groups that are going to try to leave the area soon. Maybe we can follow them out."

We helped Stan on the chow line. Soldiers were lining up, covered with snow and rubbing their hands together, trying to warm themselves.

"Things could be worse," a GI said to his friend as I handed him a cup of coffee. "We could be over with the Twenty-Eighth Infantry in Clervaux. I heard those guys got decimated."

A chill ran through me, and I looked around to see if Dottie had heard, relieved that she was talking and laughing with a couple of men at the end of the line. I decided to not tell her that news and said a silent prayer for Joe Brandon.

One soldier announced to the line that it was thirteen below zero outside, and a few others groaned and told him to put a sock in it, just as the mess hall exploded under a rain of deafening artillery shells.

Two soldiers fell down, killed right in front of me, one a young man from Connecticut that I had served only seconds before. My ears rang once more from the shells and the screams. I grabbed Viv's and Dottie's hands, and we ran out of the mess hall to find shelter. We ended up underneath the Cheyenne because there wasn't anywhere else remotely safe nearby. There was a whiteout, and the Germans continued to shell the camp as the three of us lay flat on our stomachs in the snow and mud under our truck.

I spotted Major Jones in the chaos but knew it would be potential suicide to run out to him in the middle of the attack. After about a half hour, the shelling stopped, and we gingerly crawled out from under the truck, keeping our heads down.

Major Jones was a couple hundred feet away, huddled in front of the command post tent, talking with a group of officers.

"Girls, I'm going to go talk to him," I said.

I ran through the snow and heard Viv call out, "Good luck," behind me.

"Major! Sir," I said, jogging up to him. "Sorry to interrupt, but I just wanted to ask you something. I'll keep it brief."

"Where is your damn helmet?" he asked, nodding to the men around him to give us a minute.

"I'm sorry, I ran when the mess hall exploded and forgot to grab it," I said. "Sir, any chance of us getting out of here in the Clubmobile soon? Any road openings?"

"How well do you drive?" he said, crossing his arms and looking me up and down, as if he could judge my driving skills just by looking at me.

"Better than I used to," I said, wiping the wetness off my face. "I'm good actually. Really good."

He studied me for a few more seconds and then said, "We might have a two-hour window this evening, thanks to the Belgian underground and the 101st Airborne. You're going to have to drive faster than you ever have in that thing, with just the cat eyes. The weather is supposed to clear, but the roads will be tough. A colonel and his GI driver that just arrived from another division are leaving tonight if they can; you can follow them out. You up for it?"

"Absolutely," I said. "I promised I'd get my friends out, and we have Christmas mail for hundreds of soldiers to deliver."

"All right," he said with a sigh. "It's my fault that you three ended up here in the first place. The least I can do is help you get back to your group safely."

"Thank you," I said. "We'll be ready."

"Honestly? You girls surprised me—you're braver than I thought." He gave me a small smile and a look of something like pride. "Now go tell your friends the plan and get your truck ready to go."

Chapter Twenty-Four

We were living amid relentless sounds of explosions, ack-ack, and flashing from the fighting that still surrounded us. Once we recovered our helmets from the mess hall, we didn't take them off and spent the rest of the day getting our gear packed. A couple of the GIs helped us and also kept an eye out in case things got too hot and we had to take shelter.

As we started up the Cheyenne, ready to leave that evening, Major Jones showed up, carrying white camouflage jumpsuits for us. Viv was so excited about them, she completely embarrassed him with a hug and a kiss on the cheek.

It was dusk, and the snow had mercifully stopped. The sky was clear, and the stars came out of hiding for the first time I could remember since we'd arrived in Belgium.

"All right, it looks like that two-hour window is going to hold, but you've got to go now," Major Jones said, looking at his watch. He gave us directions to the road on the other side of camp that we were going to take out.

"The jeep will be waiting for you there. The GI driving it is Private Jason Hoffman; he'll be looking for you. Remember, drive fast, keep up with them, and don't do anything foolish."

We all thanked him and went to climb into the cab.

"Fiona," he said, just as I was about to climb in.

"Yes?"

"Do you still have that incendiary device?"

"I do. You don't think I'll need it, do you?"

"Hopefully not," he said. "But if you run into trouble, you've got the device—bomb the hell out of this thing. I don't want those damn Krauts to have an ounce of petrol or coffee or anything else that might help them."

"Okay, sir," I said, already sweating from adrenaline and nerves.

"You should be okay," he said, his tone not entirely convincing. "Good luck."

It was dark, but we spotted a jeep with a trailer attached right where the major said it would be.

Private Hoffman came running over. He couldn't have been over five feet two inches.

"We've got to go—Colonel Brooks is cranky as hell. You girls keep your helmets on, okay?"

"All right, soldier," Viv said.

"You okay with this thing? Ready to drive fast?" He looked at me, bright-eyed and smiling.

"Yes, let's get the heck out of here," I said.

We drove in silence for a while, listening to the constant heavy roar of Allied planes overhead as I tried to concentrate on keeping up with the jeep on the narrow forest roads, still heavy with snow. The Cheyenne was not as agile as the jeep in this terrain, and I kept praying we wouldn't get stuck. The sounds of battle echoed in the hills and valleys, and I knew we were all listening in case anything got close enough to put us in immediate danger. After about an hour, the jeep stopped ahead of us. We pulled up behind it and waited.

"What's the holdup?" I yelled to Hoffman, who had just jumped out of the jeep to take a better look at what was in front of him. I heard him swearing.

"The goddamn bridge has been knocked out," he said, coming over to us. "We're going to have to take a detour; hoping it's not too many miles out of the way." He patted the Clubmobile door. "I know this is a beast to drive on these roads, but try to stay close."

We drove off course for what had to be over sixteen miles, the roads more treacherous than before, and I had to slow down because I was afraid of veering off into the woods.

"We're falling too far behind them," Viv said.

"I know, I'm doing my best," I answered through gritted teeth.

"I don't see them at all now. Where are they?" Dottie asked, leaning out the window to see if she could get a glimpse.

"I'm sure we'll catch up in a second," I said.

The road curved, and I spotted them a quarter mile ahead.

"There they are."

The sounds of brakes and metal screeched as the jeep crashed head-on into an enormous truck coming from the other direction.

"Oh Jesus Christ, no!" I slammed on the gas and drove as fast as I could to the scene.

The crash had knocked the jeep off the road, and it lay in a ditch, the trailer turned sideways next to it. The front end was completely smashed in.

Hoffman was pulling the colonel out of the cab with the help of the two soldiers who'd been driving the supply truck.

"He's not conscious," said Hoffman, pale and distraught, blood dripping down his face from a gash on his cheek and another above his eyebrow.

"Here, let's put him in the back of the Cheyenne," I said. "Dottie, Viv, I know it's packed back there, but we've got to make room somehow."

They ran back to make some space while I tried not to lose my footing as I helped the soldiers slowly carry the colonel back up the slippery embankment to the Cheyenne.

"I didn't even see you coming," Hoffman said to the soldiers, still horrified.

"Neither did we—these damn roads twist and turn, and you're the first ones we've seen all night. We're delivering supplies to the front, and we thought we were alone on this route," the soldier said.

"So did we," Hoffman said. He explained where we came from and our detour. "Tell me we're close to the Allied lines?"

"Sorry, you've still got a ways to go," the second soldier said.

We settled the colonel in the back of the Cheyenne on blankets, and the soldiers from the truck gave us additional first aid supplies. Hoffman stayed with him and Dottie offered to as well, also insisting on cleaning the cuts on Hoffman's face and bandaging them up for him.

"Those are going to have to be dressed as soon as possible," the first soldier said, pointing to the colonel's injuries, huge open gashes that were still bleeding profusely, one above his knee and another on his shoulder. "And that knee might be broken, judging by the swelling and the deformed look of it. There are plenty of farmhouses in these woods; you'll see the markings for the roads into them. Some are empty, some not. You might want to try to hunker down in one for at least a few hours, get him bandaged up and maybe get a little rest."

"I agree, we should," I said, looking at the poor colonel. "How's your truck?"

"It's okay; it didn't take as much damage for sure," said the first soldier. "We can still get these supplies to the front anyway."

The soldiers helped us hook up the jeep's trailer to the back of the Cheyenne, and we thanked them and said our good-byes.

"Oh and Merry Christmas!" one of them called out as they drove away.

"My God, it's Christmas Eve," Viv said, looking stunned as she climbed into the cab next to me. "For the first time in my life, I had completely forgotten."

"Me too," I said, remembering my parents and my sisters sitting around the fireplace, drinking punch and opening gifts. Thinking of Danny and Peter, wherever they were. A deep melancholy overcame me.

"All right, so find a farmhouse?" I said, taking a deep breath, gripping the wheel to ground myself in reality.

"Yes, empty house or not empty?"

"At this point, I think we should just go with the first one we find," I said.

I drove a little slower and more cautiously, now all too aware that another vehicle could come out of the darkness and hit us head-on.

"There, through the woods," Viv said, rolling down the passenger's side window and pointing ahead to the right. "I see lights; I bet there's a turn coming up for it."

We almost missed the narrow, unmarked road. When we turned down it, the trees closed in on us, snowy branches scraping both sides of the Cheyenne. They cleared in front of a stone cottage lit from within. To the right of it was a fenced-in field, a red wooden barn on the far side.

"Pray that they're friendly," I said. Dottie stayed with the colonel. Hoffman, Viv, and I approached the front door and knocked.

A boy of about thirteen years old answered and eyed us warily. He was tall and handsome with sandy-brown hair and freckles. A petite, middle-aged blonde woman came up behind him and glared at us.

"Ja? Was machst du hier?" the woman asked.

"Uh, Americans," I said, pointing to myself, wishing I spoke German.

"I thought you were Americans," the boy said, looking us over, at our mud-stained field jackets, at Hoffman's freshly bandaged face.

"You speak English," I said.

"And Dutch and French too," he said. "What are you doing here?"

I told him our tale, explaining that we had an injured officer in the back of our truck. He nodded and turned to his mother, translating for her. Her expression softened as he told her, but they were still on guard. She eyed us, deciding our fate. She looked at her son and said, *"Hol zwei Hühner.*" Then she looked at us and added, "*Bring deine Freunde hinein.*"

I looked at the son, and he smiled.

"She said I have to go get two chickens and you can bring your friends inside," he said. "I'm Fritz, and my mother's name is Elisabeth. I'll be right back." Then he ran past us to the barn.

When we opened the back of the Cheyenne, the colonel stirred and groaned, the temporary bandages Dottie had placed on his wounds soaked with blood. We carefully lifted him out of the back of the truck and carried him down the path to the front door of the cottage.

Elisabeth opened the door for us and was alarmed when she saw the colonel's condition. She motioned for us to bring him to a small settee in the corner of the large sitting area and brought over a green plaid wool blanket.

The first floor of the cottage was lit only by candlelight and had whitewashed stone walls and low ceilings with large dark beams. Next to the settee there were several chairs of various sizes assembled around a roaring fireplace. There was a big wooden table at the back of the room flanked by benches, and behind the table was a door to a small kitchen.

Viv fetched the first aid supplies, and Dottie sprinkled antiseptic sulfa powder on the colonel's wounds as I helped Hoffman bandage him up again.

"I'm going to give him a shot of morphine. He's going to be in a lot of pain when he wakes up," Hoffman said. We had all been so cold for so long, we huddled by the fire and tried to defrost ourselves.

"I had forgotten what it felt like to be warm," Viv said with a sigh.

Fritz came back with two freshly killed chickens that he presented proudly to his mother. He walked into the kitchen with her, and they continued speaking German.

"My mother's making chicken and potato stew. She said you all look too thin and pale, and that he looks close to death," Fritz said, pointing to the colonel. He sat down with us by the fire. "My father is working in Aachen, Germany, where we lived before our home was bombed. We thought you were him. I don't think he's going to make it home tonight."

There was a knock at the door just then, and Fritz's face lit up.

"Maybe he made it after all?" I said.

Fritz jumped up and went to the front door as Elisabeth came hurrying from the kitchen.

"Mehr Amerikaner?" she asked, looking at me, questioning. I shook my head—no more Americans that I knew of.

Fritz opened the door, and from where I was sitting, I caught a glimpse of three soldiers. German ones. Elisabeth glanced at us, her face white with terror. She pushed past Fritz and shut the door behind her.

Fritz was up against the door, trying to listen, terrified at what was happening on the other side.

"The penalty for harboring the enemy is execution," he whispered, trying not to cry. "They could kill us. They could kill us all."

The four of us were standing now. Hoffman had his hand on his gun, and he made his way closer to the door. We looked at each other, unsure what to do next but staying as quiet as possible. The colonel started to groan, and I prayed he didn't get any louder.

We heard Elisabeth yell in German, *"Es ist Heiligabend und hier wird nicht geschossen."*

"She told them it's the holy night and there will be no shooting here," Fritz said, his head against the door. "She's telling them they have to leave their weapons outside."

"They're coming *in*?" Viv said. "In the *house*?"

"Yes," Fritz said, looking as nervous as I felt.

The door opened, nearly knocking Fritz over, and Elisabeth walked in with the three German soldiers, their faces stony. I was struck by how young two of them were; one was tall and lanky, the other had a medium build and white-blond hair. Neither of them was more than sixteen years old. The other soldier was older and strikingly handsome, very tall with thick black hair, cobalt-blue eyes, and pale skin. He looked to be in his midtwenties.

All of us stood there in silence, and the tension in the air was so thick I could almost swat it with my hand. The colonel groaned again, and the older soldier looked over at him, and for a second his face flashed an emotion other than anger.

Elisabeth walked over to us, said something in German, and held out her hands to Hoffman.

"She said give her your weapons, they are going outside too," Fritz said.

Hoffman handed her his gun and told Fritz the colonel was not armed.

Elisabeth took the guns outside, and when she came back in, the Germans seemed a little less on guard. Maybe it was the lure of the warm fire, but the tall, skinny soldier reached into his bag and pulled out a loaf of rye bread and handed it to Elisabeth, prompting the other young soldier to pull two bottles of red wine out of his bag.

Elisabeth thanked them, and Fritz followed her into their tiny kitchen. He returned a minute later and passed out glasses of red wine, first to the Germans, then to us. We were all standing there, awkward and tense, the Germans still close to the door, ready to make a run for their weapons if necessary.

"Oh for goodness' sake, we can't do this all night." I looked at Viv, Dottie, and Hoffman and said, "Sit down."

Hoffman shot me a look, telling me he wasn't comfortable with this. "*Sit*," I said.

I pointed to the open chairs and floor space around the fire and looked at the Germans.

"Please. Sit. It's Christmas Eve."

"Thank you," the older soldier said in a strongly accented baritone voice. He translated for the younger ones, and they walked over to the fireplace, giving us nervous half smiles.

We sat quietly, warming up by the fire, sipping red wine. A silent, uneasy truce.

After a few minutes, the older soldier took a sip of wine and pointed to Colonel Brooks.

"What happened?" he asked.

Hoffman explained what had happened in the accident, and the tension in the air finally started to evaporate.

"I am a medical student, or I was. Before," he said, frowning as he looked at the colonel. "Do you want me to take a look?"

"Yes," Dottie said before any of us could protest. Hoffman looked at her, horrified.

"He needs more care. Tonight, it can't wait," Dottie said. "We have a first aid kit; he needs stitches, but I can't . . . none of us are nurses." She gave the German an agonized look.

"I gave him some morphine for the pain, and sulfa powder to prevent infection," Hoffman said in defense, but after a pause he added, "but she's right. I'm not a medic."

"Get whatever first aid supplies you have," the medical student said, standing up. "I'm Jens. This is Wolf and Axel." He pointed to the tall, lanky soldier and the shorter, blonder one.

We all made our introductions, and it was like the air came back into the room and we could breathe again.

Jens and Hoffman gathered the first aid supplies and went over to tend to Colonel Brooks, who had begun to stir even more.

"Fritz, could you please get the colonel some water if he wakes? And maybe also some clean clothes for him?" I said. "Or I could if you'll just tell me where . . ." But Fritz was already up and heading to the kitchen. Jens followed him to wash up.

"You were right, Dottie," I said, as Jens took over and tended to the colonel.

"I'm afraid he might not make it through the night," she said, sipping her wine by the fire next to Viv.

"Hopefully, he will now. God, I would sit *in* this fire if I could," Viv said. "To be this warm again makes me want to cry."

"That fact that it's Christmas makes me so homesick," Dottie said. "I miss my brothers and my parents so much."

"I'm missing my niece Gianna's first Christmas," Viv said, tears in her eyes. "My sister may never forgive me."

That melancholy feeling washed over me again, and I took a sip of wine and gave the two German soldiers an awkward smile as they observed our homesickness. I was sure they had absolutely no idea what we were saying. But when Fritz returned and sat down, they had questions.

"*Seid ihr Soldatinnen?*" asked Axel, as soon as he had a translator.

"Are you female soldiers? He wants to know," said Fritz.

I explained that we were Red Cross, pointing to the patch on my arm.

Fritz translated, and then Axel spoke again.

"He wants to know if you came here on your own, or if your country made you come," Fritz said.

"Tell him we were stupid enough to come on our own," Viv said, smiling at Axel. "No, don't tell him that; he won't understand the sarcasm."

"And ask him how old he is," Dottie said. "He looks like he's not even out of high school."

Some more banter passed between the Germans, and then Fritz said, "They're both sixteen years old. Jens is twenty-four. And they want to know why none of you are married because you look older and you're all very pretty." He was smiling, enjoying his role as translator.

"Dottie, I think you need to sing some Christmas carols," Viv said, winking at them. "These boys have too many questions."

And that's when the young German soldiers, Axel and Wolf, fell in love with Viv.

"Maybe after dinner," said Dottie.

"You sing?" Fritz said. "You have to sing some Christmas songs for us; my mother will love it. Music is her favorite thing in life."

We talked to the young soldiers and Fritz for a while, sipping wine and warming ourselves by the fire, as Jens tended to the colonel.

"Fritz!" After almost two hours, Elisabeth finally peeked out of the kitchen and called to him.

As Fritz set the table, he told us all to find a seat. Wolf and Axel chose the chairs on either side of Viv, the rest of us sat down, and Hoffman and Jens came over just as Elisabeth was placing fragrant bowls of stew in front of all of us. Fritz brought out the bread and the rest of the wine as Elisabeth folded her hands in prayer and gave us all a warning look to do the same. She bowed her head, and we all followed suit.

"Gott, wir nehmen an diese Mahlzeit, aber lass uns nicht deine Gegenwart vergessen. Du segnest, weil du uns liebst, segne auch was du uns gibst. Bitte, Gott, an diesem Heiligabend beten wir für das Ende des Krieges. Amen."

Fritz translated the prayer as soon as his mother finished: "God, as we partake of this meal, let us not forget your presence; bless us because you love us, bless also what you have given. Please, God, on this Christmas Eve, we pray for this horrible war to end. Amen."

I made the sign of the cross and looked up, and my eyes weren't the only ones glistening. We sat there for a quiet moment, our thoughts far away from this cottage in the middle of the Ardennes. Then the two younger soldiers thanked Elisabeth profusely as they reached for bread and started inhaling the food.

The first part of dinner, all you could hear was the quiet sound of spoons hitting bowls, as we were all too ravenous to even attempt polite discussion.

"Your colonel has lost a great deal of blood; his blood pressure is low," Jens said in a quiet voice to me. "You'll need to get him somewhere safe where he can get blood plasma, as well as rest and food. I'll show you your best route out; you should leave before dawn."

"Of course," I said. "Thank you for taking care of him."

"Bitte," he said.

Fritz said something to the young soldiers in German and then looked at Viv.

"You never answered their question—why aren't you all married?" He smiled mischievously.

"Tell them because all of the American men are in the war, obviously," Viv said, shaking her head. "Fiona is engaged—her fiancé's a prisoner of war over here. And Dottie has a fella in the Twenty-Eighth Infantry."

"In the Twenty-Eighth? That's where I'm from," Hoffman said. "What's his name?"

"My God, we didn't even ask. I had no idea you were in the Twenty-Eighth," I said.

"His name is Joe Brandon," Dottie said, her voice trembling. I grabbed her hand. "Do you know if he's okay? Please tell me you know something."

The Germans all watched this exchange, and I knew it didn't require translation.

"He's okay," Hoffman said. "The colonel and I were at the Twenty-Eighth's divisional command post at Wiltz, Luxembourg, when it came under severe attack. Captain Brandon and the band took up arms. They dug foxholes, picked up carbines, and fought to hold the line and stop the German advance." Hoffman looked at Jens uncomfortably when he said this. "Out of the sixty band members, there are only sixteen left."

"Jesus," Viv said. "Sixteen out of sixty."

Fritz translated this story; the younger soldiers looked terrified when they heard the last part.

Dottie was smiling as she blotted her eyes with her napkin and waved her hand in front of her face, embarrassed. "I'm sorry, I'm just so relieved." Elisabeth reached across the table, patted her on the shoulder, and nodded. Understanding without words.

"And where is your fiancé?" Fritz asked, looking at me.

"Last I heard, he was at a POW camp in East Prussia. Stalag Luft IV," I said. It was a reality I still didn't quite grasp.

Jens looked me in the eye when I said this, examining my face. "Thousands of lives interrupted," he said, taking a sip of wine. "The Allies are advancing in that area; if they get too close, they will move the prisoners."

"Move them where?" I said, feeling chilled at the thought.

"Anywhere the Allies can't liberate them," Jens said. And then, seeing the distraught look on my face, he added, "Try not to worry. This war will be over sooner, I think."

He nodded at the younger soldiers, who were now talking to Fritz in German, telling him a story and laughing, their cheeks flushed from the red wine and the warmth of the fire.

"They're sending these little boys to fight now," Jens whispered, disgust in his voice. "Next it will be kindergartners."

"I hope you're right about it ending soon," I said, my head hurting to think about somehow managing to get to East Prussia only to find that Danny had been moved somewhere else.

"Yes, me too. I am better at fixing men than . . . ," he said.

"Dottie, you promised to sing," Viv said. "For our hostess?"

"Yes, please," Fritz said, thrilled at the idea. "By the fire." He jumped up and started clearing the plates, and we all did the same, tripping over ourselves to thank Elisabeth for the first home-cooked meal we'd had in months.

We went to the Cheyenne to get Dottie's guitar, our bedrolls, and sleeping bags. We handed a couple of the bags to Jens, Axel, and Wolf to share. We also presented Elisabeth with some ground coffee for her kindness. I wished we had more to give her.

"I'll start with the most obvious choice," Dottie said, giving her guitar a quick strum when we settled in around the fire, and then she started to sing "Silent Night."

As Dottie sang, I looked over and Elisabeth had her hands clasped together on her red floral apron, tears streaming down her cheeks at the beauty of the voice and the song. The soldiers also seemed transfixed by Dottie's beautiful voice. When she finished, we all clapped, and Fritz, Axel, and Wolf gave her a standing ovation.

"Okay, now something a little more upbeat, Dots, or I'm going to be an emotional wreck," Viv said.

She was right: the song had made everyone a little gloomy. Dottie nodded in agreement and chose "Rudolph, the Red-Nosed Reindeer" next, and Fritz loved it so much he asked her to write down the words for him after she was done.

Then Axel and Wolf decided to get in on the act. They stood by the fire and sang a terrible version of "O Tannenbaum," which we all cheered for anyway. We continued to sing Christmas songs, the evening a moment's reprieve from the bitter-cold battle raging outside the door. Watching the German boys joke and laugh and try to sing with Dottie, I knew how desperately we all needed it.

After a couple of hours, I started yawning, and everyone realized that we had to get some sleep while we could. With the sleeping bags and bedrolls spread around the fireplace, I swear I fell asleep before my head hit the pillow. When I woke up a little while later, the candles were out, but the fire was still going. Everyone was fast asleep, Viv's snoring the only sound in the silence. I looked over at the settee and saw the colonel sitting up, looking at me. He had been out cold through Dottie's entire Christmas concert, but he was wide-awake now.

"Sir," I whispered as I went over to him, "would you like some water?" I handed him the glass from the little table nearby. He nodded, his hand shaking as he drank it down in one gulp. I poured him some more out of the little yellow pitcher Elisabeth had left for us.

"Where the hell are we?" he said, frowning, his quiet voice hoarse and scratchy. He had bushy eyebrows and a face pockmarked by pimples from his youth. He wiped his hand across his cheeks and looked down at his bandages.

"Who are all these people? And who are you?"

I introduced myself and told him the story of the evening, and his eyes went wide when I got to the part about the Germans. He looked at the three of them asleep on the floor, incredulous.

"The *German* stitched me up?" he whispered, pointing to Jens.

"Yes," I said. "He said you lost a lot of blood and need plasma. Also, food and rest."

"Well, I'll be damned." He was still staring at Jens, sleeping on the floor. "I do feel horrible. Jesus, I don't even remember the crash."

"We'll leave in a couple of hours, before dawn," I said. "They're giving us a map to show us the best way to the Allied lines."

"And you trust them?" Colonel Brooks asked, watching my face. His complexion even in the firelight had a gray hue, and his voice was weak.

"I do," I said.

"All right," he said, frowning. "If they send us on a wild goose chase with this map of theirs and we wind up captured or dead, it's on you."

I couldn't tell if he was kidding or not. He must have sensed it because his face softened a little, and with a slight smile he added, "But if you get us the hell out of enemy territory? You and your friends are getting Bronze Stars."

Chapter Twenty-Five

December 25, 1944

"Of course it's snowing again," Viv said, as we packed up the Cheyenne at 4:00 a.m. I had stayed up for a little while talking to the colonel, making sure he had plenty of water to drink and that his bandages were okay before I dozed off again.

"This is the first year I'm not happy about Christmas snow," Dottie said.

We let the colonel sleep while we packed up our things. The Germans were also up and ready to go, and Elisabeth gave them a bag of food she had packed. We didn't have much, but I was able to dig out some more ground coffee and K rations to give them too.

We all said our thank-yous and good-byes. They weren't "the enemy" anymore. Wolf and Axel were somber, devastated that they had to return to the realities of war. Fritz looked like he was going to cry because all of his new friends had to leave.

Viv gave the three Germans pecks on the cheek as they walked out the door, and that definitely lifted their spirits a little.

"Follow the map, and you should get out all right," Jens said. "I'd go soon, though; this snow . . ." He looked up, also sad that our reprieve from the war was over.

"I agree," I said. "Thank you. The colonel was shocked when I told him. You saved his life."

Jens looked at the colonel softly snoring on the settee. "I'm glad I could help him," he said.

I walked him out, and Axel handed him his gun. The three of them walked backward a few feet and gave us final waves good-bye before they turned and set off into the forest.

Dottie gently woke Colonel Brooks, and he insisted on walking to the Cheyenne himself, which we all took as a good sign.

"Are the Nazis still here?" he barked, rubbing his eyes as Elisabeth smiled shyly and gave him a cup of coffee.

Hoffman said, "Sir, can I help you walk?"

"Oh hell, I suppose you'll have to," the colonel said, turning white, wincing and wobbling as he tried to stand. "I think this knee's in rough shape."

I got on the other side of him, placing his arm around my shoulders, and we took our time, taking baby steps to the door and then outside.

I felt ill that we had to go back into the snow and our freezing truck, and that we still weren't in safe territory.

"Please thank your mother for being so generous and brave and compassionate," I said to Fritz, looking at Elisabeth after we were packed up and ready to go. "We will never be able to thank you enough for your kindness." When Fritz translated, Elisabeth smiled, stepped toward me, and gave me a hug.

"*Bitte,*" she said when we pulled away from each other.

"Take good care of yourselves," I said, hugging Fritz and ruffling his hair until he blushed a deep red.

Dottie agreed to stay in the back with Colonel Brooks, and Viv and Hoffman would ride up front with me to help navigate.

"Are you sure you don't want me to drive?" Hoffman asked for the tenth time.

"Look, I know you assume she's a bad driver because she's, um, a *woman*, but she's actually really damn good," Viv said. "Have you ever driven a Clubmobile before?"

"Well, no but—" Hoffman started, but Viv interrupted him.

"Well, it takes a ton of practice, and if I had to choose between you or Fiona to get us to the Allied lines? I'm putting my money on Fiona," Viv said.

"All right, fine," Hoffman said, putting his hands up in surrender.

"Hey, thanks, Viv," I said, smiling as we drove down the narrow lane we had come in on to get back to the main road. "I just need you two to tell me about any turns coming up so I don't miss them in this weather."

I wanted more than anything to drive fast, to get on the right side of the Allied lines as soon as possible, but the weather and the snowy roads wouldn't allow it. And we had learned the hard way about vehicles coming in the other direction, so I was on the lookout for those as well.

We drove for over an hour as the snow fell heavier, and I had to slow down even more, driving in the lowest gear because the Cheyenne's tires kept slipping.

"We've got to be close, right?" I said.

"The map says we are," Viv said. "According to this map, there should be a command post somewhere up ahead."

"Not that we could see it in this whiteout," I said. It was freezing, but I could feel sweat dripping under my hat. There were no more signs of cottages or shelter. I had four people with me, one seriously injured, that I had to get to safety soon. We couldn't get stuck out here. If we didn't freeze to death, we might end up shot. I was sure the next Germans we ran into wouldn't be friendly.

Suddenly, the Cheyenne started to stutter and then abruptly stalled out.

"No! No, no, no. Dottie, did you check the petrol before we left like I asked?" I yelled over my shoulder into the back.

"I did," Dottie said. "Of course I did. You asked me four times."

I closed my eyes and tried to quell the panic that was bubbling up inside of me.

"Do we have any more in the back we can add?" Viv asked. "You know, just in case that's it."

"We have some in the back," I said. "That better be it. Otherwise . . . I don't even want to think about it."

"I'll help," Hoffman said, following me outside.

"I swear I checked, Fi," Dottie said as she passed Hoffman the can of petrol.

"I know you did. How is he?" I asked.

"He needs his dressings changed again. And he's pretty weak and pale."

"We'll find that checkpoint soon," I said, not convinced at all.

Hoffman was already adding the petrol to the tank. I looked up at majestic fir trees all around us, their branches weighted down by the snow.

"This is not how this is going to end," I whispered under my breath.

"What did you say?" Hoffman asked, frowning at me.

"Talking to myself," I said. "I was just thinking that my friends and I did not come this far to end up captured by Germans or freezing to death on a road in the middle of enemy territory. I will be damned if that happens. We are getting out of here if I have to push this damn truck across the Allied lines myself."

"I don't think it will come to that," Hoffman said, giving me a small smile, sensing that I was a woman on the verge of losing it. "And I promise you I'm not asking because you're a woman or a bad driver, but if you need a break, let me know. You're actually a great driver."

"Thank you," I said. "I'm sorry . . . it's just, it's been a long week."

"You don't have to tell me," he said with a laugh. He held up the can. "She's filled up as much as she can be; hopefully that'll do it."

We climbed back in, where Viv was taking a smoke break, her hand shaking from cold or nerves or both as she inhaled a Chesterfield. She offered one to Hoffman, which he gladly accepted.

"Say a prayer that this thing starts and we're not stuck on this road," I said as I fired up the Cheyenne.

The Cheyenne spun its wheels a few times, but after I banged on the steering wheel and swore at it, we started to move forward. We drove another twenty minutes, my hands gripping the wheel as I leaned over it and kept an eye out for oncoming vehicles.

"Do you see that, Fi?" Viv said, pointing ahead. "Cat-eye lights through the snow, coming this way."

"I see them," I said, as the lights got closer.

"What if it's Germans?" Hoffman asked. The truck came closer still. I stopped the Cheyenne but kept the headlights on.

"It's impossible to tell in this weather . . . if it's Germans," I said. "I don't know, but there's no hiding from them now."

I jumped out of the cab and stood in between our tiny headlights, waving my arms and jumping up and down. The truck was a hundred feet away now, driving very slowly; it had spotted us too. It stopped. Snow had seeped into my fleece-lined boots, and it felt like icicles were forming on my toes. My hands were sore and freezing, yet I was still sweating from the stress of it all. I was desperate, ready to beg for mercy if it was the Germans, anything to get us all back to relative safety and get the colonel medical attention.

"Hello!" I yelled, cupping my hands together.

"Hello," the driver leaned out and called back. There were two men in the cab of the truck; the passenger opened his side and jumped out.

"Americans!" I said, laughing through tears. "Oh, thank God. So, we're over the line?"

"You are," said the passenger, walking over to me. "We're from the closest command post. Everyone's heard the story of your crew trapped in Vielsalm. Lots of soldiers have been keeping an eye out for you."

"I take it these are the girls everyone has been looking for?" the driver yelled to us, laughing.

"Yes," the soldier said, turning to him with a smile, then looking back at me. "That's Cal, and I'm Nate. How are you all holding up?"

I told him about the colonel's injuries, and his face got serious.

"We'll escort you to the command post and get him fixed up there," he said. I started walking away when he called out, "Oh, Fiona, Captain Moretti from the Eighty-Second wanted me to let you know he's been searching for you too."

"Wait," I said, as I tried to process his words. "Is he at the command post?"

"He was," Cal said. "But those guys were heading to the front any minute, so they might already be gone."

I got back into the Cheyenne's cab, not able to stop grinning ear to ear as the driver deftly turned the truck around so we could follow behind.

"Peter's been searching too," I said. "I can't believe it."

"Searching for *you*, through these crazy woods beyond the enemy lines?" Viv said. "Even though I'm sure that's not supposed to be his priority right now?"

"Searching for us, yes," I said.

Viv paused for a second, looking at me.

"Fiona, honey, if that's not love, I don't know what is," she said.

I didn't say anything. She was right, and I felt the now-familiar pangs of guilt settle over my euphoria. But I still desperately wanted to see Peter before he left for the front.

So I started up the Cheyenne and followed the truck down the road, hoping I'd have that opportunity.

~

We arrived at the command post a half an hour later and were greeted with cheers and applause by dozens of soldiers who had heard our story of being trapped at Vielsalm. Several of them helped lift the colonel out of the back and get him safely to the medical tent.

"Dottie!" Joe Brandon came running over, and Dottie screamed as he lifted her into his arms and twirled her around, giving her a kiss that had all the soldiers whistling.

Viv and Hoffman followed some soldiers to the mess hall. I trailed behind them at a distance. Just as I was about to enter the hall, I saw a group of soldiers walking from the other direction. One of them had a boxer's build that I would have known anywhere.

"Fiona Denning, didn't I tell you to get the hell out if things got too hot?" Peter yelled.

I ran to him and jumped into his arms. He scooped me up and kissed my salty tears, and the officers that had been walking with him laughed and cheered us before walking on without him. I buried my face in his chest, feeling safe for the first time in forever.

"How are you even here?" I looked at him when he set me down.

"I could ask the same of you."

"Thank you for searching," I said.

"Of course," he said. "You wouldn't believe how many soldiers have been looking for you three. You Red Cross girls have more fans than you even realize."

He held my hand, and it felt like a jolt of electricity was surging through my fingers. "But what were you thinking going to Vielsalm when the rest of your group was going in the opposite direction?"

I told him about the mail trucks at Bastogne, and the promise I'd made to the major at Vielsalm and how it was supposed to be a quick trip.

He sighed.

"What?" I said.

"I can't decide if you're very brave or very stupid," he said. I started to protest being called stupid but then looked over to see him quietly laughing, teasing me.

"I think naïve might be the best word," I said. "We had no idea how quickly things would turn."

"Nobody did," he said, a shadow crossing his face. "They caught us with our guard down this time."

We walked back over to the mess hall, but he stopped there, taking my elbow and pulling me behind the dining area, where we weren't in view of every soldier entering.

"I'm heading out, Fiona," he said.

"When?"

"Now," he said.

I closed my eyes. Of course he was.

"I'm not even supposed to be here," he said. "I called in a favor to stay back for a day. To look for *you*. I've got a few guys still with me, but now we've got to go."

"Where?" I whispered.

"To the front," he said. I knew that would be his answer. "We'll be gone for a while. Until it's over. And look, as soon as you get something to eat, you've got to get out of here too. Your group is in a château in Verdun, farther south; it's much safer. I know you're exhausted, but we're getting strafed here all the time. Can you drive tonight?"

"Yes," I said. "I can." I was desperate for a shower or a few hours' sleep. But it would be nicer to feel safe. The terror of being on the front had become a constant low buzz in my mind, echoing the sound of the planes roaring overhead.

"Good," he said. "Promise me you'll go as soon as you can?"

"I promise."

Peter looked around to see if anyone was watching and then grabbed both my hands.

"I need to tell you something," he said.

I bit my lip and looked up at him.

"I love you," he said. "You are the best thing that has ever happened to me. When we met, I had just gotten back from Normandy. I was in a really dark place. You pulled me back out." I opened my mouth to respond, but he lifted his hand.

"Please just let me finish. I know you have to find Danny, and who knows what will happen from there, but as hard as it is for me, I understand. If I never see you again—"

"Peter, wait—"

"No, because it's a real possibility; we both know it is," he said. "If I never see you again, just know that I love you, Fiona. I probably always will. And I wish you a long, happy life."

"Peter . . ."

I looked into his eyes wanting to say what I felt, but I couldn't bring myself to speak the words out loud. So instead I stood on my toes, put my arms around his neck, and pulled him into a passionate kiss, not even caring who saw us.

"I was in a dark place too; you helped me remember what it was like to feel happy," I said when we stopped kissing for a moment. "But Danny . . . he's always in the back of my mind. I'm committed to find-ing him. And I'm sorry . . ."

"It's okay," he said, putting his hand under my chin and tilting my head up. "I understand. Like I said, he loved you first. Go find him and rescue him. And thank you. For rescuing me."

He put his arms around me and pulled me in, and we held on to each other in the freezing cold.

"Please be safe," I said, our foreheads still touching. "And for Christ's sake, try to get through this war alive."

"I'll do my best," he said. "And thank you for the kiss. It's probably the best Christmas present I've ever had."

One last hug, a brief, final kiss good-bye, and he started walking away, backward, still looking at me. I stood there watching him, wiping my cheeks.

"Remember, no tears," he said, cupping his hands so I could hear him over the bitter wind that whipped around us. He blew me one last kiss, waved good-bye, and jogged off to round up his soldiers and head to the front.

I stood there for a minute so I could compose myself before heading into the mess hall. When I walked in, Dottie was playing the guitar, and she and Joe were leading a large group of GIs in a very raucous version of "Rudolph, the Red-Nosed Reindeer." Viv was sitting nearby, watching and laughing, but when she saw the look on my face, she came over, putting her arm around my shoulders.

"You okay, Fi?" she asked.

"I have to be," I said, letting out a breath. "Come on, let's eat and run. It's not safe for us here. We need to get back to the rest of the girls."

~

Dottie had said a tearful good-bye to Joe, once again. And we all thanked Hoffman and hugged him good-bye. The colonel was being tended to in the hospital, so we didn't even get to see him before we left. When he was ready to travel, the three of them would be heading to somewhere near Bastogne to regroup with what was left of the Twenty-Eighth.

An hour after dinner, we were gassed up and ready to go, but we sat waiting for a long time as there were important convoys coming through, and the army told us to hold off until they passed. Like everything in war, the trek to Verdun took longer than we expected, as the roads were packed with troops coming and going to the front, ambulances carrying the wounded, and vans of Nazi prisoners.

When we pulled into the large château in Verdun, it was after 10:00 p.m. The sky was clear and star-filled, and the moon was almost full. All the Clubmobiles from Group F were parked outside, and it gave me an overwhelming feeling of coming to someplace like home.

"Do you think anyone's still awake?" Dottie asked. As we slowly opened the front door, we were met with subdued cheering and barking.

"Barbara, you crazy little dog, I have missed you so much!" Dottie said, scooping up the ratty pup and hugging her tightly.

"It's a goddamn Christmas miracle!" Blanche said, teary-eyed as she and Frankie came running over and threw their arms around us, nearly knocking us to the floor with their hugs. To the right of the entryway was a large candlelit room with a roaring fireplace. Every girl from Group F was there, and a Christmas party was well underway. We were greeted with more hugs, surrounded by our friends, and I was overwhelmed with the relief and happiness of being safely back with them. There was a somber air to the group that I chalked up to everyone's holiday homesickness.

"Here." Doris of the Dixie Queen came over and handed us glasses of a bright-yellow sparkling liquid. "No eggnog available, so we made this punch. It's not particularly delicious, but it does the job."

"Quick trip to Vielsalm, huh?" Liz came over to us, her face grave, but then she broke into a smile. "I know why you did it. But I'm just so glad you three are back here safe, you have no idea."

"Me too," I said. "And I'm sorry, I never would have gone had I known . . ."

"Not even the general knew," she said.

"Frankie, I'm so glad you're back. How are you feeling?" I asked.

Frankie looked pale and thinner, with no sign of her usual high energy.

"Well, I won't be wearing a bathing suit anytime soon, but I'm . . . I'm doing okay. Happy to be out of that station hospital," she said. Her eyes filled with tears as she took a deep breath and crossed her arms, and then she started to cry.

"Oh, Frankie," I went over to her and gave her a hug.

"When does Martha get back from the London hospital?" Viv asked.

Blanche and Frankie looked at each other with sad expressions. That's when I noticed Blanche's eyes were puffy, with dark circles under them. The entire room had gone quiet at the mention of Martha's name. The despair on Liz's face told me everything before anyone said a word.

"Viv, Martha . . . she's gone," Blanche said, her face crumpling as she looked at us. "Her hands weren't healing, and she needed more skin grafts. She was still at the station hospital, and they were getting ready to ship her back home to an American hospital for surgery. The station hospital was bombed. She was in the hall, talking to some soldiers. She was the only one who didn't make it."

"Oh no. No, no, no!" Dottie put her hands up to her mouth, sank to the floor, and started sobbing as Barbara jumped onto her lap and tried to comfort her. Liz sat down next to her and put an arm around her shoulder.

Viv cursed loudly and kicked one of the chairs as she put her hands over her face, her chest heaving as she cried.

"I can't believe it," I said, feeling sick, as I wiped away the tears running down my face and hugged Frankie again. "Martha? *Our* Martha gone? Are you sure?"

"I had to identify her," Liz said in a whisper, looking up at me and nodding, her complexion white.

"We had a small ceremony. I'm so sorry we couldn't wait for you," Blanche said, shuddering as she took a breath. "It's been an awful blow. I'll forget for a little while, and then I'll hear a song or see the packs of Life Savers—she loved her Life Savers so much—and then I'll burst into tears all over again."

"And I wake up and think she's going to walk through the door from the hospital any minute," Frankie said, biting her lip. Now I knew why her eyes were so bloodshot. "And then I remember, and I just feel horribly guilty. I had just gotten out. If I had been there—"

"But thank God you weren't, Frankie," I said. "Then we might have lost you too."

"Her poor family," Dottie said, wiping her tears with a napkin.

"We have their address. Everyone's been writing them letters. Not sure if it helps much," Frankie said.

"I think it will," Liz said. "And it will help all of us."

We all sat with this news for a while, sipping our punch and grieving for our sweet friend. It was devastating, and a shock to lose one of our own. To see our happy group of six forever reduced to five.

Frankie got up and said, "I almost forgot. We have a surprise that will cheer all of us up a little. Our Christmas mail from home just showed up yesterday, including copies of *LIFE* magazine. Wait 'til—"

"Shush," Blanche said. "Don't ruin the surprise. Hey, who has one of those *LIFE* magazines handy?"

At the mention of the magazine, everyone started crowding around us, and I looked at Viv and Dottie frowning. ChiChi had tossed one to Blanche, and she had it behind her back.

"Close your eyes," Blanche said.

"What is this about?" Viv said, frowning.

"Oh for Pete's sake, just close them, Viv," Frankie said.

We all closed our eyes, and then seconds later Blanche said, "Now open them."

I opened my eyes, and all the girls were watching our reactions. Blanche was holding a *LIFE* magazine in front of our faces. And our faces were looking back from the cover. An up-close picture of the three of us taken on the day of the ceremony with Harvey Gibson in London. The cover read, *THE RED CROSS CLUBMOBILE GIRLS: BRINGING A BIT OF HOME TO THE TROOPS AT THE FRONT.*

"Holy cow, is that real?" Dottie said.

"No way. You made this," Viv said, grabbing it from Blanche. "It's a practical joke."

"That's a *really* big picture of our faces," I said, wincing.

"It's real all right," Blanche said, and a few other girls in the crowd held up their own copies, smiling. "You gals are now the famous faces of the Red Cross Clubmobilers."

"Harvey Gibson and Judith are absolutely thrilled at the publicity," Liz said. "It's been quite a hit in the States. Speaking of mail, I have to ask, were you able to preserve all of that Christmas mail?"

"We were," Dottie answered her. "Some of it is a little worse for wear, but we've got it."

"Then we really saved all five truckloads," Liz said, nodding, with an expression of relief and pride. "We did it."

"Come see, we've got more mail for you too," Liz said. "Christmas packages from home and cards and—"

"Oh, and something like two dozen letters for Viv from Harry Westwood," Blanche said.

"What?" Viv asked, her cheeks growing pink.

"I'm not kidding, he's crazy," Blanche said. "Come see."

No one was feeling much like a party with the fresh grief over Martha, but the girls had done their best to make things festive for the holiday. There was a Christmas tree in the corner by the window decorated with red bunting and cotton balls. A buffet table had been assembled, and I tried not to pile my plate too high with some of the treats we hadn't had in months, most of which had been donated from Christmas packages from home—cheese, bread, canapés made of anchovies and lobster, melba toast, nuts, figs, stuffed dates, and Christmas fruitcake.

We found some seats by the fireplace, and Blanche and Frankie brought over our mail. My parents and sisters had sent me an amazing care package that included another red wool scarf and matching socks, two new Chanel lipsticks, and several cakes of Harriet Hubbard Ayer soap. It also included jars of jellies, lollipops, cocoa packets, and a package of Mallomars, still intact, which I immediately opened and passed out to my friends.

"I haven't had one of these in ages," Dottie said, closing her eyes after biting into one.

"So Viv, are you going to open at least one letter from Harry?" I said.

"I can't decide," Viv said, twisting her mouth, trying to make up her mind.

"I'll open one for you," Blanche said. "I'm dying to know what he has to say in all those letters."

"Not yet," Viv said. "I need to enjoy my punch and think about it. What's new with Captain Guy, Blanche?"

"We're keeping in touch," Blanche said, her face lighting up at the mention of him. "He's pretty dreamy."

"What's in the package, Dottie?" Frankie said.

"It's a bunch of new records I ordered from a shop in Boston," Dottie said, lifting some out to show us. "'Rum and Coca-Cola' by the Andrews Sisters, 'Long Ago and Far Away' and 'Take the "A" Train' by my new friend Glenn Miller and his band."

"Oh my God, you haven't heard," Blanche said, looking at us. "Of course, you wouldn't have, you were cut off."

"Heard what?" Dottie asked. "Oh no . . ."

"Glenn Miller is missing. He was on a small plane heading over the channel to Paris," Blanche said.

"What?" Dottie said, hugging his record and looking like she might start crying again.

"It's true." Frankie nodded. "Everyone has been following the story. I'm afraid he's gone."

"But . . . no, he can't just be gone," Dottie said. "What about his band? They must be devastated. That night, meeting him? That was one of the best nights of my life."

We sat there in silence for a moment, and I could tell Dottie and Viv were also remembering that beautiful night in Leicester when Dottie finally revealed her talent.

"Enough sad talk; Martha wouldn't want us sitting around here crying all night. I'm getting us some more punch," Blanche said, grabbing our glasses. "And when I get back, I want to hear all about the great adventure you were just on, *especially* any romantic parts."

"And, you know, then I think we might have to put those records on and jitterbug," I said. "In honor of our beautiful friend and her dance skills that put us all to shame."

∽

Liz gave the three of us the next few days off to recover from our ordeal behind the lines. We had real mattresses for the first time in weeks, and we spent most of the time sleeping, writing letters home by the fire, or catching up with friends, sharing stories about Martha and crying when we needed to. All of Group F was devastated by her death, but for the five of us who had known her the best and loved her dearly, it was hard to comprehend that she would never be coming back to us. It was also a grim reminder for all the Clubmobile girls that we were more than just spectators observing the tragedies of war. If it could happen to Martha, it could happen to any of us.

On New Year's Eve, Group F and some soldiers stationed close by planned a party for a nearby orphanage run by French nuns, and it was a welcome distraction from the fresh grief over our friend. When we arrived, it was clear that the soldiers had been spending most of their free time there, because they were greeted by the children as if they were movie stars. They played ball and tossed the kids around as they squealed with delight. It was a brisk day, but the sun was out, so the nuns insisted on having the party outside.

Dottie, Viv, and I passed out doughnuts, hot cocoa, and little bags of candy from the Cheyenne, and watched as one of the soldiers, who was dressed like a clown, performed basic magic tricks using coins and scarves. Two little girls, one with curly black hair, the other with light-brown braids, were in the simple navy-blue smocks that many of the girls wore, under frayed wool coats that were at least one size too small. The girls were standing together enjoying the clown, mesmerized. They didn't speak to each other; instead, they just communicated with their hands, and I realized they didn't speak the same language. The clown pulled a coin out of the curly-haired girl's ear, and they both collapsed into each other giggling.

"Where are all these children from?" I asked one of the nuns who spoke English. She had dark-brown hair and gray-blue eyes and looked no older than me.

"Everywhere," she said, looking around, delighted at the sight of many of her charges seeming so happy. "France, Belgium, Germany, Luxembourg, and the Netherlands."

"Even Germany?"

"Yes," she said. She had a wistful look as she watched the two little girls. "They have suffered too much for ones so young. They have lost everything, yet they still laugh. They still love."

A jeep drove up, and I was surprised when Joe and Colonel Brooks, holding a cane, climbed out. Dottie quickly distributed the bags of candy in her hands and hurried over to greet them.

"Fiona," the colonel said. "You're one of the girls I came here to see."

"It's so good to see you. How are you feeling, Colonel Brooks?" I said, climbing down from the Cheyenne to take a break from passing out sweets. I'm not sure if he was embarrassed by it, yet I couldn't help but give him a hug.

"Better," he said, his pale complexion reddening a little at my affection. He looked much better than the last time I had seen him. He nodded to his brown wooden cane. "Can't wait to get rid of this damn thing, though. I came because I wanted to let you and your friends know that I have kept my promise. I've talked to the major general of the Twenty-Eighth, and we're writing to the War Office to recommend that the three of you receive Bronze Stars for meritorious achievement in a combat zone. Unfortunately, we're not empowered to award decorations to civilians, or I'd do it myself."

"Sir, I . . . I don't even know what to say," I said. "We were just doing what we had to. Thank you. Thank you so much."

"It's deserved. You three saved my life, according to the doctors," he said. "Well, you and that Kraut who stitched me up. I may not have let him touch me if I had been conscious."

"Bronze Stars," Dottie said, holding Joe's hand. "I have to write my parents tonight to tell them."

"Viv just went to get coffee. Here she comes, Colonel." I spotted Viv walking toward us, carrying two cups, but her eyes were on something behind us. Another truck was approaching.

When she reached us, Colonel Brooks informed her of his recommendation for the Bronze Stars. She just stared at him, moved beyond words. She put the coffee cups down and gave him a hug.

"Thank you," she said. "Thank you for the honor."

By this time, the truck had pulled into the courtyard of the orphanage and parked.

"Ah, the Brits are here too," the colonel said. "Quite the New Year's party."

"Isn't it, though?" Viv said in a soft voice, watching as a half dozen Allied soldiers got out, Harry Westwood the second to last one. He did a double take when he saw us standing with the colonel. He walked over slowly, sheepishly, not taking his eyes off Viv the whole time.

"What are you doing here?" Viv said to him, arms crossed over her chest. Her hair was tied up in a red kerchief, and she had a streak of doughnut flour on her cheek.

"We're heading to Germany like just about everyone else," he said. "We heard about the party and wanted to stop by. Did you receive any of my letters?"

"Just last night," she said. "I haven't read them yet."

"I think it might be time for the sing-along soon," Dottie said. "Joe, want to come with me and lend a hand?" Joe nodded, and they walked away.

"Viviana, might I have a word with you, alone?" Harry said, anguished. "There's so much I have to say to you."

"Harry, whatever you have to say, you can say it right here," Viv said to him. Viv shot me a look, making it clear she didn't want me leaving too.

The colonel kept looking back and forth between the two of them, not hiding his amusement at the drama playing out in front of us.

"All right, if that's the way you prefer it," Harry said. "I was a daft fool in Paris. I regret what I said about my family. I've regretted it ever since. I haven't been able to stop thinking about you, Viviana. I want you to meet my family, and I don't give a damn what they think about my being in lo—" He stopped himself and looked at me and the colonel. "Being with an American. I want you to be a part of my life, a part of my future. Please, darling, I'm begging you to give me another chance."

There was a crack in Viv's cool facade. Her eyes glistened; the pink glow in her cheeks also gave her away.

"Are you sure you can handle me, Harry Westwood?" Viv said, cocking her head, her hands now on her hips. "An American woman who's not going to bow down to you or your family even if you end up heir to the throne? I'm not exactly some delicate English rose."

"With that I would agree." Harry looked at her, then up at the sky and back to her with a smile that could launch a film career. "And I love you for all of that and more, Viviana; do you understand that? I love you. Also, I assure you there's no chance I'll end up king. So you should have no worries about that." He paused for a few moments, and she just gazed at him, her face softening, the hint of a smile on her lips.

Harry threw up his hands. "For God's sake, I'm British. We don't generally announce our feelings in front of the world like this, so please say something. Anything."

She stepped toward him and held out her hand.

"Come on," she said, a real smile now. "Help me serve some dough-nuts and candy, and we'll talk."

He smiled back and let out a huge breath as he took her hand, and the two of them headed into the Cheyenne.

The colonel looked at me with such a mischievous smile that I had to laugh.

"Hell, that was like watching one of those romantic movies my wife loves," he said, and we both started laughing. "You'll have to let me know how it ends for them."

"I will," I said. "And I have to ask you something. A favor."

"Tell me," he said. I told him the story of Danny, from the very beginning to the latest news about Stalag Luft IV.

"When the German POW camps are finally liberated, which I hope will be soon, I'd like to be there," I said. "I'm sure that the Red Cross will be sent to help. Can you pull some strings, make sure Clubmobile Group F is one of the first groups sent in?"

The colonel studied me with a combination of pride and compas-sion, like a favorite uncle.

"That's a reasonable request," he said. "I'll get you there if I can, my dear."

"Thank you so much," I said. I gave him one more hug.

"Just know that if you do find your fiancé, he won't be the same person he was when he left for war."

I thought back to Danny and me, sitting on that checkered blanket on the grass at the Bunker Hill Monument days before he left. It was a lifetime ago.

"I do understand that. And that's okay. Neither am I."

Chapter Twenty-Six

April 21, 1945

Dear Deidre, Darcy, Niamh, and Mum and Dad,
Hello from somewhere in Germany (yes, you read that right—that's all the censors will let me say!). I'm sorry it's been so long since I've written; I've barely had time to breathe these past weeks. And it's very hard to read and write by flashlight or candlelight, so I've tried to start this letter many times and given up.

In my last letter, we had just retreated to France after our adventures over Christmas. By the end of January, we were happy to be back on the front lines with the soldiers again, first "somewhere" in Belgium and now here in Germany, as this war is moving very fast these days, and I hope that's a good thing.

The counteroffensive has been nonstop, and it's exciting and rewarding to be a part of it. Relaxation is rare as we are constantly on the move, serving various units. We've been so busy, we're now having a few GIs make the doughnuts for us—which is just fine with me, Dottie, and Viv, as we're all sick of that part of the job. Our days are so long and we're so tired in the evening, we rarely even make it to dinner. Still, I wouldn't trade being here for anything, though I miss you all terribly!

All the American flags here have been flying half-staff at the news of Roosevelt's death. There is something so tragic about the fact that he didn't live to see the final chapter of this war, that he didn't see the results of the Allies' enormous sacrifices and hard work.

Our captain, Liz Anderson, has joined our friends Blanche and Frankie on their Clubmobile the Uncle Sam. The other member of their trio, our dear friend Martha, was killed when the hospital she was staying at was bombed. It's still so difficult for me to write those words. Losing Martha has devastated all of us. She was the sweetest person and a wonderful friend.

I stopped writing and stared at the peeling, pink floral wallpaper in my room. Wiping the tears from my eyes, I realized I would have to rewrite the last part of the letter. It had been almost four months since Martha's death, and we were all still feeling the loss. But sharing the news would only alarm my family.

Since Martha's passing, long days and hard work had been our solace. It was a distraction and a comfort to serve the troops, and it reminded us all of why we were there, despite the ever-present dangers.

By mid-March, we had been ordered to move into Germany near Cologne. The Nazis had put up roadblocks of double rows of logs every hundred yards or so, so getting there was like driving through an unending obstacle course. Witnessing the destruction of the German countryside had been depressing: many towns had been demolished to splinters and rubble, and a grim, deathly pallor permeated everything. The smell of dead bodies was so overwhelming, at times we had to cover our faces with our scarves.

As in France, there were refugees trudging along the roads, pushing wheelbarrows of household goods or carrying shawl bundles or shiny suitcases. Unlike in France, the condition of the German refugees varied greatly. The difference was in the extremity of the condition of the German people we saw; it was varied and shocking. Some were barefoot and emaciated, like walking corpses, while others were deeply tanned and wore German military boots.

Clubmobile Group F was now billeted in a large shell-damaged home on the outskirts of Cologne. With eight bedrooms, it was large enough for all of us, and the local GIs had rigged up stoves in the bedrooms so we weren't cold at night. We were so close to the front, some nights it was impossible to sleep with the constant blasts of artillery fire and the roar of fighter planes overhead.

I wanted to tell my sisters about all of our adventures, about being trapped in Vielsalm and Christmas Eve, about Dottie and Joe Brandon and Princess Viv finding a British aristocrat. I even wanted to tell them about Peter, who was somewhere on the front with the rest of the Eighty-Second, if he was still alive. *If.* I tried not to think about that. In any case, those stories would have to wait.

Someone knocked on the bedroom door, and I called for them to come in.

It was Liz, holding a pile of paperwork per usual.

"Everything okay?" I asked.

"It is," she said. "But we just received new orders, and I wanted to tell you first."

"Oh?" I said, feeling nervous now. I started to crack my knuckles.

"I'm not sure what your friend Colonel Brooks said, but Group F has been assigned to a Luftwaffe base over an hour away."

"What has this got to do with Colonel Brooks?"

"Several hundred Allied POWs have just been liberated over the past forty-eight hours—they've been taken to that base. It's the first word of POWs being liberated anywhere in the ETO."

"So we're going there when?" I asked.

"As soon as you're ready," she said.

The hairs on the back of my neck stood up, and I felt slightly ill.

"He honored your request, Fiona," Liz said. "We probably wouldn't have even heard about this if it wasn't for Colonel Brooks."

"He did," I said. "And I can't quite believe we're going there today."

"But are you really ready? For where we're going?" Liz said, examining my face. "This is what you've been waiting for."

"I'm ready," I said, my stomach still churning. "But I'm trying to keep my expectations low. It's not like Danny's going to walk off the first truck that arrives."

⁓

The first Clubmobile convoy to the Luftwaffe base consisted of just the Cheyenne and the Uncle Sam. It was led by none other than our friendly liaison, Captain Guy Sherry. I'm not sure how exactly the captain ended up getting assigned to our group again, and I was surprised Liz approved it, but Blanche was thrilled. Though the two of them were discreet, somehow it just made their romance all the more obvious.

We pulled up in front of the base's airdrome, which was now the US Command's quarters, and went to introduce ourselves to the officer in charge.

"They were just prisoners of war yesterday, so many of them are still in rough shape," Lieutenant Colonel Craighill told us when we met in his office. With glasses and a shock of white hair, he looked more like an Ivy League college professor than an officer.

"As of today, we have six hundred of them here, mostly British, with a few Americans and Indians." He looked at us like a man with the world on his shoulders. "I'll be honest, girls: we had set up an infirmary in this building, but other than that, we were caught unprepared for the numbers and the condition of these men. Some of them haven't eaten much in days; we're working on getting more food supplies. There's supposed to be a shipment of K rations or ten-in-one rations—hopefully both—coming soon. The Red Cross is also supposed to be shipping a huge delivery of POW relief care packages with soap and toothpaste and all those necessities, but that may not get here until next week.

"We need more water for drinking and washing; we don't even have a system for registering them and getting them assigned to barracks yet. They all need personnel records, and we need to interview each of them to make sure there're no Nazi spies or sympathizers in the bunch." He paused and then added, with sarcasm, "Other than that, things are going great."

Craighill rubbed his face in frustration before he looked us over. "Just do whatever you can for them. Make sure they write letters home, that's important. The letters will be censored, but they need to get them to their loved ones. Some of these boys have been away for a long time."

We promised we would do our best for them. As we were walking out the door, he called to Liz, "Oh, Miss Anderson, you'll need the rest of your group here tomorrow. I just received word that over two thousand more will be here in the next twenty-four hours."

"Jesus," Viv said. "This is insanity."

"They're going to need a hell of a lot more than coffee and doughnuts," I said.

"Agreed," said Liz. "We'll figure it out."

We drove the Clubmobiles out onto the airfield that had become a makeshift tent city across hundreds of acres. Men walked over to us from all directions: some clapping and cheering at the sight of us, others silent and gaping like they couldn't believe their eyes. They were covered in dust and grime. Many were so thin, their cheeks appeared hollowed out and their uniforms hung on them like rags.

"God bless them," Dottie whispered, looking out at the crowds descending upon our trucks.

"Come on up, sweetheart," I said to a shy soldier with sandy-blond hair.

"Where are you from?" I said, handing him a doughnut.

"Manchester, England," he said in a British accent, staring down at the doughnut. "I was captured at Dunkirk."

"I'm sorry, did you say Dunkirk?" I said, frowning. "But . . . that was five years ago."

His eyes filled with tears, and he just nodded. I bit the inside of my cheek like I had learned to do to keep from crying.

"Honey, we've got hot water for tea," I said, forcing myself to give him a reassuring smile. "I know how you English like your tea. Can I get you a cup?"

"Thank you," he said, wiping his dirty face with the back of his hand. "That would be . . . thank you."

Men came in steady streams for hours, lured by the smell of coffee and doughnuts. We gave out all the candy and cigarettes we had, and then with the help of Colonel Craighill and our own inventory of supplies, we put Blanche in charge of a "personal service counter" to supply the men with soap, toothbrushes, razors, and blades.

Late that afternoon, a few more trucks rolled into camp, this time all American soldiers. Viv and I walked over to greet the first truck and hand them doughnuts as they got out.

They gasped when they realized we were American girls. Blushing and speechless, they stood around us, just staring as we tried to talk to them.

"What's wrong, fellas?" I said finally, looking around at them. "We keep asking questions, but why aren't you all talking to us? You're free now. You're safe."

A soldier stepped forward, his hair so covered with dust, it was hard to determine the color. He had big brown eyes that looked too large for his gaunt face. "Miss Red Cross?" he said to me.

"Yes, sweetheart, what is it?"

"Could I touch your hand?"

"Why, of course you can," I said, my voice quiet. I smiled and held out my hand.

He reached out and took my hand in both of his and turned it over as if in awe. He looked up at me, tears running down his face, his lips trembling. And this time, no matter how much I bit my cheek or blinked, I couldn't stop my own tears from falling. I looked over at Viv, and she was crying too.

"We're here now," I said, squeezing his hand and looking around. Other soldiers were weeping too. "We didn't forget. There's a whole world out here that didn't forget you."

The day turned into night, and those scenes happened over and over again. Some ex-prisoners were elated, shaking our hands or just holding them for a moment. But more than a few broke down crying. It was impossible not to get emotional when you heard some of what they had been through. We'd no sooner get back to the Cheyenne and compose ourselves when another truck would pull up and it would start all over again.

When we had a lull, Dottie took out her guitar, and I had never seen such happiness on men's faces as she played some of the upbeat American favorites, like our old standby "Don't Sit Under the Apple Tree."

More trucks kept arriving, and we worked to do whatever we possibly could to get the men comfortable and fed and adjusted to their new reality as recovered Allied military personnel, or RAMPS, as they were now called.

"That's it, girls." Liz came over to the Cheyenne at ten o'clock. "Just told the others we should call it a day; we need to be back here with everyone at the crack of dawn tomorrow. A supply of ten-in-one rations just came in, so we're going to start a soup line in the morning. I've got a group of GIs that will build us some extra field ranges for it."

"There's another truck coming," I said, pointing to the headlights in the distance.

My feet were aching, and we were all in need of showers and sleep. I looked down at my coffee-stained uniform and mud-crusted shoes. I wanted to leave, but it was just one more. "Should we just greet them and give them whatever we have left? I'd feel terrible if they watched us drive away just as they're getting here."

Liz watched as the lights got closer and nodded. She looked as tired as I felt. "Okay, one more truck, and then we'll hit the road."

Dottie grabbed the cigarettes and candy. Viv and I both took our last trays of doughnuts from the third supply that our GI bakers had dropped off earlier.

"If any of them want coffee, send them over here," Frankie called to us from the Uncle Sam. "We've got two urns left."

"And plenty of toothbrushes and razors," Blanche added.

Viv and I stood ready to greet the soldiers as they descended from the truck. It was immediately clear that this group was in dire shape, worse than any of the others we had encountered that day. They were so thin, their chests concave and their pants practically falling off; many of them hobbled when they walked. A few smiled and thanked us, but most had dazed expressions, a look of shock that I had seen often in this war.

"Wow, American Red Cross girls," a soldier with pale-blue eyes said as he accepted a doughnut and a candy bar from me. "It's like I've gone to heaven."

"Welcome back, soldier," I said. "Feel good to be free?"

"You got that right," he said. "All these guys with me, we were all on the march together, goddamn hell on earth. They forced us to march in the freezing cold and snow when they knew the Allies were closing in." He shuddered and shook his head as if to shake out the memories. "But now we're free, and here you are with American doughnuts. I'm not even sure my stomach can handle real food after all this time."

"Well, I think we've still got some soup or warm milk and Cream of Wheat if that would be better for you," I said.

But he took a bite, tilting his head and studying my face carefully. "You look familiar, Miss Red Cross," he said. "Like I've seen your picture before."

"Maybe you saw the *LIFE* magazine photo?" I asked. "My friends and I were on the cover of a recent issue."

"Sweetheart, I haven't seen a *LIFE* magazine in two years," he said with a laugh.

"American Red Cross girls and doughnuts." Another of the more talkative soldiers got off the truck and limped over, wearing just pajamas, a German raincoat, and straw slippers. He looked terrible, but seemed overjoyed to be liberated. "Almost makes marching three hundred miles worth it."

"I think we can get you some decent clothes and shoes, honey," I said, looking at his raw, blistered feet in the slippers. "They just brought some in from a quartermaster salvage depot."

It was another hour before we were finished serving all the newly arrived soldiers from "the march." Some headed over to the Uncle Sam for coffee or to get personal supplies from Blanche. Many of them were being escorted to the infirmary to get checked out for lice or scabies and other ailments.

I nodded good-bye to the pale-blue-eyed soldier as I was walking back to the Cheyenne with Dottie and Viv, finally ready to go back to our billet and sleep.

He stopped and pointed to me again.

"I *know* I've seen you before," he said.

"Another *LIFE* magazine fan?" Viv said to him.

"No, I already told her, that wasn't it . . ." He paused for a moment, and his face got serious, and then he started shaking his head in disbelief. "My God," he said, looking into my eyes. "You're the girl from Barker's photo? Danny's fiancé?"

I heard the doughnut tray fall to the ground before I realized I had dropped it.

Dottie started picking up the stray doughnuts and putting them back on the tray, watching me as she did. Viv grabbed my hand as I stepped closer to the soldier, not believing my ears.

"What did you just say? Say it again," I said, swallowing hard and shaking, as I tried to hold back the tears.

"I'm right. The freckles, the hair. You're Fiona, aren't you?" he said, his voice quiet, taking an even closer look at my face. "From Danny Barker's photo—he kept it in his pocket. I'm Chris Sullivan; we were on the march together. From Stalag Luft IV. He was in my combine, my group. He's my friend. We helped keep each other alive, but . . ."

I felt like I was listening to his words from the other end of a tunnel. I leaned into Viv, feeling light-headed.

"Is Danny Barker alive? Where is he?" Viv said.

"Please tell me you know where he is," I said.

"Sweetheart, I'm sorry," Chris said, putting a hand on my shoulder, looking into my eyes. "He's . . . he's gone. Danny died on the march a few weeks ago."

That feeling of a tunnel, black spots in my vision, and then the next thing I knew I was waking up on the ground, my head on Viv's lap, Dottie and the soldier named Chris Sullivan kneeling next to us. And I immediately remembered why. I sat up, leaned into Viv, and sobbed in a way I hadn't since we walked off the *Queen Elizabeth*. I let the dam break on my emotions and propped myself against my friends, letting them hug me as I cried until I felt like I had no more tears left.

"I'm sorry," I said after a while, wiping my face with the back of my dirt-caked hands. "All this time, *he's* why I ended up here. And I've been trying to find out what happened to him and hoping against hope for over a year, and now . . ."

"Fiona, I'm so sorry," Chris said. He had been crying too. And I looked at the condition of him, emaciated, dressed in his ragged uniform, and yet here he was trying to comfort *me*. "I need to find Lee; he was also in our combine and one of Danny's best friends. You'll want to talk to him."

He got up, and Viv rose too and said something to him.

"Fi, let's go inside and get warm," Dottie said, grabbing my hand. It had started to drizzle, and the temperature had dropped.

"Chris and his friend will find us," Viv said.

Lieutenant Craighill led us to an empty office when Viv told him the story. He came back with a pot of coffee and some cups.

"Take all the time you need," Craighill said. "I'm so sorry, Fiona. I know this isn't the news you had hoped for."

I gave him a small smile just as Chris showed up accompanied by a tall, olive-skinned soldier with auburn hair who was probably quite handsome fifty pounds ago, but now I couldn't get past how scarecrow-thin he was.

"My God. Fiona Denning, it is an honor to meet you. I'm Lee Valenti," the soldier said, staring at me in wonder, reaching for my hand. "He showed me your picture so many times, I would know you anywhere."

"That's what I said," Chris said.

"There was a crew of us that met at the camp," Lee said. "Me, Chris, Danny, and our buddy Roger stuck together. When the Allies were closing in and they forced us on the march, we all stayed in small groups, tried to pool our resources."

"Fiona, you need to know, Danny Barker was a soldier's soldier," Chris said. "More than a few men who marched with him from Stalag Luft IV would tell you they wouldn't have survived without him. He was one of those—his attitude and his sacrifice helped us all keep going. If he found a coat, he would share it. If men were too sick to walk anymore, he would be one of the first to help carry them. He was always scavenging and bargaining for food with the Germans, because what the Nazis were giving all of us wasn't nearly enough."

"We were living on potato peels and raw turnips, not much else," Lee said with a grimace.

"Bastards," Viv said. Chris and Lee just nodded and accepted the cigarettes she offered.

"So, what happened to Danny?" I said. "Why isn't he here with you?"

The two soldiers looked at each other, trying to decide who would tell me the rest.

"He sliced open his ankle on some metal debris in the road," Chris said, taking a drag of his cigarette. "One of the Allied doctors on the march with us tried to stitch him up as best he could with what he had. But it got infected, and they didn't give the docs any sulfa powder or penicillin to treat infection—Geneva Conventions, my ass. Meanwhile, Barker's still helping carry our friend Roger, who's sick as a dog at this point, can barely walk he's so weak, and Barker's limping himself because his ankle's not good at all, but he insisted on helping."

I looked over at Viv and Dottie, and like me, they were listening and wiping away silent tears.

"We just slept on the freezing-cold ground, huddled together in fields on the side of the road. One night I woke up and I heard yelling. The guards were dragging Roger away from our group, and Dan had woken up and was screaming at them, asking where they were taking him." Chris took another cigarette from Viv, and I noticed he had the shakes.

"So, Chris and I got up and followed after them too," Lee said, continuing the story, his voice low and slow as he stared blankly ahead, reliving the movie in his mind. "They dragged Roger into a wooded area along with a few other soldiers. Meanwhile Barker's limping right behind them, shouting at them. The two of us are trying to figure out what the hell is going on, and that's when the guards started firing shots. First Roger, then Barker. The bastards . . . They said that Roger and Barker were both too sick to go on, so they executed them. Then they pointed the guns toward us and told us to get back with the group or we'd be next."

The room was quiet except for the sound of our quiet crying. Chris swore under his breath, and Lee came back from reliving it and looked at me, eyes moist.

"I'm so sorry," he said. "I have a letter in my bag. For you. I'll go get it."

Lee ran from the room to wherever his bag was. Chris put the cigarette up to his lips, his hand shaking the whole time.

"I'm sorry too," Chris said to me. "He was exactly that, a soldier's soldier. Please know that he saved lives on that march. I know that for a fact."

Lee came running back into the room and handed me the letter, and Danny's familiar messy handwriting made me start sobbing again. All the things that I had started to forget about him came back in a rush, and my heartbreak suddenly felt as raw and fresh as when I had first left Boston.

"We'll let you girls have some time to yourselves," Chris said. We all hugged each other good-bye, and it was awkward and heartfelt at the same time.

"Thank you," I whispered.

After they left, Dottie pulled me into an embrace that I couldn't leave.

"Talk to us," Viv said.

"What do you want me to say?" I said, my tears spilling out again, wondering if I'd ever be cried out. "All this time, and I find out he's really gone? All that hope I had for him, for us. And then I feel so foolish. Why did I think he'd survive when so many hadn't? Why did I think *I* would be the loved one spared the grief that thousands of others have felt? Why did I think we were so special that we would be spared?

"And I'm devastated all over again . . . and I feel *so guilty*. I keep thinking maybe if I could have done more to try to find him . . . written more letters to the International Red Cross . . . anything . . ." I just put my head in my hands. I couldn't even finish the sentence. I was physically and mentally spent.

"You need to sleep and eat and take some time off to grieve," Viv said. "Let's take you back to the house, Fiona."

"I have to write his mother . . . Oh no, they won't let me write his mother or my family about it yet, will they?"

Dottie shook her head.

"Let's go, Fiona," Dottie said. "You need to rest."

"No. Tomorrow, I'm still going to work," I said. "We need to help these POWs; Liz needs us."

Viv and Dottie gave each other a look like they were trying to manage me, and it made me crazy. And at that moment, I realized how wiped out they looked. The day had taken a toll on them too.

"Fi . . . ," Dottie said. "Let yourself grieve. Please take a day or two off."

"I know you both mean well. But I need to be busy," I said. "I don't want to sit around the house and just be alone with my thoughts right now. That would be the worst thing."

There was a pause in conversation as they both looked me over and considered.

"All right," Viv said, clearly not convinced. "*Only* if that's what you want. Just promise you'll talk to us if you need to? Take a break if you need to?"

"Yes, thank you. And I will read his letter when I'm ready," I said, tucking it in my pocket with the Purple Heart, which felt heavy with guilt. "And I'll also take some time. But right now? I'd rather get up tomorrow morning and help these men. After all, some of them were Danny's friends."

We headed to the Cheyenne and I tried to push all my feelings down, as I had for months. But this time, I knew they wouldn't stay there.

Chapter Twenty-Seven

April 27, 1945

Dear Fiona,

If you're reading this, that means things haven't gone well for me, so I hope you never do read it. Or I hope we read this together as newlyweds and both have a laugh as we throw it into the fireplace.

Today I write this from a POW camp, having been captured by the Germans when my plane crashed. I still have that photo of you from that perfect day on Bunker Hill. I'm looking at it right now.

I've thought hard about what to say in this letter, what is supposed to be my last good-bye to you, but in the end, words could never be enough. Just know that I love you, Fiona. I should have told you that every single day.

And whatever happens, I want you to be happy— that's my one request. Do all of the things we talked about. Even if I'm gone, move out of your family's home, get some pets, travel, and have some adventures. Also think about getting a new job—we both know you're too good for that mayor's office.

This is the hardest part for me to write—but please do fall in love again. Get married, have babies—all of those things. I want you to have a long, wonderful life—you'll honor me by doing that.

I'm so sorry this war cut our time together short. Thank you for the memories that have helped me get through it all. I'll be seeing you . . .

All my love,

Danny

I'd read it a hundred times, but it was still hard to grasp that I had finally, after all these months, discovered Danny's fate, discovered that he had died. Again, I wondered if every wife or fiancé was as naïve as I had been. I thought out of the thousands, he'd be one of the soldiers spared, because he was my soldier.

For the next several days after I learned the news, I channeled my grief into our work with the POWs, as more trucks of them arrived at the camp almost hourly. After the chaos of the first couple of days, the army finally began registering these poor men, interviewing them, and then assigning them to blocks of barracks upon their arrival.

The Red Cross also brought in more staff and opened a service club on the field, where men could write letters home or play cards or Ping-Pong while waiting for the planes to take them out. We worked long days, serving food, mending clothes, finding fresh clothes, and tracking down shoes and medicine and anything else they needed.

We answered hundreds of questions a day. Easy ones like, "Who won the World Series?" *The St. Louis Cardinals.* As well as more delicate ones such as, "Will my wife think I've changed too much?" or "Do you think my girlfriend still loves me?" *I think your wife will just be thrilled you're still alive . . . Of course, she still loves you.*

My friends all kept checking in with me, making sure I was okay. I was, and I wasn't. I would wake up in the morning thinking that Danny was still missing, only to remember seconds later that this time he was gone forever, and I'd have to let it sink in all over again.

After delays due to weather, they started flying the men out in huge numbers, the Brits to England, the Americans to ports of embarkation where they would then be shipped home. Seeing the absolute happiness on their faces as they left filled me with a mixture of joy and bittersweet sadness, and I had to take more than a few quiet moments alone to have a good cry.

On Friday night, Liz had called a meeting for all of Group F at the château. I had just taken a shower when Dottie knocked on the door of our bedroom and peeked in.

"Coming down?" she asked. I was in the threadbare pink pajamas that had traveled the ETO with me, my sleeping bag wrapped around my shoulders. I couldn't get warm. "I know you think we're hovering over you, because we are. You don't look good. And I'm not just talking about the weight you've lost."

I had lost weight. My uniform pants were barely staying up, but the fresh grief over Danny had made everything taste like sawdust. And I was definitely coming down with something, but I shrugged it off.

"It's just a cold," I said through chattering teeth. Dottie came in the room and put her hand on my forehead.

"You're burning up."

"It's not that bad," I said, as I started coughing.

"Uh-huh," she said, rolling her eyes. She helped me wrap the sleeping bag tighter around my shoulders, and we headed downstairs.

Everyone was socializing. Blanche waved us over. She was sitting in the front with Viv and Frankie, and they were chatting with Doris, Rosie, and ChiChi. Liz stood near the fireplace, next to something large and square covered with an army blanket. After she scanned the crowd and did a quick head count, she began to speak.

"First, I have surveys up here that the Red Cross needs all of you to fill out, to let them know what you plan to do next now that this war is mercifully winding down. Your options include heading to the Pacific, going home, or staying here with the occupation forces. Please remember that I'll be staying in the ETO, and there will be positions available in London, Paris, and Berlin at the very least."

Liz gave me a pointed look and a smile when she mentioned the ETO jobs, and I was flattered she wanted me to consider it. But did I want to stay? I tried to imagine myself living in Paris, working at the Red Cross headquarters there. My future was wide-open, which was strange and exciting and sad all at once. And judging from everyone's surprised reactions, it was the first time any of us realized we'd have to make that kind of decision so soon.

"Now, you have some time to think about it," Liz said, raising her voice above the chatter and raising her hand for quiet again. "I don't need to send these back to headquarters until the end of May, but please try to get them to me as soon as you know what your plan is."

She paused and smiled, putting her hand on the square covered by the army blanket.

"I also wanted to call you all together tonight just to say how proud I am of you and the work we have done here with the POWs," Liz said. "I think you'll agree with me when I say that while it's been some of the hardest work I've done in the ETO, it's also been some of the most rewarding." There were nods and murmurs of agreement from all over the room.

"Some statistics I think you'll be interested in: In the past week we have served sixty-four thousand doughnuts and five thousand gallons of coffee, four thousand packs of cigarettes, and fifteen thousand packs of gum." She looked around, smiling as all of us clapped.

"Most importantly, we have helped soldiers from over fifteen different countries, including Poland, Greece, China, South Africa, and Australia. Now, I don't know about you, but I think that calls for a celebration. And Lieutenant Craighill has generously provided us with champagne for the occasion."

The room erupted in cheers as Liz pulled the army blanket away to reveal two cases of champagne.

Frankie and Viv jumped up to help Liz open one of the cases and uncork a couple of bottles. A few girls ran out to their Clubmobiles and brought back as many mugs as they could carry.

"No thanks," I said, when Viv came over with two mugs, one for me and one for her.

She handed it to me anyway and then sat down on part of my sleeping bag. Frankie, Dottie, and Blanche came over to sit down with us too. It wasn't until Liz showed up with Dr. Caplan, a medical doctor from the POW infirmary, that I got suspicious.

"Dr. Caplan, what are you doing here?" I said, frowning.

"We asked Dr. Caplan to come by and take a look at you," Dottie said.

"What is this?" I said, looking around at my friends. "I've got a cold, that's all. I'm doing fine, just a little overworked."

"A little overworked?" Blanche said. "Sweetie, you haven't *stopped*, despite losing Danny."

"And I love you and your stubbornness," Viv said, "but I refuse to stand by while you work yourself to death due to grief and needless guilt. You need to knock it off."

"All right, all right," I said, holding my hands up in surrender. "You don't have to gang up on me. Doc, will you check me out?"

"Yes. And I've already written you one prescription that you must fill in two weeks' time," Dr. Caplan said.

"What?" I said. "You haven't even taken my temperature."

He handed me a piece of paper and I unfolded it.

"This is a prescription . . . ," I said, squinting as I tried to decipher his handwriting, "for a ten-day leave in Antibes?" I looked up at him, frowning. "The South of France—are you serious?"

"Yes. You need a vacation—that's an order," he said, smiling. "In two weeks, assuming you're well enough to travel by then. I'm guessing pneumonia from the looks of you."

"The South of France is actually an order for the *five* of you that I've already arranged," Liz said. "None of you have taken a break since Paris, and you need one. Things are getting under control here now, supplies are coming in, we've got more personnel. We'll be in great shape by May."

Frankie and Dottie clinked glasses as Frankie let out a whoop.

"You don't have to tell me twice," Viv said, getting up from the floor. "This calls for more champagne."

"Ten days at the beach," Blanche said. "We'll have to do some shopping when we get there; I want to burn all my clothes."

"But . . ." I tried to come up with the words, but what could I say?

Frankie grabbed my hand and squeezed it. "Fiona, you know I understand how you feel. You still need to *live*."

"I know," I said. "I just have these moments of feeling so lost. My plan was to find him. And now? I don't know what the hell I'm going to do next. Do you?"

"Yes," Frankie said. "I'm going to get on a plane and head to the French Riviera on May 11. How about we all try not to think much beyond that?"

"Couldn't agree more, Frankie," Dottie said, looking at me. "All right?"

"Okay," I said, taking a deep breath. "Let's go on vacation."

~

It was pneumonia, as Dr. Caplan had suspected. I spent the next two weeks in bed, sleeping most of the days away, and after a course of penicillin, I was feeling well enough to travel to the South of France.

"I'll be honest, Fi. If you hadn't gotten better? I was going to convince the girls we had to ditch you. I swear I have never needed a vacation more."

"Uh, thanks?" I said to Blanche, and she just smiled and put her arm around my shoulder.

The five of us had just disembarked from a C-47 in glorious Nice, France, the gorgeous sunny weather a reflection of the mood all over Europe. On April 30, Hitler had committed suicide in Berlin, and then on May 8, the Allies had formally accepted Nazi Germany's unconditional surrender of its armed forces. After six years of suffering through a harrowing war in which so much had been lost, people broke out in huge celebrations in the streets in cities and towns all over Europe. And everywhere you looked, there were smiles on faces and Allied flags draped on buildings. Though there was still fighting in the Pacific, the world was breathing a collective sigh of relief that things were drawing to a close.

The small airport in Nice was teeming with Allied military, many of whom whistled or called to us as we walked by. Several hotels along the French Riviera had been opened for officers and GIs so they could finally get some rest and relaxation.

"When we were trapped in Vielsalm, I never thought I'd feel this warm again," Viv said, her face turned up to the sun.

We got into a waiting shuttle bus for the forty-minute drive to Juan-les-Pins, a resort town just next to Antibes. We kept the windows rolled down and gasped at the beauty of the famed Côte d'Azur—the breathtaking beaches with their turquoise-blue waters, the palm trees, brilliant tropical flowers, and dazzling sunlight.

The Hôtel le Provençal was a ten-story white stucco hotel, one of five in the French Riviera that had been taken over by the Red Cross. Our driver informed us that it had been built by the American millionaire Frank Jay Gould in 1926 and that Ernest Hemingway and Charlie Chaplin had both stayed there.

Dottie, Viv, and I were given a room on the fourth floor. It had a stone balcony with a view of the sea and the mountains in the distance. Just below us was an enormous landscaped terrace with wicker chairs and tables. Off the terrace was a gravel path flanked by a low stone wall draped with bright-magenta bougainvillea. Beyond it was a small, sandy beach.

"I have never been anywhere this beautiful," Dottie said in a quiet voice as we stood on the balcony and took in the view.

"It's so stunning, it doesn't even look real," Viv said.

"Any word from Harry Westwood?" I asked Viv, wondering if she would be reuniting with him this week.

"Yes, of course," Viv said, her face lighting up. "He's coming down in a few days, staying nearby at the Hotel Eden Roc with a slew of British officers."

"Yes, *of course?*" Dottie said. "Is this getting serious, Viv?"

"Maybe." She gave us a playful grin. "You'll have to wait and see. And Joe?"

"They've opened up hotels for officers in Cannes, so that's where he'll be in a couple of days," Dottie said, chewing on her hair. She had been preoccupied lately. But all of us had been to some degree, the Red Cross survey weighing on our minds.

What would we all do next? I was still feeling adrift, even more so now that this chapter with my friends was coming to an end.

"Your turn, Fiona," Viv said, as she brought out the complimentary bottle of rosé the hotel had left in our room. "Any news about Peter Moretti that you haven't told us about?"

"Nothing," I said, sitting down on one of the chairs on the balcony, not taking my eyes off the ocean. "I don't think he made it; I think I would have heard from him if he had."

"I've heard the Eighty-Second went through hell these last few months," Viv said.

"Viv, not helpful," Dottie said, giving her a look.

"No, it's okay; I've heard the same," I said, picturing him at the command post, our last kiss, our last words. "Thousands were lost in the fighting in the Ardennes. I haven't even tried to find out if he made it out alive. I just can't take more bad news about another person I care about. And then, of course, I still feel some guilt about caring about him at all."

"Honey, I know you're still on an emotional roller coaster with all that's happened," Viv said. "But I think it's about time you stopped feeling so guilty."

"She's right," Dottie said. "We've been living in strange circumstances. Stop feeling guilty about caring for someone else that was right here with you."

Do fall in love again . . . I thought of Danny's letter, how hard it must have been for him to write those words. I hadn't realized how much I needed to hear them until I read his letter.

"You're both right, and I'm working on it," I said.

We sat there at the small iron table on our balcony, sipping our rosé and admiring the view, listening to the seagulls cry to one another.

"Even though this was not how I hoped things would turn out," I said, "I'd do it all again. I'd do it all again in a heartbeat."

"I think that makes three of us," Viv said. Dottie just nodded as we watched the sky shift into shades of pink, orange, and gold as the sun set over the Mediterranean.

∽

We spent our days swimming and sunbathing on the beach and our nights dining and dancing, alternating between Harry, Guy, and Joe's friends. I got so much sun, the freckles on my cheeks multiplied, and the blonde streak in the front of my hair bleached out. And with such delicious breads and cheeses and fresh seafood available, my appetite finally returned with a vengeance.

On our second-to-last afternoon, the five of us were sitting on the beach and it occurred to me that I felt content, even happy. Since Danny had gone missing, there had been a part of me that had been holding on to life with white knuckles, forever waiting for news about him, afraid to ever breathe easy until I knew his fate.

My mind-set was starting to shift. Frankie was right—the not knowing anything had been torture. And though my heart still ached from the loss, there was a kind of peace in the knowledge that I hadn't had before. Even though it would take me some time to completely heal, I felt a calmness I hadn't felt since before Danny left for the war.

I couldn't deny that I was still waiting on news of another soldier. In the past week, we had run into many of the officers and GIs we had met on our travels around the ETO, but so far none of our friends from the Eighty-Second.

Viv and Blanche were both asleep, stretched out on their beach chairs like cats in the sun. Frankie and Dottie had walked down to the water for a swim, and I got up to join them.

Dottie's olive skin was now a deep bronze, and she looked striking in her pale-pink bathing suit. Frankie had her curls tied in a handkerchief on her head and was wearing a navy-blue one-piece bathing suit. She was lying on her back, floating. The skin on her right thigh that had been burned still looked melted and raw, but she wasn't the least bit self-conscious. The two of them were laughing and splashing each other like little kids.

I dove in, and the salt water that hit my skin was the perfect temperature, refreshing but not frigid cold like the ocean off New England.

"We're staying here tonight because there's a great band playing on the patio," Dottie said when I floated over to them. "Joe and his friends are coming, Harry's too."

"Sounds good," I said. "I think I'll wear that new white dress I bought yesterday."

"Are you going to sing, Dots?" Frankie asked.

"Maybe," Dottie said, smiling. "I've been practicing a few new songs with Joe. It depends; some bands don't like it when someone jumps in."

"Glenn Miller didn't mind, why should they?" I said.

"No, Glenn Miller didn't mind," Dottie said with a sigh. "God bless poor Glenn Miller." They had never found his plane in the English Channel.

Dottie got out of the water and went to join our friends lying in the sun. Frankie and I swam out a little deeper, chatting and treading water, enjoying the view of the beautiful beach in the stunning golden light of the late-afternoon sun.

"I talked to Liz about the survey and what I want to do next," Frankie said as she treaded water.

"Oh?" I said. "And?"

"I'm putting in for one of the Red Cross positions in Berlin."

"Are you really?"

"Yes," Frankie said. "And I think you should join me."

I was quiet for a moment, looking up at the seagulls crying overhead as I thought about it.

"If anywhere, I was thinking of London or Paris. I hadn't even considered Berlin . . ."

"We'll be at the center of things if we go there," Frankie said. "There's so much to do still, so many soldiers and civilians to help. Liz will give you the highest recommendation, I'm sure."

"I don't know," I said. Like most of the Clubmobile girls, the question of what was next for me had been weighing on my mind. What did I want now that my future was mine alone?

"Promise me you'll think about it?" Frankie said. "I'd love for you to go with me. And I know you're feeling a little lost about what to do next, trying to figure out this unexpected future."

"I am," I said. "Thank you. I will definitely think about it."

We got out of the water and joined the group just as Viv returned with bottles of Coke for all of us.

"Well, since we're here together alone and it concerns all of you, I've got an announcement," Viv said. She was perched on her chair now, wearing a black one-piece, green-framed sunglasses, and a wide-brimmed straw hat, looking movie-star glamorous as she sipped her Coke.

Dottie looked at me; whatever Viv had to say was news to both of us too.

"I've decided, instead of going home or to the Pacific after this, I'm going to London. I'm going to work at the Red Cross club there and take some art classes." She paused as if for dramatic effect, and giving us a sly smile, she added, "Oh, and I'm also marrying Harry Westwood in three weeks."

Frankie spit out her mouthful of Coke in a messy spray, and the few people sitting around us looked up in horror. Dottie and I gasped, and Blanche jumped up, cheering and clapping.

"Viv!" I said, giving her a hug. "Oh my God, this is huge news. So, wait—are you really going to be Princess Viviana now?"

"God no," she said. "I haven't met his parents yet, but they're apparently getting used to the idea of me. They're not exactly royalty, just upper class."

"Isn't he a duke or something?" Frankie asked.

"Yes. I mean, no. He's a lord. And he also happens to be the love of my life," Viv said. "When we reunited in Verdun, I realized it. And being his wife and living with him in London? I want to pinch myself at the thought of it, I'm so happy."

She had taken off her sunglasses, and her eyes were teary, and I couldn't recall ever seeing my cool, collected friend so overcome with joy.

"Oh, Viv, I couldn't be more thrilled for you," Dottie said, getting choked up as she threw her arms around our friend.

"Details, please," Blanche said.

"It's going to be at the Hotel George V in Paris. You're all bridesmaids—my parents and sisters won't be able to come on such short notice, so I'm going to need you gals there."

"Of course," Frankie said. "Are we wearing our uniforms?"

"Absolutely not," Viv said. "No uniforms except on the guys. But you can wear whatever dresses you'd like, so that'll be easy. And we don't have a lot of time, so I need you all to help me hunt for a wedding dress. I don't care if it's twenty years old or made of parachutes, as long as it's fabulous. I've heard of a lot of Red Cross girls getting married in their uniforms lately, but that is just *not* me."

"No kidding, Viv," I said, laughing.

"Well, we are going to *celebrate* tonight," Blanche said, standing up from her chair. "I love it, the first of us getting married. Speaking of tonight, ladies, I just realized it's already four thirty. We've got to head up to the hotel to shower and change, because you know the guys will be arriving anytime now for cocktail hour."

≈

I let Dottie and Viv shower first so I could relax and take my time getting ready. By the time I got downstairs, the terrace was packed with military and Red Cross, the dance floor jammed with couples jitterbugging to the band's version of "Here We Go Again."

I saw Joe and Dottie dancing. Viv and Harry were sitting at a table with his friends, and Blanche and Frankie were at the next table with Guy's. Instead of joining them, I took a walk down the path to the beach.

The bougainvillea on the walls were covered in tiny white twinkling lights that made the gravel path look like it was out of a fairy tale. I took off my sandals and sat on the nearest beach chair, feeling the cool sand between my toes and listening to the sounds of the surf.

I was living a life I would never have recognized two years before. Sitting on a beach in the South of France, after months traveling to the front lines of the war in the European Theater.

"What's next?" I whispered to nobody but myself and the sea.

Going home didn't feel right now. I didn't want to return to my former life; it didn't even fit anymore.

Like so many others, this war had robbed me of the life I had planned, and of my first love. I decided to chart a new course now. I would stay in the ETO and apply for one of the Red Cross positions in Berlin with Frankie; that would be the best way to honor Danny's memory.

I was enjoying the quiet when I heard the sound of footsteps on the path. I grabbed my sandals to walk back, assuming it was a couple looking for privacy. Slipping my sandals back on, I stepped onto the gravel again, and when I looked up, I froze.

He stood about twenty feet away from me in the lights of the bougainvillea, still built like a boxer but a few pounds thinner now. I opened my mouth to speak but closed it, looking into his eyes, not quite believing what I was seeing.

He gave me a small wave, tilted his head with that familiar lopsided grin that made my heart burst. I squinted as hard as I could because I didn't want the tears to fall.

Do fall in love again . . . I remembered the words of Danny's last letter and silently said a prayer of thanks to him for giving me that blessing. How best to honor those we've lost? By not being afraid to live life and take risks, by daring to open your heart to possibility. By taking a chance to begin. Again.

I took a few tentative steps forward, barely breathing. He stood there, waiting for me to decide.

I ran up the path, and he picked me up into his arms and swung me around. And we stayed like that, breathing each other in, making sure of each other.

When my feet touched the ground again, we held hands and stood for a moment.

"My God, you're really here," I said, wiping the dampness from my face. "I wanted to find you again, but I was so afraid that I'd learn you were gone."

"I almost was, more than once," he said, squeezing my hands, looking at me, marveling. "I wanted to find you, but I'd convinced myself you were on your way home by now, getting married."

I looked up at him and just shook my head.

He put his hand on my cheek. "Viv just told me about what happened to Danny. Fiona, I am so sorry for your loss, for all of the pain you've gone through."

"Thank you," I said, that pang in my chest, a jumble of mixed emotions, the pain of my past love, my planned life, gone for good . . . and then the hope of what was right in front of me.

"It was horrible to hear the truth, to know that, for a time, he was here, alive, but in the end, he was lost," I said, thinking of the story of the march. "But at least I know now."

"I want you to understand," Peter said, taking his hand away from mine, nervous and searching for words. "All I want is to spend some time with you. I'm not trying to push you into anything you're not ready for . . . And if you don't want to even do that, well, I . . ."

"Peter, the fact that you're here today, alive? It feels like a miracle," I said, reaching for his hand. "And there is nothing I'd rather do than spend time with you tonight."

He smiled and let out a deep breath, relieved.

"Okay," he said, looking down at my hand in his. "Let's go." He gave me a quick kiss on my forehead, and we walked back up the path to the party hand in hand, glancing at each other with shy smiles. The terrace was even more packed with people, and the band had amped up their sound to compete with the noise of the crowds. Peter stopped when we were on the fringes.

"Do you want to get out of here?" he said, surveying the scene. "I've got a jeep; we could go for a ride. There's this fishing village . . . I even know a hotel we could stay at." I looked up at him, surprised, and he held up his hand. "I meant in *two* rooms, I . . ."

"Sounds perfect," I said. "Let me grab my bag upstairs, and I'll meet you out front." I gave him a quick kiss on the cheek, my own cheeks flushed red. I didn't even stop to see my friends, I just headed straight to our room, stuffed a change of clothes and pajamas in my bag, and left a note on the door for Viv and Dottie.

He was waiting in front of the hotel in the jeep. The valet opened the door for me, and I climbed in.

We drove along the coast of the French Riviera under a star-filled sky. I leaned out one of the windows, and the wind whipped my hair around like crazy, but I didn't care. Peter occasionally grabbed my hand, and we both kept looking at each other with a little bit of wonder.

"Where are we going?" I asked after we had been driving for over forty-five minutes.

"Villefranche-sur-Mer," he said. "It's a village some of the guys who have been here told me about. They took a drive up the coast, stayed there one night on the way to Monte Carlo."

"When did you get here?"

"Just a few hours ago," he said. "I've been asking around about the Red Cross since I got to my hotel. I had to know if you were here too." He kissed my hand. "And I still can't believe you're sitting next to me."

Villefranche-sur-Mer was a charming medieval town of terra-cotta and ochre-colored buildings with red-tiled roofs, situated on steep cobblestone streets all leading down to the harbor, the lifeblood of the village. We parked the jeep and found a small hotel with a pale-yellow facade a block up from the water on one of the narrow, ancient passageways only meant for pedestrians.

The hotel owner recommended a small restaurant across from the water, so we walked down to the harbor. The cafés along the waterfront were filled with patrons drinking wine or espresso and enjoying the view and the beautiful spring night.

We arrived at the tiny bistro with the blue awning that the hotel owner had described. A hunched, elderly woman showed us to a corner table outside. She didn't even give us menus; she just brought us a bottle of red wine and then, a little while later, came out with steaming bowls of linguine and clams.

We talked, and it felt completely strange and yet comfortable sitting across the table from Peter. When the owner cleared our plates, Peter reached across the table and grabbed my hand.

"So, tell me. I want to hear everything that has happened in your life since we said good-bye at the command post."

I started with the reunion with Group F, tearing up when I shared the devastating news about Martha. I then told him about the party for the orphans and my request to the colonel, moving on to Cologne after Belgium, and, finally, our work with the newly liberated POWs. When I got to the part where I met Danny's friends and learned about his death on the march from Stalag Luft IV, I felt my voice catch in my throat for the second time since I started talking, and he squeezed my hand harder.

"I heard about those marches," Peter said, anger in his voice. "There will be a reckoning for those guards; there has to be."

"I hope so," I said. "I'm sorry to be emotional, it's still—"

"No need to apologize," he said. "No need to ever apologize for that."

"What's happened for you since then?" I said. We were holding hands across the table now. "In some ways it feels like years since that night at the command post."

"Before I start, let's go back to the hotel before they lock the front door for the night," he said. "There's a bar with a patio there."

Peter went to pay the owner, but she just patted him on the cheek and pointed at his uniform.

"Merci beaucoup," she said. *"Merci. Bonsoir."*

And we thanked her profusely in English and French as she kissed us both.

The hotel desk clerk was leaning on his elbow, half-asleep when we arrived in the lobby. But he brought wine and a bowl of olives to our table on the patio.

We stayed up talking until late. Peter shared some of his stories from the front, including the news that he had been promoted to major. The Eighty-Second had attacked the town of Bergstein on the Rur River, among others. A couple of times he stopped short of providing details; reliving them was clearly still too much.

"We weren't even that far from each other," I said. "I'm sorry I didn't write; I was afraid I would learn you were gone."

"And, you know, I didn't write because if Danny was alive . . ."

"I know. Thank you," I said. The clock on the wall said one thirty. "I should probably go to bed," I said, not wanting to leave him but feeling like I was supposed to.

"You're probably right," Peter said, disappointment in his eyes as he grabbed my hand and pulled me up. We walked up to the second floor. Our rooms were on opposite ends of the hall.

"Good night, Fiona," he said when we stopped in front of my door. I could smell the woodsy scent of his cologne. He put his hand on my chin, tilted my head up, and kissed me, our first real kiss since the command post. We kissed slowly at first, both a little nervous, but then he wrapped his arms around me and I leaned into him, and we kissed with a passion that surprised us both.

"I better go to my room," he said, pulling away, out of breath and looking at me with an intensity that made me feel light-headed.

"Yes," I said, looking into his eyes and nodding too many times. "You probably should."

With a quick kiss good night on my forehead, he walked down to his room as if willing himself to go before he changed his mind. I let myself into my own room and put down my purse. The room was clean and neat, with whitewashed stucco walls and a tile floor, and a vase of fresh yellow roses on the nightstand.

I took off my sandals, looked at myself in the mirror, and smoothed down my hair.

With a deep breath, I reached into the pocket of the dress for the Purple Heart and closed my eyes. Before I could change my mind, I ran down the hall in my bare feet. I was about to knock on Peter's door, but he opened it first, the same intense look in his eyes.

"I was thinking if I didn't knock, I'd always regret it," I said, holding up the Purple Heart, stumbling over my words, breathless and dizzy. "I'm in love with you. I should have told you before we said good-bye last time. I love you and—"

Before I could finish he pulled me toward him and scooped me up into his arms. Holding me against his chest, he kissed me with a fierce desire as the dam of longing broke for both of us. He carried me inside and kicked the door of his room shut. His room was dark except for the moonlight streaming through the window. Peter lowered me gently onto the bed, kneeling down on it next to me, his hands tangled in my hair as we kept kissing each other desperately.

"Fiona, you're shaking," he whispered, holding my face with his hands.
"Am I?"

"Yes." He smiled. "Are you sure you want to be here?"

"I've never been so sure of anything," I said, smiling through tears.

He kissed the tears on my face, then moved down to my neck. I lifted my arms as he slowly pulled my dress up over my head, gasping at his warm hands on my bare back. I unbuttoned his shirt, tracing the scar on his chest with my fingers before I kissed it. He let out a quiet groan and pulled me down on the bed until I was underneath him, looking into his eyes again.

"Can we take our time?" I sighed, wrapping one of my legs around his as he leaned down and kissed my collarbone, gently unhooking my bra. "I just don't want this all to end . . ."

"Sweetheart, we're going to take all the time you want," he said, his voice rough as he whispered into my ear. "We've both been waiting too long for this night."

~

We didn't fall asleep until the sun was rising. When I woke up at noon, Peter was sleeping, his hand on my back, making sure of me. I wrapped myself in a blanket and walked over to the window. Villefranche was even more beautiful in the daylight, its buildings painted in brilliant shades of orange, gold, and crimson, and I could see a glimpse of the fishing boats in the harbor at the end of our narrow street.

While my grief for Danny would always be a part of me, my entire world had shifted overnight. More than once in this war, my life had changed in an instant. But today, for the first time, that change was for the good. I felt a glow of happiness and contentment that I couldn't remember ever feeling before.

"You don't even know how beautiful you are," Peter said. I looked over at the bed, and he was smiling.

"I'm a mess," I said, smiling back at him.

"You're a beautiful mess."

"I wish I wasn't going back to Germany tomorrow." I sat on the edge of the bed, missing him already.

"I know." He reached for my hand. "Sweetheart, I have to ask, what do you think you're going to do next?"

I told him about the Red Cross survey.

"With all that's happened, I don't want to go home, but I don't want to go to the Pacific either. Liz said there are definitely positions available in London, Paris, and Berlin. So I've decided to stay. I was thinking Paris, though Frankie just asked me to apply to go to Berlin with her, so I've been thinking about that."

He gave me a curious look when I said this.

I looked up at him, nervous but needing to know. "And what happens now for you? Are you going to the Pacific?"

"What happens is I've been ordered to Berlin," he said, reaching over and pulling me across the bed into his arms. "For occupation duty."

"You're kidding?" I said.

"I'm not," he murmured as he kissed me again and then looked into my eyes, his hands in my hair. "Please consider Berlin?"

"Hmm . . . I don't know," I teased, smiling as I kissed the scar above his eyebrow.

"Maybe I can convince you . . . ," he said, pressing his lips against mine with a passion that made me feel light-headed all over again.

"I'll let you try," I whispered.

~

That night, Peter drove me back to Juan-les-Pins and walked me to the door of the Provençal.

"I'll see you in Paris in three weeks," he said.

"You sure you'll be able to get the time off?"

"I'll make sure," he said. "I'm never going to let so much time pass before seeing you ever again."

"Good," I said. One last embrace, one final kiss, and my heart started to hurt. I must have looked as pained as I felt because Peter took my head in his hands.

"It's okay," he said. "This time we're not saying good-bye forever."

"I know," I said. "And I'm so happy for that."

"I love you."

"I love you," I said. "I'll see you in Paris."

I watched the jeep drive away and then walked inside, checking the terrace before heading upstairs.

"Well, look who's here." Blanche came running up to me and grabbed my hand, pulling me with her. "I'm buying you a drink, and then you are going to tell us where you have been for the past twenty-four hours, my friend."

"Okay, Blanche," I said, laughing.

"You've got a glow about you, Fi, and I know it's got nothing to do with the sun." She looked me up and down. "It's good to see. And, may I also add, it's about damn time."

"Well, well." Viv was sitting with Dottie, and I couldn't tell if they were angry or amused. "I'm glad the guys left because we wouldn't be able to have this conversation with them around. Where the hell have you been?" She swatted me with her arm.

"We got your note, but we were still a bit worried, you know," Dottie said. "You could have called the hotel at least."

"I'm so sorry," I said. "I lost track of the time. I was in Villefranche-sur-Mer. With Peter."

"I hoped so," Viv said, giving me a knowing grin.

"I know a lady never talks, but you need to at least give us a few details," Dottie said.

"More than a few," Blanche said, handing me my glass of wine as she sat down. "I want all the dirt."

"Go easy on her, Blanche," Dottie said.

"Yeah, yeah. Hey, did Dottie tell you her news yet?" Blanche asked. "Because that's big too. Lots going on at this hotel in the past couple days. I could start a Hôtel le Provençal gossip column."

"Are you engaged too?" I said, looking at Dottie.

"No," Dottie said, her cheeks turning pink.

"Dottie, what is it?"

"I got a letter," Dottie said. "From First Lieutenant Don Hayes, the new leader of Glenn Miller's band here. Before Glenn Miller went missing, he had talked about offering me a job as a soloist, to go on tour with them for the next six months. They wrote to me because they still want to extend the offer."

"Dottie!" I said, beaming from ear to ear.

"Can you believe it, Fi? *Me?*"

"Dottie, I'm so damn proud of you, I might cry," I said. "And you're going to take it?"

"I am," she said. "Joe and I talked about it; I have to take it. It's once in a lifetime. He said he'd wait for me. I know he will."

"I think of when we first got here . . ."

"I know, remember that?" Blanche said. "Martha, Frankie, and I were taking bets that you wouldn't make it, Dots."

"You did not!" Dottie said, kicking her foot.

"Oh yes, we did," Blanche said. "And please don't feel too bad, but I thought you were a goner. Actually, after the doughnut machine exploded at training? I thought you were all goners."

"Me too," Viv said, laughing.

"Where is Frankie, by the way?" I asked.

"Frankie is off exploring old town Antibes with Patrick Halloran from the Eighty-Second," Blanche said. "He's four years younger than her, but one thing I didn't realize before? He's like a male version of Frankie. The kid never stops moving."

"It's true," Viv said. "I don't know if it'll last, but it's good for her."

"So back to you," Dottie said. "I haven't seen you look this happy in over a year. And I couldn't be more thrilled about it."

"But is it serious?" Viv said, watching my expression.

"I think . . . yeah, it is," I said with a nod. I felt my face turn crimson, thinking about all that had happened.

"Good, then he's got to come to the wedding," Viv said.

"He will," I said.

"Perfect," Blanche said. "But more details on your romantic French getaway, please."

"Oh shush, Blanche," Viv said. "Can't you see you're looking at a girl who's head over heels in love?"

"You have to at least tell me that," Blanche said, eyebrows raised as she pointed her cigarette at me. "Are you? In love?"

I looked around at my friends, my face feeling flushed. I smiled and simply nodded.

"Yes."

Chapter Twenty-Eight

June 9, 1945
Paris, France

Three weeks later, the five of us were in the bridal suite at the Hotel George V in Paris, getting ready for Viv's wedding to Harry Westwood.

Frankie, Dottie, Blanche, and I were all wearing pastel-colored cocktail dresses we had purchased in Antibes or Paris for the occasion. I had found a mint-green organza dress at a small boutique in Paris when we arrived the day before. It was sleeveless with a scooped neckline and an A-line skirt. Dottie's dress was pale pink, Frankie's pastel blue, and Blanche's a light yellow.

"We look like Easter eggs," Blanche said as we stood next to each other, staring into the suite's large mirror above the dresser.

"We do not," I said, laughing as I adjusted the dragonfly comb in my hair. "Well, maybe a little."

"You look beautiful," Viv said as she walked out of the bathroom, where she had been getting changed. We all gasped. Viv, with the help of Harry's mother, had tracked down the most gorgeous ivory wedding dress—strapless with a satin sash at the waist and a tulle skirt that was floor length and covered with dotted sequins.

"Oh, Viv, look at you," Dottie said. "Wait until Harry sees you. You're stunning."

She looked gorgeous, of course, her auburn curls shining and twisted up in the front underneath a simple ivory lace veil. Her makeup was flawless as always, and her perfect, polished candy-apple-red manicure was back since we weren't making doughnuts nearly as often anymore.

"Thank you," Viv said, giving us all hugs as we showered her with compliments.

She looked in the mirror at herself and sighed.

"The only hard part is my family not being here to celebrate with me," Viv said in a quiet voice. "Thank God I have you four."

"We'll stand in for your sisters," I said, putting my arm around her shoulders.

"You girls *are* like sisters," Viv said. "I couldn't have done this without you."

"Are you sure I'm going to like this band you found for today, Dottie?" Viv asked. "It was such short notice, I'm surprised you were able to get anyone."

"I'm sure you're going to like them," Dottie said. "And no, we're not going to tell you any more, it would ruin the surprise." Dottie winked at me behind Viv's back as she straightened her veil.

"Just promise me you didn't grab an old guy with an accordion off the street or something," Viv said.

"Viv, stop asking," I said, laughing.

"Hey, were those Harry's parents I saw downstairs?" Blanche asked as I helped her put her hair in an updo. "The gray-haired Englishman and the blonde woman with the hat that looks like a giant yellow bird hanging off her head?"

"Yes, that's them," Viv said. "They're okay actually, not haughty like I expected, thank God. And I have his mother to thank for finding this dress in time."

"Where did she find it?" I asked, admiring the sequin detailing as I adjusted the skirt.

"She borrowed it from Queen Elizabeth's collection, of course," Viv said, her expression serious.

Frankie's mouth fell open, and the four of us were quiet for a few seconds as we looked at Viv in shock, but then she smiled.

"Girls, I'm kidding," Viv said, laughing. "But you should have seen the looks on your faces."

Blanche was laughing and began to say something, but then put her hand over her mouth and ran into the bathroom, the hairbrush I'd been using still in her hair. We could hear her throwing up behind the closed door. Viv, Dottie, Frankie, and I looked at each other.

"She's been throwing up like that since we left Antibes," Frankie said.

"How often? Has she seen a doctor?" I asked.

"Blanche, honey, are you up for this?" Viv asked when she came out, taking her hand. "You poor thing, if you're sick . . ."

"No, just get me some Coke and crackers and I'll be fine," Blanche said, sitting on the edge of the bed. "At least I didn't throw up on this new dress. I was waiting to tell you all this because I didn't want to upstage your day, Viv, but Guy Sherry and I are getting married in London in a few weeks."

"Well, congratulations!" Viv said, hugging her. "You're not upstaging my day at all."

"Also, the baby's due around Christmas," Blanche said as she reached for her Chesterfields and shrugged. "Whoops."

We all stood there in stunned silence for the second time in five minutes.

"I had a feeling," Frankie said, eyes wide as she kissed Blanche on the forehead and got her another Coke.

"Wow," I said, sitting down on the bed next to her. "How are you doing?"

"Well, I was in shock for a few days. It's not ideal, of course. I mean, we had talked about getting married but not this *soon*. Thank God we love each other. I'm crazy about him, as you all know."

"What are your plans? Any chance you'll be living in London too?" Viv asked.

"Well, if everything works out, I think he's going to be stationed here, in Paris," Blanche said. "If they'll have me, I'll work for the Red Cross here, at least until the baby's born. I just talked to Liz about it."

"Have you written to your parents to tell them?" Dottie asked, sitting on the other side of her.

"Not yet," Blanche said. "My mama will figure it out and want to string me up, but she just cares about New Orleans society; none of those old biddies will know." She sighed. "I think we'll be okay. Will you help me finish my hair, Fi?"

"Yes," I said, giving her a hug. "And you're going to be better than okay."

❧

At 4:15 p.m., with our bouquets of white tulips in hand, we walked downstairs and waited on the landing of the staircase. Jimmy English, accompanied by our dear Mrs. Tibbetts, had arrived the night before from Leicester. Per Viv's request, he was waiting at the bottom of the stairs, ready to escort Viv into the ceremony and give her away. Jimmy was dressed in a fine-looking navy-blue suit and seemed like a man reborn. Gone were the bloodshot eyes and beaten-down look from when we had first met him. Mrs. Tibbetts, dressed in a pretty light-blue floral dress, kissed him on the cheek and went to find a seat.

The three of us stood side by side, checking ourselves one last time in the enormous gilded mirror on the landing. It reminded me of our first day on the *Queen Elizabeth*, when they had found me crying in the bathroom. It felt like decades ago.

"You look stunning," I said to Viv in a soft voice.

"You do, Viv," Dottie said, eyes glistening.

"I didn't know I could feel this happy," Viv said, biting her lip and blinking back tears.

"Ah, the *LIFE* magazine cover girls." We all looked up, surprised to see Miss Chambers walking down the stairs. She gave us a huge smile. "You all look beautiful. Congratulations, Viviana."

"Thank you for coming, Miss Chambers," Viv said.

"Thank *you* for inviting me," Miss Chambers said. "I also want you to know that Colonel Brooks's request has been approved. You will all be receiving Bronze Stars from the US Army. So more congratulations are in order, ladies." She paused, looking at the three of us, a mixture of amusement and pride lighting her face. "As you know, I had my doubts about you three. But I couldn't be prouder of how far you've come."

We all thanked her, and she walked downstairs. The music started moments later—"Canon in D," played by a small string quartet.

"It's time, ladies," Frankie called from the bottom of the stairs. Blanche was standing next to her, shoving another cracker in her mouth.

Frankie walked down the aisle first, followed by Blanche, Dottie, and finally me.

The room where the ceremony was taking place was decorated in tulle and tulips, and many of our Red Cross and military friends were in attendance. I tried not to look desperate as I scanned the sea of faces. When I spotted Peter sitting next to Joe in the back of the room, my stomach did a little flip and I felt my face grow warm. He gave me a smile and mouthed hello, and I winked at him.

My friends and I took our places at the front, next to the Royal Air Force chaplain, Reverend Payton. Harry and his groomsmen, all in dress uniform, were on the opposite side of him. Jimmy walked Viv down the aisle, and as soon as Harry caught a glimpse of her, he bit his lip and I thought I saw a tear in his eye. The look of love between Viv and Harry was undeniable, and my heart was full for my dear friend. I spotted Harry's parents sitting in the front row, and there was no doubt they saw what everyone else had, that their son was happy and madly in love.

Jimmy kissed Viv on the cheek and sat down beside Mrs. Tibbetts, who was smiling and crying at the same time. When the ceremony was over, the whole audience cheered and threw confetti as we made our way across the lobby into the ballroom where the reception would take place.

"Are they ready?" I asked Dottie as we walked across the hall.

"Oh yeah," Dottie said, giving me a conspiratorial look.

"And are you?" I said.

"More than ever. I'm just going to go powder my face."

Dottie hurried off, and as I was walking toward the ballroom, I noticed Peter before he saw me. I ran up behind him and tapped him on the shoulder, laughing as he pulled me into a hallway off the main lobby and gave me a long, lingering kiss.

"Hello, sweetheart," he said in my ear. "I've been thinking about doing that for three weeks."

"You made it."

"I wouldn't miss it. And I got your letter about the transfer to Berlin going through right before I left," he said, holding me close. "Best news I've ever had."

"Yes, Liz said I had my pick, and I'm even getting a promotion out of the deal," I said. "We'll finally be in the same city for a while."

"For more than a while," he said, looking into my eyes.

I saw Dottie rush through the lobby behind him.

"Come on," I said, grabbing his hand. "We have the best surprise."

I felt thrilled and content as I held Peter's hand, and we walked into the ballroom together. I introduced him to Liz, ChiChi, Doris, and other friends as we made our way to the table at the front of the room. Blanche and Frankie were standing with Viv and Harry, who really did look like royalty as people came up to congratulate them.

Guy came over with a Coke and crackers for Blanche and started rubbing her back. People were whispering, looking at the number of seats and instruments on the stage in front of us.

"What band were you able to get on such short notice?" Peter said, frowning at all of us. "It looks more like an orchestra."

Joe Brandon took the stage then, holding a glass of champagne as he tapped the microphone.

"Viv and Harry," Joe said. Viv looked slightly confused, wondering why Joe was the first to give a speech. "Two things: first, I would like to propose a toast. Wishing you a life of love, health, and happiness. To Viv and Harry!"

"To Viv and Harry!" The entire room toasted the happy couple.

"Now, your best friends concocted this crazy surprise for your wedding reception, and they actually pulled it off. For your entertainment tonight, I would like to introduce . . ." He paused, and now Viv and Harry looked nervous. "The late Major Glenn Miller's American Band of the Allied Expeditionary Forces, conducted by Ray McKinley and accompanied by their new guest soloist, Dottie Sousa!"

The crowd went wild as the musicians took the stage, and Harry and Viv were clapping and cheering. Even Harry's parents looked starstruck.

"I cannot believe they're here," Viv said, laughing. "At *our* wedding."

"Are you surprised?" I said as I hugged her.

"Are you kidding? In a million years, I never thought they'd be available."

Dottie was the last to take the stage when the entire band was assembled, and the crowd went crazy cheering for her, especially all of us from Group F. Dottie adjusted her glasses, smiled, and waved.

"Thank you," she said. "I'd like to dedicate this first song to one of my best friends and her new husband on their wedding day. Viv and Harry, this one's for you."

Viv and Harry took to the dance floor as Dottie began to sing "It Had to Be You."

I caught Peter looking at me and planted a kiss on his cheek. Viv motioned for the bridal party to join them on the dance floor, so I took his hand and we walked out.

"What do you keep smiling at?" I said to Peter, his arms on my waist as we moved to the music.

"Being here with you," he said, taking a deep breath and pulling me closer. "After everything. I can barely believe how lucky I am."

"I know," I said. "And now it's on to Berlin."

"Together," he said, kissing my hair. "Finally."

We danced and then dined, and Dottie sang her heart out as the late-afternoon sun gave way to night. The band took a break, and I spotted Dottie heading out to the courtyard for some air. I kissed Peter and told him I'd be right back as I walked outside to bring her a glass of champagne. The courtyard was vast and breathtaking with an ornate black-and-white tile floor and small iron tables lit with tea-light candles that lined the perimeter. It was decorated with hundreds of oversized vases of blush-pink peonies and yellow roses as well as ornate green topiaries. The candles and the soft glow from the hotel room windows above made it all look like a modern Parisian fairyland.

Viv had already beaten me to her, and she and Dottie were sitting at a table at the far end of the courtyard, sipping champagne.

"Are you both okay?" I said.

"I just needed a few seconds to catch my breath from it all," Viv said, putting her feet up on an empty chair.

"Same here," Dottie said.

"The life of a famous singer," I said, teasing her.

"Oh please." Dottie rolled her eyes.

"This is officially the best night of my life," Viv said. Tonight there was no cool exterior; she had not stopped smiling. "And the band . . . I still can't believe it. Thank you both."

"It was Fiona's idea actually," Dottie said. "I was afraid to ask at first, sure they'd say no. I'm so glad we pulled it off."

"I figured they wouldn't disappoint their new soloist," I said.

"It also helped that they were already going to be here in Paris," Dottie said.

"I love you girls," Viv said. "Thank you for doing this with me."

"It's your wedding—of course," Dottie said.

"No, I meant thank you for joining the Red Cross with me," Viv said. "It's been hard and crazy and unconventional . . . but also amazing. I still can't believe this *is* my life now."

"I know," I said in a soft voice, gazing up at the stars. "Look at us. Look at where we are. Did you ever imagine?"

Dottie shook her head, her eyes shiny with happy tears as we took in the beauty of the courtyard.

"I'm going to miss you both so much," Viv said. "Please promise me you'll visit London as often as you can?"

"And you Berlin?"

We all agreed to do our best, but it was with the bittersweetness of us all going our separate ways and making promises that we weren't sure we could keep.

"Cheers to you and Harry," I said, clinking glasses with both of them.

"And to us, Group F, and our dear Cheyenne," Dottie said.

"And to doughnuts . . . no, forget it, not to doughnuts. I hated making those damn doughnuts," Viv said.

"Like we couldn't tell," I said, as we clinked our glasses together one last time.

We sat for a little while longer, laughing and sipping champagne among the fragrant flowers in the courtyard of the Hotel George V, enjoying each other and the warm summer night air in the City of Lights.

Historical Notes

The Beantown Girls is a work of fiction, but much of it is based on the true stories of the real Red Cross Clubmobile girls that served in the European Theater of Operations in World War II. It was enormously helpful that many of the Red Cross Clubmobile girls happened to be fantastic writers, who documented their experiences in meticulous and thoughtful ways. I used their writings, as well as archived videotaped interviews and a few invaluable books written by the women, or someone close to them. I am once again grateful to the Schlesinger Library at Harvard University for their assistance in this project and for the many boxes of well-preserved Red Cross Clubmobile diaries, letters, pictures, and other archived materials of these amazing women. A huge thank-you to my friend and research assistant Sara Brandon for her valuable help in my research efforts.

For those curious about which items are fact versus fiction, here are a few notes regarding the story:

The secret Glenn Miller concert at De Montfort Hall in Leicester, England, in September 1944 was a real event and a thrill for the Clubmobile girls that attended. Glenn Miller performed these concerts for the troops all over the European Theater. Sadly, the plane he was flying in did disappear over the English Channel in December 1944.

The army's Eighty-Second Airborne and Twenty-Eighth Infantry Divisions figure prominently in the story, and I tried to be as historically accurate as possible in terms of both the timeline and the experiences of the incredibly brave men that were part of these military divisions in Europe at that time.

As for Fiona, Viv, and Dottie, there was a Clubmobile crew that got trapped in Vielsalm, Belgium, during the early days of what would become the Battle of the Bulge. My narrative of this, as well as their escape and the saving of the Christmas mail, is all based on true stories. Several of the Clubmobile girls involved in these events received Bronze Stars.

The Christmas Eve story of American soldiers meeting lost German soldiers at a German family's cottage in the woods during the Battle of the Bulge is also based on a true story that I discovered. It appeared on an episode of *Unsolved Mysteries* in 1995 when the "boy" from the cottage was looking for the American soldiers from that night. There were no Red Cross Clubmobile girls there that evening, but I thought it was such a captivating story and fit well with *The Beantown Girls'* narrative, so I placed Fiona, Viv, and Dottie in the middle of it.

The stories of the Allied POWs that were forced to march hundreds of miles from the Stalag Luft IV POW camp is all based on heart-wrenching historical accounts. The Red Cross Clubmobile girls helped in the liberation of thousands of POWs in the ETO in 1945, and that part of the story is all based on the real Clubmobile girls' accounts of their experiences.

The Red Cross and US military did take over hotels in the South of France for soldiers and Red Cross workers to take leave at the close of the war in Europe.

The Red Cross Clubmobile girls were featured in *LIFE* magazine in February 1944, but none of them were on the cover.

Acknowledgments

Writing a story is such a solitary process, but delivering this novel to the world required a multitude of people, and I am so grateful to all of them.

To Danielle Marshall, my acquiring editor at Lake Union Publishing, thank you so much for helping to make another dream come true for me. So happy you are at the Lake Union helm!

To Alicia Clancy, my primary editor at Lake Union, I'm very grateful for your thoughtful feedback and steady hand in managing the whole editorial process. It was so lovely working with you, and I hope to again.

To Faith Black Ross, my developmental editor, what a joy it was to work with you for the second time. Your meticulous and insightful feedback makes me a better writer in every way, thank you.

To the amazing copyediting team: production manager Nicole Pomeroy and copyeditor Lindsey Alexander and to the proofreaders—you are the unsung heroes of publishing, and I could not be more grateful for your hard work and expertise.

To Gabe Dumpit and the entire Lake Union marketing team—a million thanks for everything you do to support me and all Lake Union authors.

A huge thank-you to my agent, Mark Gottlieb, for all of your help and support.

My writing community is amazing, and I am grateful for the many friends that help make this endeavor less lonely. To my fellow Lake Union authors—what an incredible tribe that I am fortunate to be a part of, and I was so happy to finally meet some of you in person this year.

To my local writer friends Susanna Baird, Jennifer Gentile, and Julie Gregori Cremins—our talks about writing are like therapy to me. Thank you for helping to keep me sane.

One of the best parts of the past couple of years has been meeting so many of the fantastic people who promote books and help get them into the hands of readers. I am so grateful to all of them. A huge thank-you to Andrea Peskind Katz—you are an author champion like no other, and I am so appreciative of everything you do for me and all authors. Suzanne Weinstein Leopold—thank you so much for your support and your friendship. To Dick Haley of Haley Booksellers, thank you for helping me connect with readers all over Massachusetts. To book lovers and promoters like Linda Zagon, Barbara Khan, Trina Burgermeister, Kristy Barret, Tamara Welch, Athena Kaye, and Lauren Margolin—authors and readers are so lucky to have you in their lives, thank you for all that you do.

To the many New England librarians who have been such amazing supporters from the start, thank you. Your help and support means so much to this local girl.

Thank you to my parents, Tom and Beth Healey—for everything you do to support me and our family, and for being my number one fans in writing and in life. To my daughters, Madeleine and Ellie—you inspire me every single day and will always be my biggest accomplishments.

None of this would be possible without my husband, Charlie Ungashick. Thank you for helping me find the time and space to write, even if that means ordering a lot of takeout meals! Before I had even published a single magazine article, you always pushed me to think bigger and aim higher with my writing goals. Thank you for never doubting these dreams could come true. My favorite story is ours.